A Parcel of Rogues

Niall Illingworth

Grosvenor House
Publishing Limited

This book is published by
Grosvenor House Publishing Ltd
Link House
140 The Broadway, Tolworth, Surrey, KT6 7HT.
www.grosvenorhousepublishing.co.uk

A CIP record for this book
is available from the British Library

ISBN 978-1-78623-624-1

For mum, and in loving memory of dad.

'Also by the Same Author'

Where the Larkspur Grow

Acknowledgements:

Thank you to the many readers of my first novel who were kind enough to say that they'd enjoyed reading it. Without that positive feedback I don't think I would have had the energy to write this book. Writers, I've learned, are no different from people generally: we appreciate being appreciated.

I'm also grateful to those who provided constructive comments about my writing. I'm hoping I've been able to incorporate at least some of them in this second book.

To Erin, Steve, Debs, Stuart and Gordon, my thanks for being my guinea pigs and for ploughing through the early drafts of this novel. Finally, can I say a special word of thanks to Eunice, who undertook the considerable task of proof reading all 98,000 words. My grammar may still not be perfect, but it has been improved immeasurably by your efforts.

Chapter 1

September 1992

The fall had come early to Greenbrier County. The night air was now noticeably cooler and for late September the breeze carried a bite and a reminder that dark winter days were not far away. Fox squirrels traversed the forest canopy busying themselves gathering autumn's bounty for the long months ahead. A penetrating dampness enveloped the woodland floor and willow and river birch trees dipped their branch ends into the inky cold water of the Greenbrier river. Above, a single yellow buckeye leaf pirouetted down an invisible spiral of breeze, the first to fall this season, a corpse that had once been summer.

Charlie Jarret pulled up the collar of his jacket before carefully dropping the last handful of maggots into the plastic pouch of his catapult. Taking aim, he fired the wriggling feast across the river to the deep pool that lay in front of an ancient beech tree. He set the line clip on his rod and positioned it carefully on the rest. Taking the thermos flask out of his tackle bag he poured himself a coffee, placed his crutch on the ground, then eased himself into his trusty old fishing chair. To his right towered the imposing structure of the Greenbrier bridge. The moon was bright and full, and in the stillness of the night its light filtered through the intricate structure of the bridge's three metal arches, casting long dark shadows across the width of the river.

Charlie glanced to his left. Tied to the trunk of a large willow tree, fifty yards or so up river, was the remains of a washed-out pink ribbon that hugged the grey twisted trunk like a cummerbund. The remnants of three faded bouquets clung to the wretched tree, their cellophane wrapped blooms, an ever-present reminder of the horror that had visited that spot all those years ago.

Charlie had fished this spot many times before but never this late into September. The river was running slow after the recent dry spell, so conditions were nigh on perfect. Charlie knew that tonight was his best chance. Brownie had told him that a 7lb walleye had been caught near to the bridge a couple of days ago and there were reports of even bigger fish having been seen in the river. With rain forecast it was now or never as far as Charlie was concerned. All he had to do was sit and wait.

He was first aware of the sound of an engine running. Car doors slammed, and various voices could be heard talking excitedly amongst themselves.

'Just the bridge to go Nathan, then you've done it bro,' said a voice from above. It was difficult to tell how many of them were up there, but from the laughter and chatter Charlie reckoned there might be at least half a dozen.

'Remember, you've to do both sides of the bridge or it doesn't count,' squealed a high-pitched voice. 'And you must be carrying the head, it can stay in the bag, but you can't put it down. This is fucking brilliant Nathan, you're smashing it.'

What the fuck is going on, wondered Charlie as the whooping and hollering grew ever louder.

'Another few feet and you're there. Come on Nathan you can do it.'

Seconds later another voice shouted,

'You've nailed it Nathan. You're the fucking big dog now, you're the man Nathan.'

'Mic Sgith,' yelled all the voices in unison. 'Mic Sgith,' they shouted again and again.

Charlie stared up at the bridge. Silhouetted against the moonlight and standing on the narrow parapet that ran the length of the bridge was the figure of a teenage boy dressed in shorts and a singlet. He was holding a canvas bag. Disembodied voices from behind him started to chant.

'Nathan, Nathan, Nathan,' they thundered.

The boy turned and nodded. Reaching into the bag he pulled out the head of a small deer. Holding it by one antler the boy swung it above his head several times before hurling it into the dark waters of the river below.

'What the actual fuck!' shouted Charlie, 'I've just spent the last twenty minutes baiting that pool and now you've gone and spooked every fish between here and Fairlea, you asshole.'

*

The staircase leading up to Curtis Wyles' office was steep and not particularly well lit. The Dionach paused at the foot of the stairs and removed a small black leather notebook from his inside jacket pocket. Squinting in the dim light, he carefully thumbed through the well-worn book. On page forty-six he found what he was looking for. The Dionach stared at the page.

'178 referrals,' he hissed contemptuously, 'the class of 1960 really were shit.'

The receptionist in the small and rather dull panelled office asked him to take a seat while she phoned Mr Wyles to let him know that his appointment had arrived. Putting down the phone she peered over her bifocal glasses and smiled.

'Mr Buckley, Mr Wyles is ready to see you now, please go in.'

The Dionach opened the door pausing briefly as he scanned the room. Purposefully, he strode forward coming to a halt in front of an imposing oak desk that was smothered in files and various pieces of paper. Curtis Wyles stood up, smiled broadly and thrust out his hand to greet his visitor.

'It's great to see you Dionach,' said Curtis as the two men shook hands. 'It must be five years since I last saw you at the reunion dinner.' Curtis carefully looked the Dionach up and down.

'You know, I don't think you've changed a bit, and as for that suit the creases are still razor sharp. And I never did understand how anyone could have such shiny shoes and, more to the point, keep them so shiny. Look at them they're immaculate.' The Dionach stood tall but didn't reply.

'Please have a seat,' said Curtis pulling a leather padded chair from the front of the desk. 'I'm just about to have my morning coffee, would you care for one?'

Buckley nodded. 'Milk and one sugar would be most acceptable thank you.' Curtis started to laugh.

'Only one sugar, what happened to that famous sweet tooth of yours? Cook was always despairing that we kept running out of sugar and she always tried to blame you.'

Buckley nodded again.

'I think cook and Mrs Buckley must have been in cahoots. But their nagging must have paid off, I've been down to one sugar for years now. Done wonders to help keep the waistline in check,' said Buckley patting his stomach.

'I know I could do with losing another stone but it's not easy when you get to my age. You've got to have some pleasure in life. Anyway, as you might remember, I'm thrawn that way, I don't give up easily.'

Curtis looked bemused.

'Thrawn, not sure that's one I'm familiar with. Is it another of your famous Scottish words?'

'Certainly is,' replied Buckley with just the hint of a smile. 'I've got a whole notebook full of them. Just another thing I've got to thank the Founder for.'

'I take it that it means dogged or something like that?' replied Curtis.

'More like stubborn, said Buckley, 'But dogged is close enough.'

Curtis took a sip of his coffee and sat down.

'Thrawn! I like it. Those Scot's words of yours have a habit of describing things perfectly. I think my favourite is dreich. And apposite for today don't you think?' said Curtis looking out the window.

'It's become 'a thing' in our family, I use dreich all the time. As I said you couldn't find a better word to describe this weather.' Buckley smiled and nodded.

'Couldn't agree more. The last couple of days have been lousy and that easterly wind has a real edge to it. It's very cold for September.'

'Remind me?' said Curtis. 'Dionach, is that not Gaelic for a caretaker? I should know but I've forgotten, sorry.' Buckley fixed Curtis with a piercing stare.

'Caretaker!' he scoffed. 'No, Mr Wyles, it is not. It's a Gaelic word for a guardian or protector.' Curtis knew he had touched a nerve. He had seen the Dionach annoyed before, but before he could change the subject Buckley continued.

'A caretaker is a person who looks after a building. A guardian, Mr Wyles, has a far more important role. He is required to protect and defend.'

'Apologies Donald, I meant no offence,' said Curtis sheepishly.

'None taken,' replied Buckley. 'But the Founder didn't take kindly to any other term. It had to be Dionach. He saw the Dionach as being the cornerstone of his school. The protector and upholder of its standards and ethics. Within the college, just like my father before me, I am the Dionach. I'm not Mr Buckley and never Donald, just the Dionach. That discipline and attention to detail is what made Marsco College great. Makes it great I should say as I still regard it as so, albeit I fear that may all be about to change.'

Curtis sensed that something was bothering his friend. He could see the worry in his eyes.

'It was a fantastic school. It gave me my love of the outdoors and taught me so much about life that has stood me in good stead for all these years,' said Curtis trying to lift the mood. 'And may I say, I hope that will continue for many years to come.'

Buckley sat bolt upright in his chair clasping his hands on his lap.

'Amen to that,' he whispered with a gentle nod.

'So, my friend, to business. What brings you all the way from White Sulphur Springs to see me today?' The

Dionach paused for a moment before leaning forward in his chair.

'Advice, Mr Wyles, I need your advice.'

'Of course,' said Curtis, 'If I can be of assistance, I'd be glad to help. Is it a legal matter that you're looking for help with?'

'In a roundabout way I suppose it is.' said the Dionach.

'Well hopefully you've come to the right place. How about you try and tell me what's on your mind and I'll try my best to advise you accordingly,' said Curtis reassuringly.

*

In the detectives' office of Lewisburg police department, Charlie Finch was dictating witness statements onto a dictaphone when the door opened.

'Charlie, have you got a minute?' asked Mike Rawlingson from the doorway.

'Sure,' said Charlie looking up from his desk, 'what's up?'

Mike smiled at his colleague.

'Sorry to interrupt, but the chief wants to see you in his office right away.'

Charlie put down the dictaphone and switched off the machine. His automatic response in such situations was to wonder what he might have done wrong to merit a summons to the chief's office, as it wouldn't be the first time, he'd experienced the sharp tongue and angst of his chief of police. But at that precise moment Charlie couldn't think of anything that he'd done wrong. Before he had time to contemplate further, Mike continued.

'Nothing to worry about, in fact quite the opposite. I think he might have some good news for a change, so you'd better get up there.' Charlie looked quizzically at his boss.

'Are you coming?' asked Charlie putting on his jacket.

'Not this time,' said Mike with a chuckle, 'you're going solo today.'

'Not sure I like the sound of that,' said Charlie as he reached the office door. 'Is this in any way connected to our earlier conversation?'

'It might be, but we'll talk more when you get back. Now get a move on will you, Bull Wilder isn't a man you keep waiting.'

As Charlie approached Bull's office, he could see the chief sitting writing at his desk. Charlie knocked gently on the door.

'Come,' said the chief without lifting his head. 'Take a seat Charlie, I'll be with you in a minute, I've a report to present to the Police Authority this afternoon and I'm on the last paragraph.'

Charlie didn't say anything but for the next couple of minutes he sat and perused the large collection of photographs and certificates that adorned the spacious office. Most of the photographs showed the chief in his police uniform. The different insignia on his shirts denoted his steady rise through the ranks. As far as Charlie could see only two photos were not police related. On the corner of the desk was a silver framed photo of the chief with his wife and young son. The boy appeared to be aged about ten. Charlie smiled to himself. The familiar resemblance was remarkable. The boy was short and stocky like his father, but it was their hair that was so striking. Both father and son sported a flattop cut with razor sharp sides. The likeness was uncanny.

On the wall immediately behind the chief was a framed black and white photograph of five smartly dressed young men aged about eighteen. Charlie recognised that the chief was the boy in the centre of the photograph. His flattop haircut looked just the same as it did today. Each of the boys was wearing a checked jacket, collar and tie and a waistcoat. The ensemble was finished off with a pair of dark coloured trousers and shoes. There was no question that they looked smart, but Charlie thought they had an air of arrogance about them as each boy's chin was held high and their chests were puffed out like preening peacocks. Charlie strained his eyes to read the caption at the bottom of the photograph. It read, Mic Sgith, Marsco College, 1960. Well, I never knew that, thought Charlie to himself. Bull Wilder was educated at Marsco, helps explain why he is such a sanctimonious shit I suppose.

'Right Charlie, I'll come straight to the point,' said the chief brusquely. 'I suppose Mike has told you about Susan's situation.' Charlie nodded. 'Well, while she undergoes her cancer treatment, I've agreed that Mike can work 8-4 Monday to Friday. Frees him up to look after his son at the weekends and of course, we'll be flexible if he needs to take Susan for appointments in Charleston.'

'That's excellent sir, I know that will make things considerably easier,' said Charlie quietly.

'Of course, one man's loss is another man's gain, so I've decided that you will be promoted to acting lieutenant until such times as Mike is able to resume full duties. How do you like the sound of that?' asked the chief looking Charlie straight in the eye. Charlie sat back in his chair not saying anything.

'At least look as if you're pleased man,' said Wilder. 'I've plenty other detectives I could give it to if you don't want it.' he continued.

'No, no, of course I want it sir. I just wasn't expecting it to be honest. But, I'm thrilled sir. Just sorry about how it has come about, but I'm delighted to be given the opportunity.' said a clearly stunned Charlie.

'Good. Well that's agreed then. You start tomorrow, and don't fuck it up or it will be a very long time before you get another chance. Do you understand me?'

'Absolutely sir, I'll give it 100% you can be assured of that.'

By the time Charlie got back to his office Mike was sitting in his chair with his feet up on the desk reading the paper.

'I take it you had something to do with this?' asked Charlie suspiciously. Mike frowned and gave a gentle nod.

'But hey listen, that's only because Bull asked me who I thought should get it. Relax will you, it's a great opportunity for you and it suits my needs just fine. The docs say that after her operation Susan will need a course of radiation treatment. But the prognosis is very positive, I could be back in the saddle in six months or so. Look, opportunities like this don't present themselves every day. And anyway, it's a recognition of your hard work and of your ability as a detective. You should be delighted.'

'Believe me I am,' said Charlie pulling up a chair and sitting down. 'It's just the circumstances. It's difficult to be happy given Susan's situation.'

'That's not an issue, Susan is going to be thrilled when I tell you're being made acting lieutenant. The doctors have told her staying positive is important, so this news will give her a right lift, honestly, I'm not joshing you.' Charlie looked at his boss and smiled.

'Anyway, I'm not going anywhere, so if you need any advice, which I don't think you will, I won't be far away. But I'm not sure there will be too much excitement for you to deal with, since we cleared up the Maisie Foster murder case things have been quiet round here, certainly in terms of major investigations.' added Mike.

'Let's hope it stays that way,' said Charlie with a grin.

'Come on, grab your bag I'm taking you to Bursley's for a beer.' said Mike patting his friend on the back.

'Nice one, rank seems to bring some privileges. I could get used to this.'

Chapter 2

'Fine then,' said the Dionach, 'I'll get straight to the point. You will have heard that Ewart Wilder has been appointed the new chair of the Board of Governors.'

Curtis nodded, 'Yes I'd heard that.'

'Well, when you add that to the fact that he's already the president of the Old Marsconions, he's suddenly become a very powerful man, and more to the point, a man who's clearly intent on flexing his muscles.' continued the Dionach.

'In what way has he, to use your own words, been flexing his muscles?' asked Curtis reverting to lawyer mode and leaning back in his chair.

The Dionach stood up and leant his considerable frame on Curtis's desk.

'Yesterday, Wilder handed me a letter informing me that my employment at the school will terminate on my next birthday and at that time myself and my family will be expected to vacate the lodge house and move out of the college. He said that it had been discussed and agreed with the Board of Governors.'

'I see,' said Curtis who was now writing some notes on a pad. 'And I take it this news has come completely out of the blue?'

'Totally,' said the Dionach. 'I'll be seventy on my next birthday and I know most people retire before then, but my father was seventy-two when he finally stopped. But he went of his own accord. I've officially been the Dionach since 1963 when I took over from him, but for the next twelve years he continued to work alongside me, till he decided it was time to retire. But the point is nobody forced him to go.'

Curtis looked at the Dionach. His face was flushed and the veins at both sides of his temples bulged prominently. He was clearly finding this stressful.

'Mr Wyles, there have only been two Dionachs since the Founder started the school in 1917. My father and now me. My son was supposed to take over from me, but, as you know, he's not able to do so. So, forgive me if I'm taking this personally. After seventy-five years loyal service by my family I think I'm entitled to. I was named after the Founder, the college is in my blood, it's all I've ever known Mr Wyles.'

For a few moments Curtis didn't say anything. On the face of it he could see how upsetting this was for his friend. But his lawyer's intuition was telling him that there was more to this than met the eye. He needed to understand why the Dionach was so upset. Surely, thought Curtis, when you're approaching seventy it can't be that surprising that others are expecting you to retire. And as for the lodge, that is part of the college estate, it doesn't seem unreasonable for that to be made available to the next incumbent to the job. Curtis didn't want to appear cold and uncaring. But if he was going to be able to help, he needed to know more.

'I can see that this has come as a complete surprise and the suddenness, well, of course, that's been upsetting. But I'll be honest Donald, I'm struggling to see that Wilder's done anything illegal, I'm sorry if that sounds harsh,' said Curtis. 'Look, I'll level with you. I happen to know there's no love lost between you and Bull Wilder, but that came from others, not him. I didn't know him well at school, but he joined the Buffalos when he was working at police headquarters in Charleston, so for a couple of years I saw him very regularly at lodge meetings. He's direct, abrupt and probably a bit of a bully. Not an ideal quality for a chief of police I'll grant you. But for the record, I never heard him badmouthing you and he certainly never told me why the pair of you didn't get on. So, if I'm going to be able to help, you're going to have to explain to me why that animosity exists?'

Buckley sat down again and stroked his chin.

'He holds a grudge against me,' said Buckley quietly. 'You see his son, Jason, applied to be the Sligachan scholar five years ago. But, unlike his father, he didn't get chosen and Wilder blames me for that.'

Curtis gave Buckley a knowing look.

'And does he have any justification for blaming you, Donald?'

Buckley gave a deep sigh and looked up at the ceiling.

'Ewart Wilder's a cheat Mr Wyles, and more to the point he knows that I know that he's a cheat. You see he cheated when he applied for the scholarship in 1955 and he should never have been given it. I found out because Seth saw what he did and told me. I informed the selection panel, but they wouldn't listen. They said that because Seth is autistic, and his speech is so poor they couldn't accept anything he said as evidence. That hurt Mr Wyles, I can tell you. My son would never lie. But they didn't want to believe Seth, they always felt he

14

was an embarrassment to the school. They didn't even like the fact that I allowed him to tend the gardens. They would have preferred him to have been kept completely out of sight.

The boy who should have got that scholarship was Ralph Portman, but he was a bit too rough around the edges for their liking. From what my father later told me if the Founder had still been alive, he would have chosen Portman in a heartbeat. But he wasn't what the panel were looking for. As it turned out it suited them to give it to Wilder, irrespective of the fact that he'd cheated,' said Buckley.

'You say he cheated, what exactly did he do?' asked Curtis who was now taking copious notes.

'Well back then, Mr Wyles, there were four elements to the scholarship assessment. Nowadays, there are only three. An exam, the mountain run and a panel interview. But as you know the Founder laid great store on a boy's resilience and self-sufficiency and because of his love of the wilderness we used to include a fourth test, usually some type of survival technique like gutting a fish or making a fire. That year the additional test was to skin a rabbit,' explained Buckley.

'Doctor Roberts, who was the Principal back then, stopped the extra test in the late sixties as he wanted a greater emphasis on the academic side of things, skinning rabbits didn't really fit in with his ethos for the school.' Curtis looked up and grimaced.

'Hearing that I'm glad I didn't try for the scholarship. My father wanted me to but my mother, God bless her, just told him to get his chequebook out and pay the fees. Apologies,' said Curtis, 'I digress. I think you were about to explain how Wilder cheated.'

'Indeed,' said Buckley taking off his glasses. 'In those days the exam and the run were done in the morning. We then had an hour lunch break before the interviews and the practical test. That allowed for the boys to see round the school and familiarise themselves with the place. Well that was what was supposed to happen. I can remember it very clearly, Mr Wyles. I'd gone to the dining hall for my lunch. I was never in the habit of locking my door, but it was definitely closed. I'd left a typed note on my desk outlining the details of the test for that afternoon. As it happened, Seth was outside my office working in the garden. Through the window he saw Wilder enter my office and go up to my desk where he picked up and read the typed note. Immediately afterwards, Wilder went next door to the library and found a book on how to trap and skin animals. Again, Seth saw him in the library with the book.

Later that day, after the assessments had all finished, I found the book he'd been looking at. You see he hadn't replaced it in the right section. The book had a red dot on its spine but Wilder had put it back in a section that were all colour coded yellow. I even checked with the Librarian and she was adamant that the book hadn't been borrowed by anyone in months and she never misplaced a book. You see, Mr Wyles, at the practical test, Wilder was head and shoulders better than the other boys. There's a specific way to skin a rabbit. You cut the feet off and slice the skin up the belly to the head. If you know how it's quite straightforward and you can peel the fur off in one piece. Wilder's attempt was almost perfect. The others all made a right pig's breakfast of it. Please understand, Mr Wyles, making me retire and having my family evicted from their home is his way of getting back at me.'

Curtis looked confused.

'I think I must be missing something, Donald. Wilder got his scholarship and went on to be head of school, so why after nearly forty years, does he still hold a grudge? It's not like he lost out on anything is it?'

The Dionach clasped his hands together and gave a little sigh.

'Forgive me, Mr Wyles, I should have explained this more clearly. All that about, Wilder was just the background. The grudge really exists because he blames me for the fact that his son, Jason, wasn't awarded the scholarship when he applied five years ago. And that stopped the Wilders being the first father and son to have both been Sligachan scholars. That's what really irked him.'

'Okay, yes you did say that,' said Curtis writing more notes on his pad. 'But let's cut to the chase. This is the critical bit, does Ewart Wilder have any cause to blame you for that?'

'No,' said the Dionach indignantly, 'I don't believe he has. None of the criteria for the scholarship, and by that, I mean any of the assessments, are set in stone. They can be flexible. One year we dropped the fourth test completely because the fish they were supposed to gut had gone rotten, so you see, Mr Wyles, we have to be adaptable.' Curtis pursed his lips.

'My lawyer's instinct is now telling me you are starting to prevaricate. So, if you don't mind, Just, tell me what happened to prevent Wilder's son getting the scholarship.'

'We didn't do the mountain run,' said the Dionach awkwardly. 'We did a swim in the lake instead. Out to the pontoon and back. And Ryan Portman easily beat Jason Wilder in the swim. As the exam and interview scores had been close it was Portman's prowess in the swim that swung it for him, and he was awarded the scholarship. And that was that really,' said the Dionach putting his hands behind his head and leaning back in his chair.

'Really,' said Curtis sarcastically, 'that was that.' He frowned and stared at the Dionach for several moments not saying anything.

'Donald, I well remember his father Ralph at school. He won all the swimming prizes, every year. He was a fantastic swimmer, he swam like a fish. Something that I'd wager is common to the Portman family. I also happen to know that for the last couple of years Ryan has worked at the outdoor pool in Williamsburg during the summer vacation. I know that as a fact because I met him there when I visited with my family. I bumped into his father at the pool and he introduced me to his son. And before you say anything, you don't get to be a life guard if you're not a strong swimmer. But somehow, I think you know all this.' The Dionach nodded slowly.

'Let me guess, you dreamt up some excuse as to why you couldn't do the mountain run that year, and as you knew Ryan would be a better swimmer than Wilder's boy, it conveniently meant you could thwart Jason's scholarship ambitions. Am I right, Donald?'

'Pretty much,' said Buckley with a sly smile. 'I phoned the police to inform them that a mountain lion had been spotted by some walkers while out hiking earlier in the day. That provided me with the reason I needed to change the run to a swim. It wouldn't have been safe you see.'

'Well it wouldn't have been safe if it had been true. But to my knowledge there never have been mountain lions in Greenbrier County. I take it you just made that story up?' asked, Curtis draining the last dregs from his coffee cup.

The Dionach looked down at his feet and nodded. Then he started to laugh.

'Sharp practice maybe, but I wouldn't call it cheating, Mr Wyles. Summary justice don't you think? And pretty sweet that it was Ralph Portman's son who got the scholarship instead of Wilder's boy. Makes up for Ralph losing out to Ewart all those years ago.' said Buckley still chuckling.

'Yes, I can see there is a certain irony to that,' said Curtis scratching his head. 'And I bet it breaks your heart to think that Ewart Wilder has had to pay full fees for the last six years.'

'Yep, I'm devasted by that,' said Buckley struggling to contain his glee. 'No more than the man deserves, he's a complete shit.'

Curtis looked up from his desk and gave the Dionach a knowing look.

'Seriously, Donald, regardless of what you or I may think, I'm struggling to see how any of this helps your case. I mean you not having to retire or move out of the house. In fact, from what you've told me, I'm beginning to understand why Wilder's so annoyed about it all. By the way, and this is just a thought, what about the house by the lake? I know it's currently used to store the boats and canoes, but wouldn't that be an option? Even if it were only on a temporary basis. Have you discussed that as a possibility with Wilder? Surely the school could find somewhere else to store the boats and equipment?'

The Dionach smiled and shook his head.

'You would have thought so. That would have been a perfect solution, well in terms of where we might live, but you see, Mr Wyles, Wilder and the board have agreed to turn the lake house into a dormitory to be used by the head of school and his four house captains. The work is already underway. They're spending thousands adding extra bedrooms and another bathroom. Funny how all this is happening at the same time I'm being told that I'll have to retire and move out. As I said, Mr Wyles, Wilder is determined to get back at me for what happened to his son.'

Curtis pulled a face and rested his chin on his hands.

'That is all very unfortunate, but as unreasonable as this is going to sound, there's nothing in what you've told me that would stand a cat's chance in hell in a court. In fact, it would never see the inside of a court, they just wouldn't entertain it. So, despite everything you've told me, unless there is something else, I can't see how I can begin to help you.'

'There is something else,' said Buckley in a serious voice. Curtis put down his pen and looked up.

'Okay, I'm listening, go on.'

'I believe there is a letter, written by the Founder and given personally to my father, that explicitly states that while Marsco College exists, the Buckley family will continue to occupy the lodge house and carry out the duties of the Dionach at the school.'

Curtis folded his arms and leant forward on his desk.

'Now that sounds a whole lot more interesting. But you said you believe there to be a letter. I take it by that that you don't actually have the letter?'

'That is correct, Mr Wyles, but I am in the process of trying to establish its whereabouts. Up till now I'd never given it that much thought. Father had mentioned it a couple of times years ago, but I don't recall ever seeing the letter. I just knew that it existed. Then in my father's latter years, probably for the last five before he died, he had dementia, I don't suppose he could remember the letter and certainly not where he put it. But he was a hoarder and I never knew him to throw anything out, so I think we will still have it somewhere, it's just that at this precise moment I don't know where that somewhere might be.'

'This is much more like it, Donald. Something we can potentially get our teeth into,' said Curtis animatedly. 'But it all hinges on you being able to find the letter. Without it you don't have much of a case, well any case if I'm honest. But this could be a game changer, particularly if, as you suggest, it makes specific provision for your family to remain in the house and of course, continue the Dionach dynasty. Look, I'm coming to the seventy-fifth anniversary dinner at the beginning of next month. That gives you a week or so to hopefully find it. Give me a call as soon as you manage to lay your hands on it. But we'll talk more when I see you at the dinner.'

Buckley nodded. 'I really appreciate your help, Mr Wyles.'

'Talking of the dinner, I take it you'll be giving us a couple of the Bard's songs?'

Buckley smiled and nodded. 'It might be my last chance, so I suppose I should try and make the most of it.'

'Now don't say that, all is not lost, not by a long way. I think we may just be getting somewhere now. But we do need you to find that letter.' 'I understand that,

Mr Wyles, and I'm going to turn the house upside down in an effort to find it.' The Dionach stood up to shake hands with Curtis. 'And I want you to know, I'm very grateful for your time and help.'

The Dionach turned to leave but paused at the doorway. Reaching into his jacket pocket he took out his diary.

'Remind me, Mr Wyles, what was your graduation year?'

'1961, the year after Wilder,' replied Curtis.

The Dionach skimmed through the pages then smiled.

'Only fifty-seven referrals all year, that's the second lowest in the history of the college. You know that's 121 fewer than Wilder's mob. And what's more, their total doesn't even take into consideration the incident at the Greenbrier bridge. What a parcel of rogues they were.'

Chapter 3

As usual at that time of the evening, Bursley's Bar was packed with office workers stopping off for a drink on their way home. Charlie scanned the room looking for an empty table and a broad smile broke out across his face. Sitting at a table in the far corner were Chris, Angela and Phil Coutts. Charlie waved to his friends.

'I should have known,' said Charlie patting Mike on the back. 'I'm going to have to sharpen up if I'm going to make a success of this new job. How many years have we worked together?' said Charlie shaking his head.

'Quite a few, but there was no way we could let this pass without celebrating with a few of your buddies. Now, what are you having?'

'The usual,' replied Charlie.

'Two Stroh's when you get a minute,' said Mike to the barman who was clearing some glasses from the counter. Mike turned around just in time to see his other colleagues raising their empty glasses.

'Tell you what, better make that five, seems like my timing is as good as ever,' added Mike with a sigh. Charlie laughed.

'Comes with the territory, responsibilities of being the boss you see,' said Charlie with a wink.

'Well why are you not getting them in then?' asked Mike with faux outrage. 'You're the boss now!'

'Ah, you see, that's where you're wrong. My promotion doesn't take effect until the morning,' replied Charlie quick as a flash.

'Huh, appears there is nothing wrong with your reactions when it comes to avoiding getting a round in.' said Mike sarcastically as he placed the five glasses of beer on a tray. Charlie laughed and slapped his boss on the back.

'Relax will you, I'll be getting the next one in.'

'Oi, watch what you're doing,' said Mike desperately trying not to spill any of the beer, 'now make yourself useful and pass these around before that thirsty horde makes a grab for this tray and spills even more than you have already.'

After a kiss from Angela and a handshake from the others, the five friends clinked and raised their glasses as Mike proposed a toast to Charlie, congratulating him on his promotion, and wishing him well in his new role.

'And, on a personal note,' said Mike, 'can I just add, that I'm very much looking forward to my extra half hour in bed and not having to sit through Bull's morning meeting rants and the insufferable contributions of sycophantic weasels like Mitchell and Price.'

'You're really selling it to him boss,' said Chris between mouthfuls of his beer.

'Shit,' said Charlie looking perplexed, 'I never thought about the early start to prepare for the meeting. Mrs Finch is really going to love this, I usually drop the kids off for school in the mornings, that isn't going to work now is it?' Charlie looked despondent.

'Ah, the unseen consequences of high office,' said Phil with a smile. 'But don't be worrying about that just now. Apart from Mike you now outrank all of us, so I suppose we all work for you now, I'm sure we'll be able to work something out. There's always a way Charlie.'

'Appreciate that,' said Charlie with a nod. 'It's going to be a steep learning curve and take a bit of getting used to that's for sure. It's funny, but it's simple things like that that you never consider. But hey, it's all good, what's not to like, acting lieutenant who would have thought it. Listen Phil, changing the subject, a little bird told me that that you were putting your ticket in. Surely not. I didn't think you were old enough to retire.' said Charlie.

'Not sure who you've been talking to but nothings decided yet. I'm just thinking about it. I've got the service to retire and I'll let you know that I'm fifty-two, so plenty old enough. It'll not be this year though. Sometime next year perhaps, but I want to wait until Sam is properly settled in the job before I go. I know that's a bit ridiculous to say, but I suppose it's a fatherly thing. I just want to see that's he's going to be okay, especially after the start he's had.' said Phil quietly.

'Of course, that's perfectly understandable. How's he doing anyway? I'd heard he'd been in hospital. If you don't mind me asking what happened? I know he was at the training college and had some sort of reaction, but that's about all I know.'

'It was just such a weird thing. They were doing a practical exercise involving some sort of drug search. Apparently, Sam found the piece of cannabis down the sock of the instructor but about ten minutes later he started to feel sick and his hands and arms broke out in large hives. The most concerning thing was his tongue started to swell and he was having difficulty swallowing. They called an ambulance and he was rushed to the hospital. The doctor who saw him was pretty sure he'd suffered some form of anaphylactic shock. It seems it was brought on by the cannabis resin. Very unusual but not unheard of they said. Anyway, the doc treating him said he'd never encountered it before, well not one brought on by touching cannabis. But the good news is he's made a full recovery and been back at work for a few weeks.'

'Good grief, I hadn't appreciated it was so serious,' said Charlie puffing out his cheeks. 'Well, one thing's for sure, he isn't destined for a career in narcotics!'

'No, I don't suppose he is. When he's operational he's supposed to carry extra thick rubber gloves, in case he has to search anybody for drugs,' said Phil with a smile.

'Since he started, he's been working with Neil Planner on general patrol duties which I'm pleased about. Neil's a sound guy and has endless patience, he'll need it too, Sam can get a bit hyper sometimes and is full on. When he was a child we wondered if he might have ADHD. It turned out he doesn't, but they did diagnose that he had mild dyslexia, so writing police reports and doing exams is always going to be challenging for him. But on the flip side of that he's absolutely brilliant with figures.' Charlie laughed.

'Yes, I'd heard that. I was speaking to Neil the other day and he told me about the shift night out in Ronceverte, all of them arguing because they couldn't work out how much change they should each get back after the food and drinks were paid for. Quick as you like Sam piped up $3.83 or something like that. Turns out he'd worked it out in his head. They couldn't believe it, so they checked it with a calculator, and he was spot on, to the exact cent. Quite amazing, Neil couldn't believe how quickly he'd worked it out.' Phil nodded and laughed.

'I know, it's just how his brain is wired. He's got a remarkable ability for numbers. I think it must be connected to his dyslexia. It somehow compensates for his struggles with words and spelling. Poor at one thing brilliant at another. Just as well they hadn't asked him to write down the drinks order, goodness knows what he might have come back from the bar with.'

'Perhaps he should have been an accountant,' said Charlie, 'sounds like bean counting would have been right up his street.' Phil gave a wry smile.

'It wouldn't have suited him. He could handle the figures no problem but sitting in an office all day, that would make him demented. As I said he's a bit of a live wire so a job that lets him get out and about is much more his thing.'

'He sounds like an interesting guy, I'd like to meet him. You should have invited him along, would have helped bring the age profile down a bit, as both you and Mike are cracking on a bit,' said Charlie with a chuckle.

'He would have enjoyed it too I'm sure, but he's on annual leave this week and he's away to Oklahoma to a friend's wedding, someone he met at college apparently.'

'Oklahoma,' exclaimed Charlie, 'how's he getting there, it's miles away?'

Phil smiled and gently shook his head.

'He's driving. I know, I know, it's utter madness but he worked out the cost of flying, Amtrak and the bus and he reckons driving is the cheapest option, so he's away in his car. Just hope it makes it as it's a ten-year old Toyota.'

'Jeezo, Phil, that must be nearly a twenty-hour drive, and the same back of course, he'll be the best part of four days just driving. He'll be exhausted when he gets back.'

Phil raised his eyebrows and smiled again.

'I tried to explain all that to him, but he wasn't for changing his mind. I did say his brain was wired a little differently. Anyway, you won't have to wait too long to meet him, he's due to go on a fortnight's attachment working with you detectives in November, and as you're now the boss, you'll get to decide what to do with him.'

'I'll look forward to that,' said Charlie patting Phil on the shoulder. 'Maybe I'll just lock him in an office and get him to scrutinise all the department's overtime and expenses claims, at least that way I'll know they'll be accurate, and it would be one less thing for Bull to have a pop at me about.'

The two friends laughed and drained their glasses.

'Same again?' asked Charlie raising his glass in the direction of his colleagues.

'Sure,' said four voices in unison.

'This new boss shows considerable promise don't you think,' said Angela nudging Chris on his arm.

'Certainly does,' replied Chris. 'Much more amenable than that old curmudgeon we used to have as our leader!'

Mike tilted his head and glowered as the others burst into laughter.

*

It was a little after six, when Ewart Wilder drew up outside his house in a quiet cul-de-sac on the west side of Fairlea.

'Complete waste of money if you ask me,' muttered Wilder as he pressed the key fob for the umpteenth time attempting to operate the electronic security gates that his wife, Bridget, had insisted they had installed at the entrance to their impressive four bedroomed villa.

'Every night's the freaking same, no use having the damn things if they don't work properly,' his frustration and blood pressure rising in equal measure with each failed attempt. Eventually the gates started to part. Before they had fully opened Wilder sped through spinning his wheels and scattering pebbles into flowerbeds and across the immaculately cut lawn.

He braked sharply coming to a halt in front of the double garage that adjoined the white fronted Georgian Colonial property. Already late, he grabbed his briefcase and hurried towards the front door. Noticing his wife's car, he stopped abruptly then walked suspiciously across the driveway to the vehicle that was parked underneath three enormous pine trees.

'How many fucking times does she need to be told?' fumed Wilder as he placed his finger into the sticky resin and pine needles that covered the roof of the car. 'Every other week she does it. Fuck! Perhaps she does it just to annoy me.' he muttered. 'Surely nobody can be that stupid!'

'Where have you been?' asked Bridget taking a plate of macaroni cheese out of the oven as her husband walked into the kitchen. 'Not sure you'll even have time to eat this. Were you remembering that you've got a board of governors meeting at the school at seven?'

'What do you mean, where have you been? I've been at the god damn office dealing with any amount of garbage, and yes I was remembering about the meeting.' said Wilder picking up a fork and theatrically plunging it into the blackened top of the macaroni.

'It would have been fine if you'd been home at half five like you said you would. I had it ready for then, but since you are forty minutes late it's dry and a bit burnt. Just leave it if you don't want it,' said Bridget calmly.

Twenty years of marriage had taught her that getting into an argument with Ewart Wilder was a futile exercise. He would never back down and as for seeing the other person's point of view, well that wasn't in his locker. He was irascible and operated on a very short fuse. Despite his volatile temper their marriage had mainly been a happy one. They had a much-loved son; a beautiful home and her husband was chief of police. There was much to be content with. Her spouse's high office brought a certain cachet that Bridget relished. Everyone in Fairlea knew who Bridget Wilder was and that sat well with her.

'I could make you up a sandwich which you could eat on the way over if you'd like?' said Bridget in a conciliatory voice.

'No, it's fine,' said Wilder between mouthfuls of the macaroni. 'This is a bit dry, but I've tasted worse. Don't think I'll finish it, but it will keep me going till after the meeting. I might pick up a burger on the way home.'

'Whatever suits best darling,' said Bridget rubbing the back of her husband's shoulders. 'By the way Jason phoned earlier, he said he might try and catch you after the meeting, but he has a lacrosse match in Williamsburg and isn't sure if he'll get back before you have to leave. Either way he was phoning to let us know that he's made up his mind, and Duke will be his first choice for university next year. If he doesn't get into Duke, he's going to try Tuft's. He asked me to let you know.'

'Duke or Tuft's eh, our son doesn't do anything by half measures does he. Duke is just about the most expensive university out there and Tuft's isn't a kick up the pants away from it. Oh well, six years of boarding fees at Marsco followed by four years at university, but hey, it's all good, it's just money after all.' said Wilder sarcastically.

'Oh, give over will you. He's our only son and of course we'll want the best for him. And when he's rich and successful, I'm sure he'll want to keep his old father in the style you've become accustomed to.' replied Bridget. Wilder shook his head and laughed.

'You are joking, aren't you? I can live pretty frugally, it's you that he has to worry about. He can just give me a pill and be done with it when I'm an old git. You on the other hand will cost a fortune. Bet you'll want Calvin Klein incontinence pants, nothing but the best for Mrs Wilder!'

'Now you're just being gross, Ewart. I may like nice things but that's just being vulgar.' said Bridget as she loaded plates into the dishwasher.

'Look at the time, you better get a move on if you've to be there for seven. And just one more thing before you go, I've arranged a viewing for the lake house at Fayetteville on Saturday. I did tell you so no excuses. You promised that this would be the year we could get a lake house and this one looks like it might be ideal. So, please, don't go and arrange anything for Saturday morning, I said we'd be there at ten.'

The road to White Sulphur Springs was quiet and the drive to the college took no more than twenty minutes. Seems strange, thought Wilder, as he meandered his way past the fields and small farmsteads that edged the foothills of the Allegheny Mountains, my son only lives eleven miles from the school, but he's still required to board. There can't be many kids at boarding schools who live only a twenty-minute drive away. It would save a fortune if he'd been able to attend as a day pupil. Wilder was genuinely concerned as to how he was going to pay for everything. He might have a decent salary, but with university fees and the probability of a second property to pay for, money was going to be tight. And that's all on top of what Bridget is already spending. That woman has an insatiable appetite for stuff. Expensive stuff, and stuff that we don't need. Wilder's head began to hurt just thinking about it.

It had always been a requirement for pupils at Marsco to board, but as he parked his car and made his way across the gravel forecourt to the imposing stone building in which most of the classrooms and offices were located, any notion that that should change immediately evaporated. Just look at this place, thought Wilder, its magnificent. For several moments he stood quietly soaking up the ambiance of this special place.

The main school building was built in the Scottish baronial style. Its lavish towers and decorative corbelling, a nod to its French renaissance influence. Though built largely of brick, the facing stones were made of buff coloured sandstone quarried locally in Summers County. Decades of exposure to the elements had given the stone a greyish tinge. On the crow's steps of the gable end where the prevailing wind was harshest, the stone was pitted and granular giving lie to the fact that the building was not even a hundred years old.

Wilder turned and peered down the manicured lawn to the lake and forest beyond. In the far distance the imposing presence of Greenbrier Mountain, stood proud and sentinel in the fading light. The mountain, almost a mirror image of Marsco, the crowning jewel of the Red Cuillin range, and from whom the school took its name, was a constant reminder of the Founder and his boyhood home on the Isle of Skye.

To the left of the lake next to the football and lacrosse pitches stood Dunvegan, Wilder's old house and dormitory. He smiled to himself as he remembered the bitter rivalry and inter-house competitions that punctuated life at Marsco throughout the school year. Blood, sweat and even some tears had been shed ensuring Dunvegan were crowned house champions when Wilder was head of school. Nothing but victory would do and Portree, Kyleakin and Glenbrittle, the other three houses, hadn't had a look in, he had made sure of that. By the start of the summer term Dunvegan had the Founder's Cup all sewn up. That wasn't going to be the case this year. The first month of the Michaelmas term suggested that things would be tight. For the first time in years it looked like all houses would be in the running for this year's trophy.

I'll have to have a word with Jason, thought Wilder, as his son, like his father before him, was house captain of Dunvegan. It's six years since we last won the cup, that's way too long and it's about time that situation changed.

Ewart Wilder firmly believed that he wouldn't be the man he was if he hadn't attended Marsco. It was fortunate that he won the scholarship, as without it, his parents would never have been able to afford the fees. As was the case with all Sligachan scholars, there was an expectation that they would accede to become head of school in their final year. To be awarded the scholarship each recipient had undergone an intensive selection process and proved their capabilities across a range of disciplines. It was a fundamental belief of the Founder that the school would only flourish and have its ethos and principles upheld, if it was under the leadership of its best boys. In that way he could keep the 'bloodline' pure and the school would continue to prosper.

Never in the history of the school had the Sligachan scholar not taken up the position as head of school, but in September 1960 that rite of passage hung by a thread. What happened that fateful night at Greenbrier bridge was never properly established. If it had been Wilder would certainly not have been head boy. In all likelihood, he would also have been stripped of the scholarship and been expelled from the school. But nothing was ever proved. Many had their own thoughts as to what had happened that night, but in the absence of any wrongdoing being established by the police, not a word was spoken and Wilder took up the office he believed was his right.

Entering the school building through the arched doorway, Wilder made his way up the sweeping staircase which ran off both sides of the large reception hall. Carpeted in McCaig tartan, an attractive pattern of dark blue and green squares overlaid with a thin red crosshatch, the staircases met at a narrow landing above which hung an enormous oil painting. More than seven feet high and five feet across, the painting had been commissioned by the Founder and had hung in its current position since the college opened in 1917. Set in an ornate golden frame, the foreground of the painting depicted a small white walled cottage with three figures standing to its side. Beyond the cottage a winding path rose gently up the slopes of Glen Sligachan to the centrepiece of the painting and the brooding presence of Marsco. Guarded on either side by Beinn Dearg Mhor and Ruadh Stac, dark thunder clouds and a menacing sky shrouded the mountain giving it a strange, almost mystical appearance, like some creation from Tolkien's middle earth.

On a brass plaque at the bottom of the painting were the words Duthaich nan Diathan[1]. Wilder smiled to himself. He had been thirteen when he had first seen the painting. During a tour of the school the Dionach had gone to great lengths to explain the importance of the picture to the boys gathered at the top of the stairs. His words had fallen largely on deaf ears as their minds were focused firmly on the scholarship assessments that lay ahead. Several years later, as head of school, Wilder found himself explaining the significance of the painting to parents and benefactors who visited the school each year as part of the annual Founders day celebrations.

Donald Alban McCaig, had been born in Sligachan on the Island of Skye in 1879. Until the age of eighteen he had lived in a cottage at the head of the glen with his mother and father. Learning only his native Gaelic as a small child, he had been nearly ten before he had become fluent in English. A necessity his father said, if he was going to be able to communicate with the affluent English visitors, who arrived each autumn to shoot grouse and stalk deer on the nearby Strathaird estate. A polite and industrious boy could earn good

---

[1] Translated from Gaelic this means 'God's country'.

money in tips grouse beating or carrying the guns for wealthy patrons, but only if he spoke English. Without it the Laird wouldn't entertain you and your money-making opportunities would be seriously restricted.

Around the same age he learned English, Donald started to accompany his father on his regular excursions into the hills and mountains around their cottage that made up the Red Cuillin range. It was during those formative years of hiking and hunting that he developed his skills of self-reliance and his love of the outdoors. Occasionally, such adventures would necessitate that they spent the night on the mountain and he well remembered bivouacking on the hillside with no more than an outcrop of rock and a deer hide for protection. Soon, the young Donald was being sent out into the hills on his own to camp, snare mountain hares and fish for wild brown trout in the numerous small lochs that nestled between the hills. You learned to grow up fast when faced with such challenges. Throughout those childhood years, the presence of Marsco was never far away. He could see the mountain through his bedroom window and during the endless daylight hours of summer, it was the first thing he saw in the morning and the last thing he saw at night.

Marsco had also provided him with his first stag. Aged twelve, and under the watchful eye of his father, he had stalked and shot his first deer on boggy ground just below Bealach. It had been a clean kill and when his father cut off his trophy's ear and bloodied his face, there was no prouder boy on Skye.

But the idyll of island life was not to last. Work was scarce, and other than assisting his father on their croft and occasional work as a ghillie for the local estate, there was no work to be had. There was barely enough food to feed two mouths let alone three. No one was therefore surprised when, just after his eighteenth birthday, Donald announced that he'd decided to emigrate and seek a new life in the United States. He knew it was the right decision but leaving his beloved Skye left him with a heavy heart. His departure being all the more poignant as it would be the last-time he would see his parents alive. Twenty months after leaving home, both of his parents were dead. They developed tuberculosis during the ferociously cold winter of 1899 and passed away within nine days of each other. By the time news of their deaths reached Donald they had been joined by five other victims in the small graveyard at Bracadale.

By late October 1897, Donald had arrived in New York and found work as a barman in the prestigious Waldorf hotel on the corner of fifth avenue and thirty-third street. Opened in 1893, the majestic ten storey building was frequented by the great and the good of New York society. It was there, while serving after dinner drinks in the Empire Room one evening, that Donald McCaig got his big break. He happened to remark to the gentleman hosting the dinner that, if he didn't mind him saying, he had made a fine choice of whisky. The man broke off his conversation and stared at Donald over the rim of his spectacles.

'Judging by your accent, I take it you know Talisker and Skye then?' said the gentleman stroking a neatly trimmed white beard.

'Yes sir, I do,' replied Donald politely. 'I'm from Skye and my uncle used to work at the distillery at Carbost.'

That simple exchange of pleasantries was about to change Donald McCaig's life forever. The man who had ordered the Talisker turned out to be none other than Andrew Carnegie, the Scottish steel magnate, who by then was well on the way to becoming one of the richest men in the country. What happened thereafter is a little unclear, but what is known is that Donald McCaig was offered a job and shortly afterwards moved to Pittsburgh, to take up a position with the Carnegie Steel Company. He was not yet twenty years old.

Some say that the Greenbrier Steel Corporation, the company Donald founded in 1902, was started with $100,000 given to him as a gift by Carnegie in 1901, when he sold his steel empire to J.P.Morgan, making Carnegie the richest man in America. Whether that story was apocryphal or not, it remains a fact that Donald McCaig went on to become a very wealthy businessman in his own right, with steel from his Greenbrier mill, building bridges and supplying construction projects throughout West Virginia and the length and breadth of the eastern seaboard.

As well as a shrewd head for business, there was something else that Donald shared with Carnegie. He had a generous heart and a desire to share his wealth for the benefit of others. Although still only a young man, no-one was really surprised that Donald McCaig had never married. There just wasn't the time. Every waking hour was given over to steelmaking. Round the clock, fifty-two weeks a year, the mill was never idle. Like his mentor, McCaig used the Bessemer process to turn molten pig iron into high quality steel. He made his first million by the age of twenty-five and in a little over fifteen years, he had created a thriving business employing more than 300 men. By his thirtieth birthday his personal wealth had swelled to an eye watering $40 million. With no family of his own, Donald started to look for other ways to use his fortune.

There can be no doubt that his own philanthropy was inspired by the actions of Carnegie. Like his mentor, McCaig started to distribute his money to numerous local charities and worthy causes. He also made sure that he didn't forget his childhood home in Skye. The island, and Sligachan in particular, being the beneficiary of several sizable donations. By example, the tiny graveyard at Barcadale where his parents were buried, received $50,000 dollars to ensure the proper upkeep of the church and grounds. By the fall of 1915 several million dollars had been given away.

It was, however, a chance encounter when out hillwalking with a friend one beautiful April morning that an unexpected opportunity presented itself. Returning to his vehicle after an ascent of the Greenbrier, his favourite of the Allegheny Mountains, Donald noticed a 'For Sale' sign fixed to a palisade fence a short distance from his car. Through the gaps in the fence he could see a large baronial style mansion. Several other outbuildings stood on beautifully manicured lawns to the side of the house and in the far distance he could see a lake and what appeared to be a boathouse.

For several years, Donald had harboured an ambition to start a school for boys. Built on an ethos of self-reliance and resilience, he wished to create an environment where as well as a rigorous academic grounding, boys could be taught many of the life skills that he had learned with his father in Skye all those years ago. He knew how fortunate he had been to have met Andrew Carnegie, and not a day went by that he wasn't grateful for that stroke of good fortune. But he was equally sure, that if it hadn't been for his father, and the opportunities given to him to experience the harsh realities of life in the mountains, he would never have become the success he now was.

Within two months of that fateful day, he had purchased the property and set about the monumental task of converting the house into a boarding school for boys. Eighteen months and several million dollars later the school was ready to receive its first pupils. On 4th October 1917, eighty-four boys entered the gates of Marsco College, named of course after the mountain that had dominated so much of his early life. The name and location of the school proved particularly apposite, as the Greenbrier mountain that provided a magnificent back drop to the school, had a striking physical likeness to Marsco. The two mountains were also of a similar height, it couldn't have been more perfect as far as Donald McCaig was concerned.

*

'Excuse me Mr Wilder,' gasped a clearly out of breath boy as Ewart opened the door into a spacious room at the top of the stairs.

'Sorry to bother you, sir. But I've a message from Mr McKean, he's asked me to tell you that the Dionach won't be able to make this evening's meeting, something urgent has come up and he's had to go to Lewisburg. Mr McKean asked me to give you this. He says it's the Dionach's report.' Wilder snatched the handwritten note from the boy.

'He didn't give you anything else to give me?' snapped Wilder without a word of thanks to the boy. 'I was expecting the archive! The Dionach was supposed to be bringing me the archive.' he continued, his voice laced with exasperation.

'I'm very sorry sir, but Mr McKean said to tell you that the Dionach couldn't find it, but he was going to keep looking for it and get it to you as soon as he could.'

'Did he now!' said Wilder angrily shaking his head. The boy looked down at his shoes not saying anything. 'I take it you are duty team tonight?'

'That's correct sir, Mr McKean and Glenbrittle are duty team all week,' replied the boy nervously.

'Right then, I need you to have Mr McKean meet me here after my meeting. It should last about an hour, so have him meet me at eight and tell him to make sure he has his keys with him, do you understand?' The boy nodded and scurried away down the stairs.

'What's up Ewart?' asked a white-haired man who was sitting reading a set of previous minutes at the far end of the large mahogany conference table that dominated the room. 'You don't look best pleased.'

'That is something of an under-statement,' said Wilder sardonically as he started to unpack his briefcase. 'That man is going to drive me to distraction. You know this is all to do with us telling Buckley that he will have to retire and vacate the lodge house next year. It's his way of getting back at us.'

'Sorry but you've lost me now, what's he supposed to have done?' asked the white-haired man.

'He's not coming to the meeting tonight, apparently he's got some urgent appointment in Lewisburg. But he's at it, I know he is. Look? He's given us a handwritten report. Well, I say report, but it's no more than two pages of undecipherable scribbles. The Dionach's report is a standing item on this agenda. Always has been as far as I'm aware. And what's more he was supposed to have the archive for me tonight. I can't write my speech for the dinner without it. That son of a bitch is starting to test my patience. But if he thinks I, or this committee for that matter, are going to change our minds, then the man's more stupid than I thought he was.'

'I see,' said the white-haired man studiously avoiding eye contact as he returned to reading his papers.

By the time the other four members of the governors committee had arrived Wilder had just about regained his composure. Most of the next hour was taken up discussing arrangements for the seventy-fifth anniversary dinner that was now just over a week away. The committee's secretary informed the meeting that 138 former pupils had now confirmed their attendance. Adding on thirty-nine staff, the head of school and the four house captains, that meant that 182 would be sitting down to dinner. Everyone agreed that that was a splendid response and Wilder asked the secretary to make a note of the committee's appreciation in the minutes.

The only point from the Dionach's report that Wilder deemed worthy of mentioning, was the fact that for the third time this year, intruders had been seen within the school grounds near to the lake. As no activity had been reported at any of the school buildings, most round the table agreed, it was likely to be poachers after trout from the lake, which had been an ongoing problem for many years. After a brief discussion, it was unanimously agreed there was a need for vigilance, especially in the lead up to the dinner.

It was quarter past eight by the time the meeting concluded, Mr McKean had been waiting patiently at the top of the stairs for the last twenty minutes.

'Have you brought your keys?' asked Wilder without a word of apology for the meeting having run over.

'Yes sir, I have them here,' said McKean holding up a large bunch of keys.

'Good, then I need you to open the Dionach's office for me.'

'Okay,' said McKean hesitantly, 'have you left something in it?'

'No,' said Wilder trying his best to remain calm, 'I just want to check something. And given he's not here, I need you to open the door for me.' continued Wilder who was less than impressed with the tone of McKean's voice.

'Are you sure his office is locked?' asked McKean innocently.

'Well why don't we go and find out,' said Wilder whose increasing level of frustration was apparent by the flushed colour of his cheeks.

'Just as well you brought the keys then,' said Wilder with a smirk after finding the door to the office locked.

'Indeed,' said McKean searching through the bunch of keys. Having found the appropriate key, he unlocked the door and stood at the entrance to the office while Wilder prowled the room.

'Well colour me surprised,' said Wilder lifting a large leather-bound book from a shelf at the back of the Dionach's desk. 'Unless I'm very much mistaken this appears to be the college archive Mr McKean, the one you had reported to me that the Dionach couldn't find.' McKean shrugged his shoulders.

'I'm only reporting what the Dionach told me, Mr Wilder. If you have an issue with that can I suggest that you take that up with the Dionach.'

'Oh, I will, Mr McKean, you don't need to worry about that.'

'Will there be anything else sir?' asked McKean in a perfunctory voice.

'Nothing else, Mr McKean thank you. You've been most helpful.'

As McKean turned to leave, he paused for a moment.

'Sorry sir, but there is something else, apologies but I forgot to pass on that your son telephoned to say that he wouldn't make it back before you had to leave. Anyway, he asked me to tell you that they lost to Williamsburg in overtime. Oh well, better luck next time eh. Just as well it's only a game.'

Chapter 4

The light drizzle that had started to fall through the night had now turned to heavy and persistent rain. Charlie Jarret hunched up his shoulders and pulled his neck down, attempting to prevent the rain from running down the back of his jacket. But it was to no avail. The collar and back of his shirt were already saturated, and the cold dampness was starting to chill his kidneys. A dull ache had replaced the sharp pain of earlier, but Charlie still winced as he looked down at his left ankle. It was clearly broken and lying at such an unnatural angle that it looked like his foot was on back to front.

With a calliper on his other leg and without his crutch, Charlie knew he was in trouble. He had made several feeble attempts to crawl up the steep side of the ditch, but the pain from his ankle was excruciating. He'd be lucky if he moved more than a couple of feet. With nothing to hold onto it looked an impossible task. Lying on his back looking up at the leaden sky he had no idea how he could get out of his predicament. He was starting to feel scared, and to make matters worse he didn't have a clue where he was.

It had been no more than half an hour from the time they bundled him into the pick-up to the time they callously pushed him into the ditch. Even though he was in considerable pain, Charlie hadn't lost consciousness at any time and he'd looked at his watch immediately after he found himself at the bottom of the ditch, it had been just after ten to two. He remembered it had been about a quarter past one when he'd set his rod and settled into his fishing chair. So, wherever he was, he couldn't be much more than thirty minutes from Greenbrier bridge. Of course, it had been pitch-black, and he hadn't recognised any buildings or other landmarks as he lay in the back of the pick-up. He couldn't tell if they'd driven him north, south, east or west. Judging by the lack of vehicle traffic on the road above him, Charlie reckoned it was likely that he was on some remote track high up in the Allegheny mountains, but more than that he couldn't say.

The ditch must have been at least fifteen-feet deep and it's banks were covered in long lush grass. He couldn't see the road, but he knew it couldn't be far above him as he had heard the occasional sound of a vehicle as it sped past heading to goodness knows where. A foot or so behind where he was lying was a stone wall, roughly constructed of large and uneven boulders. Judging by the lichen that covered the stones it looked very old and it continued for as far as he could see.

His first plan of escape had not proved at all successful. He had shouted at the top of his voice whenever he heard a vehicle approaching. But his cries fell on deaf ears. Thinking about it now he realised that plan was never going to work. It was nearly October, cold and it had been raining for hours. No one was going to be driving past with their windows open. Shouting at cars was futile, he needed another plan.

Numerous bull thistles were growing out of fissures at the base of the wall immediately behind where he was lying. Each time he tried to move, their sharp spines scratched at his hands and any other part of exposed flesh. It was impossible to find a position that was out of their reach. Charlie put his hand in his jacket pocket and took out a half-eaten packet of Jolly Ranchers. The blackcurrant candy tasted good and provided a moments distraction from his ordeal. It was strange, but he didn't feel hungry. He had worked out that it must have been more than twelve hours since he'd last eaten, but fear does funny things to you, making you feel hungry just isn't one of them. What it does do, is focus the mind, clarifies your thinking. Like some sixth sense you understand what you must do, the survival instinct is overwhelming, it needed to be if Charlie was going to find a way out of this hell-hole.

Lying on the ground next to the biggest thistle, a few feet to his right were half a dozen small rocks about the size of a tennis ball. If he could manoeuvre himself a little closer, he reckoned he could use the edge of his calliper to drag the loose stones towards him. As there was nothing wrong with his throwing arm, he thought he might be able to throw the rocks over the ditch to the road beyond. Well that was his plan. If he was very lucky, he might hit, or at least come close to hitting, a passing car which would then stop and come to investigate. He would then start to shout and scream, and this nightmare might finally be over.

Half an hour later he had managed to drag the stones to his side. Six attempts, that's all I've got thought Charlie. If this didn't work, he hadn't a clue what else he could do. He was a gambler by nature and had always enjoyed a bet on the horses or a game of cards. Most Friday nights through the winter, he and a few friends would buy a box of beer and play poker until the small hours. He was a risk taker and used to going all in. He hadn't won in a while, but he was an optimist. He had to be, life had thrown a lot at him. He had worn a calliper on his leg since developing polio as a small child, his father had died when he was still a baby and the family had always been dirt poor. His mother, well she had so many problems it was difficult to know where to begin. Charlie had never had it easy, he was due a break and perhaps his luck was about to change.

Being unable to stand was going to make throwing the stones difficult. He wondered if he might be able to kneel, but with his shattered ankle that proved impossible. The only way he was going to be able to throw the rock was to lie on his left side bracing himself with his arm. If he could lever himself a foot or so off the ground, he might create enough room to generate the power needed to propel the rock to the road above. Not wanting to waste any of his six chances, Charlie decided he would rehearse the process, only without an actual rock.

He had imagined that balancing his weight on his side was going to be his biggest problem, but that proved to be the least of his worries. As he pulled his throwing arm back his knuckles smacked into the wall behind him. He hadn't allowed enough clearance and now he was nursing three bleeding and badly scraped knuckles. Charlie managed an ironic laugh. What else could go wrong? There was something strangely comedic about the seriousness of his situation. Look on the bright side, he thought. At least you didn't waste one of your rocks during that cock up.

Having waited nearly twenty minutes for a vehicle to appear his first throw turned into a complete anti-climax.

The rock didn't make it above the height of the ditch and buried itself in a clump of thick grass. Throws two and three had been a little better in so much as they both made it over the ditch. That was at least something, but neither stone had caused a car to stop and come and investigate. With only three rocks remaining Charlie decided not to throw any more. Instead he would wait till later in the afternoon in the hope that the road might become busier as people might be returning home from work. That was the hope anyway.

Charlie knew that by now his brother, Henry would have come looking for him. It had been Henry who had dropped him at the bridge last night so no doubt he would have returned there to look for him when he hadn't returned home. Henry's best friend, Eustace Brownlie, would likely be out looking for him too, but none of that provided much comfort as they wouldn't have a clue as to where to start to look for him. They will have found my fishing gear, thought Charlie. But they will think that I slipped on the muddy bank and drowned myself in the river. No way will they have any idea that I'm stuck in a ditch up some fucking mountain.

'Fuck,' screamed Charlie at the top of his voice. 'Fuck, fuck, fuck.'

For the first time it struck home that he might not get out of here. Water was starting to lie in small puddles at the bottom of the ditch. At that moment they were no more than an inch deep, but if the rain didn't ease up, they would start to rise rapidly.

'Well isn't that just fucking terrific, thirty-nine fucking years on this planet and I'm destined to drown in a fucking ditch. Ain't life a bitch.'

*

49

Five hundred miles away in Indiana, Sam Coutts was eight hours into his mammoth road trip. Okay, so, let's just say there are approximately forty milk duds in a box, and I average about five boxes a week so that's 200, times fifty-two is 10,400. Wow! That's a lot of milk duds to eat in a year, thought Sam putting down the empty candy box on the passenger seat.

It was now after six-thirty and he was just approaching the outskirts of Boonville. Indiana was the third state of the journey and two more lay ahead before he reached his destination in Tulsa. After more than eight hours at the wheel he was just looking forward to getting to Boonville, where he planned to spend the night. It had been a long day and all those hours of driving were starting to take its toll. He was feeling ravenous, but he had it on good authority that Jamieson's Motel served the best steak and fries in the state. It was that thought that was keeping him going.

For someone who was not yet twenty-three, it would be fair to say that Sam Coutts was a little odd. Stick thin with short wiry blond hair, he had a somewhat unusual dress sense. Nothing he wore ever seemed to match and everything always seemed at least one size too big. Sam Coutts was just a little different. As a young child growing up, he had been painfully shy, he didn't have many close friends and his early school years had been a struggle on account of his dyslexia. He had been slow in learning to read and his spelling really wasn't very good. He was in fourth grade before he was properly diagnosed. He had Miss Campbell to thank for that. She knew immediately that something wasn't right. His prowess with numbers and mental arithmetic was starting to shine through and in those subjects, he was streets ahead of the other children in the class. She knew he was a bright kid and her hunch proved to be correct when his test results confirmed that he was dyslexic. After that diagnosis things started to improve. With the proper support his reading and writing got steadily better and with it his confidence.

Throughout his teenage years, English, particularly any written work, continued to be a trial. However, by the end of high school he had managed to scrape together the necessary qualifications to allow him to go to college and study statistics. Four years later, armed with his degree, a sizeable student debt and some new friendships, it was time to step into the real world and find a job. To nobody's surprise Sam chose not to take an office job, but rather he decided to follow in his father's footsteps and join the police. He was fortunate to have been posted to his father's office in Lewisburg where many of his dad's friends kept an eye out for him. For the last six months he had been learning the job on uniform patrol duties and with no two days ever the same, he was as happy as a sandboy.

Most of Sam's friends would have passed the tedium of such a long journey listening to the radio or playing their CD's. But after eight hours behind the wheel he still hadn't turned the radio on. He liked nature, so he had passed some of the time enjoying the beautiful countryside. Past the horse studs of Kentucky, and through Indiana's endless fields of golden corn and ripening pumpkins there had been a lot to see. It was, however, his fascination with numbers, that kept his hyperactive mind alert and focused.

Although he had more than half the journey still to go, he had already stopped twice for fuel. 457 miles and 16 gallons of gas meant he was averaging 28.5 miles to the gallon. Sam wasn't impressed. His ten-year old Toyota was turning into a gas guzzler. Sam had done the arithmetic in his head and then recorded the details in a notebook he kept at the side of his driver's seat. Numbers and statistics were his friends. He had no difficulty working out complicated calculations without the need for a calculator or even a pen and paper. Sam would happily admit that he was obsessed with figures. And it was not just restricted to car journeys. Just about everything he did was recorded and turned into a statistic. If he walked to the shops, he would record the time it took to walk there and back. He used to drive his friends crazy when they went for a round of golf as he recorded every score in his notebook. Not just his but theirs as well. He did the same thing when they went out for a drink or to a restaurant. Each item and its cost were recorded in his book. To those that didn't know him it could all seem just a little bit creepy. It wasn't a great surprise then that Sam was still single. He had friends who were girls, but they made sure that they kept Sam at arms-length. So far, his nerdiness had not proved attractive to the opposite sex, but he remained hopeful. One thing was certain, he was never going to change his ways. He just needed to meet someone who shared his love of numbers.

As he drew up outside the motel it was approaching seven o'clock. After checking in he dumped his bag on his bed and headed for the diner.

'Steak and fries, a side of corn and a strawberry milkshake,' repeated the smiley waitress, 'is that everything?'

'It is for now,' replied Sam with a beaming smile, 'but I've got my eye on a slice of that lemon meringue pie, but we'll see how I get on. I hear the steaks are big in here.'

'You could say that,' said the waitress. 'This is a trucker's motel and truckers don't do small portions, it's steaks the size of your hat, or it isn't worth calling a steak.'

Sam was confused. He had never heard that expression before and as the only two people in the diner who were wearing hats had baseball caps on, he was concerned that his steak might not be very big after all. He needn't have worried. Half an hour later he was done. The T-Bone had hung over all sides of his plate and even though he was hungry as a bear he couldn't finish it.

'I don't suppose you'll be wanting that pie then?' said the waitress with a laugh. Sam leant back in his chair and puffed out his cheeks.

'Nope,' he replied. 'But I'll take another milkshake please. It might help shift that steak. It was really good, but I'm stuffed now. And do you think you could bring the cheque at the same time thanks.'

As Sam waited for his cheque his attention was caught by a large red and white truck that had just pulled off the highway into the car park. It was the West Virginian licence plate that he had noticed first but as the truck parked up, he saw the familiar words 'Deans Haulage' written on its side. He smiled to himself. Small world he thought. Five hundred miles from home and a truck from Huntersville rocks up.

Sam watched as the driver jumped down from the cab and made his way to the diner. The waitress waved at the man as he approached the door.

'Do you know that guy?' asked Sam as the waitress put down his cheque.

'Not really, but he was in here about six weeks ago. I remember him because of his Orioles cap. My mother is from Baltimore and I'm an Orioles fan, so we chatted about baseball. Great team in the seventies but they suck now. Haven't won anything in years. Why you asking?'

Sam shrugged his shoulders.

'No reason really, it's just that I live pretty close to where that haulage company is based. Just wasn't expecting to see someone from where I'm from so far away I suppose.'

The man sat on a stool at the counter and the waitress poured him a coffee. Sam picked up his cheque and started to laugh.

'$17.29, perfect, that's just perfect. Made my day that has,' said Sam handing the waitress a twenty-dollar bill. The waitress frowned.

'What has? You've lost me know.'

'1729 it's a magic number. The only number that can be expressed as the sum of the cubes of two different sets of numbers. They call it Ramanujan's number because he discovered it. Srinivas Ramanujan was an Indian mathematician.'

The waitress scratched her head.

'I'll take you word for that,' she said in a nonplussed voice. Then she continued, 'Do you know what's an even better number?'

'No,' replied Sam, his interest suddenly pricked.

'864.5,' said the waitress with a mischievous smile.

'Never heard of 864.5 being a special number. Why would that be?' asked Sam who was clearly intrigued.

'Because it would have been half of your cheque and paying $8.64 for your steak instead of $17.29 would have been pretty special don't you think?'

The man in the Orioles' cap burst out laughing spluttering coffee all over the counter.

'That'll teach you to be a smart-ass son,' said the man giving Sam a friendly pat on the back. Sam wasn't sure what to say. He certainly wasn't trying to be smart.

'Look, I'm just joking with you. But you've got to hand it to her, that was a darn smart reply she gave you.'

Sam smiled and nodded. 'Yep, I suppose it was.'

'You ordered the nachos and salsa, right?' said the waitress putting down a plate piled high with tortilla chips.

'Wrong,' said the truck driver pulling a face. 'Hate all that Mexican muck! I ordered the philly sandwich.'

'Apologies,' said the waitress removing the plate and giving it to a guy at the other end of the counter. 'Your sandwich will only be a couple of minutes.'

'No hurry,' said the driver with a smile. 'Where you from son? That's a West Virginian accent unless I'm very much mistaken!'

'Yup, you're spot on. I'm from Fairlea, Greenbrier County. Not that far from Huntersville. In fact, I know of the Deans estate where your firm is based.'

'Small world right enough, eh.' Sam smiled and nodded.

'And what takes you to Boonville?' asked the man. 'Middle of nowhere this is.'

'I'm heading to a friend's wedding in Tulsa, just breaking the journey here, it's a bit of a trek to Oklahoma,' said Sam pulling up a stool.

'Tell me about it. I'm on my way back from Mexico. Crossed the border at Nogales, and two nights and 1,600 miles later I've reached here. Still got the best part of 500 miles to go. That's what you call a journey son. Your trip to Tulsa is chicken feed!' Sam and the man both started to laugh.

'Wow, that's an epic journey alright. What were you taking to Mexico?'

'Broiler chickens, corn and tobacco this time but it varies. Depends on the time of year what crops I carry. Just started this run. This is only my second trip to Mexico. The boss wants it as a regular route. I hope it's not too regular, 2,000 plus miles and three overnights, wouldn't want to do that every week.'

Sam blew out his cheeks and shook his head. 'No, I bet you don't. Look can I buy you a beer?'

'Certainly can,' said the man with a grin, 'I refuse nothing but blows.'

'Two beers when you get a moment please,' said Sam waving a ten-dollar bill trying to get the waitresses attention.

From the other end of the counter the waitress put her hand to her mouth and shouted.

'330, that's another magic number.'

'Take it that's the price of two beers,' replied Sam quick as a flash.

'Sure is.' said the waitress placing two bottles on the counter. 'But 400 would be even more special.'

'Is that because it includes seventy cents as a tip?'

The waitress winked and smiled.

'You're sure picking this up quickly, you can come again anytime.'

Chapter 5

Charlie Finch was sitting at his kitchen table dabbing a piece of tissue on his chin. Somehow, he had managed to cut himself shaving and now he was feeling agitated as he couldn't get it to stop bleeding. I didn't need to do that on this of all days, he thought as he poured milk onto a bowl of Cheerios. Today he was up a little earlier than usual in preparation for his first day as acting lieutenant. He was feeling apprehensive and had butterflies in his stomach. Mike's were big shoes to fill and even if his new job was only going to be for six months or so, it still came with considerable responsibilities.

Charlie was still struggling to reconcile that he was the beneficiary of his friend's misfortune and Susan's illness was weighing heavily on his mind. At thirty-seven he was young to take on the role of senior detective and with less than ten years in the department, his rapid elevation had put more than one nose out of joint. That didn't worry him unduly, Charlie knew who they were and believed he had their measure. Anyway, he had a small team of colleagues who were one hundred percent loyal and his most trusted friend, Mike, would be just along the corridor for a word of advice if needed.

'How are you feeling?' asked his wife, Alison, who had appeared wearing her dressing gown and slippers.

'A bit nervous if I'm being honest,' replied Charlie. 'I wasn't expecting to but I am. And I could have done without cutting myself shaving.'

'At least it's not on your shirt.' said Alison inspecting the nick on her husband's chin. 'And don't worry about the nerves, that's perfectly understandable. It's a big job, but you're going to do just fine. You wouldn't have got it if Wilder didn't think you were up to it. Anyway, I think you look very smart in your grey suit.'

'Might be better if you thought I looked very competent, that's probably more important than looking smart.' said Charlie with a nervous laugh.

'Well I think you look both, how's that then,' said Alison kissing her husband on the top of his head.

'Look, why don't you get going, better being early on your first day. I'm dropping the kids off at school, so there's no reason for you to hang about. Get in sharp and get yourself organised.'

Charlie looked at his wife and smiled.

'Only one flaw in that cunning plan, I left my car at the office last night, remember? I must have had at least four beers at Bursley's, so I wasn't going to be driving home. Anyway, Mike's arranged for Susan to run us in this morning, which is good of her, especially considering she picked us up last night as well.'

Alison pulled up a chair and sat at the breakfast bar.

'She's a terrific lady alright, and that's typical of the woman. She won't let her illness get in the way of her life, she's one of the nicest and most determined people I know, she'll fight that cancer head on. And I'll tell you this Charlie Finch, Mike will appreciate that you're taking his job for a while. It will help him to support Susan and that's what's important just now.'

said Alison standing up and looking out of the side window.

'That looks like it might be them now. Yes, Susan's waving, it's definitely them.'

The journey to the police office took no more than fifteen minutes. Susan pulled up at the front door and leant across and gave Mike a kiss.

'Thanks for the lift,' said Charlie getting out the rear of the car. 'Twice in the space of a day, you must feel like a taxi service, but it was very good of you.'

'Not a problem, just happy to help. And good luck today, I know you're going to do just great.' shouted Susan as she pulled away.

'I'm going to swing by the front office and have a word with Phil before heading up. Stick the kettle on and make us a coffee will you, I won't be long.' said Charlie grinning.

'I take it that's a lawful order lieutenant?' replied Mike with a chuckle.

'Yep, it sure is. The first of many, so you better get used to it.'

'Righto sir,' said Mike standing to attention and saluting, 'I'll get straight onto it.'

Phil was in the front office reading an incident report when Charlie walked in.

'Morning Phil, anything doing overnight?'

'Lieutenant Finch, good morning to you. Great night last night. Just a pity we had to come to work this morning. Too many beers for me on a midweek night, I'm feeling it a bit this morning. Must be getting old!' Charlie nodded and smiled.

'On the plus side there's nothing much to report this morning. Well not on the crime side of things,' continued Phil. 'Just a burglary overnight to a cash and carry in Alderson and an assault in Ronceverte. Some guy smashed a pool cue over his friend's head in a bar. Injuries aren't serious, and the uniforms have dealt with it.' added Phil.

'Okay,' said Charlie picking up the incident report, 'that all sounds pretty routine. Just what I was looking for, a nice quiet start. Any suspects for the break-in at the cash and carry? Sounds just like the thing Screech and Eustace would do.'

'You would have thought,' replied Phil, 'but I don't think so this time. The only things that have been stolen are boxes of chocolate and trays of muffins. Sounds like kids. They didn't touch the steaks that were in a freezer or the electrical goods that were at the back of the premises. They smashed a window, which activated the alarm. They just climbed in grabbed the stuff and ran off. Simple as that.'

'Thanks, that's all noted. And you weren't kidding were you, there's next to nothing in the crime file,' said Charlie picking up a ring binder from Phil's desk. "If we can keep it this quiet for the next six months or so, that would do very nicely.'

'Funny that you mentioned Screech in relation to the burglary.' said Phil. 'The only other thing of note that has come in is a missing person enquiry. And its Screech Jarret's brother who's missing. Screech came into the office yesterday afternoon with Brownie to report that his brother, Charlie, hadn't returned from a fishing trip at the Greenbrier Bridge. They spent the morning looking for him and came in afterwards to make the report. We must have just missed them when we left for Bursley's. We've got uniformed officers down there just now, but I've a feeling this one isn't going to end well. They've found all his fishing gear on the riverbank, just no sign of Charlie.'

'Charlie Jarret is that the guy who has a calliper on his leg?' asked Charlie.

'That's him. He's got a couple of convictions. Minor stuff though. He's certainly not a seasoned criminal like his brother. Drunk and disorderly and a couple of thefts. But nothing recent. The last one was over three years ago.'

Charlie nodded. 'Yep, I've met him a couple of times, when I've been at the house looking for Screech. Can you dig out the Missing Person file and send it up when you get a moment, I'll give it the once over?'

'Sure will, boss. Just as soon as the uniforms are finished with it. Sergeant Lang is giving the troops a briefing just now.'

'Thanks Phil. And less of the boss bit, will you? It's making me nervous.'

*

'Not a problem, Phil, I'll let him know,' said Mike putting down the phone as Charlie walked into the detectives' office.

'What's up?' asked Charlie raising an eyebrow.

'Just after you left Phil, he got a radio message to say the uniforms have found Charlie Jarret's crutch lying in some reeds on the other side of the river. They're now asking if the detectives want to take a look.'

'Think I'd better' said Charlie biting the end of his thumb.

'They've not found a body, but it does seem strange that his crutch is on the other side of the river from his fishing gear. The river must be nearly fifty feet wide at the bridge.' added Mike.

'Huh,' said Charlie sitting down at his desk. 'On the face of it, I can't think of a reason to explain how it got to the other side of the river. Maybe it floated across. Would a crutch float? Not sure that it would! It certainly seems a bit weird right enough. I'll head down with Angela after the chief's meeting. It shouldn't take too long as there's nothing of note crime wise to talk about. I might be able to kill two birds with one stone as well. I've a statement to get in Fairlea regarding that domestic assault last week. It'll let me get that case tidied up. We'll stop by the bridge on our way over.'

*

'The water sure is muddy after all that rain,' said Angela as she stood on the bridge with Charlie peering down at the murky soup below. 'Might be a while till it clears enough to let us see the bottom. I take it we would be able to see the bottom? Funny, I've stood on this spot many times, but I can't say for certain if you can see the bottom. Just shows you how much attention I pay.'

'Yep, it's a pity, it's going to make a search of the river a lot more difficult. By the way, do you know who the sergeant over there is? I don't recognise him.'

'That's Hugh Robertson. Good guy. Used to work over at White Sulphur Springs but transferred to our office a few weeks ago. Hugh.' shouted Angela from the bridge.

Sergeant Robertson looked up and gave a wave.

'Hugh, this is my boss, Lieutenant Finch,' said Angela patting Charlie's arm.

'Morning, sir,' said Sergeant Robertson with a nod. Charlie returned the acknowledgement.

'What can you tell us sergeant?'

'Well sir, I can tell you that it appears that nothing's been stolen. All his gear seems to be here. A couple of rods and he's got an expensive Penn reel in his bag. I do a bit of fishing myself and that reel must be worth nearly a hundred dollars. None of his stuff appears to have been touched. There's still coffee in a cup by his chair. I'm afraid it looks like he must have fallen in. Apparently, he wears a calliper so if he's gone in then it looks like he's drowned. I suppose if he was wearing boots, he might have waded in to free his line or something like that and slipped. The bank at the water's edge is really muddy.'

'Starting to look that way,' said Charlie. 'Have we traced any witnesses? Do we know if anyone saw him after Screech dropped him off?'

'Not had much of a chance to speak to anyone yet, but from what Screech told me earlier, no-one seems to have seen him.' said Sergeant Robertson.

'Alright, fine, that's all noted, but before I ask you to do this, have you been able to have a good look at the crutch? I mean, I take it there isn't any blood on it or anything else like that?' asked Charlie.

Sergeant Robertson shook his head.

'Nothing on it that I could see. There's certainly no blood on it. It's soaking wet and covered in mud. Why, do you think it's been used as a weapon?' asked Sergeant Robertson who was now clambering up the muddy bank to the bridge.

'No, not really,' said Charlie, 'but I wanted to check before I get you to do something for me.'

'Do what?' asked Sergeant Robertson who was now on the bridge.

'I want to see if the crutch will float. I'd do it myself, but I don't want to ruin these shoes. So, can you go across to the other side and put the crutch into some shallow water?'

'Sure, not a problem,' said Sergeant Robertson, 'just give me a minute.' A minute or so later Sergeant Robertson had scrambled down the far bank and was placing the crutch into some slack water at the side of the reed bed.

'Well, it doesn't float,' shouted Sergeant Robertson. 'For what it's worth, it sank like a stone!'

'Might be worth a great deal,' replied Charlie, 'I think it proves that someone has put it there. Could have been put there by Charlie Jarret of course, but it's more likely that someone has thrown it over there.' continued Charlie. 'And if that someone wasn't Jarret then that puts an altogether different light on his disappearance. Listen, you said you did a bit a fishing. Have you ever fished this bit of the river?'

'Yep, a few times, but that was quite some time ago. Why do you ask?'

'Because I'd like to know how deep the river is.' said Charlie.

'As I remember most of it is fairly shallow. The deepest part by far is the pool on the far side to the left of the reeds. Must be seven or eight feet there. The rest of it is no more than three or four feet as I recall.'

'Okay, fine. I want you to find us a boat and dredge it. The section from that large beech to where it starts to get shallow on those stones about a hundred yards downstream. And get two of your officers to walk down and check either bank. For at least a mile. That will do us for starters anyway.' said Charlie.

'No problem, sir, I'll get that organised. I can get a rowing boat from Tom Davis; his place is just a little up river and I know he has a boat. We'll need a grappling hook if we're going to dredge but I'm pretty sure he'll have one of those as well. That should let us get the job done.'

By now Angela had wandered to the end of the bridge and was paying close attention to a muddy track that led down to where the fishing rod was still sitting on its rest.

'Boss, this track has got several footprints on it. The bridge must have offered some protection from the rain as they look fresh. Look at these two,' said Angela pointing at the ground. 'They've definitely been made by the same shoe. Or boot should I say. Judging by the pointed toe, I'd say that's it's been made by a cowboy boot. But look here at the heel! It's got a very distinctive mark on it.'

Charlie stared at the footprints. 'Good work Angela,' said Charlie approvingly. 'It could be significant right enough. Whoever made it was missing an insert, some sort of logo has come out of the heel. Well that's what it looks like to me.'

'Yeah, I would agree,' said Angela. 'And as one of the prints is facing down and the other up, it looks like someone has gone down to the river from here and then come back up the same way.'

'It certainly does,' replied Charlie rubbing his chin. 'Just a pity the other prints aren't as clear. But just looking at the different sizes, it looks like several people were on this track. Let's get them protected and get scenes of crime down to photograph them.'

'I'll get on it right away,' said Angela taking her police radio out of her jacket pocket.

'And good work again Angela. If they were in anyway connected to Jarret's disappearance, I'd bet my bottom dollar that they were also responsible for the crutch ending up on the other side of the river. This might not be a straightforward missing person enquiry after all.'

*

Ninety minutes later and with his statement in the bag, Charlie was in McDonalds about to order two coffees when he saw Angela gesticulating for him to return to the car.

'What's up?' said Charlie as he opened the car door.

'Radio message from Hugh, he's asking us to return to the bridge immediately. They've found something.' replied Angela.

As they parked their car on some hard standing to the side of the bridge, Charlie noticed two familiar figures looking over the bridge at the officers below. It was Screech Jarret and Eustace Brownlie. About fifty yards upstream of the bridge, Sergeant Robertson and two uniformed officers were standing next to a rowing boat that was pulled onto some stones at the edge of the water.

'I think you'd better come down lieutenant, we've found something. It's not our missing person but you're going to want to see this.' said Sergeant Robertson.

'Sounds intriguing,' said Angela turning to Charlie, 'and don't worry about your shoes, its only mud, it'll clean off.'

Charlie and Angela slithered down the muddy bank making sure they kept well away from the footprints that were now covered by several plastic boxes.

'Okay, sergeant what have you found?' asked Charlie.

'This,' said Sergeant Robertson, lifting a deer's head by its antler from the side of the boat.

'Yikes,' shrieked Angela, recoiling in mock horror, 'that's horrible.'

'We pulled it up with the grappling hook from the middle of the river about twenty feet this side of the bridge. Gave me a bit of a fright when it first appeared through the muddy water. For a split second I thought it was the head of our man. That sounds kind of stupid now given it has two freaking antlers growing out of its head.'

'Don't be daft,' said Charlie, 'I know exactly what you mean. It's like that moment just before you first see a dead body. You know it's there, but until you see it, your mind is racing and imagining all sorts of terrible things. Well mine does.'

'Spot on lieutenant. It was just like that moment. I think that everyone who has ever been a cop knows that feeling.'

'Look, it's missing an ear!' said Angela who was now bending down and giving the macabre scene her full attention. 'It doesn't look like its been in the water that long either, there's no decomposition of the soft tissues. Even the eyes look fresh, they've not even gone that milky way they often do.'

'Appears you may have missed your vocation detective. Perhaps you should have been a forensic scientist!' said Charlie with a laugh.

'No thanks.' replied Angela, 'I'll stick to the detective side of things. But it is fascinating don't you think?'

'Take a look at the bone in the neck.' said Sergeant Robertson holding up the head. 'It appears to be a very clean cut. Like it might have been done with a saw. The ear on the other hand has been more roughly removed, judging by that ragged edge. It looks to me if that has been cut with some sort of knife. Most likely a hunting knife. Oh, and one last thing. This animal has been killed outwith the hunting season. That doesn't start around here for another couple of weeks.'

'Interesting,' said Charlie as he made some notes in his pocketbook.

'So why would it be missing an ear?' asked Angela.

'Well, quite often, especially when it's your first kill, they cut off an ear and the hunter's face is wiped with the animal's blood. They call it being 'blooded'.' explained Sergeant Robertson. 'It's like some type of rite of passage. Fathers often do it to their sons after they've shot their first deer. It's a centuries old tradition. I don't think it's as common these days, but I know it still goes on.'

'Okay I can see that,' said Charlie. 'But why have they cut the poor critter's, head off, what's the purpose of that?'

Sergeant Robertson shrugged his shoulders.

'Good question. I have no idea. But if they've taken a saw with them to cut it off then it ain't been done by accident.'

'And why would you then throw it into the Greenbrier river? Makes no sense to me.' added Angela.

'Could be some sort of satanic ritual I suppose,' said Charlie thinking out loud. 'I've seen that type of thing in films loads of times.'

'Steady on lieutenant,' said Angela chuckling, 'this is little old Fairlea, things like that don't happen round here.'

'First time for everything,' replied Charlie, 'and if you've a better explanation, I'm all ears.' Sergeant Robertson started to laugh.

'Nice pun lieutenant. But seriously, you might just be right. There must be a reason why it ended up here. In the absence of any better explanation I'd say you might not be too wide of the mark.'

'Sure, of course,' said Angela trying to backtrack. 'I was just being facetious. I wasn't trying to rule anything out.'

'It's fine Angela, I know what you meant. But at this stage of the enquiry everything will need to be considered. But if Charlie Jarret isn't in the river, then where is he? I don't want to read too much into this, but that deer's head could well be connected to his disappearance. Looks like my quiet first day isn't going to be so quiet after all.'

'What's going on officer?' shouted a voice from the bridge.

With the distraction of the deer's head, Charlie had forgotten that Screech and Brownie had been watching them from above.

'Just give me a minute then I'll come up and speak to you.' shouted Charlie. 'One last thing then before I head off sergeant. Can you make sure that scenes of crime photograph the head as well as the footprints? And can you ask them to take the head back to the lab? I'm particularly interested to know more about what's made those cuts. They might also be able to tell us how long the thing has been in the river.'

'Will do lieutenant. Expect it will liven up their day. Can't be every day they get called out to examine a deer's head.' Angela started laughing but then a thought occurred to her.

'I've got some heavy-duty paper bags in our car, you'll need to use one of them.

Whatever you do don't put it in a plastic bag or they will have a fit! I was at the lecture last week, anything involving blood or other bodily fluids must be transported in paper bags.'

'Glad you mentioned that Angela, I missed that talk, and being truthful I wasn't remembering. So that's one ticking off you've saved me.'

'Always happy to help our uniform colleagues,' replied Angela with a wink as she scrambled up the bank to her car to look for the bags.

'Sorry to have kept you, Henry.' said Charlie as he approached the friends who were now sitting on the parapet.

'I take it you've not found him then?' said Screech with his familiar wide-eyed stare. 'I might only have one eye, but I could see from here that that was a deer's head they dredged up.'

'And a white-tailed buck at that,' added Eustace.

'Plenty white-tailed deer in the forests around here.' continued Screech.

'Any idea why its head should end up in the river next to where your brother was fishing?' asked Charlie.

'Nope,' replied Screech. 'Isn't that your job detective?'

'Yep, I guess it is,' said Charlie. 'I was just hoping you might know something about it, that's all.'

'You think it's connected to my brother's disappearance, don't you?' said Screech leaning forward and fixing Charlie with a stare.

'I never said that, Henry. I'm just trying to make sense of what's gone on here. Finding your brother is my number one priority, but I'll level with you, we don't know where he is and it's now nearly twenty-four hours since you reported him missing, so I do have concerns for his well-being.'

'So, how are we going to find him then?' asked Screech.

'The honest answer, I don't know yet,' replied Charlie. 'We've dredged the section of river either side of the bridge and we've searched the riverbanks for a mile downstream and there's no trace.'

'Are you sure he's not in the river?' asked Screech.

'No, I'm not 100% sure. But we'll have to wait until the water is less muddy, then we should be able to say one way or another. But If we're going to be able to find him, I think we're going to need your help.'

'Why should we help you? I remember you, detective,' said Eustace suspiciously. 'You tried to pin the murder of that Foster girl on us. I've not forgotten that.'

Charlie frowned and gently shook his head.

'If you recall, you were charged with the theft of the scaffolding poles. We then interviewed you about the murder, but you were released as soon as we were able to prove that you weren't involved. And if you're still hacked off about that, then I'm sorry, but I was just doing my job.' said Charlie coldly.

Eustace was about to argue when Henry put his arm across his friend's chest.

'Leave it Eustace. He's right, they did let us go. We did time for stealing them poles, but they dropped the murder charge. Anyway, now's not the time for old grudges. We've got to find my brother and we need their help, but they need our help just as much.'

'You're right there,' said Charlie nodding his head. 'And just so you're aware, I'm going to extend the search downstream and include the woods on both sides of the river. And as I said, we'll continue to monitor the river. The sergeant over there is taking the rods and all your brother's fishing gear back to the police office now. If this turns into a criminal investigation, I might need it as evidence. But it's just precautionary at the moment.'

'Fine, and I appreciate the update.' said Screech.

'Not a problem,' replied Charlie. 'Look, I take it you've been making your own enquiries since you reported your brother missing. Have you turned up anything that I need to know about?'

'Well, if you're asking if anybody saw or spoke to him after I dropped him off the answer appears to be no, I suppose that's not really surprising, early hours of the morning in the middle of nowhere, nobody's going to pass by. Well not on foot anyway.'

Charlie pursed his lips and nodded slowly.

'I might have turned up one thing that could help us though.' said Screech.

Charlie raised his eyebrows, 'And what's that?'

'Well this morning I spoke to Bradley Coombs. He's a good friend of Charlie's. He says he saw a pick-up parked next to the bridge the night he went missing. In fact, he said there might have been two vehicles as he thought a car was parked behind the pick-up. He said he was listening to his music and not giving it much attention. But he did say he didn't see anyone at the vehicles.'

'Huh, that is interesting,' said Charlie taking some notes. 'Did he say what time it was when he passed?'

'He said he was on his way home from work so must have been about 0115 hrs. Not that long after I dropped Charlie off.'

'Did he mention anything else. Make of vehicle, colour, number plates, that kind of thing?' asked Charlie.

'He just said the pick-up was dark coloured, black, brown or possibly dark blue, but he couldn't remember the make and said nothing about the plates.' added Screech.

'What about the other vehicle, did he say anything about that?'

'Not really. Only that he thought it was a small saloon and light coloured. More than that he couldn't say.'

Charlie looked perplexed.

'A dark coloured pick-up! Half the pick-ups in the county must be dark coloured and there must be hundreds of them. Without knowing the type of vehicle, its going to make tracing it a whole lot more difficult. But listen, I'm grateful for your help.' said Charlie, who had now been joined on the bridge by Angela. 'That's been useful. We'll obviously need to follow this up with Bradley and get a proper statement from him. Do you happen to know his address?'

Screech shook his head.

'I'm not sure where he's currently staying, but I often see him at his uncle's shed on Church Street, you might get him there. I know he works part-time as a delivery driver and uses the shed to store his parcels.'

Eustace burst out laughing.

'You'll know the shed, detective. It was the one that used to have all them stolen Christmas trees in it. You never got us for that one, did you?' said Eustace who was finding the situation immensely funny. Charlie tilted his head and sighed.

'No, you got away with one that time, Eustace. We thought it was you, but we just couldn't prove it at the time.' said Charlie in a serious voice.

By now Eustace was almost beside himself with glee and laughing so much tears were rolling down his cheeks.

'Ha-ha,' he shrieked slapping his thigh, 'Eustace Brownlie and Henry Jarret made you look like fools that day alright, didn't we? We'd been stealing them for weeks and you never caught us.'

Charlie bit his lip and stared at Eustace, a deep penetrating stare.

'Of course, you do realise that while that crime was never solved it still remains on file.'

Eustace stopped laughing and glanced across to Screech hoping his friend was going to offer some reassurance, but none was forthcoming.

'And what you've just told us Eustace could be considered a confession of guilt. Looks like you arrived just in time Detective Brown, you'll be able to corroborate that admission.'

Angela smiled as Eustace's face drained of colour. Screech shook his head.

'Eustace Brownlie, you've just confirmed what I've always known; you are a fucking idiot.'

'We'll be in touch,' said Charlie with a wave as he and Angela walked back to their car. 'We'll swing past the shed on our way back to the office and try and grab a word with Bradley.'

'It's a bit early for Christmas trees but you never know, we'll take a look while we're there,' shouted Angela as the detectives got into their vehicle.

'Shit Henry, I'm sorry, I didn't mean no harm. I just thought it was funny that we'd got one over on the cops for once. That's all it was Henry. I'm sorry, but I'm a dumbass, you know that. Where you going now?' asked

Eustace as he watched his friend disappear down the side of the bridge to an area of stones at the edge of the river.

'As far away from you as possible.' shouted Henry. 'You're a numbskull Eustace. You never learn. How many times have I told you to just keep your mouth shut? But you'll like a kid in a candy store, you just can't help yourself.'

Eustace didn't reply but sat on the parapet and folded his arms. His petted lip and frown would have turned milk sour. He sat in a huff, like a small child who had just been chastised by its parent.

Standing by the water's edge Henry's thoughts returned to his younger brother. Surely, he wouldn't have fallen in. Charlie was an experienced fisherman. He'd fished this spot dozens of times before and he'd never got himself into difficulties. Henry was convinced that something else must have happened. He was worried, but the fact that the police hadn't recovered his body at least gave him some hope. As he contemplated what to do next, he bent down and picked up a couple of stones which he tossed aimlessly into the river. As he bent down to pick up another stone his eye was drawn to an object lying amongst the pebbles. It was a small button. Beige in colour and made of horn, the edge of the button was serrated and much darker in colour. Delicately carved on the front was the shape of a mountain with a thistle superimposed in front of it.

'What you found Henry?' asked Eustace who had got over his huff and made his way down to the river.

'It's just a button,' said Henry holding it up to show Eustace.

'I'd say that's made from a deer's antler,' said Eustace examining the button. 'The colour and ridges on its side makes me think it's made from an antler. And look here, it's still got some of its thread attached.' said Eustace holding the button in the palm of his hand.

'For once in your life I think you may be right,' said Henry patting his friend on his back.

'What about the carving on the front of it, what do you think that's about?' asked Eustace.

'Can't say, replied Henry, 'although the thistle kind of suggests it might have a Scottish connection. Who knows? It's strange though, there is something very familiar about it, but I can't think what it is.'

'Do you think it's got anything to do with Henry's disappearance?' asked Eustace.

'Doubt it, but you never know,' said Henry putting the button in his trouser pocket. 'It's just a lovely thing, someone went to a lot of trouble to carve that.'

Chapter 6

Sitting on the stone wall about twenty yards from where Charlie was lying was a large black crow. He had seen it a couple of times earlier in the day breaking acorns on the wall. But this time was different. Trapped under its talons was a squirming frog, thrusting out its limbs in all directions desperately trying to free itself from its captor. Escape looked impossible. The bird nonchalantly preened its wing feathers with its thick stubby beak paying little attention to its prey. Its iridescent feathers shimmered in the early evening sunlight. Jet black with highlights of green and purple, the crow looked magnificent. Suddenly and brutally the bird despatched its victim. Three rapid pecks to the head, like a pneumatic drill smashing tarmac, and it was done. The crow ripped a leg from the lifeless corpse, repeatedly jabbing at the raw flesh as it picked off small morsels, bit by bit.

It was strange, but Charlie realised he was no longer shivering. His clothes were still soaked through from yesterday's rain but the bitter coldness of earlier had left him. He now had no pain. The dull ache from his shattered foot had subsided hours ago and his hands were now numb and devoid of feeling. The last of his six stones lay next to him. The despair and anger he had felt earlier had slowly ebbed away. Now his overwhelming emotion was one of quiet resignation. Charlie was exhausted, he just wanted to go to sleep. He could feel his body shutting down, like a battery losing its charge, his very essence was slowly draining away, his senses no longer sharp, he was struggling to think straight. He was stuck in some twilight zone, no man's land, the space between life and death.

What does a man do when he's facing death thought Charlie, as he lay staring at the sky; they pray to God. Though he had never been a religious man, for a time, when he had been dating Erin Coulter, he had regularly attended worship at the Methodist church where Erin had gone since she was a child. He liked the pastor and often found himself reflecting on his thought-provoking sermons. He even enjoyed singing the great Wesley hymns that dominated Sunday services. His attendance came to an end when the relationship with Erin broke down. Afterwards Charlie didn't feel inclined to go. He wasn't hostile to the church by any means, just a little ambivalent. He always seemed to have something better to do on a Sunday morning.

Right now, he might be staring into the abyss, but he still had no great expectation of what God might do for him. Why should God be bothered with me if I couldn't be bothered with him reasoned Charlie. He knew religion wasn't a 'quid pro quo', but conversely, surely a loving God, the one he remembered hearing about when sitting in church with Erin, wasn't going to reject him because he hadn't been a regular attender, or a true believer. Charlie wondered just how much of a believer you needed to be to get a ticket to the ball. He wasn't sure, but he knew it was time to pray.

In the quiet stillness he closed his eyes, but the words just wouldn't come. Tears filled his eyes. He wanted to ask for forgiveness, he had sinned many times and done things he knew were wrong. He had hurt others. His friends and family. Even his beloved mother who had nurtured him, despite her own years of despair, had not been spared. Charlie felt ashamed. He couldn't find the courage to pray for himself. He deserved the wrath of God not his forgiveness. Instead he prayed to the God of mercy and asked that his brother, Henry and his darling mother, might be protected and cared for. His prayer was short, perfunctory even, but it had said all that he wanted to say. He felt relieved, a weight had been lifted from his shoulders, he had made his peace.

Now barely conscious, Charlie stared at the crow through misted eyes. It appeared to be shrouded in a strange light, so bright it was like looking at the sun. Charlie squinted at the bird which stretched and flexed its enormous wings like some giant phoenix. He felt a sense of calm sweep over him. He looked up to the heavens. The sky was blue and cotton wool clouds drifted gently by, an ever-changing canvas of silvery white swirls, transitory and eternal. He felt the touch of his mother brush his cheek and her sweet breath whispered in his ear. Wrapped in her loving arms Charlie felt no fear. He closed his eyes as sleep approached. His brother was calling his name, running excitedly towards him through the corn field next to the house, the playground of their childhood, a safe and happy place.

The gentle sound of a piano playing, evocative of times past, seeped into his consciousness. It was Beethoven's Fur Elise, his mother's favourite piece, so familiar and comforting. High in the heavens above him another voice came, an unfamiliar voice yet kind and compelling. It was calling his name. It was the voice of his father. Charlie felt ready. It was time to leave this earthly plain and soar on the phoenix's wings to the dreamland above. To cool waters and Elysian Fields, the paradise that his mortal years had so cruelly denied.

Chapter 7

'Firstly, can I say I'm delighted to see you remembered to park away from those damned pine trees,' said Ewart Wilder putting down his briefcase and removing his jacket. Bridget turned and looked at her husband.

'And secondly, darling. What else is it that you wanted to say?' asked Bridget, her voice dripping with sarcasm as she wiped her hands dry on her apron. Wilder looked bemused.

'Did you really want to say, how lovely to see you, how was your day darling?' Bridget Wilder hadn't cared for the tone of her husband's voice one bit. 'I'm not some disobedient teenager or one of your subordinate officers, Ewart. I'm your wife, if you hadn't noticed, and I don't care to be spoken to like that.'

Wilder put his arms around her neck and kissed her gently on her cheek keen to make amends.

'Apologies,' he said it's just...'

'I know what you meant. I would just like to be given the respect I think I deserve that's all. Now let that be the end of this conversation. Your dinner's ready and I've made your favourite, so pour me a glass of wine and pull up a stool.'

Wilder did as he was instructed. There weren't many people who could speak to him like that and not suffer a stinging retort, but his wife was one of them. Bridget had the measure of her husband.

'It's delicious darling,' said Wilder between mouthfuls of the steaming lasagne. Got just the right amount of garlic, perfect.'

'Excellent,' said Bridget, 'good to know that I can do something right.' Wilder smiled weakly and continued eating. 'And how was your day in the hot seat dear. Anything of note been happening in the world of policing?'

Wilder shook his head.

'No, not really. It's been quiet for weeks. I don't think I can remember a time when there's been so little crime. Not since I became chief anyway.'

'Well, that's got to be a good thing hasn't it? I mean the police authority must be pleased even if you don't seem to be.' replied Bridget.

'No, I didn't mean to give that impression. It's a good thing of course, but when it's as quiet as this I always feel I must be missing something, that's all. Puts me on edge a little.'

'What was going on at the Greenbrier Bridge?' asked Bridget as she sipped her wine. 'I passed by on my way to the shops at lunchtime and there were several officers at the water's edge, another couple were out in a rowing boat.'

'They were looking for a missing person,' replied Wilder. 'Screech Jarret's younger brother was fishing at the bridge and we think he's slipped in. We've been dredging the river for a couple of days now. Jarret wears a calliper, so we think he's got into difficulties and drowned. Only we can't find his body but I'm pretty sure he's in there. Charlie Finch, who's my new acting lieutenant, isn't so sure but there isn't another explanation. He's been gone more than two days, when the level of the water falls and isn't so muddy, we'll find him. Lieutenant Finch is getting a little ahead of himself, but he's keen to do well so I'm not holding that against him.'

'Oh, that's horrible,' replied Bridget. 'His poor family must be worried sick.'

'Hmm,' muttered Wilder. 'Just a pity it wasn't Screech that was missing, he's one real badass. His brother's no angel but Screech is a one-man crime wave. Well two, if you include his sidekick Eustace Brownlie. The two of them are joined at the hip. Crime would be permanently down if Screech had drowned and not his brother!'

'Hush your mouth, Ewart Wilder, that's a quite dreadful thing to say. He's somebody's son, and you just shouldn't say things like that.'

Wilder frowned. 'I'm sorry that you find that offensive, Bridget, but Screech Jarret is scum. He's a fraudster and a habitual thief. This town wouldn't miss Screech Jarret, not for a single minute.'

'Okay, let's just change the subject, I'm sorry I brought it up. Anyway, are you still intending to go over to the school this evening?'

'I'm going to have to,' replied Wilder. 'I could do with staying here and working on my speech, but I'm meeting the Dionach and Chef to go over the final arrangements. I'll try and catch Jason while I'm there. Have you had a chance to read the prospectus from Duke yet? I'm still trying to get my head around those fees. $15,000 just for the tuition. That's before you've paid for accommodation, meals or bought a book. It's going to be mega expensive.'

'He'll need to get a loan. I know he's expecting to, but we'll support him as best we can, I don't want him saddled with debt when he graduates.' said Bridget softly. Wilder scoffed and refilled his cup of coffee.

No time like the present, thought Bridget reaching across the work surface and rubbing her husband's hand. Might as well mention the lake house if we're going to be talking about money.

'Are you remembering about the house at Fayetteville? I said we'd let them know one way or another by the weekend. It'll be perfect for us. You said so yourself Ewart. We've got some savings and with your salary, I know we can manage all of this.'

'I'm not so sure,' said Wilder putting on his jacket.

Bridget smiled and lowered her lashes running the tip of her tongue across her lips.

'You won't be late home will you darling?' asked Bridget.

'I shouldn't think so,' replied Wilder, his attention now caught by the allure of his wife. 'Why you asking?'

'Oh, I don't know,' said Bridget seductively, 'I thought you might like to meet me in the hot tub later, that's all. There're at least two glasses left in this bottle, would be a shame to waste it. Unfortunately, I've mislaid my costume, so I might have to do without it.'

Wilder broke into a beaming smile.

'I'll phone you when I'm about to leave. And don't go looking too hard for that bikini, you hear me,' said Wilder heading out the door.

'I wasn't intending to,' said Bridget blowing a kiss to her husband.

By the time Wilder arrived in the school dining room, the Dionach and chef were already perusing the menu over a cup of coffee. The Dionach's son, Seth, was also sitting at the table leafing through a book about butterflies. Wilder pulled up a chair and sat down.

'I think Mr Wilder, this is what we had discussed,' said chef handing Wilder a copy of the menu. 'We'd better hope so, as the beef was delivered this morning,' he added with a chuckle. Wilder studied the menu for a moment before nodding his head.

'Yes, lentil soup, followed by the rib of beef and seasonal vegetables, and rounded off with cranachan. Yep, that's what we agreed.' said Wilder. 'How will you be cooking the beef, chef? I take it we're not ordering individually.'

'What, with 182 covers, I should damn well hope not,' said chef indignantly. 'It'll be cooked medium-rare, the way beef should be cooked. And any philistine who wants it well done will just have to lump it. I ain't ruining top quality beef for anyone.'

'Quite right, chef' said the Dionach slapping him on the back.

'Okay, that's all fine,' added Wilder. 'And the place settings Dionach, what about them?'

The Dionach stood up and went across to a small table in the corner of the room. 'It will look something like this,' he said pointing at the table that was set with cutlery, plates and various glasses. 'And everyone will have a menu and order of events at their place rolled up and tied with a ribbon of McCaig tartan.'

Wilder picked up the scroll and untied the ribbon.

'Looks good Dionach, a good choice of font I'd say. It looks the part.' Wilder stared at the paper, 'What's this then?' he said tapping the paper with his knuckle. 'A Man's a Man for a That', fine. You sing that at every

Burn's supper but, 'A Parcel of Rogues', that's a new one on me. I'm sure I've never heard you sing it before. Is it even Scottish?'

The Dionach smiled. 'It certainly is sir, it's another one by Burns only not as well known. I thought, as it's the 75th anniversary, I'd do something new. I hope you don't have a problem with that?'

Wilder shrugged his shoulders and shook his head.

'So, just to confirm, sir. Your speech and the toast to the college will be before the meal and the music and songs afterwards?'

'That's correct,' said Wilder. 'I think that works best. It gets too raucous if you do the speeches after the meal. By the time some of those guys get a few malts down their necks it could get messy. And if I've spent hours preparing the damned speech, they at least can do me the courtesy of listening to it sober!'

'Yes, I agree with that. Speeches before the meal works best.' said the Dionach who was now watching his son out the corner of his eye.

'Seth, please, put that down, it's not for playing with.' said the Dionach sternly. Seth looked at his father and put down the glass tumbler and went and sat down again.

'It's the light sparkling off the crystal that's fascinating him. Seth loves that sort of thing. Anything that sparkles or has bright colours will always attract his attention, but I'm sorry, he meant no harm.'

'Not a problem,' said Wilder picking up and examining the glass. Wilder smiled and nodded several times. 'I like it, I like it a lot,' he said holding the glass up to the light. 'Whoever engraved it has done a good job. The mountain and the thistle are very striking. And

'Marsco College, 75th anniversary dinner, 4th October 1992,' is perfect. Simple and not too fussy. I think everyone will be delighted to get one of these as a memento of the evening. Gentlemen you've done a fine job. I'm delighted.'

Praise indeed thought the Dionach and chef to themselves, as neither were used to such pleasantries from the head of governors. Must be on a promise, thought chef as he headed back to the kitchen, can't think of anything else to explain it.

'Sir, if you have a minute, I was hoping I could have a word in private? I've a couple of things I'd like to discuss with you. It won't take long.' said the Dionach with just the suggestion of a smile.

Wilder looked at the Dionach suspiciously. He had noticed that tonight he'd been noticeably more cheerful than of late. Much more agreeable and certainly less grumpy than he had been since being told by the board that he'd have to retire and move out of the lodge. Wilder wondered what was going on. His police intuition made him think that something was afoot.

'Yes, that will be fine, but I have to see Jason beforehand. I said I'd meet him in the library at eight, and its just after that now,' said Wilder looking at his watch.

'If it's all right with you then can I ask that you stop by at the lodge house after you're finished with Jason? I've got something I want to show you.'

Wilder was curious, but he hadn't an inkling what the Dionach was on about.

'Fine then, I'll see you in about twenty minutes,' he said striding off in the direction of the library.

It had gone quarter to nine when Wilder knocked on the door at the lodge. The Dionach opened the door and ushered him into the small lounge at the rear of the house. 'Will you have a dram, sir? I was about to pour myself one.'

'No, you're fine. I've a meeting with Mrs Wilder that I must get back for, so I'm hoping this won't take too long,' said Wilder brusquely.

'No, I won't keep you unduly, sir. I know you're a busy man. Firstly, I was hoping you would grant me a day off. I know its short notice, but I've just heard that my maiden aunt has passed away and the funeral is this Thursday in Ripley. I'd like to take my wife and Seth to represent the family as I don't suppose there will be many mourners. I would travel up after dinner on Wednesday and be back by mid-morning on Friday. I know it's not ideal with the dinner on Friday evening, but I'd like to attend. I'll guarantee to be home by lunchtime Friday.' said the Dionach.

'Granted.' said Wilder without further comment. 'And the second thing, you said you had something to show me.'

The Dionach nodded. Pulling back the curtain he removed a small key that was hanging on a hook behind it. The Dionach bent down and unlocked a wooden cabinet that was standing in the corner of the room. He removed a small box from the middle shelf. Made of Spanish cedar, the creamy white lid was made of mother-of-pearl and had a porcelain-like lustre. Inscribed on a brass plaque on the front of the box was the words, 'To Donald McCaig, a trusted colleague and loyal friend, from Andrew Carnegie, 23.11.01.'

'This cigar box was given to my father by the Founder shortly before he died in 1947. As you can see from the inscription it was originally a gift to the Founder from

Andrew Carnegie. It was my father's prized possession,' explained the Dionach. Wilder stared at the box.

'And very nice it is too,' said Wilder sardonically. 'But you didn't ask me to drop by just to look at a cigar box. So, what else are you going to tell me?' The Dionach clenched his teeth and nodded gently.

'I wanted to show you this.' Carefully, he slid out a narrow drawer from the base of the box and removed a folded-up piece of paper.

'This, Mr Wilder, is a letter, written in the Founder's hand. It was given to my father to mark thirty years loyal service to the school. In it the Founder states that in recognition of that loyalty, the position of Dionach at Marsco, shall remain within the Buckley family for however long the family should want it. It also states, Mr Wilder, that so long as they continue to carry out the duties of the Dionach, the family will be entitled to occupy the lodge house.' Wilder tilted his head and stroked his chin. For several moments he didn't say anything.

'Can I see your letter?' asked Wilder holding out his hand.

'No, Mr Wilder I'm sorry but you can't. It's the only copy I've got at the moment, so if you don't mind, I'll keep hold of it just now.'

'That's fine,' said Wilder without emotion, 'but tell me this, why didn't you mention this letter before?'

'I didn't know where it was, sir. I knew it existed, but I didn't want to say anything until I could lay hands on it. And now that I have it, if it's all right with you, I'd like it discussed at the next governors' meeting in November.'

'Of course,' replied Wilder. 'In the circumstances that would be entirely appropriate. I'll make sure that we do that.'

The Dionach was taken aback by the reasonableness of his response. He had anticipated much more resistance from his foe and now he felt perturbed. This had all been a little too straightforward.

'It's certainly a beautiful box, the iridescence of the pearl in this light is quite stunning. I can see hints of grey and green. In fact, from over here, it almost appears pink. When you consider its provenance, I can see why your father prized it so highly.' said Wilder taking his car key out of his pocket.

'It is a lovely thing, that is for sure,' said the Dionach locking the box in the cabinet and hanging up the key. 'And I'd like to thank you for granting my time off and for listening to what I had to say, it's much appreciated.'

'Not a problem,' replied Wilder, 'I hope the funeral goes as well as it can do in the circumstances. I'll see you at the dinner on Friday, it's going to be a great occasion.'

Chapter 8

In his office on the third floor of Lewisburg police office, Chief Wilder was growing ever more irate. Sergeant Coutts was not answering his phone.

'Where the devil have you been?' sneered Wilder when Sergeant Coutts eventually picked up the receiver.

'Sorry to have kept you waiting, sir, but I was dealing with a member of the public at the front counter.'

'Never mind about that,' said the chief impatiently, 'I need you to find Wayne Mitchell for me and have him report to my office immediately, understand?'

'Yes, sir. I think he may be in the canteen. I saw him about ten minutes ago, I'll go look for him now and get him to come and see you.'

Over in the detectives' office Mike Rawlingson was marking up the availability roster.

'Better be on your guard this morning, Charlie, looks like Bull is in one of his moods. He tore a strip off me, just because I was slightly late bringing in the crime file. So, keep your head down at the morning meeting. Here, I've made up the duty roster for the next week.'

'Thanks,' said Charlie taking the report and sitting down at a desk. 'And I appreciate the heads up. The man's like a volcano, you just never know when he's going to erupt.'

'Well you better put your hard hat on because it's looking kinda like he might go off on one today, somethings clearly annoyed him.'

'I'll be careful. I'll use all those diplomatic skills you taught me to keep a lid on things.' They both started to laugh. 'Anyway, more importantly how's Susan? Isn't it today you've got to take her to Charleston for her treatment?' asked Charlie.

'She's doing well thanks. She's a very resilient lady. And the treatment's tomorrow. I'll work on a bit tonight as I won't be in at all tomorrow.' replied Mike.

'You will not. All the extra hours you've given the job over the years. You'll go at your usual time. No, in fact, you'll go at three and that, Mike is an order.'

Mike looked up and smiled at his friend.

'So, tell me Lieutenant, three days into the new job, how are you settling in?'

Charlie rested his chin on his hands. 'Fine, I think. I'm enjoying it but it's been a quiet start. Well, apart from the missing person enquiry.'

'Yeah, how's that going? Angela told me about the deer's head that the cops had dredged up. What's your take on that?'

Charlie smiled to himself. That was just typical of Mike and just another illustration of why he was such a good boss. Charlie was going to ask Mike the same question, but Mike was in too quickly, keen to give the acting lieutenant his place and first go at an explanation.

'I'm really not sure being honest. If Jarret had been in the river, I would have expected to find him by now. The water's much less muddy, but there's been no trace of him. Same with the search of the banks and woods. Without his crutch and wearing a calliper, I don't suppose he could walk very far, but again we've turned up nothing. I'm beginning to think me might have been abducted.'

Mike blew out his cheeks and raised his eyebrows.

'I agree it's looking less likely that he's in the river. But abduction, what would be the reason for that, there would need to be a reason?'

Charlie shrugged his shoulders.

'You would have thought. But I can't think of any reason, it's not as if anyone could hold him to ransom. The Jarrets don't have any money.'

'What about witnesses, have you traced any?' asked Mike.

'Only potential witness is a young guy called Bradley Coombs, he's the nephew of old man Coombs, he of the infamous Christmas tree saga.' Mike nodded and smiled knowingly. 'Well, apparently he drove over the bridge on his way home from work about 0115 hrs. He says he saw a pick-up and what he thinks was another vehicle parked near the bridge when he passed. We've taken a statement from him, but the details are quite sketchy. He certainly didn't see anyone at the time, and I suppose it's not that unusual to have vehicles parked at the bridge.'

'It is at one fifteen in the morning!' exclaimed Mike.

'Well yeah, I suppose. But other than saying it was a dark coloured pick-up, black, brown, possibly navy blue. You can see our difficulty. We've got next to nothing to go on.'

'Yep, it's a strange one right enough. So, back to the deer's head, what's your theory about that?'

'Don't really have one, other than its possibly part of some macabre ritual. But I'm keeping an open mind just

93

at the minute. The head is currently at the lab and I'm waiting for Dave Richardson to get back to me. It looks like it was removed with a saw, while the ear that's missing appears to have been cut off with a knife. Not sure how any of that is going to help this enquiry, but I know the head didn't end up in the river by accident. I don't want to leap to any conclusions and say that it's linked to Charlie Jarret's disappearance, but, then again, it could be.'

Mike sat back in his chair clasping his hands behind his head.

'I'd go along with all that. Best not to rule anything out at this stage. Your theory about the deer could well be right. I certainly don't have a better explanation for it, but it's a weird one right enough. I suppose you've spoken to Screech and his sidekick. What are they saying about it?'

'They seem as mystified as us. They've been out looking for him for three days now. I know Screech is starting to fear the worst. I don't blame him, I've got a bad feeling in my bones about this one,' said Charlie despondently.

'I think you might be right; it's not looking great that's for sure. But keep close tabs on Screech and Eustace you hear me. If anyone can find him it will be those two, I know Screech and Charlie are close, so he'll be working night and day to find him.'

*

'Come in and sit down, and make sure you shut the door behind you,' barked Wilder to Wayne Mitchell who was standing in the doorway like a guilty schoolboy. Obediently, he closed the door and went and sat down in front of Wilder's desk. He twiddled his thumbs nervously while the chief scribbled notes on a pad.

Sycophancy is not an uncommon trait in the police force, but over the years, Wayne Mitchell had managed to turn it into something of an art form and taken it to another level altogether. Universally loathed by the other officers, everyone knew that Mitchell had spent years crawling up Wilder's ass and was only in the job because the chief had gone out on a limb to protect him. When Mitchell had spectacularly fucked up during the Maisie Foster murder enquiry, he had been disciplined at the behest of Mike Rawlingson for neglect of duty. In other circumstances, Mitchell's actions might have prevented Mike and Charlie from solving the case and stopped a guilty man going to jail.

Everyone at the station knew that Mitchell was lucky to still be in a job, and that was only because Wilder had intervened on his behalf. But like many sycophants, he still had his uses. He was a snitch and things that should never reach the chief's ear, only did so curtesy of Wayne Mitchell. In truth, the chief had little time for him, but he was prepared to tolerate him as he was a rich and dependable source of intelligence. That allowed Wilder to keep one step ahead of the many malcontents, who secretly wished the worst for their autocratic chief of police.

Wilder put down his pen and fixed Mitchell with a deep penetrating stare. Mitchell squirmed in his chair, snared by his master's gaze. He felt hot and uncomfortable and small beads of sweat started to appear on his crimson face. He had no idea why he had been summoned to the chief's office. He felt trapped, a captive to his boss. He wanted to run but there was nowhere to run to. He was at the chief's beck and call and, as usual, he was willing to do anything that his master requested.

'Remind me?' said Wilder. 'How long is it since you appeared at that discipline hearing?'

Mitchell bit his lip and looked at his feet.

'More than five years, sir.' He replied quietly. Wilder leant forward.

'And would you consider that you've now 'tholed your assize'?' Mitchell looked confused. He hadn't a clue what that was supposed to mean.

'It's a Scots legal phrase, we learnt at school,' explained Wilder. 'In a roundabout way it means do you think you've now paid your debt. Particularly apt in your situation don't you think?'

Mitchell was still none the wiser but nodded in agreement.

Wilder got up from his desk and walked over to the window.

'I believe in second chances Mitchell. Five years is a long time. Long enough for you to reflect on the stupidity of your actions.' Michell forced a weak smile and nodded.

'I dug you out a hole back then. I risked my reputation for you. Never forget that. You owe me big time,' continued Wilder.

'I won't forget, sir.' said Mitchell who was still looking at his feet. 'I really appreciate what you did for me.'

'Good,' said Wilder looking out of the window. 'Because today I'm going to give you the opportunity to pay me back for that loyalty, do you understand?'

'Yes sir, of course, sir.' said Mitchell nodding furiously.

'Fine then.' said Wilder. 'But before we go any further let me make clear that what I'm offering you is non-negotiable. Do what I'm going to ask, and you'll be well rewarded. If you're successful, in two weeks from now I'm going to make you a sergeant. If you're not up for it, you'll stay in that backwater where you're working now for the rest of your career. Understand?'

Mitchell sat bolt upright. What the hell was going on. He had the necessary qualifications to be a sergeant, but at that precise moment he would have said he had more chance of winning the lottery than being promoted.

'I believe that you've done your time, so this is going to be your big chance. Your only chance. Do I make myself clear?'

Mitchell looked incredulous. This was just surreal. There must be a half-dozen officers waiting to be made up to sergeant. How were they going to react? They hate me enough already he thought. This would just seal the deal. What's the catch? There must be a catch. The chief hasn't suddenly gone soft and decided to promote me. What's the pay-off he wondered. He wasn't going to have to wait long to find out.

'I need you to do something for me,' said Wilder sitting back down at his desk. 'This is strictly confidential, between you and me. Nobody else is going to know. And if they ever find out, I'll drop you like a stone, your life won't be worth living. We can't afford to fuck this up. Have I made myself clear?'

'Perfectly clear, sir.'

'Good, then listen carefully and I'll explain what I need you to do. Just one thing though before I start. Do you know the trout fishery out at Grassy Meadows?'

Mitchell nodded but was still not sure where any of this was going.

'There's a guy who works there called Crawford Alan, he's a friend of mine, ask for him and tell him I sent you when you get there. He's going to give you a trout.'

Chapter 9

Henry Jarret was lying on his bed listening to his music. He was tired after another fruitless day of searching. He needed his own sanctuary as his poor mother sat in her chair by the kitchen window weeping. She hadn't stopped crying since Charlie disappeared four days ago and although he was heartfelt sorry for her, it was doing his head in.

For the umpteenth time that afternoon, he took out the button and stared at it. Rolling it over and over between his fingers. It was starting to drive him to distraction. The engraving on the front seemed so familiar, yet he still couldn't place it.

In a small frame on his chest of drawers was an old black and white photo of his father. It was a little faded and must have been nearly fifty years old. Looking at the photo Henry thought how like his father Charlie was. He felt a lump rise in his throat. His brother had never got to know his dad as Joe Jarret had been killed in a mining accident when Charlie was only months old. That's a terrible thing thought Henry, a son should get to know and spend time with his father. It just ain't right.

Tears started to well up in his eyes as he realised that he could barely remember his father. He had not yet had his fifth birthday when the accident happened, so he only had the vaguest recollection of what he had been like. The sadness was crushing and for several minutes he sat motionless on the bed weeping. Drying his eyes with a tissue, he stared at the photograph of his father once again. Then like a thunderbolt it struck him.

'Eureka!' he shouted.

Suddenly, he knew where he'd seen the engraving on the button. Henry jumped off the bed and grabbed his jacket and truck keys.

'I'm heading out Ma, I've got something needing doing, I'm away to get Eustace, not sure when I'll be back.'

The shack where Eustace lived stood on the edge of some woods on the far side of town. The flimsy construction was no more than some planks of woods roughly nailed together. Several sheets of corrugated metal were meshed together with chicken wire to form a makeshift roof. In heavy rain it was prone to leaking and standing within the one roomed building you could see daylight through the gaps in the planks. In winter, when the wind was from the east, the tiny shack was like an ice box.

Eustace had no electricity or running water. His toilet was a latrine pit by some bushes at the rear of the property. Eustace Brownlie had been bedevilled by poverty all his life and while Fairlea was not a prosperous town, the living conditions he endured were about as bad as it got in Greenbrier County.

'Eustace, Eustace, are you there?' yelled Screech through the rickety front door.

Eustace rolled over on the camp bed that stood in the far corner of the room. Pretending not to hear he pulled his blanket and coat up over his head. He was exhausted after four days of searching and now he just wanted to sleep.

'Get up Eustace we've got somewhere to go, I can see you're in there,' shouted Screech who was now rattling the door handle.

'Alright, alright' came a tiny voice from within. 'This had better be good Henry, we're only a couple of hours back and you're wanting us out again.' Eustace opened the door and let Screech in.

'What's happened to your voice my friend? It's all croaky, I can hardly hear you.'

'Think I've got a sore throat coming on, feels that way anyway,' replied Eustace.

'Never mind about that now, we've got somewhere we need to visit,' said Screech helping his friend on with his jacket. 'That button I found. I've remembered where I've seen it. Come on get in the truck, we're heading there now.'

'Heading where?' asked Eustace getting into the passenger seat.

'Fairlea cemetery, that's where,' replied Screech starting the engine and turning the truck around. 'And I'll tell you one more thing Eustace, you losing your voice is going to be a real bonus, you won't be able to fuck things up like you usually do,' laughed Screech slapping his friend on the thigh. Eustace shook his head and said nothing.

'Damn it,' said Screech as he parked the truck in the car park at the side of the cemetery. 'They had better not be locked.' Screech jumped down from the truck and strode across to the imposing wrought iron gates that formed the entrance to the graveyard. 'Right, good they're not locked.' he said pushing the gates open. 'What are you waiting for?' asked Screech turning around to see where Eustace was. 'Get a move on will you, get your ass over here.'

'Don't know why you dragged me out here,' said a clearly unimpressed Eustace. 'I thought we were supposed to be looking for Charlie. Well I can tell you something, we ain't going to find him in here! What has some carving on a button got to do with anything?' asked Eustace sullenly.

'Might be diddly-squat,' snapped Screech. 'But we've looked just about everywhere these last four days with fuck all success. So, as our friends in the police might say, we're now following a different line of enquiry. Might prove to be nothing at all, but unless you've got any better ideas let's see where this takes us.'

Eustace shrugged his shoulders. 'Okay, fine. I wasn't trying to be difficult, I just want to find Charlie,' said Eustace dejectedly.

'I know you do my friend, and I'm grateful for your help. Look, it's just over here. Every time I visit my dad's grave I pass it. No wonder I thought it was familiar. I must have passed it hundreds of times over the years,' said Screech hurrying along the gravel path.

'You would have thought it would be bigger, what with all his money,' said Eustace staring at the plain granite headstone that marked the final resting place of Donald Alban McCaig. 'I know he was worth millions, but if I had his money, my stone would be huge like the one over there,' said Eustace pointing across to an imposing white marble obelisk that must have been nearly ten foot tall.

'Don't suppose he was really that bothered, him being dead and all that.' chuckled Screech. The two friends stood for a few moments looking at the stone. The inscription read,

In Loving Memory of
Donald Alban McCaig, Born 13th March 1879
in Sligachan, Skye
Died 10th December 1958 in Fairlea, W.V
Founder of the Greenbrier Steel Corporation and
Marsco College
Alba Moiteil agus Mac an Eilein Sgitheanaich[2]

Although the stone was nearly thirty-five years old, the letters of the inscription looked like they had been written yesterday. At the foot of the stone lay a bunch of thistles, their purple heads still fresh and vibrant. The thistles had been carefully tied with a ribbon of tartan. Someone was obviously taking great care to ensure that the grave was cared for.

Carved within a circle near the top of the stone was the picture of a mountain with a stylised thistle in front of it.

'At least I was right about where I'd seen it,' said Screech holding up the button. 'Look, the engraving on it is an exact match. I think I was also right about the thistle being Scottish. McCaig's a Scottish name and he was born on Skye, I know that's a Scottish Island.'

'I'll take your word for it,' replied Eustace.

'Not sure why he's got a mountain carved on his stone,' continued Screech.

'Maybe there are mountains on Skye.' said Eustace. Screech gave his friend a withering look.

'You didn't know Skye was in Scotland so what do you know about Scottish mountains!'

---

[2] Translated from Gaelic this means 'Proud Scot and son of Skye'.

'Nothing,' said Eustace, 'it was only a guess. But I can tell you where Marsco College is, it's on the back road out of White Sulphur Springs.'

'You're right, and you and I are heading over there tomorrow. We'll wait till it's dark and park in the visitor centre on the mountain road. That way we can cut through the forest to the school and no one will see us?'

'Okay fine.' said Eustace quietly. 'But can you take me home now, my throat feels like I've swallowed glass, and I need to get some sleep.'

*

The rear window smashed easily with one strike of the centre punch. He'd hardly made a noise but all the same he stood back in the shadows of the garden wall to make sure that nobody had heard him. After a minute or so he reached into his jacket pocket and removed a neatly folded white plastic bag. Carefully he unwrapped the bag and removed the fish. Wilder had been very specific. The trout was to be left on the back lawn, just a few feet from the rear of the house. Using an underarm throw, Mitchell lobbed the fish onto the grass as he had been instructed.

With great care he put his arm through the broken window and released the window catch. It was tight, but he managed to squeeze himself through the narrow gap. He ignored the key fob behind the curtain and made his way across the room to where the cabinet stood. The leaky white light of the waning moon cut through the darkness allowing him to complete his task.

Putting down his bag, Mitchell took out a small crowbar. The door jemmied open without difficulty and he found what he was after sitting on the middle shelf.

He removed the cigar box and opened the bottom drawer, good, the letter was there. It wasn't a particularly big box, but it was quite wide and try as he might he couldn't get it into his bag. His thick gloves weren't helping so he removed them and loosened the neck of the bag, so it was wide enough for the box to fit in. So far so good he thought. Moving carefully round the room he picked up a carriage clock, a pair of earrings and a lady's watch that was sitting on the mantlepiece. This had to look like a proper burglary.

Lying on a small table next to a leather armchair were several sheets of paper. Mitchell stopped and reached into his jacket for his flashlight. This could be what Bull said to look out for. A smile broke out across his face as he started to read the papers. Bingo, he thought, these are photocopies of the letter.

Suddenly, there was a noise. Mitchell stood rock still and switched off the flashlight. Through a side window he could see the figure of a man walking a dog on a lead. They were heading towards the lodge. He grabbed the letters and thrust them into his jacket pocket. Snatching up his bag, he scrambled out through the window. As he went to move away, he realised that the cord of his duffel bag was caught on the window handle. Repeatedly he pulled at the cord, but it was stuck fast.

'Shit, oh for fuck's sake come on,' he cursed, frantically pulling at the cord. By now he could hear the crunching sound of feet coming up the gravel path at the front of the house. With one last determined tug the cord snapped, Mitchell hurtled backwards landing on his back in the soft mud of a rose bed.

'Who the hell are you?' shouted a voice from the darkness. The beam from a flashlight lit up Mitchell's face.

He recoiled and immediately turned away, desperate not to be identified.

'You stay right there you hear me,' said the man slipping the lead of a large alsatian dog and holding it by its collar. The snarling beast barked furiously and lurched forwards in its eagerness to get to Mitchell.

'One move and I'm setting the dog on you,' shouted the man.

Mitchell grabbed his bag and fled across the lawn. He vaulted the six-foot rear wall hardly breaking stride and made a be-line up the hill towards the woods. If he could make it to the trees, he'd have a chance he thought. He could hear the howl of the dog behind him but he daren't look back. His breath came in short spurts as he sprinted up the hill. His heart pounding and his lungs burning by his efforts to reach safety. Through the trees he ran with his hands in front of his face to protect him from protruding branches that scratched and stabbed at him from all directions.

Mitchell never saw the tree root that sent him crashing to the ground. Covered in soft mud, a feeling of panic now threatened to overwhelm him. As he fell, he'd let go of the bag, instinctively putting his hands out to break his fall. Now in almost complete darkness he couldn't see the bag. Frantically he reached around trying to locate it. Where the fuck was it? He was torn as to what to do. It must have only been seconds, but he couldn't risk searching any longer or his pursuers would be upon him. He stood up to continue running and there it was. Like eyes adjusting to a dark room, he could make out the shape of the bag lying a few feet in front of him. Hardly believing his luck, he scooped up the bag and sprinted away into the darkness.

By the time he reached the perimeter wall he was exhausted. He slumped against the cold stone trying to catch his breath. Mitchell knew how close he'd come to disaster. His vehicle was parked some distance away but just now he needed to rest. In the stillness of the night there was not a sound to be heard. He huddled against the wall and waited. Five minutes passed, and he was breathing normally again. All was quiet. There was no sign of anybody.

Having convinced himself that he wasn't being followed Mitchell made his way back to his vehicle. As a further precaution he took a circuitous route home and by the time he reached his lock-up it was after two. He hadn't passed another vehicle on his journey home. After locking his pick-up in the garage, he climbed the staircase leading to his first floor flat.

He struggled to open the door as his hands were still shaking. He badly needed a drink. The first shot of bourbon hardly touched the sides. He refilled his glass and drained a second shot. The neat liquor burnt the back of his throat but at least he could feel his nerves slowly starting to subside. That had been too close for comfort. If he'd been caught it wasn't his promotion, he need worry about, he would have been looking at a jail sentence. That prospect sent a shiver down his spine as he knew fine well what happened to cops in prison. I ain't doing anything like that again, I don't care what Bull Wilder says. I've paid my debt, we're even after this, thought Mitchell. I've risked my neck for what? Some damned letter! He pulled out the photocopies from inside his jacket. He read the letter but was still none the wiser as to why it was so important.

Putting down his glass Mitchell reached into the bag. A look of horror swept over his face.

'No way. You've got to be fucking kidding man,' he wailed banging his fist on the table in anger. He tipped the contents of the bag onto the kitchen table.

'Why didn't that fucking carriage clock, or those stupid earrings fall out.' he cried kicking a chair over in frustration. 'Fuck, why does it always happen to me. It must have come out when I tripped and fell. It's somewhere in the middle of that fucking forest, but it will have to stay there, I don't have a fucking clue where it is and I ain't going back to look for it.'

Chapter 10

The following morning Mike Rawlingson was in the office much earlier than normal. He wanted to finish the report that he'd started yesterday. Susan was currently between consultations and other than a dry mouth and a loss of appetite, was coping well with her radiation treatment. She was resting at home and didn't need Mike fussing around her. She was more than happy for her husband to put in a few extra hours, particularly if it was going to help his friend out.

Charlie hadn't asked him to prepare the report, but he had the time and he knew that this morning the chief would want a positional statement regarding the missing person enquiry. In truth there wasn't that much to report, but years of ploughing through pages of long-term missing person enquiries had taught Mike the benefit of having a brief synopsis report outlining the actions taken to date. It was easy to lose track of exactly what had been done and, just as importantly, what enquiries still needed undertaken or to be completed. He was just finishing the report when Dave Richardson popped his head round the door looking for Charlie.

'He's not in yet Dave, but he'll not be far away. Is that the report on the deer's head by any chance?'

'Yep, and the photographs of the footprints that were found on the path next to the bridge.'

'Did you find anything interesting?' asked Mike switching on the kettle. 'Just about to have a coffee, would you like one?'

'Why not,' said Dave pulling up a chair. 'We found a couple of things of interest that I'll need to speak to Charlie about, so I might as well have one while I'm waiting'

'Doesn't look like you'll have to wait long, I can see him walking across the car park,' said Mike pouring the remnants of yesterday's coffee into the rubber plant on the windowsill.

'Am I late?' asked Charlie looking slightly confused as he hung up his jacket.

Mike laughed. 'No, I'm in early,' he said handing Charlie his report.

'Jeez, you didn't have to do that,' said Charlie scanning the three-page document.

'Not a problem, I knew you had the missing person review this morning, and I remember all too well what a pain in the ass it was trying to make sense of those reports. If the enquiry goes on more than a few days, it ends up looking like a dog's dinner, there are so many entries in it.'

Charlie smiled and nodded. 'I know exactly what you mean, and every group updates its own actions, so the handwriting is usually impossible to read. I appreciate you taking the trouble to plough through it all.'

'Happy to help, you've done it often enough for me in the past. Anyway, more importantly Dave's got the photos and his report on the deer's head,' added Mike.

'I was hoping that was why you were here,' said Charlie unpacking his briefcase. 'So, what can you tell us?'

'Let's start with the footprints,' said Dave passing Charlie some photographs. 'Angela was right, the one with the missing inset was made by a cowboy boot and it's a size eight, so below average size if it was made by an adult. The inset itself is of a lion rampant. I think I've tracked down the company that makes them. They're called Moore's. They're based in Pittsburgh and they manufacture thousands of rubber soles for shoes and boots, so I don't think that'll be of any great help. The other prints that you found were all bigger. A size ten and an eleven but they weren't particularly clear and I'm struggling to tell you much more about them other than they were made by a shoe or boot with a heel. They definitely weren't made by sneakers. There were other prints as you can see but I can't do anything with them as they are mainly skid marks.'

'Are you able to say how many people made these prints?' asked Charlie.

'I can't say with any certainty I'm afraid. But there were at least three different prints on the path. It's likely there were more, but I can't say that for definite.' replied Dave. 'I can tell you they were freshly made though. I'd say no more than a few hours either side of when your man went missing.'

Charlie nodded. 'That's good to know, it means they could well be connected to his disappearance. Anything else about the prints?'

'No, that's your lot.' said Dave.

'And what about the deer's head?' asked Mike, 'what can you tell us about that?'

Dave removed another set of photographs from his folder.

'I can tell you it's the head of a male white-tailed deer and that it hadn't been in the river long. Anything up to a day but certainly no longer. There was no decomposition of any note. If it had been in the river for any length of time fish, or more likely crayfish, would have started eating it and there was no evidence of that.' explained Dave.

'Can you tell us anything about how the head and ear were removed?' asked Charlie. Dave nodded as he took a large mouthful of coffee.

'This is the most interesting bit. Can't say much about the ear other than it was roughly cut with a knife. One with a straight edged blade, most probably a hunting knife. The neck bone on the other hand was cut using a saw with a thin serrated blade. Something like a hacksaw.' Dave passed the photos to Charlie and Mike.

'I've had these blown up, but if you look carefully you can see quite clearly what I'm about to explain.' Charlie and Mike peered at the photographs.

'Firstly, I want you to look at the score marks that I've indicated by the letter 'A',' said Dave. 'It looks like it was a bit of a false start because that kerf is not at all deep.'

'What's a kerf when it's at home?' asked Mike who was finding this fascinating.

'Sorry, I should have said. The kerf is the name for the groove left by the saw. I reckon they must have hit a spur, that would have been difficult to cut through, so they decided to cut just below it.'

'A bit like when you hit a knot sawing wood then.' said Mike.

'Just like that.' replied Dave. 'Look closely at the mark the saw's made. See how it's ever so slightly jagged and then it runs straight for a tiny bit before it's jagged again.' Charlie and Mike both nodded. 'Well, that's because the saw blade is missing some teeth and probably quite blunt. I reckon three or maybe four teeth are missing from that blade.' said Dave.

'Huh,' said Charlie scratching his head.

'Now, have a look at the next photograph. This is one I've mocked up. I used a new hack saw that is obviously sharp and has all its teeth. I used a bit of deer bone, about the same width as the one we're interested in. If you look carefully, you'll see that the striation pattern is completely different. It's uniform throughout, there's no deviation in it.' said Dave.

'Well I'll be damned,' said Mike holding up the photographs side by side.

'I've learnt something new today.' added Charlie who was now writing some notes on a pad.

'So, let me get this straight,' said Mike. 'The deer's neck bone was cut with a serrated saw blade, that was blunt and missing some of its teeth, is that correct?'

'That's about the strength of it.' replied Dave. 'If you can find me that blade, I should be able to prove it was the one that cut that head off. Anyway, you'll find all that in the report I've typed up.'

Charlie stood up and patted Dave on the shoulder.

'I'm grateful to you Dave, as usual that's been most useful. Not sure what us detectives would do without you.'

'Not a problem, just happy to help,' said Dave as he headed out the door.

'Great guy Dave. A real enthusiast and nothing's ever too much trouble.' said Mike.

'Worth his weight in gold that's for sure.' added Charlie. 'We've got him to thank that we were able to solve the Maisie Foster murder. If he hadn't taken it upon himself to check that blood sample, we might still have an innocent man in jail. Doesn't bear thinking about does it?' Mike nodded in agreement.

'While you're here, have you had a chance to go through the overnight crime report yet?' asked Charlie.

'Yep. I'd Just finished going over it when Dave appeared. The only one you really need to know about is a burglary at Marsco College over at White Sulphur Springs. The lodge house was broken into in the early hours. The family who live in the house were away overnight, but the gardener was looking after their dog and was returning after a late-night walk when he disturbed the intruder.'

'Much taken?' asked Charlie.

'Doesn't look like it, but we won't really know until the householder gets back later this afternoon. Apparently, the family were away overnight at a relative's funeral. The gardener was going to give chase, but the intruder headed into the forest and he thought better of it. There is one thing's that a bit odd about it all though,' said Mike.

'What's that then,' asked Charlie looking up.

'Well, apparently the uniforms who attended found a fish on the back lawn. A whole fish. It hadn't been gutted or anything.'

'That does seem a bit weird,' said Charlie writing some notes. 'Could it have been stolen out the fridge or something like that?' asked Charlie.

'Don't think so. The cops asked the gardener that but according to him, Mr Buckley who's the householder, doesn't like fish, so he thinks it's unlikely. They seem to think it might be a trout, but they're not sure, so Hugh

Robertson is heading over to have a look. He's a bit of a fisherman apparently.'

'We'll get it photographed in situ as part of the scenes of crime,' said Charlie.

'A deer's head and now a trout, poor old Dave won't know what the hell is going on,' said Mike laughing.

'He's not the only one,' replied Charlie.

'Just checking but isn't Marsco College where Bull went to school?' asked Charlie.

'That's correct,' replied Mike. 'That's why I wanted you to know about the burglary.'

Charlie nodded and sat back down. 'I only found out that he'd gone there the other week when I saw a photograph of him and his school buddies in his office. Marsco's pretty exclusive, must have cost a fortune.' said Charlie.

Mike chuckled. 'Didn't cost his folks a cent. Bull won the scholarship and got in for nothing. He's having to pay fees now right enough, his son's in his last year at the school.'

'Well, well, well you learn something every day, I didn't know that.'

Mike shook his head. 'I can't believe I never told you any of this before. But hey, there you go, it must have just slipped my mind. And if you didn't know that you're not going to be aware of this,' continued Mike.

'Be aware of what?' asked Charlie with a puzzled look on his face.

'Wilder's not just a former pupil, he's currently president of the Old Marsconians club and a few months ago took over as chair of the board of governors. So, you can see, he's going to take a keen interest in this one.'

'Holy shit, I'm glad you told me all this, that might have been embarrassing. He's bound to go into full Bull Wilder rant mode about this one.' said Charlie.

Mike smiled. 'And just one last thing lieutenant, it's the seventy-fifth anniversary of the college tomorrow and they're holding a big dinner. Bull's giving the speech to the college, he's been working on it for the last week and is stressed enough about it, so have your wits about you. This is likely to send him off the deep end!'

Charlie frowned as he gathered up his various reports.

'And to think lieutenant, just last week you were moaning about how quiet things were. Now you've got a long-term missing person, a break-in to the chief's school and the deer's head mystery to solve. Things are hotting up nicely don't you think?' said Mike leaning back in his chair and putting his feet on his desk.

'Thanks a lot, my friend, but haven't you forgotten something? You didn't mention the trout!'

'Of course,' said Mike cheekily, 'I knew there was something fishy about that.'

Chapter 11

Twenty miles north in Huntersville, the newest and biggest member of the fleet was reversing down a narrow path to a compound deep in the forest of the sprawling Deans estate.

'You're doing fine,' shouted Ralph Portman, who was guiding the massive truck to its destination at the compound's gates. 'Another twenty feet or so, and we're there. Keep coming, keep coming,' he said using his hands to guide the massive vehicle the last few feet.

'That'll do you,' he said banging the rear door and giving a thumbs up to the driver. The driver jumped down from the cab and walked to the rear of the truck where he high fived Portman.

'I wouldn't fancy tackling that last section if it were dark,' said the man removing his Orioles cap and wiping the sweat from his brow. 'That was tight. I don't think I could have had more than a foot clearance either side.'

'No, you're right. That would be nearly impossible in the dark. I'll make a note of that. We knew it would be snug but it's going to have to be done in daylight and somebody must be on hand to assist when you're reversing that last bit to the gates. But it's all good, no harm done, it's the first trip after all, we're learning as we go on.' The driver nodded.

'How was the trip then, any problems?' asked Portman. The driver puffed out his cheeks and gave a wry smile.

'A bit of a scare at the border, I had to use the cash to buy off the Mexican guard. He was sniffing about the boxes in the back. I told him they had Tequila in them that we hadn't paid tax on. I bought him off for $200 but we're going to have to get that sorted.'

Portman scratched the back of his head and nodded. 'Do you think he believed you about the Tequila?'

'I think so. I don't think he would have found the false container, but it's not worth the risk. We can't use the no tax trick too often. We need to get over the border without any checks or this might become too risky.'

Portman bit on his lip. 'I've got an idea about how we might be able to fix that problem, so leave that with me.'

Portman pulled an envelope stuffed with cash from his jacket pocket and handed it to the driver.

'Just a little thank you for your endeavours my friend, and I don't expect to see you here till next Wednesday. A few days off after such a long trip will be welcome, I'm sure.'

The driver smiled and waved the envelope in the air.

'Appreciate that Mr Portman. I might take the wife for an over-night in Charleston. keep her sweet, and you never know I might get lucky.'

'Well before you get carried away thinking about that, we have one more job to do. We need to move them into the compound. Make sure they know that they've to have their heads covered when they come out, you understand?'

The driver nodded. They were told that when I picked them up, but I'll explain it again. One of them speaks pretty good English.'

*

Charlie was busy dictating a statement when the chief walked into his office.

'Is there any update regarding the burglary at the school? I'm heading home early as I've to be over there for 1830 hrs. The dinner starts at half seven but I've things to organise first. I don't want to arrive there without a comprehensive update. Everyone is going to be asking about it.'

'No, of course,' said Charlie looking up from his desk. 'Not much I can tell you that you didn't know about from this morning's meeting. Although Angela is just off the phone to say the householder Mr Buckley has arrived home.'

'What's he got to say about it?' asked Wilder pulling up a chair and sitting down.

'Apparently he's really going off on one. Angela says it's impossible to interview him at the moment as he keeps cursing and swearing. I know he's had his home broken into, but his reaction sounds a bit extreme.'

'Not always the most stable of characters is Mr Buckley,' said the chief knowingly. 'He's getting on a bit now and his fuse is increasingly short. Once he's had a chance to calm down, he'll be all right. Anything else I need to know?'

'According to Angela he seems particularly upset at a cigar box that appears to have been stolen. It was in a cabinet that was broken into and he keeps shouting and swearing about it. I suppose it might have been very valuable. I know a lady's watch is also missing but we don't have a full list of the stolen items yet.' said Charlie. 'There is something else though that's potentially of interest.'

'Oh, what's that?' asked the chief.

'It's to do with the fish that was found on the lawn,' said Charlie. Before he could continue the chief interrupted.

'Yes, the fish, I've been thinking about that. At our last governors' meeting we discussed the problem we had been having with poachers. They're a real pain in the ass. It's happened several times this year already. Perhaps whoever broke into the lodge had also been poaching at the lake and dropped the trout as they tried to get away. You did say they had been disturbed.'

'Yes, sir, I did say that. But there's something strange about that.' said Charlie.

The chief frowned. 'What do you mean strange?'

'Well this morning when I was reading the initial report left by the nightshift cops it said they weren't sure what type of fish it was. So, I asked Sergeant Robertson to go and take a look as he's a keen fisherman. The thing is, sir, he's saying that the trout on the lawn is a rainbow trout.'

'So, what?' said the chief looking pensive.

'Well, according to Sergeant Robertson, there aren't any rainbow trout in the lake. He's spoken to the gardener who also looks after the lake and according to him the lake only holds brown trout. Much prized apparently. All the fish in the lake are descendants of the original fish that were imported from Scotland, not long after the school opened.'

'Could a stray one have got in?' asked Wilder sternly.

'It's possible of course, but Sergeant Robertson says rainbow trout are much more likely to come from stocked fisheries where they are fed intensively so they grow big for recreational fishermen. He says that the lake at Marsco is fed by a stream that runs down from the Greenbrier mountain, so he can't explain how the rainbow trout would have got in the lake. If poachers dropped it after breaking into the lodge it would almost certainly have been a brown trout, and as it isn't, we're at a loss to explain it.' said Charlie.

'Probably not going to be that important in the greater scheme of things,' said Wilder not wanting to dwell on it. 'And what about scenes of crime, anything from them?'

'Still too early to say, but it looks like whoever did it was wearing gloves. They haven't found any prints at the point of entry, but I'll have to wait for their report to know for sure.'

'I see,' said Wilder nodding.

'There are some footprints in a rose bed where we think the intruder fell coming out of the house. According to the witness who disturbed him, there appeared to be only one man. The footprints in the flower bed support that as they are all the same size and have the same tread pattern. I should have the photographs to show you when you're back in on Monday, sir.'

'Good. That seems pretty comprehensive lieutenant. Phone me at home if anything significant comes in over the weekend. I want to know about it right away you understand?'

'Understood, sir,' said Charlie standing up. 'And I hope the dinner and your speech goes well tonight. It sounds like it should be a good night.'

'Really looking forward to this one,' replied the chief. 'We have reunion dinners every five years, but this one will be even more special as my son will be attending. The head of school and his house captains get to go this year as it's the seventy-fifth anniversary. And as Jason is house captain of Dunvegan, he'll be there. If I recall correctly, there will be one hundred and eighty-two sitting down for dinner. Its been a real logistical challenge to get it organised, but it's going to be worth it.' said the chief pulling a blue and green tartan tie out of his pocket.

'Before I go, I want your opinion on this tie? This is my tie from my last year at the school. I'll admit it's a little threadbare but other than that, I can't see much wrong with it. Mrs Wilder gave me implicit instructions this morning that I was to stop by Carruthers in Lewisburg and pick up another one. But I think I'll save myself twenty dollars and keep hold of this one, what do you think?'

Charlie stared at the tie. It was certainly well worn, and the bottom edge was quite frayed. Not wanting to annoy the chief, Charlie decided to be diplomatic.

'Doesn't look too bad to me, Sir. I might keep it tucked into my waistcoat though. That way the frayed edge won't show.' Wilder broke into a broad grin.

'Good advice lieutenant, I agree. That's twenty dollars you've saved me.' He said with a wave as he headed out the door.

Chapter 12

It was late afternoon when Screech drew up outside Eustace's place. He checked that both flashlights were working before placing them under his seat in a canvas bag. By the time we get up to the school it will be after half six and that will only leave us an hour of daylight at best. We're going to need those flashlights thought Screech.

The passenger door opened and in climbed Eustace wearing a padded camouflage jacket, green scarf and a black balaclava. Screech looked at his friend and shook his head.

'It's a bit fresh tonight but it ain't that cold. You look like you're dressed for an arctic expedition.'

'I need to keep warm,' replied Eustace in a barely decipherable whisper. I've no voice and my throat, it feels like I've swallowed a box of tacks. I don't want no flu, so I've layered up just in case.'

'Fair enough. Looks like it was just as well that I brought this along,' said Screech reaching into his bag and pulling out a half bottle of bourbon. 'You're going to need it for medicinal purposes.'

Eustace laughed and nodded enthusiastically. He might not be feeling on top of his game, but Eustace Brownlie never turned down an invitation for a drink.

'Two great minds think alike,' whispered Eustace taking a bottle of Wild Turkey out his inside pocket.

'Well I'll be darned. Two great minds right enough,' said Screech with a high five to his friend.

The sign at the car park said closed as Screech turned off the narrow road that wound its way to the summit of the Greenbrier mountain. The car park was popular with walkers and tourists who came to enjoy the network of forest trails and viewing points that were a feature of this beautiful county. At this time in October, the visitor centre and café closed at five, so when Screech parked up next to the toilet block there was nobody about.

'Come over and have a look at this,' said Screech handing Eustace the pair of binoculars that had been hanging round his neck. 'If you look through that gap in the trees you can see the lake and the school buildings beyond it. This is a good place to approach from. Nobody's going to see us. The trees go right down to the edge of the lake and we should get a good view from there.'

'What exactly are we looking for?' asked Eustace in the tiniest of voices.

'Not entirely sure if I'm honest,' replied Screech, 'but after five days of looking for Charlie, I'm prepared to try anything. I know I found the button next to where his fishing gear was, so I guess I'm hoping that. Well, I'm just hoping Eustace. Hoping he may still be alive, that's all.' Eustace nodded but didn't say anything. He could see how upsetting this was for his friend.

The path down from the car park was steep but the ground under foot was firm and progress swift. There is something magical about a deciduous forest in the fall and as they picked a route through the trees, the two friends had time to marvel at the wonders of nature. In the warm evening air, maples, oak and beech resplendent in their autumn palette formed a kaleido-scope of colour. Sycamore seeds, caught in the evening breeze, helicoptered their way gently to the ground while golden chanterelles and morel mushrooms prolif-erated in the smorgasbord of decaying vegetation, their gnarly purple heads a contradiction to this most appe-tising of Appalachian fungi.

Eustace stopped abruptly as they entered a clearing. Between some clumps of thick grass, he had spotted something. He went over and bent down to look, recoiling immediately. The stench of maggot infested flesh was overpowering. Eustace turned away and retched. Screech stood rooted to the spot. Gripped by fear he was barely able to breathe. Eustace stumbled his way back to the path covering his nose to avoid the foul smell. Henry closed his eyes and prayed.

'It's not Charlie, it's okay, it's not him,' whispered Eustace grabbing his friend by the arm. Henry opened his eyes and smiled weakly. 'It's a deer carcass and its missing its head. I reckon we've found where the head in the river came from. Don't get too close, its rancid and crawling with maggots.'

'For a moment there I was sure it was him,' said Henry sitting down on a tree stump. 'It's really weird but I couldn't move I was so scared. Does that sound stupid?' Eustace shook his head.

'No,' he whispered. 'He's your brother, it just shows you care.'

Henry looked up and smiled. 'You're a good man Eustace Brownlie, and sometimes much wiser than I give you credit for.' Eustace smiled and nodded.

'I'm still not sure what all this means.' said Henry. 'But the button, and now finding the deer carcass tells me that we might be onto something. Whoever cut that buck's head off took it to the bridge and threw it into the river I reckon. We know Charlie was there, so I think whoever took the head knows what happened to my brother.' Eustace nodded in agreement.

'Come on, we better get a move on before it gets too dark,' said Henry. 'Who knows what we might find when we get down there.'

By the time they reached the edge of the treeline it was just before seven.

'Not sure what the hell is going on,' said Henry, 'but it looks like there must be some sort of event judging by the number of cars that are coming down the drive. They seem to be using the football pitch as a car park. You see that building over there?' Henry pointed across the lake to a large building that was set a few yards back from the water's edge. Eustace nodded.

'That looks like a boathouse. If we get ourselves behind it, we should be close enough to see what's going on. Come on follow me, and make sure nobody sees you.'

The boathouse was made of wood and painted grey. It had a pitched roof and a veranda that ran the width of the house. A wooden jetty led directly from the veranda to the lake. Two rowing boats, freshly painted in the blue and green colours of Marsco, were tied to the jetty. On the veranda sat several rolls of insulating material and a large pile of plasterboard sheets.

'Doesn't look much like a boathouse to me!' exclaimed Eustace peering in a side window. 'There ain't no boats in it for a start. And someone's fitted a new bathroom and I can see a bedroom next to that. I'd say this is being turned into a house.'

'Never mind that, it doesn't matter what it is, but look over there,' said Screech pointing to an area of hard standing next to the house, can you see it?'

'See what?' replied Eustace who wasn't following what his friend was on about.

'The blue Ford pick-up, stupid. Bradley said he'd seen a dark coloured pick-up parked at the bridge the night Charlie went missing. Well, that's a dark pick-up and you just found the deer's carcass. I think we're onto something, this could be the truck we're looking for. Hurry up, we need to get a closer look at that truck. And keep your head down you hear me.'

Eustace nodded. Crouching down he followed Screech to the vehicle.

'Look at this,' said Eustace in a croaky voice pointing at a sticker on the windscreen.

'Shhh,' said Screech nodding and putting his finger to his lips.

The circular sticker had a picture of a mountain with a thistle in front of it. Written round the edge in stylised letters were the words Mic Sgith, 1992.

'It's the same design that's on the button and McCaig's gravestone in Fairlea.' Before Screech could continue, he was aware of male voices coming towards him. 'Quickly,' said Screech grabbing Eustace by the arm. 'Someone's coming, get back to the boathouse now.'

Staying low the two friends hurried back keeping the pick-up between them and the approaching men.

Screech peeped round the side of the building.

'Shit, they're coming towards the house. Here take my bag and get under the jetty. And don't say a word understand?'

Eustace nodded and slithered down the grass embankment at the side of the house. Screech followed, and the pair squeezed themselves through the lattice of crossbeams and stanchions that supported the wooden structure.

'Fucking posh punks, they've even got a marquee for their drivers, so they can all get wasted at their dinner. Did you see the spread in that tent?' said the first man. The other man nodded. 'Can you imagine what the dinner must be like? Fucking lobster and caviar, I wouldn't put it past them. Sure as hell glad I didn't go to a school like that, I would have hated it,' said a voice from the veranda above.

'Yup, me too.' said another voice. 'And that fat motherfucker driving the Ferrari who yelled at me for parking too close to the Merc got what he deserved, he just wanted to call me black boy. I know he did, you can always tell. The racist ones can't hide it.'

'You got him though bro,' said the first voice, 'that asshole will be sorry when he finds his car's been keyed.'

'Shit, you know we've got four hours to wait till this thing is over and we get paid. Get those Buds and snacks out man, this is gonna be a long wait.'

Eustace looked at Screech and shrugged his shoulders. They both knew they had no option other than to sit it out. It was going to be a long night. Eustace reached into his jacket and took out his bottle of bourbon. He took off the cap and handed the bottle to Screech. Henry took two large swigs before handing the bottle back. Both friends smiled. What else was there to do. At least we've another bottle when we've finished this one thought Eustace spreading himself out and making himself comfortable. Screech was about to do the same when he heard a rustling sound a few feet away. He peered into the rapidly fading light. He thought he could hear something scratching on wood. A pair of eyes blinked back at him.

'No fucking way man,' whispered Screech, 'that had better not be a rat. I fucking hate rats!'

*

The dining room was now empty except for two figures who were deep in conversation at the top table. The remnants of a splendid dinner were there for all to see. Empty wine and whisky bottles littered the tables and the fug of cigar smoke hung in the air. Waitresses, immaculately dressed in black uniforms, busied themselves clearing tables while two men loaded speakers and microphones onto a trolley.

'Fine speech Ewart,' said Ralph Portman topping up his glass for a last whisky. 'You did the Founder and the school proud. I know how much work must have gone into preparing that,' said Portman taking a puff from his cigar.

'Thanks, I appreciate that,' said Wilder leaning back in his chair. 'An important landmark for the school today, so I wanted to do it justice. I've got a lot to thank Marsco for.'

'You and me both,' said Portman raising his glass. 'Let's hope we're both still around for its centenary.'

'I'll drink to that,' said Wilder clinking glasses with his companion.

'Changing the subject for a moment, what the fuck do you think the Dionach was on about? I thought he was going to explode at one point. That rant before he sang the second song was a bit near the bone. I thought

129

he was supposed to be explaining how Burns came to write it, seemed more like a dig at you from where I was sitting,' said Portman.

'I think that was how he intended it to come across. He's still pissed that the board is making him retire next year and, of course, the burglary at the lodge hasn't helped. I think it's got to him and he's stressed out his box. I'm letting this latest outburst go given the circumstances, but if that son of a bitch does it again, I'm having him, nobody speaks to me like that.'

'No, that was completely out of order, but I can kind of understand why he's upset, he's never known anything else but this school, man and boy, it's in his blood. Still, that doesn't excuse what he said. We've both known him a long time, I'll have a word, tell him to calm down. Bad enough saying things like that one to one. But in front of all those guests, it's not on. As I said I'll speak to him.' Wilder nodded his approval.

'On a more positive note it was great to have the boys with us, I know they understand the history of this place, but to see over a hundred old boys, from all over the country, must have made an impression.' said Portman.

'It can't fail to,' said Wilder. 'That's what makes this school so special. If you're a Marsconian you get it, the ethos, that sense of belonging, you just get it.'

For several moments neither man said anything as they thought about times long past and a place that meant so much to them, a place seared deep in their hearts. It was Portman who eventually broke the silence.

'Listen, Ewart, while it's just the two of us, there's something else I want to talk to you about.'

Wilder looked up quizzically.

'Go on, I'm listening.'

'It's to do with money, or rather the lack of money.' said Portman.

Wilder looked expressionless and didn't say anything. He wasn't sure where this conversation was going.

'Jason was at the estate last week and he told me he's applying for Duke next year. He also told me you're getting grief from Bridget because she wants you to buy a lake house at Fayetteville. The thing is, he said you were concerned about how you were going to pay for it all. That's a lot of additional expenditure my friend.'

'Sounds like my son's got a loose tongue. I'll need to speak to him about that,' replied Wilder coldly. 'Anyway, I'm not sure what any of this has got to do with you.'

'It's got nothing to do with me, you're right. But I've got a proposition to put to you that would help both of us. It helps my business interests and would mean a lot of extra cash for you. Easy money. Money that would help pay those college fees and another mortgage.'

Wilder leant forward resting his chin on his hand and stared at Portman. Money for what? 'Cause there's always a what.'

'For turning a blind eye. And for brokering a deal. If you fix those two things there's $2,000 a month for you. Deposited straight to your bank account, regular as clockwork.'

'Turn a blind eye to what exactly?' asked Wilder suspiciously.

'To vehicle checks on my trucks that's what. Your cops are killing me. Drivers are getting done for the slightest thing and one of my men now has a ban pending because of the endorsements on his licence.

If I lose another driver, I can't keep all the trucks on the road and the business loses money, big money. I can't afford for that to happen.' explained Portman.

'Tell your drivers to keep their noses clean and they won't get endorsements then,' said Wilder dismissively.

'It's not as simple as that. They're getting done for the tiniest indiscretion. Ever since that young girl was knocked down and killed over in Lewisburg, they've been persecuting us. It wasn't even one of my trucks that killed the girl. Every day they're getting stopped, its relentless. Two of your cops, Planner and Coutts, are over us like a rash. Every ticket I see has their names on it.'

Wilder bit his lip and thought for a moment.

'Okay then, even if I did need the money, what makes you think I'd do that for you, what you're asking is clearly not kosher. It could cost me my job, and that's before you've even told me what else you want.'

'You owe me Ewart,' replied Portman stubbing out his cigar. 'Big time.'

'You think?' replied Wilder with a sneer.

'Yep, I think you do.' said Portman seriously. 'I know you cheated at the scholarship interviews. I've known that for years, the Dionach told me. But I've kept my counsel on that. But more importantly, you owe me for not snitching on you when the cops interviewed us about that night at the bridge. One word from me and you would have been expelled from the school. You'd never have made police chief either. Somehow, I think you know all of that. So, yes, I reckon you owe me, and now it's time to call in that dept. What do you say?'

Wilder sipped his whisky and stroked his chin.

'And the second thing you want me to do, explain exactly what that is?'

Portman leant forward checking nobody else was listening.

'I need you to speak to Eduardo Lopez, your Mexican friend, the one you brought to the Founders day barbeque last year when he was on a course at the police college with you. I know he's Chief of Police in Nogales.'

'And what of it?' said Wilder.

'I'm looking to open up a lucrative new route to Mexico. One that's going to earn me a lot of money. We're going to be crossing the border at Nogales. One trip every four to six weeks. I will be able to provide exact times and dates, but I need a guarantee that the truck will get through, no checks, no searches. I need you to fix that with Lopez.'

'Why, what are you carrying?' asked Wilder.

'Do you really want to know? I'll tell you if you do, but as I said, all I need you to do is set it up and then contact Lopez each time we intend to make the crossing. You get $2,000 and he gets $1,000. Every time we make a successful trip. He told me at the barbeque that there wasn't a Mexican who couldn't be bought off, I think it's time we put that to the test.'

Wilder sat back in his chair not saying anything. He'd decided he didn't need to know what was being carried. The less he knew the easier it would be to distance himself from this if he needed to. The money on offer was appealing. An extra two grand each month would more than pay for the lake house, and cover most of the Duke fees as well.

'When do you need to know?' asked Wilder getting up from the table.

'Within the week,' replied Portman standing up. 'And if you agree, I'll make an immediate deposit of

$2,000 to your account as a gesture of goodwill.' Portman held out his hand and the two men shook hands.

'That was an interesting chat, I'll be in touch.' said Wilder putting on his jacket. 'Now where the hell has my glass gone? I'm sure it was here on the table during the dinner. I opened the box to have a look at it and now its disappeared.'

'I don't see mine either,' said Portman looking under the table. 'If some asshole has taken my glass there will be hell to pay.'

*

'That looks like most of the cars are now away.' said Screech looking through the jetty to the football pitch where the steady stream of taillights disappearing up the drive towards the main gates had slowed to a trickle. 'It's difficult to tell because it's so dark but it looks like there's just a few stragglers left, time for us to make a move.'

Eustace grimaced and stretched his shoulders. They had been stuck under the jetty for over four hours and now he was as stiff as a board and his throat felt like he'd swallowed sandpaper. Just as they were about to move, they heard voices talking above them. Screech put his finger to his lips.

'I'm going to drop my dad back at Huntersville. Lucky for him I've got that swimming competition next week, as otherwise I would have torn into those beers and not been able to drive him,' said the first voice. 'I'm going to stay over and come back in the morning. It would be too late by the time I get back tonight. Listen, does your dad need a lift?'

'No, you're, fine. He told me he'd arranged for one of the night shift patrol cars to pick him up. Perks of the job, eh.' said the second voice.

'Yep, rank brings its privileges right enough. What you looking so worried about? I'll be back in good time for the game.' said the first voice.

'You'd better be,' said the second voice laughing, 'or coach will go off on one. Big Game tomorrow, if we lose, we won't make the play offs, and if you think that coach will be mad, wait till you see what my father will be like. They won the cup in their final year didn't they. He's expecting the same from us.'

'I think they won everything, well according to them they did, there was nobody quite like the class of 1960, they were special!' said the first voice.

'Yep, special in all sorts of ways,' said the second voice laughing.

Screech and Eustace watched as the taller of the boys got into the pick-up and drove round the lake to the gravel forecourt in front of the main school building. The other boy watched him go before entering the boathouse.

Screech turned and looked at Eustace.

'I've got a feeling in my bones bout this, we're onto something now, I'm sure of it. We'll get back to the pick-up and head over to Huntersville and see what's going on.' Eustace nodded.

'We can park on the high road at the back of the estate,' whispered Eustace whose voice had now all but disappeared. 'Be just like old times when we were up there stealing them Christmas trees,' he said chuckling to himself.

*

135

By the time Screech pulled off the road at the back of the Deans estate it was nearly two.

'You forget how dark it gets when you're out the town and away from streetlights,' said Screech handing Eustace one of the flashlights from his bag. 'We can use these while we're still in the forest, but as soon as we see the house it's lights off understand. You never know who might be around.' As they were about to move off the hoot of an owl split the night air.

'That's a screech owl that is!' exclaimed Eustace confidently. Identifying birds was one of the few subjects he was any good at. Screech narrowed his one good eye and glared at Eustace.

'You trying to be funny?'

Eustace shook his head. Screech hated his nickname, given to him as a child when he lost an eye after being hit in the face by a well-directed rock. Despite his wide-eyed stare, the result of an ill-fitting artificial eye, that in all honesty did give him a remarkable resemblance to an owl, his oldest friend was not given to teasing him about it. In fact, Eustace was about the only person, other than Henry's mother and Charlie, who never called him Screech.

'Wasn't being funny,' said Eustace earnestly, 'but that was definitely a screech owl.'

'Okay, never mind.' said Screech shaking his head. 'Just remember to switch the flashlight off if we hear anybody, or when we see the house, got it?' said Screech.

'Got it,' said Eustace putting his thumb up.

Progress was slow as the pair made their way through the hundreds of fir trees that dominated the curtilage of the estate. No longer grown commercially, the trees had been left to grow wild as the estate diversified its interests into haulage and more lucrative ventures several years ago. Now the trees grew tall and provided homes for the forest's inhabitants. As they navigated through the forest the heady scent of pine resin gave way to the sweet smell of sassafras and black birch as the wood thinned to its natural state.

They were first aware of a yellow glow. A haze of artificial light filtering through the trees. But it wasn't coming from the house. Screech and Eustace switched off their flashlights. If that's not the house, then what the hell is it? thought Screech as they crept ever closer.

'Whoa!' said Eustace as they reached the edge of the trees. The two friends stood motionless staring at a large and rather austere looking single storey building.

'It looks to me like some sort of prison compound. That fence must be fifteen feet high and it's got barbed wire on the top. Somebody doesn't want you getting in or out of that place by the looks of it.' said Screech.

'Do you think there's a chance Charlie might be in there?' whispered Eustace.

'It's possible. I sure as hell hope so.' replied Screech. Eustace grabbed Screech's shoulder and pointed at the security cameras that were attached to four metal stanchions whose lights illuminated the rectangular compound.

'Yeah, I see them. We'll keep the trees as cover and work our way around it.' said Screech. 'We can't risk being picked up by one of those cameras. If they've gone to the trouble of building that, you can bet your bottom dollar that those cameras are being monitored somewhere.'

It was at least a quarter of a mile from the compound to the house. En route they passed the yard where six trucks were parked in regimental fashion, freshly washed and resplendent in their red and white livery. The house itself was an enormous three storied property made of sandstone. Its gable end was clothed in a shock of orange tinged Virginia Creeper. Each shuttered window housed a terracotta window box, filled with pink and white geraniums, flowering defiantly despite the chill of early October. The house was in darkness except for one bedroom on the second floor.

Screech and Eustace stood in the shadows underneath the roof overhang of the vast triple garage. From there they had a clear view of the blue pick-up that was parked near to the side-door of the house. Screech wasn't sure what he was going to do. Of course, he wanted a closer inspection of the vehicle, but most of all he wanted to get a proper look at who was driving the truck. That might have to wait, as for now it appeared there was nobody about. Gesturing for Eustace to follow, Screech tiptoed towards the pick-up.

He'd only gone a few yards when there was an enormous crash behind him. Eustace had caught his foot on a garden hose and stumbled forward. Unable to keep his balance, he fell headlong into some wooden shelves sending tins of paint, glass jars and a metal watering can crashing to the ground. Screech spun round to see his friend lying prostrate on the gravel.

'Someone's out there!' shouted a voice. 'Ryan get the dog and go to the side door. Joe, Ben, get up, we've got intruders.'

Screech knew they were now in serious trouble. If they were caught, they could be sure of a beating, their reputation would see to that. If he ran now, he had time to slip into the night and escape through the maze of trees. But he wasn't going to leave without his friend. Bonds are strong after forty years of kinship and right now Eustace needed his help. Screech ran to his stricken friend who was sitting in the darkness trying to put his boot back on that had been ripped off in his fall. Precious seconds passed as Eustace frantically pulled at his boot.

Behind them house lights switched on and a dog started to bark. Fear gripped both men as the sound of boots on gravel thundered towards them. Abandoning his boot, Eustace sprinted towards the woods pursued by a man brandishing a golf club. Instinctively, Screech ran the other side of the garage and across the lawn. Safety was less than seventy yards away, but in the darkness, he never saw his foe. The butt of the rifle crunched into the side of his head. Poleaxed, Screech fell to the ground, his cheek and temporal plates shattered by the force of the blow. Unconscious and with blood oozing out of his right ear, he lay motionless on the grass.

Eustace could feel his heart pounding as he stumbled ever deeper into the woods. He daren't look back, but with his energy levels depleting he knew he couldn't run much further. He wasn't sure if he was still being chased. He couldn't hear any voices and the barking dog seemed some distance away. Just another minute and I'll stop thought Eustace. Get my breath back and head back to the truck and meet Henry. He'll be there, he's fitter than me, he'll be there.

In the darkness Eustace never saw the trap. His bootless foot stood on the plate and the metal jaws snapped shut around his ankle sending him sprawling to the ground. Eustace wanted to scream, the pain was excruciating, searing through his body like a hot knife.

He writhed in agony covering his mouth to suppress his cries. In the blackness, Eustace pulled at the steel jaws desperate to release himself from its vice like grip. They wouldn't budge and with every move its teeth bit deeper into his ankle. He was going nowhere. He started to feel faint and quite sick. The vomit came up in waves. Turning his head to the side the contents of his stomach erupted out of his mouth covering the shoulder and sleeve of his jacket. He winced in pain as he shuffled away from the evil smelling pile and attempted to spit the sour taste of bile from his mouth.

Several minutes passed and no one appeared. Perhaps his pursuer had given up and returned to the house. As if things couldn't be any worse, he was now starting to feel cold. A clammy sweat dampened his brow and he was shivering uncontrollably. He pulled down his balaclava and zipped up his jacket. He reckoned if he could manage the pain, he could lie still until it was daylight. Then he might have a chance of freeing himself if he could see what he was doing. He had no other option other than to lie there and wait.

No more than ten minutes had passed before Eustace was aware of voices coming towards him. He screwed up his eyes and put his hand to his face to protect himself from the glare of the flashlight. Blinded by the beam, he couldn't see who was holding the flashlight, but he heard their laughter and smelt the foul breath of a panting dog inches from his face.

'Well lookey here,' said a voice. 'What a fucking surprise. Who else would it be? Like tweedle-dee and tweedle-dum, if you get Screech Jarret, you're bound to find Eustace fucking Brownlie. Caught in a coyote trap without his boot. Well I'll be damned,' said the voice.

'Help me. Please help me,' mouthed Eustace reaching out his hand, but no words came. His voice now mute, the final indignity of his calamitous situation. One of the males moved towards Eustace.

'Leave him be,' barked the other man. 'He can stay there till the morning. He ain't going anywhere. Teach that scumbag a lesson. You don't mess with the Portman's. Get that Brownlie, you don't fuck with us.'

Chapter 13

The Dionach was asleep in an armchair when Mrs Buckley came down the stairs. On a table in front of him sat a tumbler and an empty bottle of Talisker. Next to the bottle were three boxes containing crystal glasses, prized mementos of last night's dinner.

'Donald, Donald.' cried Mrs Buckley, 'it's after eight and look at the state you're in.' The Dionach opened an eye and groaned. 'Get yourself upstairs to bed now and sleep that off. How much whisky have you had? You're supposed to be supervising the clearing of the dining room in an hour.' said Mrs Buckley clearly annoyed. 'Seth and I will see to that, but you better be up and at it by lunchtime, you hear me, or there will be hell to pay.'

The Dionach groaned again as he raised his ample frame from the chair and headed for the stairs. 'Can you bring me a glass of water and some Tylenol, my head's killing me?' he muttered.

'Serves you damned right, hardly surprising you've got a sore head, judging by all that whisky you've drunk. Seth Buckley, get yourself down here. Your father's not feeling well, I need you to walk the dog. You hear me? You can have some breakfast when you get back.'

Mrs Buckley was whisking eggs in the kitchen when Seth came down the stairs. Noticing the boxes on the table he opened one and removed the crystal glass which glinted in the morning sunlight streaming through the window. Seth grinned and squealed. He placed the glass inside his jacket and whistled for the dog which came bounding in from the kitchen.

'Make sure you give him a decent walk now. Take him up into the woods and let him have a good run. He didn't get much of a walk yesterday, so he needs a decent run.' said Mrs Buckley kissing her son on the cheek. 'I'll have pancakes and bacon ready for you when you get back, so at least a half hour walk. Okay?' Seth smiled at his mother as he grabbed the dog's lead and headed for the woods at the rear of the lodge.

*

At Lewisburg police department, Angela was talking to Phil Coutts in the detectives' office.

'You'd better call him,' said Phil reading through an incident print out. 'He's going to want know ASAP. As for Bull, I'd let Charlie decide that, but I expect he'll ring him straight away, especially as Screech and Brownie are involved. What a way to go though, caught in a coyote trap. It says here that the doc suspects he's had a heart attack. The wound on his ankle hasn't killed him but a heart attack brought on by shock will be the likely cause. Of course, we won't know for sure until the autopsy.' Angela nodded as she picked up the phone.

'Boss, hi it's Angela. Sorry to bother you on a Saturday, but I think you'd better get down here. There's been an incident at the Deans estate in Huntersville. Appears to be some sort of break-in gone wrong. Screech Jarret is in a serious condition in hospital and Eustace Brownlie is dead. He appears to have got caught in a coyote trap, running away from the burglary.

Doc thinks he may have had a heart attack. A couple of estate workers found him this morning when they were checking the woods. No, Wilder doesn't know yet. You're the first person I've called. Okay, I'll have the incident for you when you get in. See you in half an hour then.'

'I think I'll give Mike a call. He'll want to know.' said Phil. 'He must have charged that pair dozens of times, but I know he doesn't hold any malice against them. Not like Bull. Mike told me that Susan was going to Harpers Ferry this weekend to visit an old school friend, so he'll want to come in and help.'

'By the sounds of it we're going need as many hands as we can get for this one. You stick the kettle on, I'll go and get an up to date incident printed off for Charlie coming in. Can't believe Eustace is dead.' said Angela shaking her head.

'Doesn't sound great for Screech either,' said Phil heading for the door, 'he could easily go the same way as his friend. What a start to the weekend eh?'

*

Fifteen minutes into his walk and Seth was approaching the stone wall that marked the boundary and highpoint of the school's estate. He was about to turn around and head back down the hill to the lodge when something caught his eye. Lying in some fescue grass by the roots of a large beech tree was a wooden box. Seth bent down and picked up the box. Its beautiful mother of pearl inlay shimmered seductively as it caught the sunlight. Seth held up the box triumphantly and squealed in delight.

Breaking almost to a run, he headed purposefully through the woods coming to a stop next to the trunk of a dead cedar tree. The top of the trunk was jagged and burnt, a tell-tale sign that it had been struck by lightning. Cautiously, Seth checked to make sure that nobody was around. Having assured himself that no-one was watching, he found a toe-hole near the base of the tree and hauled himself up onto one of the lowest branches. From there he reached up to an old woodpecker hole that had long since been deserted. Very carefully he placed the box into the hole. Taking the crystal glass from inside his jacket he repeated the process.

Back on firm ground Seth clapped his hands and made several strange screeching noises. Shifting his weight from foot to foot he was in a state of near ecstasy. This was his special place, a place that only he knew about. Somewhere he could store his precious things. Today he had two more treasures to covet and protect. Today was a good day, a very good day.

The delicious smell of bacon and pancakes filled the air as he locked the door of the dog's kennel.

'Good timing son,' shouted his mother form the kitchen door. 'These are just ready, sit yourself down and get tucked in. When you're finished, I'm going to need you to help me up at the school. Your father's in the doghouse, so I need your help if that's alright.'

Seth nodded then stared out the window. His father wasn't in the doghouse, the dog was. Gnawing on its bone as it usually did. Seth had no idea what his mother was on about. But it didn't matter. His pancakes were delicious, and today he'd added two additions to his stash of special things. He tingled at the thought of it and that made him very happy.

*

'For goodness sake Mike, there was no need for you to come in,' said Charlie spotting his friend studying the incident print out over a coffee in the corner of the detectives' office. 'You're on restricted duties to prevent you having to come in on days like these.' Mike looked up and smiled.

'Honestly it's not a problem. Susan and Keegan are up at Harpers for the weekend, and I've nothing better to do, so don't fret, just happy to help where you need me. I can't believe that Brownie's dead though. He was a prolific thief, but he didn't deserve to die like that. Sounds horrific. Caught in a leg trap and without his boot. Sends shivers down my spine, it must have been agony.'

Charlie nodded then poured himself a coffee and sat down.

'What a horrible way to die. There's a suggestion that he may have died of a heart attack. In the circumstances that might prove to be a blessing.' He said. 'What's the latest on Screech. Do we have an update from the hospital yet?'

'Chris is down there now,' replied Angela. 'Last update was the doctors are thinking of putting Screech into an induced coma. They're concerned about the swelling in his brain.'

'Now that is serious,' said Mike looking up. 'They only do that if they need to protect and control the pressure in the brain. Even if he pulls through there will be no guarantee that he won't have suffered brain damage.'

'Do we know what he was hit with?' asked Charlie.

'The butt of a rifle apparently,' replied Angela. 'Sergeant Lang is still at the house. He spoke to a guy called Ralph Portman, who apparently hit Screech as he was coming around the side of the building. He says Screech had smashed a window and stolen cash and a watch from a downstairs lounge. Portman is claiming he hit him in self-defence as he was about to be attacked.'

'Doesn't sound like Screech. Well not the attacking part. Never known him to have assaulted anybody and we've arrested him dozens of times.' said Charlie.

'It says here that the uniforms who attended found $120 dollars in his jacket pocket along with a Rolex watch which Portman is claiming is his. He says he'd left the money and the watch on a desk in the lounge.' explained Phil who had come back up from the uniform bar. 'Also, his right wrist was badly cut. Presumably cut it reaching through the broken glass trying to get the window open.'

'Can we stop presuming please,' said Charlie. 'Far too early to be speculating as to what might or might not have happened.' Mike looked on approvingly. He had taught Charlie well. He could almost hear himself saying exactly those same words if he'd been in Charlie's shoes.

'Sorry, Charlie.' said Phil, 'I shouldn't get ahead of myself at this stage. Listen, it's not on your print out, boss, but while I was in the control room a radio message came in that a patrol car has found Screech's pick-up in the visitor car park on the high road at the back of the estate. It's going to be lifted and brought here for scenes of crime.'

Charlie nodded, 'Fine. I take it there's nothing suspicious about the vehicle?'

'Doesn't appear to be.' replied Phil. 'Just routine. But in the circumstances better to get it properly checked.'

'Do you know, none of this is making a lot of sense to me,' said Charlie rubbing his chin. 'The pair of them have spent the best part of the last week looking for Screech's brother. Just seems a bit odd that they break into a house when they're still looking for him. And why that house? I wonder what took them over to Huntersville in the middle of the night? A bit further away than their usual patch. And when was their last conviction for a burglary? Must be some time ago. Stealing from yards is much more their thing. Not breaking into houses.'

'I've got their conviction sheets here,' said Phil holding up several sheets of paper. Phil studied the papers. 'You're not wrong boss, last one I can see was over three years ago. Several thefts since then and one break-in to a timber yard. But no domestic burglaries in all that time.'

'Perhaps they just got lucky and never got caught,' said Mike sarcastically. 'But it looks like their luck run out last night, big time. I can tell you something about Ralph Portman though. He was in the same year as Bull at Marsco College. He's in the photograph that hangs behind Wilder's desk when Bull was head of school.'

'I know who you're talking about.' said Phil. 'He was in the office not that long ago complaining about the number of times his drivers were getting stopped. He runs Deans Haulage and I know he's been living in the house since old man Deans died. He occupies most of the house while Mrs Deans lives in a couple of rooms on one wing. And one last thing, Portman's son, Ryan, is dating Deans' granddaughter. I know that because Sam charged her with jumping a red light and Portman's boy was with her in the car.'

'Talking of Wilder what's he got to say about all of this?' asked Mike.

'Well he's not exactly upset about it, let's put it that way.' replied Charlie. 'I think it would be fair to say that he thinks the pair got what was coming to them.'

'What a callous son of a bitch he is,' muttered Phil.

'He's convinced himself it's going to do wonders for our crime figures, especially if Screech doesn't pull through. It beats me how anyone can become a chief of police with such a cold hearted and cynical view of the world.' said Charlie.

'That's precisely why Wilder, and others like him, rise to high office. Detached, pragmatic and above all else scheming. Always looking for what's best for them. They don't really give a shit as to who gets hurt on their way to the top.' added Mike.

'Well you can stuff that for a game of soldiers,' said Phil. 'If that's what it takes then you're welcome to it. I may be just a sergeant, but I'd like to think I've still got some humanity left in me.'

'You don't have to worry on that score,' said Charlie patting his friend on the back, 'compared to Wilder you look like Mother Theresa.'

'Not sure how much of a compliment that is,' said Phil with a scowl.

'Anyway, getting back to Wilder, he seemed disappointed when I told him it was very unlikely that they were responsible for the break-in at the school. He would happily have pinned that on them too, till I reminded him that that burglary appeared to have only involved one person. And anyway, according to Dave Richardson the footprints found in the rose bed at the lodge are a size eight. Both Screech and Brownie have size ten feet, so those prints don't belong to them.' said Charlie.

'Talking about the lodge burglary, did Dave say if they'd got any fingerprints from inside the house?' asked Mike.

'No fingerprints, but they got a good footprint from the lounge carpet. Again, size eight, like the ones they found outside. The pattern on the sole suggests it was made by a pair of Doc Martins, like the pair you've got on,' said Charlie pointing to Phil's shoes.

'Hope you're not suggesting I'm a suspect,' said Phil only half joking.

'What size are your shoes then?' asked Angela mischievously. Mike and Charlie turned and stared at Phil.

'Size nine,' spluttered Phil taking off his shoe to prove he wasn't lying.

'Relax will you,' said Charlie laughing. 'If you were a suspect then this job would really go to hell in a hand cart. Mother Theresa would never have got herself involved in anything criminal and we've already established, you're just like her, so we can safely rule you out as a suspect.'

'Phew,' said Phil blowing out his cheeks and wiping his brow in mock relief. The others started to laugh. None of them knew where these enquiries would take them, but even in the throes of serious incidents like these, you had to find a way to let off steam and relieve tension. This had been one of those moments. Everyone in the room knew it was having a laugh at each other's expense that made them such a tight-knit and effective unit. They would need every ounce of their professional expertise if they were to get to the bottom of what was becoming an increasingly complicated enquiry.

*

'Yes, yes, he is in, Mr Wyles. He's upstairs at the minute but if you hold on, I'll give him a call and you can speak to him.' Mrs Buckley put the phone down and went to the foot of the stairs. 'Donald. Donald. Can you come and take this call? It's Curtis Wyles on the phone.'

The Dionach made a groaning noise from the top of the stairs.

'He won't be a minute Mr Wyles. No, he never said, but I think he's okay. A little too much to drink but other than that I think he's fine.' continued Mrs Buckley as she waited for her husband to appear.

Judging by the moans he made coming down the stairs and his dishevelled appearance, it did not look like the Dionach had rid himself of his hangover.

'Pull yourself together, Donald.' said Mrs Buckley covering the mouthpiece of the phone. 'It's gone twelve and look at the state you're still in. Now sit down and take this call from Mr Wyles. I'm not sure what you got up to last night, but he's concerned about your welfare and wants to know you're alright.'

The Dionach grabbed the phone and slumped down into a chair.

'Good afternoon, Mr Wyles, what can I do for you?'

'Just thought I'd give you a call to make sure you were alright,' said Curtis. 'It's a long time since I've seen you so angry, and after what you told me last night, I was concerned that you might go and do something rash.'

The Dionach slowly shook his head.

'No, honestly I'm fine. Just a bit of a sore head that's all. And I'm remembering what you said. I've not contacted the police about it.'

'I think that's wise at this stage Donald. Making an allegation like that against the chief of police is a very serious matter. That's not to say that it doesn't look highly suspicious. Particularly with the break-in occurring the following day. But as I said to you last night, in the absence of any firm evidence, I suggest that we let the police investigation take its course at this stage. Now that doesn't mean that we can't revisit this. It just means that now is not the time to be making those allegations. I'm saying that, both as your lawyer and your friend.'

'And it's sensible advice Mr Wyles. You can rest assured I won't be speaking to the police without consulting you first.'

'By all means speak to them, just don't make the accusation. I expect the cops will be back in contact soon enough. They'll want to confirm exactly what has been stolen, and I hope they will give you an update regarding the scenes of crime examination that you said they'd undertaken. So, when they do get in touch, I want you to write everything they say down. You hear me? Every last detail. You never know, it may turn out to be useful.'

'Yes, yes I understand, I'll make sure I do that, Mr Wyles.'

'Oh, and one last thing,' said Curtis, 'did you happen to catch the local news on the radio this morning?'

'Afraid I've not had a chance yet,' said the Dionach, 'I've been trying to sleep off my sore head. Why, what's happened?'

'Well, they're reporting that someone has been found dead after a break-in at the Huntersville estate, no real details as yet, but am I right in thinking that's the old Deans estate where Ralph Portman works?' asked Curtis.

'It sure is,' said a clearly stunned Dionach. I wonder what the hell's gone on there.'

'Difficult to say and we probably shouldn't surmise,' replied Curtis, 'but it's strange when you think that we were speaking to him at the dinner last night.'

'You don't think it's connected to my break-in, do you?' asked the Dionach.

'I couldn't possibly say, but stranger things have happened.'

*

Over In the detectives' office, Angela was putting on her coat while Charlie gathered up a pile of files from his desk.

'You don't mind if I tag along do you?' asked Mike as he rinsed out his coffee cup.

'Not at all,' said Charlie. 'You're more than welcome. We're going to swing past the hospital first and see if we can get a word with the doctor before heading over to Huntersville. Dave said he'd be there for the scenes of crime, but he expected to be finished around two. It would be good to grab a word with him while he's still at the locus.'

'Better get going then, it's twelve-thirty now,' said Angela, 'we'll be pushing it to get to Huntersville by two if we don't leave now.'

'Anyone up for a bite to eat at Ming's afterwards? I was about to have breakfast when you called, so I'm starving now.' said Charlie.

'I'm in,' said Mike with an approving nod.

'Me too,' replied Angela, 'love Ming's.'

Forty minutes later the three officers were walking back to their vehicle in the car park of the Fairlea County Hospital. The update provided by the doctor had been bleak.

'If I picked up what the doc said correctly, Screech could be kept in a coma for weeks,' said Angela. 'He looked pretty glum, didn't he? I didn't get the impression that he was hopeful of a full recovery, did you?'

'Nope. The prognosis doesn't look great.' replied Charlie.

'Hardly surprising when you hear of the damage that's been done to his skull. Sounds like his head has crumpled like a soda can. That rifle butt must have hit him with some force,' added Mike.

'Do you know one of the sad things about all of this?' asked Charlie.

'What's that then?' replied Mike.

'Well, if you disregard his own predicament, which is bad enough, it's the fact that he's unaware that his best friend is dead. Looks increasingly like his younger brother might have gone the same way, and he knows none of that.' said Charlie.

'And he might never know, I got the distinct impression from the doctor that he thinks there will be some brain damage even if he does pull through.' said Mike.

'Think of his poor mother, said Angela. 'How is she going to cope? She might lose both her sons in tragic circumstances, and she's stuck in that house. A prisoner of her own mental health issues. Dirt poor and with no one to look after her. Some folk just get a raw deal in this world, don't they?'

Charlie and Mike nodded but didn't say anything. There was nothing more needing to be said.

Over at Huntersville, Dave Richardson was sitting on the tailgate of the scenes of crime van removing a pair of disposable paper shoes when Charlie and the others arrived at the house.

'Just in time, lieutenant, I've about finished here and was getting ready to head back to the office.'

'Glad I caught you then,' said Charlie with a smile. 'What can you tell us?'

'Well, the point of entry is definitely that window,' said Dave pointing to a window frame that was covered in the silvery grey residue of fingerprint powder. 'The windows been smashed from the outside, someone has then reached in and opened it by the handle and entered the room. There were shards of glass with blood on them lying on the carpet underneath the window. They've obviously been seized for further examination.'

'Okay, good,' said Charlie writing some notes in his folder. 'Any joy with fingerprints?'

'We've got several on pieces of broken glass and a couple from the frame itself. They could, of course, have been made by the householders. You'll need to arrange for them to come in for elimination prints, but I'm hopeful some will be our suspects.'

'Anything from the desk or the room itself?' asked Mike.

'No. That's the funny thing. There's no blood on the carpet or on the desk. No footprints either. Really struggling to get any sort of print from the desk. But the blood's a strange one. The culprit has obviously cut themselves on the broken glass but other than the blood underneath the window there's not a speck to be found.' said Dave.

'Might they have wrapped a hanky or something else round their wrist if they'd cut it when they broke the window.' said Angela.

'Hmm, good point, it's a definite possibility,' said Charlie chewing on the end of his pen. 'We should have checked that when we were at the hospital. Get a message to Chris and have him go to the hospital and check if Screech had a blood-stained hanky or anything like that on him when he arrived at the hospital. And after that, get in contact with Sergeant Lang. The incident said his team had done the initial search of the grounds. I'm sure he would have said if they'd found anything, but check it out all the same, would you?' said Charlie looking at Angela.

'Sure, I'll get a radio message to him right away.'

'What are you thinking now?' asked Mike, who could always tell when Charlie was preoccupied in thought.

'Just give me a moment,' replied Charlie who was staring studiously at the broken window. 'Dave, before you go can you confirm that you're finished with the window, I mean in terms of your examination. Is it alright for me to touch it?' Dave looked quizzically at Charlie.

'Yep, we're finished with it. But I'm not sure why you would want to touch it, you'll get filthy. It's covered in fingerprint powder.'

'No, that's fine, as long as you're all done. I don't want to destroy any potential evidence.'

'No, you carry on lieutenant, you won't be compromising any evidence.' said Dave with a chuckle.

Mike turned to Angela and shook his head. Angela raised her eyebrows. Neither of them had a clue what Charlie was thinking.

'Angela, can you take off your coat and roll up your sleeves? I don't want you to get your clothes dirty.' said Charlie.

'Not sure how appropriate that is, sir.' said Angela with a grin. 'I mean getting your subordinates to remove their clothes.' Mike burst out laughing.

'No, no I didn't....' before Charlie could explain Angela cut over him.

'I'm just joshing you; I know you didn't mean that, but I'm curious as to what you're thinking.'

'Just bear with me, will you?' said Charlie. Angela smiled and nodded.

'I know the window's broken, but I want you to imagine that you've just smashed the glass. Can you now go and open the window, as if you were going to climb in. But please be careful there are still some jagged edges, I don't want you cutting yourself.'

Mike was intrigued, he hadn't any idea what his colleague was up to. He watched intently as Angela approached the window. She rolled up the right-hand sleeve of her blouse and was about to place her hand on the window handle when she stood back. Something wasn't right. Angela stared at the window and tapped her chin. After a few seconds she rolled up her other sleeve and then reached in and opened the window. She was about to step through the aperture when Charlie stopped her.

'That's fine, Angela, you can stop there.' said Charlie smiling. 'You've just confirmed something that I think could be important.'

Angela looked confused. 'I'm not getting this,' she said shaking her head.

'Not sure I am either if I'm honest,' said Mike. 'I think you're going to have to tell us why that might be important.'

'Okay then, I will.' announced Charlie confidently. 'You're right-handed aren't you Angela?' Angela nodded. 'And yet you opened the window with your left hand.' said Charlie.

'I did but I wasn't going to. I changed my mind and decided to use my left hand when I saw the way the handle was. It's very close to the wall on the left side there. Reaching across with my right hand would have been quite awkward, it just seemed easier to use my left.'

'Exactly,' said Charlie. 'I'm right-handed but I would have done the same.'

'Bingo. I think I've got this Lieutenant Finch,' said Mike animatedly. 'And may I say, smart thinking on your part, I must have taught you well.'

'Can you just tell me what the pair of you are on about?', said Angela unable to hide her frustration.

'Screech is left-handed,' continued Mike, 'but the cut is on his right wrist. If he is left handed why didn't he open it with his preferred hand. You've just proved how awkward it would be to open it with your right hand and you're right-handed!'

'Of course, it doesn't prove he didn't open it with his left hand and then somehow managed to cut himself on his right wrist. But it's certainly a bit odd don't you think. If Screech Jarret broke that window, I'm sure he would have opened it with his left hand. It's just another thing that doesn't seem to add up,' said Charlie.

'Jeezo, guys. That would never have occurred to me. I've got a lot to learn.' said Angela despondently.

'I wouldn't worry about it if I were you. You'll pick these things up as you get more experience. That's how I did it, working with Mike over the years. But as you can see, the problem Mike now has, is it appears that as the years pass, you start to forget things. It's an age thing you see!' said Charlie.

'Hey cheeky, I didn't forget. It just took me a little longer to work it out.' replied Mike. Charlie chuckled as he wiped his fingers with a handkerchief.

'Okay, as I said to Phil, let's not get ahead of ourselves. It's worth noting, but until we've taken all the witness statements and seen Dave's report, we won't be able to say one way or another how significant it might be. And decision made, we'll leave the witness statements till tomorrow. My stomach thinks its throat's been cut, so I'll have to eat something soon. Before that though, I want to have a look at where Brownie was found.' said Charlie turning around to look for Angela.

Angela had wondered off and was now speaking to a uniformed officer at the front door of the house. She waved to her colleagues to come over.

'According to this officer, Brownie's boot was found on the gravel over there. The trap where he was found dead is only a five-minute walk into the forest. Apparently, there's a path nearly all the way, he says we can't miss it.'

As they rounded a corner on the meandering path, they could see a rectangle of yellow barrier tape strung between several large trees a couple of hundred metres ahead of them. Two uniformed officers were standing on the path chatting.

'Afternoon lieutenant,' said the older officer as the detectives approached. Charlie nodded in acknowledgement.

'Just want a quick look, we won't touch anything.'

'That's fine, sir, we're just waiting for the photographer. Dave Richardson said she'd be here by three. After she's finished, we've to seize the trap and take it back to the office, unless you're going to tell us differently.'

'No, that sounds fine.' said Charlie lifting the barrier tape for the others to go under.

'Oh, Good grief, look at the jaws on that thing! They look razor sharp. Poor guy, what a way to go,' said Angela shaking her head.

'I just hope he did have a heart attack and died straight away.' said Mike quietly. 'Doesn't bear thinking about being stuck in that contraption.'

Charlie nodded. 'Hopefully the autopsy will tell us more, you've just got to hope that the shock of it all brought on a heart attack and he didn't suffer. Sod's law that it was his foot without a boot that stepped on it.'

Angela winced at the thought. 'Why couldn't he just have released the trap?' she asked. 'There must be an easy way to get it off surely.'

'Who knows.' replied Mike. 'You might have thought he could have got the thing off his ankle. But remember it would have been pitch black. It would be difficult if he couldn't see.'

'Unfortunately, the reason for that might have to remain a mystery,' said Charlie, 'I don't think the witnesses are going to be able to answer that one.'

Chapter 14

The following Monday, Mike was up early and making porridge and a smoothie for Susan.

'I think the amount of syrup I'm having to put on this is going to negate any of the benefits the doctor said it would do for me,' said Susan kissing her husband on the cheek and pulling up a bar stool. 'I just can't face it without the syrup. It's like eating wallpaper paste.'

Mike laughed. 'I'm sure it's still going to do you some good. Syrup or no syrup.'

Susan sighed and shook her head.

'I need to get back on the wagon after that weekend. Drank way too much wine and ate like a King. Anna's a great host and we had some laughs reminiscing about our school days, but she says she's going to have me back up before Christmas and she's going to make sure that Colette can make that weekend.' said Susan taking a spoonful of porridge from the bowl. 'I'll have to start preparing now for that trip, Colette does nothing by half measures.'

'I think It's just brilliant that you're feeling up to going and meeting your friends. It's got to be good for you. Laughter is the best medicine as they say.'

Susan put down her spoon and looked up.

'Changing the subject for a moment, tell me how's Charlie getting on in his new job?' Mike put down his cup.

'He's doing great. Yeah, he's doing really well. Because you were away, I spent a lot of time with him over the weekend. I can see a big change in him already. He's got a good head on him, thinks clearly and the others, of course, like him which always helps.' Mike started to laugh.

'What's so funny?'

'Well, it's funny because after his first few days he had been complaining about how quiet it was. I can tell you he isn't complaining now. The last ten days have been manic for him. But that's a good thing. It will test whether he's up to spinning a few plates. He's got several enquiries on the go now, so he's got his hands full. But I've every confidence in him. He'll handle it just fine. I'll tell you something else, he's got the measure of Wilder. He doesn't let him get under his skin the way I did, and believe me, that's a good thing.'

'I know it's none of my business, but it sounds quite dreadful what happened to Eustace and Screech. There's nothing more sinister to that is there? You always said they were a pair of rogues, but neither of them was violent. How come Eustace is dead and Screech might end up the same way? It's just horrible.' Mike looked at his wife and shrugged his shoulders.

'It's awful what's happened, but it does just look like a break-in that's gone wrong. It happens. You know I can't say too much at this stage, but Charlie is keeping an open mind, that's all we can do.'

'I know,' said Susan smiling. 'I've got every faith in both of you. I know you'll find out what happened to them.' Susan yawned and stretched her arms.

'I don't think I've got the weekend out of my system yet; it seems to have taken a bit more out of me than I thought.'

'Why don't you go back to bed for a couple of hours, just take it easy, the doctor said you weren't to overdo things. Anyway, I could do with getting in sharp today. I've got the witness statements from the Huntersville break-in to review for Charlie, and the morning report will take longer to pull together this morning as it was so busy at the weekend.'

'You better get going then darling, I'm not going back to bed, but I will lie out on the couch for an hour or so and read my book.'

*

It was a beautiful October morning. The air was warm and the scent of grass, freshly cut along the Lewisburg road, filled the cab of Mike's station wagon. Since the murder of Maisie Foster, he could never drive past the road end that lead up to Dararra Farm without thinking about Josh Heggerty and, of course, poor Maisie. What a tragedy that was he thought. Five years on, Josh was happily married to Becca, Maisie's sister, and now they had a child of their own. That was a comfort, but he still shuddered at the thought of Josh's wrongful conviction. Four years is a long time to spend in prison for a crime you didn't commit. It had been a chastening experience for Mike, and for Charlie too. They had made mistakes during that investigation, critical errors that they weren't proud of. But you learn from your mistakes and, he always felt they had become better detectives because of that enquiry.

He was only a couple of miles out of Lewisburg and on a long straight section of road when he became aware of a large truck travelling towards him. Suddenly, almost out of thin air, three deer bolted from the undergrowth into the path of his vehicle. They were no more than twenty feet in front of him. Mike slammed on his brakes to avoid hitting the beasts. With locked brakes and squealing tyres, he fought to keep his vehicle from veering into the path of the oncoming truck.

He heard the bang and in his rear mirror and saw the unfortunate deer hurtling through the air. The truck slewed violently, crossing into the other carriageway before swinging back and careering into the dirt verge. The sound of the truck's tyres bursting was deafening. Mike pulled into the side of the road and ran back to the truck. A serpentine of black tracks and burnt rubber criss-crossed the road like some huge snake, a reminder of how close they had come to tragedy. The truck was lying at an angle of about twenty degrees. Another few feet and it would have toppled over into the drainage ditch. Two tyres on the driver's side were shredded and the front grill and windscreen were smattered in blood and tissue from the unfortunate animal.

'I think I only hit one,' said the driver as he jumped down from the cab. 'Just as well by the look of things as he peered at the damage to the front of his vehicle. Can't imagine what would have happened if I'd hit all three of them,' he said removing his Orioles cap and wiping his brow.

'Are you okay?' asked Mike, 'You must have got a right fright. I know I did. They just seemed to appear from nowhere. There's nothing you can do either. Just hit the brakes and hope.' The driver nodded.

'I'm fine thanks. Occupational hazard when you're a trucker. Hasn't happened to me for a while, but this time of year is always risky as there are so many deer about. And if you hit a big buck, like this one,' said the driver pulling a large piece of broken antler from his grill, 'they can be heavy beasts and do a lot of damage. Still, it could have been worse. That's the way I try and look at things.'

Mike nodded. 'Just glad you're Okay.' He was about to explain that he was a police officer, when in the distance, he saw blue flashing lights and the familiar sight of a highway patrol vehicle coming towards them.

'Colleagues of mine,' said Mike with a smile. 'I was heading to the office and was just about to suggest that I give them a call, but hey, no need.'

Mike and the truck driver watched as the patrol car parked a short distance behind the truck and two uniformed officers got out. It was Neil Planner and Sam Coutts.

'A passing motorist flagged as down and told us that there'd been an accident, is everyone okay, nobody injured?' asked officer Planner.

'We're both fine,' said Mike and the driver simultaneously.

'Oh, it's yourself, sir' said officer Planner noticing Mike. 'I didn't recognise you for a moment. Not used to seeing you in these circumstances.'

'No, I know what you mean,' said Mike. 'But I think we both had a narrow escape. Three deer bolted across the road. I managed to avoid them but as you can see, my friend here wasn't so fortunate. He's going to need some assistance; he's got two burst tyres for his trouble.'

Officer Planner smiled and nodded. 'No problem, we'll get that sorted.'

'We use AE Recovery in Lewisburg for all our local stuff if that helps. Deans Haulage has an account with them. I've got a number but if you could contact them for me, I'd appreciate it.' said the driver gratefully. Officer Planner whistled to Sam who was placing a police accident sign and some cones in the roadway.

'Sam, can you get onto the control room and get then to contact AE Recovery, we're going to need them to attend, and tell them to bring two 245/70 R tyres while they're at it will you?'

'On it now,' said Sam with a wave of acknowledgement.

'If you've got things under control here, I'll get on my way if you don't mind. I'm already late but if I get a shift on, I could still make the morning meeting.' said Mike checking his pockets for his car keys.

'Yep, that's fine,' said officer Planner. 'We'll be here for a while getting details, but I can catch you back at the office if I need anything from yourself.' As Mike headed back to his car, he passed Sam who was writing details of the truck in his pocketbook.

'Morning, sir.' said Sam looking up with a grin.

'What are you looking so pleased about,' asked Mike.

'I've just remembered where I've seen that truck. It was in Indiana, when I stopped off on my way to a friend's wedding. It's definitely the same truck, I never forget a plate number.' continued Sam.

As Sam approached the truck, he noticed the driver's baseball cap. It's him for sure thought Sam. No doubt about it. I wonder if he'll recognise me? After a minute or so it was apparent that the driver hadn't a clue who Sam was. Although he was looking straight at him there wasn't a flicker of recognition. In truth, that wasn't all that surprising. Sam remembered his father telling him that people often didn't recognise him when he had his uniform on. Especially if he was wearing his cap. It must be a context thing thought Sam, I never told him I was a cop when we met, so he's not connecting the two things. That, or perhaps I just don't have a memorable face. More likely to be that thought Sam, smiling to himself. He decided not to remind the driver that they had met before. Neil had told him that sometimes it paid to keep your cards close to your chest, don't give unnecessary information away. For whatever reason Sam felt this was one of those moments.

'What's in your truck and where are you heading?' asked Neil making small talk with the driver.

'Truck's empty just now, well apart from a box of provisions I've just picked up for myself from Kroger's. I'm heading to Bloomington to pick up a load of pumpkins, doesn't look I'm going to make it back tonight unless that recovery vehicle gets here soon. It takes a bit of time changing these tyres I can tell you.' Officer Planner nodded.

'Yep, that's for sure, I've attended enough of these blow outs in my time. Fingers crossed it won't be too long. Listen, can you open the back so I can check the trailer? And I'm also going to need to see your driver's licence and logbook, have you got them with you?' The driver nodded as he opened the trailer doors.

'The documents are in the cab; I'll just go and get them.'

'Fine,' said Neil climbing into the rear of the trailer. The trailer was empty except for one large cardboard box which had fallen on its side. Several bottles and numerous food packets had spilled out and were lying on the floor. Neil picked up the packets of tortillas, cheese and bottles of hot sauce and returned them to the box.

'I've just started this journey, so today's trip isn't marked up yet. I know it should be, but I usually start my log when I stop for a break.' said the driver handing Neil the documents.

'That's fine, said Neil jumping down from the trailer. 'This is just routine, nothing to worry about, you weren't to blame for the accident.' Neil handed the logbook to Sam.

'You must love your Mexican food?' said Neil laughing. 'That amount of chilli sauce would keep most folks going for years.' The driver smiled.

'Yeah, it's not just me, but the whole family like it and that's the best stuff, authentic Mexican. Would you like a bottle to try?' asked the driver.

'No, you're, fine thanks. I can't do anything too spicy, doesn't agree with my stomach.' replied Neil.

Sam looked quizzically at the man. It had only been ten days or so since they'd met in the motel at Boonville. Sam was sure that at that time the driver had made some remark about not liking Mexican food. In fact, he was sure that he'd called it Mexican muck. Yet here he was with a box stuffed with Mexican food for him and his family. This wasn't making any sense.

As Neil recorded details from the driver's licence, Sam studied the logbook. Since landing in hospital after handling cannabis during a drugs exercise at the police college, Sam and Neil had done their best to avoid drug searches. Instead they focused their time on traffic offenders. All this meant that they had become particularly adept at navigating through the finer details of road traffic legislation. As a young officer eager to impress, Sam had to show he was industrious and hardworking. In the rural backwaters of Greenbrier

County, traffic offences were an everyday occurrence, so he busied himself reporting all manner of obscure offences.

In his first few months in the job, Sam had become something of an expert. Most officers couldn't be bothered by the complexities of traffic legislation. It just wasn't sexy enough. If it wasn't a drunk driving offence, then most weren't interested. The seemingly never-ending regulations that dealt with the minutiae of axle weights and maximum loads, operator's licences and lighting offences was not for them. Sam on the other hand lapped it up. Facts, figures and mundane details were right up his street and with his forensic memory and ability with numbers he was well suited to it.

As Sam flipped through the pages of the logbook, something struck him straight away. There were no mistakes or greasy marks that were typical of the other log books he'd checked. Although this book was two thirds full, it was pristine. Sam couldn't see a single entry that had been scored through. This was the sort of book you'd mock-up if you were using it for training purposes, it was perfect, a little too perfect. Sam turned the pages back to September 26th, the day he'd met the trucker in Boonville. The total number of miles recorded for that day was 311 with the final destination given as the Deans depot in Huntersville. How could that be thought Sam scratching his head? On the 26th, that truck and the two of us were at Jamieson's Motel. Sam flipped back another page. The 25th showed the truck had done 324 miles and finished up in Akron, Ohio. The day before that the truck had been in Des Moines, Iowa.

This was just plain weird thought Sam. The driver told me he'd crossed the border at Nogales. That's got to be the best part of 1,500 miles from Des Moines. Sam walked round the vehicle and double checked the truck licence plate and trailer number. Both checked out against the numbers in the log book. Sam was about to speak to Neil about the discrepancies when the AE Recovery truck arrived.

'Looks like you might have a chance of making it to Bloomington and back after all,' said Neil.

'If they can change two tyres in an hour then I've got half a chance,' replied the driver making a thumbs up sign.

Forty-five minutes later the truck was on its way and Neil and Sam were headed to Ike's diner for their break. Sam was starving and looking forward to demolishing a stack of pancakes and bacon. Neil had stuck him on traffic control while the truck's tyres were changed. The road had become much busier with traffic as folk headed to work and parents dropped their kids at the school a mile down the road. Sam had been fully engaged ensuring that everyone got past the accident scene safely. Now with the thought of finally getting his breakfast he had forgotten to mention the logbook to Neil.

Chapter 15

Mike had arrived in the office just after eight-thirty, but as the chief's morning meeting was already in full swing there was no way he was going to interrupt. He had seen the chief's conniptions at first hand. Now was not the time to be walking in late. The meeting room was the chief's domain, his stage. A place where he imposed his authority without challenge. You needed to know when and how to take the chief on. The morning meeting was not that place. Mike had seen experienced officers eviscerated by the chief's interrogation. He might be a megalomaniac but there was no doubting his brain. He was sharp. Not much got past the chief and woe betide anyone who appeared at that meeting ill prepared. The chief could sense weakness a mile away and he would pounce on the unprepared like a cat stalking a mouse. The unfortunate soul would then be tormented and publicly humiliated much to the amusement of the chief. He was in charge and everyone in that room knew it.

'Well, what did you make of that? If I hadn't heard it with my own ears, I wouldn't have believed it.' said Charlie shaking his head. Mike looked up from his desk wondering what he had missed.

'That son of a bitch should buy a lottery ticket. He's bound to win. Excuse my French, but that is fucking unbelievable, no wonder Angela's upset.' said Phil switching on the kettle.

'I'll give her a few minutes to compose herself and if she's not back, I'll ask Sarah to go check on her.' replied Charlie. Mike hadn't a clue what was going on but by the sound of things he must have missed a spectacular morning meeting.

'I'll tell you one thing,' said Phil handing Charlie a coffee. 'He's got some balls that chief of ours. Made that announcement without a hint of embarrassment. He must have felt every pair of eyes burning into him like a laser, but not a flinch. He's a shit alright, but I just think he doesn't care.'

Charlie started to laugh. 'You were nearly right Phil, but there was one idiot in the room grinning like the complete clown he is. He didn't even have the sense to keep his mouth shut and say nothing.'

'Can one of you explain what the hell you're going on about?' asked Mike. 'By the sounds of it I missed an interesting meeting. And apologies for being late but I nearly hit a deer on the way in. The truck coming the other way wasn't so fortunate and smashed into it, so I stopped to see nobody was hurt. Your boy turned up,' said Mike nodding at Phil. I left him and Neil dealing with it, but my start to the morning sounds boring compared to yours, so what's up?' Charlie looked incredulously at Mike and shook his head.

'The chief has made Wayne Mitchell a sergeant. Moved him in to take immediate charge of roads policing. Steve Joice has been royally shafted. He's been moved to god knows where to accommodate Mitchell.' said Charlie clearly annoyed. Mike stood wide mouthed.

'For Fuck's sake, that is unbelievable. He's a complete incompetent and every man and his dog know he's lucky to still be in the job. Fucking sergeant. No wonder Angela's upset.'

'She'll not be the only one. I can think of at least five cops off the top of the head who are qualified to be a sergeant and he goes and promotes a total imbecile and, as I said, without a hint of embarrassment.' said Phil angrily.

'Probably just as well you weren't there,' said Charlie patting Mike on the back. 'I don't think you would have been able to keep your counsel somehow and all hell would have been set loose.'

Mike didn't reply. He stood motionless looking astonished trying to make sense of what he'd just heard.

'You know what's also strange,' said Phil getting up to give Angela a seat as she walked in the door. 'He made the announcement about Mitchell at the start of the meeting. Why do that? You would have thought he'd have kept it till the end. Nobody was concentrating after that, I know I wasn't and there was loads of important stuff from the weekend to be discussed. Just seems really odd to me.'

'Yeah, you're right, I picked up on that too. I was trying my best to concentrate but I admit I was struggling to follow some of the other reports.'

'Can't help you there,' said Angela with a wry smile. 'It was all I could do to just sit there. I didn't want to be in that room with that dick! You've got to wonder what's the point of sitting exams and working hard, if the chief is going to promote a cretin like Mitchell. Complete joke.'

'Try not to take it personally,' said Mike pouring Angela a coffee. 'I know it must feel like it, but it's not a reflection on your abilities, believe me.'

Angela smiled and nodded. 'I know you're right, but it's not just me. Chris, Jamey and Sarah have all been qualified for ages and that's just from the detective side of things, there's plenty more on the uniform side who are going to be severely pissed by that decision. Feel sorry for those who will have to work for him.' Continued Angela.

'That'll be Sam then,' replied Phil with a sigh. 'Wayne Mitchell's going to be his boss for the foreseeable future.'

Angela rolled her eyes. 'God help him with that.'

'Look, putting the Mitchell debacle to one side for a minute, did I hear the chief right? He's scaling back the Huntersville enquiry. Doesn't want a full search of the forest.' said Charlie.

'Yeah, I heard that bit,' said Phil nodding. 'He reckons that with one suspect dead and the other in a coma in the hospital, it's a done deal.'

'He wants the additional resources to focus on his new initiative,' said Angela. 'I heard that bit because that fucking idiot, Mitchell's getting a key role.'

'I didn't know what he was on about, we don't have a drug problem do we? Well, not one that justifies that level of response.' said Phil.

'Seemed strange to me. I thought he might have run it past me before announcing it, but hey, that's Bull Wilder for you. It's his way or the highway!' muttered Charlie.

'The really stupid bit is that he's diverting road patrols away from dealing with traffic stops and offences. That's their bread and butter and essential I can tell you and much more of a priority than drugs are around here.' added Angela.

'It won't suit Sam that's for sure. He's a little paranoid about having another episode like the one at the college.' said Phil.

'Don't blame him,' said Charlie. 'He's going to have to be very careful.' The others nodded in agreement.

'Has anyone seen Chris?' asked Charlie. 'I thought he might be back from the hospital by now.'

'He'll be here in a minute, he's just parking up,' replied Mike looking out the window. 'Looks like he's been to Annie Mack's. That looks suspiciously like a bag of doughnuts he's got with him.'

'Hope he's got plenty then,' said Angela. 'I'm comfort eating after that fiasco this morning. So, I'll need about four for myself.' The others smiled and laughed.

'Nothing wrong with your eyesight Mike,' said Phil as Chris walked in with an enormous bag of doughnuts.

'I'm eagle eyed when things are far away but can't read a report without my glasses when it's in front of my nose,' chuckled Mike as Chris passed round the tasty treats.

'How did you get on at the hospital, did you get all the property?' asked Charlie.

Chris nodded. 'Yep, got it all. $120 and the Rolex. That's all that appears to have been stolen. I've double checked with Ralph Portman, he's now positive that nothing else was taken. As for Screech's own property, all he had on him was a five dollar note, his keys, a packet of Marlboro tobacco and a fancy button. That was it. The good news is, there looks like there might be a print on the watch face. Of course, it might prove to be Portman's, but I'll take it down to Dave after I've finished this,' said Chris taking a mouthful of doughnut. Charlie raised an eyebrow and looked at Chris.

'If the watch was found in Screech's pocket then a fingerprint on the face is really neither here nor there,' added Charlie. 'The fact it was recovered from his jacket pocket is the important thing from an evidential point of view. But belt and braces, I suppose. It's all good.'

Chris sat back in his chair and gave a despondent sigh. Charlie was right. The fingerprint was not going to be crucial in this case. It was their awareness of little details like that that both Charlie and Mike were so good at. You could see why they had both done well. They were smart detectives, always alert, always thinking. Chris would need to up his game if he were to make sergeant anytime soon, he thought. And that's before Wilder has his say on the matter.

Chapter 16

Four Weeks Later

'Where did you get that suit?' asked Mike looking Sam up and down. 'It's huge. It looks like it would fit two of you.'

An embarrassed Sam didn't know what to say. He just stood and shrugged his shoulders.

'I'm sorry, but It's the only suit I've got,' replied Sam sheepishly. 'I got it for my graduation, but I've lost a few pounds since then. I think it was all the exercise at the police college that did it. That and not eating properly as the food was terrible.'

Mike smiled and patted Sam on the arm. 'Look I'm just messing with you. The suit's fine, a little roomy but you look smart. Folk will think you're a real detective.' said Mike.

'That would be good.' replied Sam. 'I've been looking forward to this attachment for months. I can't wait to get started.' As Sam and Mike were chatting Charlie walked into the room carrying several files.

'Something up?' asked Mike looking up from his desk.

'Could be,' said Charlie putting down the files, 'but then again it might prove to be nothing at all.'

'Sounds interesting,' said Mike.

'Not sure how interesting it'll be, but It looks like someone might have hacked into the accounts of one hundred and eighty-five Citizen Bank customers. One of whom just happens to be our illustrious leader, Mr Ewart Wilder.' explained Charlie.

'Ah,' said Mike giving Charlie a knowing look.

'None of that is helped by the fact that the chief is currently on vacation in Mexico. Very last minute, he decided to surprise Mrs Wilder for their twentieth wedding anniversary. He's fairly splashing the cash. A week in Mexico and a new lake house to boot. Nice work if you can get it,' said Charlie.

'Didn't have the chief down as an old romantic,' laughed Mike. 'I guess he's none the wiser about any of this?' Charlie shook his head.

'I've left a message at his hotel asking him to give me a call so I can update him. It might be that he hasn't been affected, but the bank is concerned that at least some of the accounts have been compromised. Only one way to find out. We're going to have to plough through all these accounts and check them.' Sam's ears pricked up. That sounded right up his street.

'What on earth have you done to yourself?' asked Charlie as Mike limped across the office carrying a box of paper for the photocopier.

'Turned my ankle playing squash with Keegan. I know, I know a stupid thing to be doing when you're as old and unfit as I am.' Charlie laughed.

'Well, that wasn't quite what I was going to say, but yeah, I suppose that's close enough. I take it you're not going to be coming to the funeral then?'

'Afraid I'll have to give it a miss, especially as I hear it's a burial. I don't think standing by a grave will do me any good. Anyway, Chris was in earlier and he said he was going with you. I'll stay here and make a start on those accounts if you'd like. Sam here can give me a hand.' Charlie nodded and looked across to Sam.

'Apologies, I didn't mean to ignore you,' said Charlie thrusting out a hand to shake hands with his newest member of staff. 'Good to have you with us for a couple of weeks. Your dad was just saying how you were looking forward to having a break from roads policing.'

Sam wasn't sure how to respond so he just nodded and smiled. He certainly didn't want to get off on the wrong foot and start complaining about his lot. But the truth be told he was desperate for a break. Since Sergeant Mitchell had become his boss things had become very difficult. Neil, his friend and partner, was miserable and nothing they did ever seemed to be right. Mitchell was never off their case. Sam hadn't reported a single case in the last week. Actively discouraged from stopping trucks and reporting traffic offences, Operation Clarion, the so-called drugs initiative, had proved to be a disaster. Poorly led and with no proper intelligence to direct them, Sam and Neil had been left to their own devices and each day a little more motivation drained out of them. It was dispiriting and unrewarding. For the first time since he joined, Sam hadn't looked forward to going to his work. This two-week secondment couldn't have come at a better time. It was time to recharge his batteries, experience something completely different and learn some new skills. Sam was itching to get started.

'I wasn't intending to go to the burial, just the church service. But on reflection I think I will,' said Charlie. 'I can't see many people being at the service, so I think it's appropriate for us to go.'

'Yes, I agree,' said Mike. 'He could be a real pain in the butt. If It wasn't tied down, he'd likely steal it. But he had some endearing qualities as well. He'd had a tough life, and I couldn't help feeling sorry for him.' Charlie nodded.

'Sad too that Screech won't be there. His one true friend and he's stuck in hospital.'

'By the way, what's the latest on Screech. Is he still in the coma?' asked Mike.

'Apparently not.' replied Charlie. 'They brought him out the coma on Tuesday. He's aware of what happened to Eustace, but its going to be a while till he gets out the hospital.'

'Well, that's progress I suppose,' said Mike. 'Is he saying anything about the burglary?'

'He's not really saying anything at the moment. Chris tried to speak with him yesterday, but his speech is so poor, he can't seem to get his words in the right order. The doc is hopeful that might improve with time, but he can't help us yet. It's still not clear whether his memory has been affected. I'm afraid we'll just have to wait and see.' said Charlie. 'He does understand though. He got pretty upset when Chris told him about his friend.'

'Boss, if you're ready, I think we should get going.' said Chris sticking his head round the door. 'The service is at ten and it's gone nine-fifteen now.'

'Be right with you,' said Charlie doing up his top button and straightening his tie. As he reached the door Charlie turned back to speak to Mike. 'And good luck with those reports guys, I think you've drawn the short straw with that lot.'

'Oh, don't worry about us,' said Mike sarcastically, 'they're still going to be here when you get back, so you'll get your turn, we'll make sure of that.'

Charlie smiled. 'Oh, I don't know. I might have to delegate them to my subordinates. Why have a dog and bark yourself?'

*

'I think we'll park in the cemetery car park and walk back to the church,' said Charlie. 'It's less than ten minutes away and it's a glorious morning. Anyway, I could do with the walk.'

'Fine by me,' replied Chris pulling off the main road into the car park.

As the two detectives walked along the narrow footpath that led to the church, Chris smiled as he sniffed the warm air. A plume of woodsmoke drifted lazily over a fence and across the path in front of them. Its spicy sweet aroma a childhood memory for Chris of burning birch logs with his grandfather. Above them a half dozen barn swallows clung to a telephone wire, the last stragglers from summer, reluctant to give up their perch and begin the long journey south to their winter home in the Cordillera mountains of Bolivia. Over to their left, basking on the corrugated roof of a crumbling outbuilding, was an ancient tabby cat getting heat into its aging bones, hoping that an unsuspecting swallow, distracted by the prospect of its epic journey, might happen across its path.

'I love this time of year,' said Chris taking off his jacket and putting it over his shoulder. The temperature is still lovely and warm. But more than that, everywhere you look the trees are just a riot of colour. Amber, scarlet, gold, it's just beautiful.'

Charlie grinned and shook his head.

'And here was me thinking you were just a crusty old detective like the rest of us. Not a sensitive soul with such an appreciation of nature.'

'Steady on boss. I wouldn't go that far. I just said I liked this time of the year.' replied Chris somewhat defensively.

As they approached the church, they could see a cluster of people talking together in the neat garden at the front of the wood panelled building. Further down the path an elderly lady was being supported on either arm by two men. The lady was very stooped and wearing a threadbare blue coat. Progress was painfully slow as she shuffled up the path with tiny steps.

'Jeezo,' said Charlie. 'I wasn't expecting to see her here. If I'm not mistaken that's Mrs Jarret, Screech's and Charlie's mother. Well I'll be damned. She must have made a special effort to be here. I don't think she's been out of her house in years because of her agoraphobia.'

'Pretty impressive then if that's the case,' replied Chris.

'She will want to be here for her son. She'll know how upset he'll be at the death of his best friend. It just must be so difficult for her, especially as her younger boy is still missing. That takes guts to do what she's doing. You've got to admire her courage.' said Charlie.

'Yep, people can be so resilient sometimes, even in the most difficult of circumstances.'

Charlie nodded in agreement.

'It also looks like there are going to be more people here than we were expecting. It just goes to show, Brownie had more friends than perhaps we gave him credit for,' said Charlie as they headed into the church.

Inside the church ten rows of pews were divided on either side by a central aisle. At the front of the church, on a raised platform, stood a plain wooden table, a lectern and half a dozen chairs. On the wall above the platform hung a large wooden cross. Charlie and Chris took a seat towards the rear of the church. At a rough count there were more than twenty people present, that was more than double what Charlie had been expecting.

Neither Charlie or Chris were church goers. Chris had only been in church for funerals and the marriage of his cousin. Charlie on the other hand, had dutifully attended Sunday school with his older sister in his younger years. But aged thirteen, his parents decided he was old enough to make his own mind up and, like most boys his age, Charlie decided he would play ball with his friends and hang out at the mall. Charlie hadn't even been married in church, yet despite nearly twenty-five years away, there was something familiar and comforting about the service.

The minister, an elderly man in his seventies with white straggly hair, spoke warmly about Eustace Brownlie. His homily, a powerful message of man's fallibility and God's enduring love and hope for the future. Such a simple truth, preached with conviction and honesty, resonated with Charlie. God didn't judge unfairly and despite being fully aware of his failings, God would not forsake Eustace. He knew and loved Eustace Brownlie.

'People,' the minister continued, 'are often quick to see the worst in others.' He explained that not everyone here today would be aware that for the last ten years, the beautiful gardens of this church, that you walked through to get here, were tended by Eustace. Most weeks, except for those when he was detained at the President's pleasure, he cut the grass and weeded the flower beds, in gratitude for the love and support shown to him by members of this congregation who brought him hot meals and warm clothing.

Faces smiled and laughed at the minister's kind metaphor. All present knew of Eustace's frequent spells in prison, but they also knew that was not what defined the man. His willingness to reciprocate, to give something back in return for the love and kindness that he had been shown, was the reason they were here today. Eustace Brownlie had touched their lives, and they gave thanks to God for that.

After the service concluded, the mourners made the short journey back down the path to the cemetery where they gathered around a freshly dug grave near to the perimeter wall.

At the graveside a youngish lady, smartly dressed in a green dress, sang the opening verse of Amazing Grace.

'Amazing Grace, how sweet the sound that saved a wretch like me

I once was lost, but now am found

T'was blind but now I see.'

How appropriate thought Charlie, as the other mourners joined in the second verse. 'How sweet the sound that saved a wretch like me'. The words seemed to somehow capture the essence of his old foe. At the end of the hymn the minister led the mourners in a closing prayer. Charlie smiled to himself. He felt uplifted. Funerals are almost always sad occasions, but somehow this felt different. As they walked back slowly through the graveyard, Charlie felt good. A poor man, who had suffered more than most, had been given a dignified send off by people who cared for him. Good people, who chose to see beyond the thief and petty criminal that Chris and Charlie knew.

This morning had been good for Charlie's soul. Police work exposes you to sights that most folk never see. If you're not careful it can envelop you, drag you down, leaving you cynical and suspicious. Today, a man by the name of Eustace Brownlie, managed to erode a little of that cynicism and Charlie knew that was a good thing.

Charlie was nearly at the gate when he realised that Chris was no longer with him. Turning around, he saw his colleague standing on the path looking at a beautifully manicured grave. Chris waved for Charlie to come over.

'What have you found?' asked Charlie as he approached the gravestone.

'This headstone,' said Chris pointing at the stone, 'It's the grave of Donald McCaig, founder of Marsco College. Bull's old school.' Charlie nodded.

'I'd heard of him, but I couldn't have told you that he was buried here. And I didn't know that he had owned the Greenbrier Steel Corporation, he must have been worth millions.' said Chris.

'It's got nice carvings and the gold lettering is very striking. But It's a very modest grave for someone who must have been so wealthy don't you think?' said Charlie after reading the inscription on the stone.

'Sure is,' replied Chris, 'but I kind of like that don't you? Not showy nor pretentious. I can't stand rich people who feel the need to show off their money.'

'Just as well I'm neither rich nor pretentious then,' said Charlie smiling. 'And I'll tell you something else, somebody's taking great care to look after it. It's immaculate, there's not a blade of grass out of place. And the thistles and tartan ribbon, someone's making sure that his Scottish roots aren't forgotten.'

'Strange isn't it, how we were at the college the other day and now we find ourselves standing at the graveside of its founder,' said Chris.

'Hadn't given it a lot of thought but I suppose it is,' replied Charlie. 'Police work has a habit of turning up coincidences like that, don't you think? It's one of the things that makes this job so interesting.' Chris nodded looking at his watch.

'But we better get a shift on boss, or we'll miss the Annie Mack sandwich run, and we can't have that.'

'And that's another thing about policing, one minute you can be engrossed thinking about a serious enquiry, and the next you're thinking about your stomach and what's for lunch.' said Charlie laughing.

'Summed up the job pretty well with that analogy I'd say,' said Chris unlocking the car. 'An army can't march on an empty stomach, and a police officer can't think straight if he doesn't get his lunch.' he laughed.

'Well, get a shift on then and we'll make it back before the sandwich run,' said Charlie, 'I'm starving now you've started talking about food.'

*

'Perfect timing by the looks of things,' said Charlie spying Sam walking across the car park. 'Toot the horn and get him to wait. I'll nip out and see him, what are you wanting?'

'Rueben's and a diet coke,' replied Chris thrusting a five dollar note into Charlie's hand.

'I see the new boy's been sent to get the lunch,' laughed Charlie catching up with Sam. 'Nothing changes does it.'

Sam smiled. 'It's not a problem, sir. Can I get you and Chris something?'

'Two Rueben's a coke and a sprite would do nicely,' said Charlie handing over a ten-dollar bill. 'Listen, how did you get on with the bank accounts this morning?'

'Good thanks. Lieutenant Rawlingson took some time to explain what we were looking for and we've devised a system that will let us work through the paperwork systematically. I found it fascinating. We must work to a process or we'll almost certainly miss stuff or duplicate what's already been done. I think we've agreed how we're going to tackle it, so I reckon we've made a decent start.'

Charlie smiled and nodded. He liked what he'd just heard. Sam had clearly been listening to Mike. That wasn't always the case with young officers arriving for secondments. Some had watched too many detective programs on T.V and came with a confidence not matched by their ability. The capacity to listen, keep an open mind and work methodically through enquiries was a pre-requisite of being a good detective. If first impressions were anything to go by, Sam Coutts might just have what it takes.

'How was the service?' asked Mike as Charlie and Chris walked into the office.

'You know I found it surprisingly uplifting.' said Charlie taking off his jacket. 'Yeah, it was really good. Must have been more than twenty people there, including Mrs Jarret, which was a shock given her agoraphobia.'

'And I bet you didn't know that Brownie had tended the gardens at the Baptist church for the last ten years.' added Chris.

'Really?' said Mike raising his eyebrows.

'Just shows that you should never judge a book by its cover,' said Charlie. 'Gave me a bit of a reality check if I'm being honest, there is good in just about everyone. It's just that in this job we sometimes only ever see the bad side of things. So, in a way, Eustace Brownlie taught me a useful lesson, I'm glad we went.'

'I caught Sam heading to Annie Mack's and he told me you'd made a good start sorting out how you're going to tackle the bank enquiry.' said Charlie. Mike nodded.

'I'll tell you something, they weren't joking when they said he's a whiz with figures. After I explained what we needed to do he knocked up a spreadsheet in next to no time and he's already started cross referencing dates and account numbers. You should see him, he's as happy as a pig in ……, well you know what I mean. I don't think it will take us as long as I first thought to plough through all the accounts.'

'I'm impressed,' replied Charlie, 'but there's no hurry. The bank is now monitoring all those accounts so any discrepancies we find are going to be historic. From what I can gather the bank suspect it might be an inside job. It's going to take a bit of time getting through them, but the manager is aware of that, so no need to bust a gut, I'd rather we took our time and got it right.'

'Sounds good' said Mike.

'By the way, any word from our illustrious leader?' asked Charlie. Mike shook his head.

'Nothing yet. I expect he's too busy experiencing the cultural delights of Cancun.'

'Shouldn't think so,' chuckled Charlie, 'don't think our leader would recognise culture even if it walked up and kicked him in the ass.' Just then, Sam arrived carrying a box full of sandwiches and drinks.

'You're being unusually quiet, Angela.' remarked Charlie as Sam passed round the sandwiches. After a moment's silence Angela looked up and put down the report she'd been studying for the last ten minutes.

'Did somebody say something?'

'I was just wondering what you were reading, that's all,' replied Charlie. 'You seem to be engrossed in it whatever it is.' Angela smiled as she started to unwrap her baguette.

'It's the forensic report on the fish that was found at the burglary at the lodge house. Dave sent it up as he'd just got it back from the lab in Charleston. I was reviewing the case file anyway, but this is fascinating. There's three pages here on the autopsy done on that damned fish.'

'Enlighten us then,' said Chris between mouthfuls of his lunch. 'What's so interesting?'

'Well, apart from confirming that it's a rainbow trout, I can tell you that it's female and weighs 2lb 3oz. The bit I think is most interesting is this bit here,' said Angela turning to the second page. 'It says that the fish had only been dead for a few hours as its stomach was full of undigested pellets. They've even included a photograph. Don't you just love the level of details these guys give you?'

'Well it didn't come from any fish shop that's for sure. Not if its stomach was full of food. All their fish are gutted,' said Mike who, as an occasional fisherman, liked to think he knew what he was talking about.

'Just as well you buy them like that, it's bad enough when they still have their heads on. It's the eyes I don't like. But I wouldn't eat fish if I had to gut them myself. Can't be doing with all that blood and sliminess.' said Angela.

'It certainly suggests that the fish has come from a commercial fishery, wild fish don't end up with a belly full of pellets.' added Mike. 'Does the report say anything about the pellets. What they were made of for example?' Angela turned the page of the report and nodded.

'It says here that the pellets are made of starch, digestible protein and plant oils. They are also high in lipids whatever those are.'

'I think lipids are fatty acids and are connected to the production of omega 3. It's something like that.' remarked Sam. 'I remember studying it in biology. But I don't know much more I'm afraid, biology wasn't my strongest subject at school.'

'Who knew I had such a knowledgeable team,' said Charlie laughing. 'I'm learning new things about fish every day. Not sure how useful it's going to be but it's all good, every day's a school day.'

'And you can add on the stuff we learnt about kerfs and saw marks when Dave was explaining how that deer's head had been cut off.' said Mike. 'Fascinating, well I think it is.' Mike was about to explain why he found it so interesting when the phone on Chris's desk rang. Chris looked up and indicated for the others to be quiet.

'Hi Phil, yes it's Chris speaking. Yep, he's here, but go on. Yes, it certainly sounds like it, it can't be anyone else. Where about on the mountain road are they?'

The others stopped eating their lunch and looked across to Chris. This was no ordinary call. Even Sam could sense something important was afoot. As he listened Chris scribbled some notes on a pad.

'Can you print off the incident and I'll ask Sam to come down and pick it up. Yep, if you could.' Chris looked at his watch. 'It's after twenty-past now, can you say to them that we'll be there by two. Just to confirm Phil, you said that Dave and the forensic team were already aware. Yep, that's fine, I'll get Charlie to call him.' Chris put down the phone.

'What's up?' asked Charlie.

'More bad news boss. That was Phil. A trash truck picking up litter on the mountain road have come across a body lying in a ditch. Uniforms are up there now, I'm afraid it's Charlie Jarret. The body has a calliper on its right leg.'

Charlie grimaced and gently shook his head. Normally he wouldn't be willing to confirm the report without a formal identification. But this wasn't an ordinary case. They only had one missing person on their books, and everyone knew he wore a calliper on his leg. There was no mistake, they had found Charlie Jarret.

'This is turning out to be some day. Eustace Brownlie's funeral in the morning and his best friend's younger brother found dead in the afternoon. Can't imagine what this is going to do to Mrs Jarret, the poor woman.' said Charlie. For a few moments nobody said anything.

'Sam, do you mind going down to the front office and picking up the incident?' asked Chris.

'Not a problem,' said Sam getting up from his chair.

'Just hold on for now, Sam. We'll pick it up on our way out. Better finish your sandwich, and then grab your jacket and a clipboard. Don't know when we'll next get a chance to eat. It looks like you've picked a good week to start your secondment, there's going to be plenty going on to keep you busy.' said Charlie.

A frisson of excitement went up Sam's spine. He'd never met Charlie Jarret, but he knew all about the missing person enquiry. Judging by the hive of activity taking place around him as the others looked out logbooks, production bags and disposable gloves, this looked like they were preparing for a criminal investigation, and a serious one at that. It was exactly what Sam had been hoping for. He didn't, of course, wish any harm to Charlie Jarret, but his misfortune looked like providing Sam with his first proper taste of detective work.

'Don't you want me to stay in the office and make a start on the bank accounts?' volunteered Sam hoping that he at least sounded a little sincere.

'The accounts can wait,' replied Charlie. 'This will be good experience for you. But remember and keep your hands in your pockets when we get up there.' Mike smiled but Sam looked confused. 'That way you won't be tempted to touch anything. We've already drawn a blank trying to trace any witnesses into his disappearance, so forensics might prove to be our best shot. If you keep your hands in your pockets you won't contaminate any potential evidence.' added Charlie.

'I'll do that, sir.' said Sam in a serious voice.

'He says that to all our new starts,' said Mike reassuringly. 'It's partly for my benefit. You see, when he was a young detective, I was forever saying the same thing to him, and now it's just become a habit. It's good advice, and advice that you should follow, but he says it partly to let me know he's never forgotten that lesson.'

Chris and Angela smiled as they remembered receiving the same advice.

'Looks like your initial hunch that he may have been abducted was right after all,' said Mike. Charlie nodded.

'Well, I was right about him not being in the river, and unless he walked from Greenbrier Bridge to the mountain road, it does look like he was abducted. Hope nobody's got plans for tonight, we may be here for a while.' The others shook their heads.

'Mike do you mind holding the fort here?' asked Charlie lifting the phone.

'No, that's fine. I can stay on till whenever, message me if you need anything.' replied Mike. Charlie smiled and gave a thumbs up sign as he picked up the phone.

'Dave, it's Charlie, glad I caught you.........'

Chapter 17

A uniformed officer was attaching yellow barrier tape to a road sign pole when the detectives arrived in two vehicles which they parked on the opposite side of the road.

'Can you grab the Logbook Angela and make sure the officer knows that no one enters the scene without it being logged. And I mean no-one. It doesn't matter what rank they are; every visit will be accounted for.'

'We should be fine,' replied Angela, 'that looks like Jerry Curran securing the cordon, he's an old hand and knows what he's doing, but I'll pass on your instructions.'

'Sam, can you check the incident?' asked Charlie, 'who does it say is the supervisory officer who's supposed to be here?'

Sam peered at the print-out. 'It says that Sergeant Lang should be here. That looks like it might be him speaking to the truck driver over there.'

'Yep, that's him,' replied Charlie, 'I'll grab a quick word before we do anything else. You wait here and don't enter the cordoned off area, you hear me?'

'Loud and clear,' replied Sam putting his hands in his pocket.

'Afternoon lieutenant,' said Sergeant Lang on seeing Charlie approaching.

'Afternoon Gordon, what can you tell me then?' Sergeant Lang turned and pointed to the man standing next to him.

'This is Will Kerrigan; he found the body when he was picking up litter from the side of the road. He then telephoned us to report it. That was about two hours ago. He has a colleague but he's sitting in the cab a bit shook up. He'd never seen a dead body before and is feeling a bit faint.'

'That's understandable. It's not as if you would be expecting to come across a body when you turn up for work.' said Charlie.

'Second one I've found since I started with the cleansing department.' said Kerrigan animatedly. 'Found an old hobo in a garbage container about ten years back. But that was completely different. He was fresh. Well, I say fresh, he stank to high heaven, but that was because he hadn't had a wash in months, not because he had been dead for very long. If you see what I mean lieutenant.'

'I understand what you're saying Mr Kerrigan.'

'This guy's a bit of a mess,' continued Kerrigan, 'I haven't touched him you understand. I knew what to do as I always watch Columbo, he's forever finding dead bodies. He never touches them though, but he uses his pen to move things around.'

I've got a right one here, thought Charlie. 'You didn't move anything with your pen when you were down there did you?' asked Charlie suspiciously. Kerrigan laughed.

'No, sir, I did not. I got such a freaking fright when I saw him, half of his face is missing. He's got no eyes, looks like some critter or a bird's been at him.'

Charlie looked at Sergeant Lang who gave a rueful nod.

'He's a bit of a mess I'm afraid. Do you want to have a look?'

'I think I'm going to need to,' replied Charlie waving at Sam to come across.

'It's a little less steep over there,' said Sergeant Lang pointing to some shrubs that were growing just beyond the cordoned off area. 'If we climb the wall over there, we can approach the body from the field, and we shouldn't disturb the locus. He's lying facing the wall so you should get a good view from there.'

'That sounds like a good plan, I take it you've already been down and had a look?' asked Charlie.

Gordon nodded. 'Just to confirm that he was dead.'

'Yeah, of course, I wasn't suggesting anything else.' said Charlie. 'I was just wondering if there was anything else you could tell us.'

'Well, I'm no doctor, but I can tell you that his left ankle is broken. His foot is twisted at a crazy angle. Kind of suggests that he might have broken it falling into the ditch. The side is pretty steep next to where he is lying.'

Charlie, Gordon and Sam stood silently looking at the corpse from the other side of the wall. Sam winced as he looked at the body. He had been to several sudden deaths since he'd joined the job and so had seen dead bodies. He hadn't though, encountered one that was in a state of decomposition and had been ravaged by some wild creature. It was like a scene from a horror movie.

'You okay?' asked Charlie tapping Sam on his arm.

'Yeah, I'm fine, sir.' replied Sam.

'Not one of the more pleasant tasks we have to undertake but a necessary one. It's always good to see a body in situ. Dave and the team will be along to photograph and carry out a full forensic examination, but nothing beats seeing the scene for yourself.' explained Charlie.

'What a way to go, I hope he didn't suffer.' said Gordon.

'Well, I don't think the broken ankle would have killed him. But with a calliper and a foot like that I don't suppose he had much chance of being able to get up the side of the ditch. God, Its tragic. What, fifteen, twenty feet at most, from the road where someone would have found him. Let's hope he died quickly of hypothermia or something like that. The post-mortem should tell us that.' added Charlie.

'Do you think the rock that's lying next to him is significant?' asked Sam. 'It's just that I noticed a couple of similar sized rocks lying by the side of the road. He could have been trying to throw them up there to get someone's attention. Particularly as it doesn't look like he could move far with his ankle like that.'

Charlie had noticed the rock lying next to the body, but he hadn't seen the ones at the roadside. He was impressed. It might prove to be completely inconsequential, but for such a young and inexperienced officer, Sam Coutts was already displaying qualities that suggested he would make a good detective.

'Well spotted,' replied Charlie. 'It's noticing the little details like that that can make all the difference to enquiries. Too early to say if it's got any significance to this investigation, but we'll make sure that we get the rocks photographed, just in case.'

'Doesn't look like you'll have to wait too long. That looks like Dave and the team talking to Angela. I'll go up and speak to him and show him how to get down to here if you like.' said Gordon.

'Appreciate that,' replied Charlie who was now drawing a rough sketch on his clipboard.

'Can I ask what you're doing lieutenant?' asked Sam curiously.

'Just something I learned from Mike years ago. It's just a quick drawing of the locus. Position of the body relative to the wall and the ditch, rough distances that kind of thing. We'll get detailed photographs later, but it's always handy to have a sketch to refresh your memory. I've lost count of the times when it's proved useful. Just another good habit of detective work I suppose.'

Sam nodded. In his first couple of days working with Mike and Charlie, he had learned more than he had in all the time since Sergeant Mitchell had taken over as his line manager. The only thing Sam had learned from Mitchell was how not to do things. He was hopeless. This, on the other hand, was completely different. He was working with hardworking and knowledgeable detectives who were more than willing to share their experience. Sam wished that he could join the detectives full time. If nothing else, his secondment was going to indicate where he wanted his police career to go. It would have the added bonus of taking him as far away from Wayne Mitchell as possible, which in Sam's book could only be a good thing.

'Gordon wasn't kidding,' said Dave as he joined Charlie and Sam at the wall. 'He said it wasn't pretty and he's not wrong. Pretty gruesome.'

'Any thoughts what caused those injuries to his face?' asked Charlie. Dave leaned over the wall and stared at the stricken corpse.

'Almost certainly a bird. Most likely a crow. They dine on carrion and this after all, is just another piece of meat that provides easy pickings for a hungry predator.'

'Just out of interest, what makes you think it's a crow, and not for example a hawk?' asked Charlie.

'Good question lieutenant. But if you look at the side of his face you can see what looks like stabbing injuries. That's typical of crows. Raptors have a sharp hooked bill that rips flesh. Crows' beaks are thick and not as sharp. They tend to stab at their prey.'

'And what about the eyes, would they have been removed by a crow?'

'That's the give-away, I'm afraid. Crows will target the eyes and soft tissue parts. You'll notice most of the lips have gone too. In the wild carrion crows will often peck out the eyes of new born lambs. It's a rich protein source and an easy meal for them. Nature in the raw can appear to be very cruel.'

'We'll do the usual photographs and full examination of the body, I'll let you know when we are in a position to have the body removed, I expect you'll want to have someone at the mortuary to book him in.' said Dave.

'I've already teed Chris up for that, so if you can let him know, that would be good.' replied Charlie.

'Won't be for a while yet, we've a few hours work here first. I'm going to get a tent set up, weather forecast is saying fifty per cent chance of rain. By the way can you touch base with Angela when you head up? She thinks she may have found something that might be important.'

'Will do,' said Charlie, 'I'll catch you back at the office later and get an update, I think we're heading for a late night.'

Angela was putting on a pair of protective gloves when Charlie scrambled up the ditch to the roadside.

'What you got then?' asked Charlie.

Angela opened a black plastic trash bag and tipped the contents onto the grass verge.

'I was talking to the truck driver and he said he'd just started to fill a new bag of trash when he discovered the body.' said Angela sifting through a small pile of plastic bottles and cardboard containers.

'Ah,' said Angela carefully picking up an empty bottle of chocolate milk and two burger boxes. 'This is what I'm looking for. He said he'd picked up these items just before he discovered the body. He said they were lying at the edge of the road directly above the body.' Angela examined the bottle closely.

'Yes, look at this boss. The sell by date says 28th September. That's two days after Charlie Jarret went missing. Must have been purchased around the time he disappeared. Chocolate milk can't have much of a shelf life so could only be a few days either side. And look, these burger boxes are marked with a Sheetz label. There's a Sheetz gas station in Ronceverte, that's only a fifteen-minute drive from here.'

Charlie nodded slowly. 'You could be on to something right enough. It could just be trash thrown from a passing vehicle and have no relevance, but it's going to need to be checked out. All this other stuff looks like its been lying about for ages. You can hardly make out the labels they're so faded.'

'I'll get a statement from the truck driver and his colleague and swing past the gas station on the way back to the office if you'd like. I'll take Sam with me. Be good experience for him.' said Angela.

'Yeah, do that. Chris will go to the mortuary, so I'll head back to the office and get things started there.' said Charlie. 'Any issues give me a shout and check with Dave will you before you leave. I don't suppose we'll get any prints off any of this, not after they've been exposed to the elements for this length of time, but you never know. He'll want to photograph them before we take them to the office, so if you sort that before you go, I'd appreciate it.'

*

It was after four by the time Charlie got back to the office.

'You've just missed a call from our leader,' said Mike looking up from his desk in the detectives' office. 'He's literally just off the phone.'

'What did he have to say about his bank account potentially being compromised. Did he go off on one?' asked Charlie hanging up his jacket.

'Surprisingly no. In fact, I'd say he was remarkably sanguine. Not like Bull at all.' replied Mike. Charlie started to chuckle.

'He did say he'd checked his account and there was nothing untoward about it. He's certain no money has been taken from the account that shouldn't have.' added Mike.

Charlie nodded. 'Did you tell him about Charlie Jarret?'

'No, I didn't. I hadn't heard from you or the others and without you confirming the identity I wasn't about to speculate with Bull. Been down that road too many times before. Anyway, he's back in a couple of days, I didn't want to ruin his holiday worrying about work.'

Charlie nearly choked on the mouthful of coffee he'd just taken.

'Now I know you're being sarcastic. Since when did you give a monkey's about ruining Bull's vacation?' Mike smirked but didn't reply.

'But you're right, it can wait until he gets back.' added Charlie.

'Anyway, how did you get on?' asked Mike, 'are you any the wiser as to how he ended up dead in a ditch on the mountain road?'

'Well, I'm pretty sure someone took him from the bridge and drove him up there. If I was a betting man, I'd say someone then pushed him from the roadside into the ditch. It's very steep and he's ended up at the bottom of the ditch next to a stone wall. His left ankle was clearly broken, it was facing completely the wrong way, must have been agony.'

Mike screwed up his face at the thought.

'Poor guy was in some state,' continued Charlie. 'His eyes and half his face are away, Dave thinks birds, most likely crows, have been at him. But that would have happened after death, looks like with his calliper and broken ankle he couldn't get out of the ditch and has died of exposure.'

'Good grief, what a way to go,' said Mike quietly. 'But why would anyone abduct him and drive him up there. What's the motive? There's got to be a reason.' continued Mike.

'You would have thought. But it certainly wasn't for money, he was as poor as a church mouse. But finding a motive will be key to solving this case. It's no longer a missing person enquiry, this is now a serious criminal investigation.'

Mike nodded. 'Anything you're needing me to do just now?'

'You could start setting up the incident room, that would be a help. And pull in another couple from the book to work on this enquiry. Twelve hour shifts as of tomorrow.' said Charlie.

'I'll get on it straight away. So that's you, Chris, Angela and Sam, plus two from the book, is that right?'

'That's it. And if you could oversee the incident room that would be great,' added Charlie.

'That's going to take me back a bit, haven't done that role in years, but sure, whatever you need.'

As Mike was speaking the phone on Charlie's desk rang.

'Oh, hi Angela, how'd you get on?' said Charlie answering the phone. Mike watched on intently as for the next few minutes Charlie conversed with Angela. By the time he put down the phone he had scribbled down several pages of notes.

'It could be that we might have got our first break,' said Charlie putting down his pen. 'Angela and Sam are over at the Sheetz gas station in Ronceverte. We recovered burger boxes and a chocolate milk bottle near to where the body was lying. The sell by date on the bottle tied in with roughly the time he went missing and the burger boxes had Sheetz labels on them. Angela is now saying that she's got the till roll from the night he went missing. Four burgers, three cokes and a Doctor Pepper were purchased from the store at 0134 hours. Then eleven minutes later someone else bought another two burgers and a bottle of chocolate milk. That's roughly an hour and a half after Screech dropped his brother at the bridge.' Mike smiled and nodded.

'She also said there was CCTV from the store,' continued Charlie.

'Bingo,' said Mike thumping his desk with his fist.

'Don't get too excited. She says for some reason the camera was pointing at the floor, something to do with the bracket being loose, but anyway it's only captured images from the knee down. But it's not all bad news, she says at 0134 hrs the camera has captured at least three people standing by the till. And get this, one of them is wearing cowboy boots. Ten minutes later another person wearing cowboy boots appears at the till.'

'Hmm, that ties in with the prints you had photographed at the bridge, doesn't it?' asked Mike, 'I'm sure two of the prints were made by cowboy boots.'

'Correct, they were. That's a cracking bit of work by Angela. It would be too much of a coincidence for this not to be connected to Charlie Jarret's disappearance. Angela told me that none of the images showed anyone with a calliper on their leg which suggests he wasn't in the store.' Mike bit his lip and rubbed his brow.

'Let me just get this clear, Angela is saying that six burgers were bought, but in two transactions that were eleven minutes apart. That seems a bit strange. You would have thought they would have all been bought together.' Charlie shrugged his shoulders.

'I don't suppose any of the burgers were bought for Jarret, but it does suggest that there might have been six of them.'

Mike nodded. 'We can't say for sure that there were six of them, they could have turned up at different times, then again the two transactions might not be connected at all.'

'That's possible,' said Charlie. 'But for now, let's assume there were six of them. That would make seven if you include Jarret.' said Mike.

'Correct.' replied Charlie. 'So, if there were seven in total, it suggests to me that they travelled in two vehicles.'

'Seven could travel in a pick-up. Three in the front and four in the back.' said Mike. 'Remember Bradley Coombs said he passed a dark coloured pick-up on his way home that night.'

'True, but he also said he thought there was another vehicle parked at the bridge, a smaller saloon car. If he was right about that then I think both those vehicles are connected to Jarret's abduction.'

'Who are you phoning now?' asked Mike as Charlie lifted the receiver.

'The control room, I want a message passed to Angela, we didn't discuss if she'd checked for CCTV outside the building. If we're right about the vehicles, then with a bit of luck cameras might have caught them arriving or leaving the garage. They sure as hell didn't get up to the mountain road without a vehicle. Fingers crossed eh.'

*

'You sure you don't mind?' said Charlie handing Mike a beer.

'Nope,' said Mike taking a large gulp. 'Susan's at her music group tonight and you're right, it might be a while till we get a chance for a beer. What time did Angela say she would be here?'

'Anytime now,' said Charlie looking at his watch. 'And Chris shouldn't be far behind, when I spoke to

Dave, he said the body had left to go to the mortuary so checking him in shouldn't take too long.'

Five minutes later Angela and Sam walked into the bar.

'Any joy?' asked Charlie hopefully. The dead pan expression on his colleagues faces gave the game away.

'Afraid not,' said Angela pulling up a chair. 'We checked both the outside camera tapes. Apparently, one hasn't been working properly for months, I had a look at it, but it was all grainy and you couldn't make anything out. The other one didn't show any vehicles, well apart from the car belonging to the guy who was working nightshift that day. We've still to contact him, but according to the manager, he's a bit of a dozy type and not the brightest bulb in the box, but hey, you never know.'

Charlie puffed out his cheeks and gave a knowing look. 'Sod's law. I expect their vehicles were parked at the side covered by the dud camera.'

'Unfortunately, there aren't any other cameras between the garage and where Charlie Jarret was found. We double checked on our way over here,' added Sam, 'and as there is really only one road you can take to get there, I don't think we missed anything.'

'That's a good piece of work by both of you today.' said Charlie. 'Mike's at the bar getting a round in. Better let him know what you're having, you don't want to miss the boss buying a drink. We'll not stay too long tonight, early start tomorrow. I want everyone in for a briefing at seven.'

'Understood,' said Angela sticking two fingers up and mouthing to Mike that she and Sam would both have a beer. A couple of minutes later Chris walked into the bar.

'Good timing as usual,' said Mike returning with the drinks. 'What are you having?'

'Just a coke thanks.' replied Chris sitting down at the table.

'Any issues at the hospital?' asked Charlie.

'No. No issues,' replied Chris. 'But I may have turned up something that could be useful.' Chris reached into his pocket and pulled out a small plastic bag.

'What is it?' asked Mike staring at the bag, 'I can't see anything.'

'It's some green thread,' replied Chris. 'I removed it at the mortuary, it was sticking to the Velcro on Jarret's jacket. I don't know how Dave missed it.'

'What makes you think it might be significant?' asked Charlie sceptically as he examined the plastic bag, 'it's just a few threads of cotton.'

'I know that,' said Chris, whose enthusiasm for his find didn't seem to be shared by his colleagues. 'But do you remember the button that Screech had on him? The one with the mountain and the thistle engraved on it?'

'Sure,' said Charlie, 'I remember it.'

'Well, that button had green thread like this attached to it. I'm going to lodge it with Dave. I want to know if the thread on Jarret's jacket is the same as the stuff that was attached to the button.'

'Yeah, well that's fair enough,' said Charlie. 'Who knows what the forensic team might be able to tell us. Look, I wasn't trying to be dismissive, so apologies if that's how it came across. I was expecting, well, I don't know what I was expecting, but it certainly wasn't thread. But you're right, let's lodge it and get it analysed. Only way to tell if it's got any significance.'

Chris smiled. 'I've to call in at the office before I head home, I'll try and get a word with Dave if he's still about. It's amazing what they can tell you, just look what they did for Angela's fish!' The others laughed.

'And, if it's alright with you boss, I'm going to pay the cemetery caretaker a visit tomorrow. The mountain and thistle on the button are the same design that was on the gravestone of that guy who founded Marsco College. We were just looking at it this morning when we were leaving Brownie's funeral. It didn't register at the time, but when I got back to the office and checked the button, I realised they were the same. God damn it, now I can't remember the guy's name.' said Chris scratching his head.

'McCaig. Donald McCaig. And that's a good idea. While you're there try and find out who has been tending that grave. I'd like to speak to whoever that is.' added Charlie.

*

'You're in early,' said the cleaner removing her bucket and mop to let Mike enter the detectives' office.

'Not as early as some by the looks of things,' said Mike noticing the office light was on. 'I take it our new lieutenant has made an early start today?' said Mike opening the door.

The cleaner shook her head.

'I haven't seen Charlie this morning. That's Phil Coutts boy who's in there. I started mopping the corridor floor just before six and he was sitting working away at a desk then. Must be keen eh. Either that or he can't sleep.' said the cleaner with a chuckle.

'Definitely the former. He takes after his father. Conscientious and hardworking, much like yourself,' said Mike with a wink.

'Flattery will get your everywhere,' said the cleaner with a wave as she headed for the lift.

'How long have you been here?' asked Mike hanging up his jacket. 'I take it you did go home last night?'

Sam looked up and smiled.

'About an hour and a half. I wanted to make a start on those accounts. I was up anyway so it seemed like a good opportunity. I've got about twenty done. Not found anything unusual yet, but its early days.'

Mike nodded. 'Seriously Sam, I don't want to discourage you from hard work, but we're now onto twelve-hour days, adding on another couple of hours is going to make it a mighty long day. You'll end up exhausted and not fit for anything.'

'Don't worry about me. I never sleep more than six hours. I'm always up early and doing something. Anyway, after two months of working for Sergeant Mitchell, I'm just glad of the opportunity. Working for him was as slow as a week in the jail. He actively discouraged you from getting involved with things.'

'That bad eh?' replied Mike.

'Afraid so,' said Sam putting the files back into the folder. 'Oh, I meant to ask you, what's the reason why these files have the account holders' details blacked out?'

'That's fairly standard practice. You'll notice you've got photocopies there. Lieutenant Finch has the originals, he's had the personal information redacted for security reasons. It's nothing against you, but we do it routinely with sensitive enquiries like this. Much easier to keep things confidential that way,' added

Mike. Before Sam had a chance to respond, Charlie walked in the door.

'Twenty to seven and I'm only third in!' he exclaimed.

'Fourth actually boss, I saw you parking up when I was speaking to Zoe down at the lab.' said a clearly amused Chris who had just walked in the door.

'Good grief. Looks like I'm working with a bunch of insomniacs. Let's hope your investigatory skills are as good as your time keeping. If they are, we might have half a chance of solving this case.' said Charlie filling the kettle at the sink. 'Time for a quick coffee and then up and at them. Anything in the overnight crime file that I need to know about?'

*

The caretaker's house sat next to the information board on the town side of the cemetery. Having got no reply at the door Chris wandered through the wrought iron gates and up the slope of the centre path to where three men were standing next to a small truck.

'Would any of you be the caretaker by any chance?' asked Chris as he approached the men.

'That would be me,' said the smaller of the men who was dressed in a dark suit and cap. The other two men ignored Chris and removed spades and wooden boards from the rear of the truck.

'And who might you be?' replied the man tilting his cap back on his head. Chris produced his police badge and introduced himself. The man looked at the badge and nodded.

'Remember what I told you,' said the man turning to the other two men. 'It's a family lair and there are already two in there. You won't have to go too deep to find them, but be careful, I don't want a repeat of the last time.'

Chris thought better of asking what all that meant and followed the man back to the house.

'I'm having a coffee; would you care for one?'

'That would be good,' said Chris sitting down at a table in the small kitchen. 'Just milk for me please.' As the man made the coffee Chris explained why he was there.

'I'd say it's the best kept grave in the cemetery,' said the man handing Chris his coffee. 'That grass is cut and edged once a week, every week. Well certainly from spring through to the fall. Even in the winter he still calls every week to check it.'

'Who calls?' asked Chris taking out his notebook.

'Mr Buckley.' Replied the man. 'He's a caretaker like me, over at Marsco College. And every week, after he's cut the grass, he lays a small bunch of thistles by the headstone, always neatly tied with ribbon of the same tartan. I've been working here for fourteen years and he's been doing it ever since I came. He may have been doing it for much longer than that. I should make a point of asking him next time I see him.'

'Does he always come on the same day?' asked Chris.

'He's usually here on a Thursday morning. Anytime between ten and eleven. But occasionally the day can vary. But not often, I can tell you that. And woe betide anyone who interferes with the grave.'

Chris looked bemused. 'Interferes with the grave, what do you mean by that?'

'Perhaps interfere might not be the right word, but he doesn't take kindly to any behaviour that, shall we say, disrespects the grave.'

211

'And does that happen?' asked Chris starting to write some notes in his book.

'I've seen him yell at a small child who ran over the edge of the grave. And a couple of months back he really went off on one. He was furious. He came banging on my door. He was holding an animal's ear. He was adamant it was a deer's ear. I couldn't have told you, put it was certainly an animal's ear. All covered in blood it was. He was ranting and raving as someone had left it lying on top of the grave. He wanted to know if I knew anything about it, or if I'd seen anyone.'

'And did you. I mean did you know or see anything?' asked Chris trying to make sure he wrote all of this down.

'Not a thing.' replied the man.

'I see,' said Chris putting down his pen. 'I don't suppose you can tell me what day that happened?'

The man smiled. That I can help you with. It was my birthday. It was the 24th September, which was a Thursday.'

Chris sat back in his chair gently nodding his head. The 24th was the day Charlie Jarret was reported missing. And the deer's head that Hugh Robertson pulled out of the river the following day was missing an ear. Wait till the boss hears about this thought Chris.

'I'm grateful to you, that's been very helpful.'

'Not sure how it helps, but if you say it does then I'm happy to have been of assistance.'

'By the way, if you don't mind me asking, what did you mean when you said to your colleagues that you didn't want a repeat of last time. Did they put a spade through a coffin?' The caretaker laughed.

'If only,' he replied, 'it was worse than that. The dozy fool went and fell in. landed on top of the coffin splitting the lid clean in two.'

'Woah, I wouldn't fancy that,' gasped Chris.

'I'm pretty sure he won't do it again,' said the caretaker. 'He'd only just started with us when that happened. He was traumatised for the rest of the day and couldn't dig a grave for a week. He's over it now, but I like to remind them, help keeps them on their toes if you know what I mean.'

Chris smiled. 'Yeah, I think I know exactly what you mean.'

Chapter 18

'Let me get this right then,' said Charlie who was talking to Chris and Mike in his office. 'The caretaker is saying that the grave is looked after by Donald Buckley, who works at Marsco College. And he found a deer's ear lying on McCaig's grave on the morning of the 24th September, the same day Screech reported his brother missing.' Chris nodded. 'And he's sure of the date because the 24th was his birthday. Have I got that right?'

'Hundred percent.' replied Chris.

For several moments Charlie didn't say anything. He stood looking out the window deep in concentration. Eventually he spoke.

'First of all, that's a cracking bit of work Chris. It clearly suggests that the deer's head is connected to Jarret's disappearance. Do me a favour will you and go and get the master keys from Phil?'

'Sure,' said Chris, 'but what will I tell him when he asks me why I want them?'

'Just tell him I need them to access Bull's office. And get him to phone me straight away.'

'On it now, boss.' replied Chris heading out the door.

'Now I'm curious,' said Mike. 'Why do you need to get into Bull's office? You do know that Phil will have to record that in his log.'

'I know,' replied Charlie, 'that's why I asked Chris to get Phil to phone me. I'm needing a favour. I don't want it recorded.'

'Well, I'm sure he'll do you that favour, but I'm still none the wiser why you need into his office.' added Mike.

'You know the photograph above his desk, the one of him when he was at Marsco?' continued Charlie.

'Yeah, I know the one you mean,' said Mike pulling up a chair.

'Well I want to know the names of the boys that are in that photograph. I know Bull and Ralph Portman are in it. But if I remember there are another three boys in that picture, and I want to know who they are. I'm sure all the names are written on a plaque at the bottom of the photograph.' continued Charlie.

'Are you thinking they're connected to Jarret's death?' asked Mike who was trying to understand where his friend was going with this.

'I'm just covering all the bases, as you would say.' replied Charlie. 'We've had a break in to the lodge house at Marsco and then there was burglary at the Deans estate, reported by Portman if you remember. That ended with Brownie dead and Screech seriously injured after a rifle butt smashed into his head. There are just too many strange coincidences. We know Bull and Portman are connected through the school. I'm thinking out loud now, but something tells me there's a connection to the college in all of this. The chief will be back at work in a couple of days, so now seems like a good time to take a closer look at that photograph.'

'Can't argue with that,' said Mike.

In a little more than two months, Mike had seen Charlie flourish in his new role. He was much more confident in himself and there was a maturity about him that wasn't there before. His thought process was clear and considered. Mike knew he had made the right decision in suggesting Charlie should be the acting lieutenant. If he could find the answers to all of this, he really would make his mark as a detective.

'Can you find Sam and give him the heads up for me? When I've got the names from that picture, I'm heading over to Marsco with Chris and I think Sam should come along. I want a word with Donald Buckley.' Mike nodded. As he got up to go and look for Sam, the phone on Charlie's desk rang.

'Hi Phil, thanks for the quick response. Look, I need to ask you for a favour.'

*

'It's funny isn't it,' said Chris as he drove through the entrance to the college and parked on the gravel car park in front of the main entrance. 'They were carved on the gate pillars as we came in and look, it's on the stonework above the front door. They're all over the place.' Sam stared up at the oval shaped carving above the entrance that depicted a thistle with a mountain standing behind it.

'I was here with Angela after the break-in to the lodge and I never noticed them. Now they seem to be everywhere.' added Chris.

'You did see them,' said Charlie, 'but because they didn't mean anything at the time they didn't register. The brain's a funny thing right enough.'

'Well mine certainly is. I sometimes think that part of mine isn't functioning properly.' added Chris quietly. Sam started to laugh.

216

'We're just different. We don't all think or see things the same way,' explained Charlie as they walked across the forecourt. 'Just as well really. It's good to have a team with different skill sets. It's one of the reasons why I think we've got such a strong team. The whole is greater than the sum of the parts. We complement each other.'

Entering through the stone archway the three officers made their way across the hall to the school office. The door was lying open and a smartly dressed lady in her early sixties was sitting at a desk typing. Charlie tapped on the door. The lady looked up and smiled.

'Can I help you gentlemen, I'm the college secretary?'

Charlie returned her smile and pointed to his badge as he introduced himself and his colleagues.

'I was hoping to catch a word with Mr Buckley, I believe he's the school's caretaker.' The lady put her finger to her lips and made a shushing noise at Charlie.

'Don't use the 'C' word she whispered. It's taboo within the college. His title is the Dionach.' said the lady pointing to a door across the hall. The detectives looked across the hall to a door which had the word Dionach written on it in large gold lettering.

'It's from the Gaelic, it means a guardian or protector. There has been a Dionach at the college since the Founder started the school in 1917. It was Mr Buckley's father to begin with and since 1963 it's been Donald. The Buckleys have been the Dionach at Marsco for seventy-five years. They're very particular about it, so you can see why we never use the 'C' word.' Charlie nodded and smiled.

'And what about yourself, I'm sorry I didn't ask your name, have you worked at the college a long time.'

'Apologies but that was rude of me not to introduce myself. I'm Jean Henderson. I started working here in 1959 and have been the secretary since 1974.'

'A long time right enough,' said Charlie.

'Not quite as long as Mr Buckley, but other than him, I am the longest serving member of staff. Another eighteen months and it will be time to retire, not that I'm wishing it away you understand. It's a great place to work, but there comes a time when it's time to go. There's a big world out there that I want to explore.'

'Another thirteen years before I can go,' said Charlie, 'but you're right, lots of things to look forward to in retirement.'

'I'm sorry,' said Jean looking out her window, 'I seem to have taken you a bit off subject. You said you wanted to speak to Mr Buckley. I know he's not in his office and as he doesn't appear to be with Seth. I think he may be up in the top wood with Mr Thomas, our gardener. He said they were going to cut firewood sometime today, so I think that's where he'll be.'

'Seth is his son isn't he. Would he be able to tell us where his dad is?' asked Charlie peering out the window at Seth who was dressed in a pair of overalls and busy trimming the edge of a rose bed.

'I'm afraid that's unlikely.' said Jean. 'Seth has autism and next to no speech. He's also painfully shy, especially with people he doesn't know.'

As she was speaking Sam started to frantically pat down and search his pockets.

'You lost something?' asked Chris who could tell Sam was becoming agitated.

'I must have dropped it,' he said in a worried voice.

'Dropped what?' asked Chris as Sam checked his pockets for the third time.

'My police badge. I had it when I came out the car, but it must have fallen off my jacket pocket somewhere.' Just then Sam noticed Seth through the office window. He had stopped edging the grass and was now picking up something that was lying by the edge of the lawn.

'He's got my badge!' exclaimed Sam. 'Excuse me lieutenant, ma'am, but I'll need to go and retrieve my badge, it appears that guy has found it.' said Sam pointing out the window.

By the time Sam got around to the rose bed, Seth was nowhere to be seen. Where the hell can he be? He can't have gone far. It only took me seconds to get here. As Sam scanned all around, he heard a gate slamming shut behind him. Over a stone wall, Sam could see the figure of a man in green-overalls scurrying up the hill towards the woods. That's him thought Sam. Where the hell's he going with my badge? By the time Sam got through the gate the man had disappeared into the forest. Sam started to run. He couldn't see the man, but he could hear him. Several high-pitched squeals broke the silence. He was over to his right. Sam navigated his way through the trees and suddenly there he was. No more than a hundred yards ahead of him. Sam was intrigued. Where the heck was he going? For the next five minutes Sam followed at a safe distance making sure he wasn't seen.

From behind a bush, Sam watched as the man stopped next to a dead tree. Having convinced himself nobody was watching the man climbed up the trunk onto a low hanging branch. Reaching into his pocket he took out Sam's badge and placed it carefully into a hole about twelve feet from the ground. Sam stayed hidden

219

as the man climbed down and scurried his way back down the path and out of sight. Having waited a minute to make sure he wasn't coming back, Sam made his way to the dead tree. Carefully he climbed to a branch that was high enough to allow him to access the hole. He reached up and put his hand into the hole that was the size of a small watermelon.

Sam held his breath as gingerly he navigated the hole with his fingers, momentarily apprehensive about what he might find. Straightaway he felt metal and the softness of smooth leather. He knew it was his badge. As he probed further down the hole, he could feel several other items. He ran his finger over the rim of what appeared to be a glass. His fingertips tracing the contours of the cut crystal. He then felt the sharp edge of what he thought was a box. The top of the box was silky smooth, but the sides had the texture of wood. Taking great care, he started to remove the items. Out came his badge, followed by a glass tumbler and then finally a beautiful wooden box with a mother of pearl top. He was sure there were more items in the hole, but as they were deeper down, he wasn't confident that he would be able to get them out. They would have to stay there for now.

Back on terra firma, Sam examined the glass and box. He'd overheard Mike talking about the anniversary dinner that the chief had attended and realised from the engraving that the glass must be a memento of that. But it was the cigar box that now had his attention. Angela had mentioned that a cigar box had been stolen during the burglary at the lodge, this must be it he thought. He tingled with excitement as he realised the significance of his discovery. As he read the inscription on the brass plate, he noticed what he thought was a fingerprint. He angled the box so that the sunlight caught the plate. There was no mistake. Sure enough, there appeared to be a large thumb print on the corner of the brass plate. Very carefully Sam took off his jacket and wrapped it around the box and glass. These will need to be examined for prints he thought, you never know the one on the plate might belong to our thief!

In the school office, Charlie and Chris were still chatting to Jean Henderson.

'It's not a problem,' said Charlie, 'We will catch the Dimmock, another time.'

'The Dionach,' said Jean with a broad grin. 'But pretty close and well done for trying.'

Charlie screwed up his nose and raised his eyebrows. 'Dionach. Right I'll try and remember that. But listen, while we're here, there is something else I wanted to ask you,' said Charlie taking a piece of paper from his inside jacket pocket.'

'Oh, what's that?' asked Jean getting up from her chair.

'Do the following names mean anything to you?' asked Charlie handing over the piece of paper. 'I already know who Ewart Wilder and Ralph Portman are, it's really the other three I'm interested in.'

Jean studied the paper. 'Yes indeed,' she said sitting back down at her desk. 'I know all three of them. Well technically only two now. Vince Sanders died in a car accident many years ago. I think it was during his first or second year at university. Brian Swartz now lives in Melbourne, Australia. He emigrated about fifteen years ago. He used to come to the reunion dinners, but understandably, he wasn't able to be at the seventy-fifth, although of course he was invited.'

Chris was scribbling notes on a pad while Jean was speaking.

'Ah, Edward Broadley, now he is a gentleman. I haven't seen him since he left the college. I know he's now a dentist and lives up in Harrisburg. I was very sorry he didn't come to the dinner, but I wasn't surprised. He sent me a nice e-mail declining the invitation.' Charlie closed his folder and stood up.

'Can I ask why you weren't surprised he didn't attend?'

'He wasn't like the other boys,' replied Jean, 'they were all sporty types. You would call them Jocks now. No, Edward was much more studious. Quite sensitive and he took the death of Mark Tyler very badly. So much so that I know he changed his university application from West Virginia State to Penn University in Pennsylvania. He just wanted to get away. I don't think he's ever been back at Marsco.' Charlie was intrigued. He wasn't aware that a boy had died.

'I take it Edward was friends with the boy that died then? I'm sorry, but I don't know anything about that, can you tell us what happened?' asked Charlie.

'They were in the same house, although Edward was the year above Mark. They had been good friends for years. I can remember it very well,' replied Jean. 'It happened in the fall of 1960. My second year at the school. It was a real tragedy, he drowned near to the Greenbrier bridge. Nobody really knows what happened and I don't think the police ever got to the bottom of it. I'm surprised you don't know any of this, but I suppose it was a long time ago now.'

'A bit before our time right enough, but I've a couple of colleagues who might recall the event, I'll need to check with them when I see them. But please carry on, you said he drowned near to the bridge.'

'Lots of people had their own theories as to what happened. But I know they found him with a head injury,' continued Jean. 'Personally, I think he had been climbing on the bridge when he slipped and banged his head. I can remember it had been raining hard that night so the bridge would have been slippery. If he knocked himself out hitting the bridge, he wouldn't have stood a chance when he fell into the water. Gosh it was really sad.'

Charlie and Chris nodded sympathetically.

'Talking about it now brings it all back. What made it even worse was the fact he'd been the Sligachan scholar. He was supposed to become the head of school the following year, so you can see it had a huge impact on everyone.' Charlie pulled up a chair and sat down.

'It's always sad when a young person loses their life, I can see how upsetting that would have been at the time.' said Charlie genuinely trying to be empathetic. 'But if you don't mind me asking, you said that others had their own theories as to what happened. You've told us what you think happened, but what were others saying?'

For a moment Jean didn't say anything. She sat looking at the ceiling. Charlie sensed her discomfort.

'I'm not really wanting to speculate and other people I'm sure will tell you what they think. But without naming anyone, there were rumours at the time, that the members of Mic Sgith were out of school that night and some say Mark was with them when they left.'

It was clear to Charlie that Jean was finding this very uncomfortable.

'Look, I'm sorry lieutenant, but I don't want to say anything more. There was a police investigation at the time, but nothing was proved, so it's just speculation. Now I wish I hadn't told you. I don't approve of tittle tattle,' said Jean putting her head into her hands.

'I'm sorry, I didn't mean to make you feel uncomfortable, we won't pursue this any further. But two quick questions if I may,' said Charlie. 'Mic Sgith. Can you tell us what that means? And if you had Edward Broadley's home address, I would be most grateful.' Jean looked up and smiled.

'Now I can certainly help you with those questions. Mic Sgith is a Gaelic expression. I think it means Sons of Skye. We don't call them that now but in 1960, the head of school and his four house captains gave themselves the name Mic Sgith. It was supposed to be a tribute to the Founder, who hailed from the Isle of Skye. But like many things, it all got a little out of hand. That group of boys thought they ruled the school. Thinking back, I don't think the term was used again after young Mark was killed. The headmaster at the time clamped down hard. He didn't approve, so I suppose it disappeared. They were called various things after that, but never Mic Sgith.'

Chris raised his eyebrows and gave Charlie a knowing look.

'Just give me a minute and I'll find you that address.' said Jean pulling out a folder from a filing cabinet next to her desk. As she was leafing through the folder, Sam walked in carrying the items still wrapped in his jacket.

'I see you've got your badge back,' said Chris noticing the badge on Sam's shirt pocket. 'But what have you got wrapped in there that's so precious?' asked Chris pointing at the jacket.

'It's a cigar box and a crystal glass. They were in a tree in the woods. I think it's the box that was stolen during the lodge burglary. I'm pretty sure there are still other items in the tree, but I couldn't reach them.' said Sam.

'Let's have a look at the box,' said Charlie who had been writing down the address that the secretary had just found. Sam unwrapped his jacket and showed Charlie the box.

'I think it has a fingerprint on the brass plate. I'm hoping it might be our thief, but I suppose it's more likely to belong to Mr Buckley.' said Sam angling the box so the light caught the fingerprint.

'You could well be right, you never know, either way it's going to need to be checked. But that does look like the stolen box.' replied Charlie.

'Does it have a drawer at the bottom of it? I remember Buckley was fuming about the box being stolen. Something to do with a letter he said had been in a drawer.' said Chris.

'Let's have a look and see then,' said Charlie taking a handkerchief out of his pocket. With great care he opened the drawer. 'Looks like it's here right enough, but I'm not going to touch it. It's possible we might get a print from it. Good effort though Sam. Recovering stolen property and getting your badge back constitutes a good morning's work.' Sam didn't say anything, but a beaming smile broke out across his face, at that precise moment he felt ten foot tall.

Charlie thanked the secretary for her assistance and asked that she let Mr Buckley know that someone would be back to see him, probably tomorrow, all being well.

'I didn't want to say in front of the secretary,' said Sam as they walked back to their car. 'But my badge was in the tree along with the box and glass. The man who was cutting the grass, who, if I picked you up right, is Buckley's son, put my badge in a hole in the tree. I followed him into the woods and saw him do it. Do you think that means he's our thief?'

'You would have thought, wouldn't you, but I'm pretty sure he's not.' said Charlie. Sam looked confused. 'If I recall correctly, Seth Buckley was away overnight at a family funeral with his mother and father on the night of the burglary.'

'Spot on boss.' said Chris, 'I took the report with Angela the following day and that's correct, the three of them had been away at a funeral.'

'You said you thought there might be other items in the tree,' said Charlie.

'I'm almost certain there are.' replied Sam.

'Well that being the case, we'll get hold of a ladder and you can check that out tomorrow,' said Charlie. Sam smiled and gave an approving nod.

They were more than half-way back to Lewisburg when Chris suddenly banged the steering wheel in frustration.

'God damn it,' he said shaking his head angrily. 'I'd forget my head if it wasn't screwed on.'

'What's the problem?' asked Charlie opening one eye having dozed off in the passenger seat.

'I forgot to show the secretary a picture of the button, I was about to when Sam came back with the box and then I just forgot.' said Chris banging the steering wheel again.

'Sorry about that,' said Sam sheepishly from the back seat.

'Don't you apologise, It's not your fault.' said Charlie. 'In fact, it's as much my fault as anybody's, but it's not a problem. We've to go back and see Buckley anyway so it can be done then. But this is a good learning point for you Sam. It shows how easy it is to forget something. And in our line of work that something could prove to be crucial. We have to be switched on one hundred percent of the time, but its nothing we can't sort, so no harm done.'

When they got back to the office Mike was painstakingly working his way through the pile of bank statements.

'Slowly getting there,' he said as Charlie and the others hung up their jackets.

'Have you found anything unusual yet?' asked Charlie lifting a mug up to see if Mike wanted a coffee.

'Not a darn thing, but I'll have a coffee thanks. How did you get on?'

'Yeah, good thanks,' replied Charlie. 'I've got an address for one of the boys in Bull's photograph which I'm going to follow up on. And eagle-eyed Sam here managed to retrieve the cigar box which had been stolen during the break-in.'

'How did you manage that?' asked Mike. Sam laughed.

'Bit of a long story but I'll tell you later. I'm just going to the lab with Chris to see if we can get a lift off the box, looks like there might be a cracking print on the plate.'

'Let's hope so,' said Mike. 'That would be a real bonus.'

'I shouldn't be too long; I'll give you a hand with those accounts when I get back.' said Sam as he and Chris headed out the office.

'No rush,' replied Mike, 'they'll still be here when you get back.'

Charlie handed Mike his coffee and sat down at his desk.

'By the way, the autopsy report for Charlie Jarret is on your desk, Dave came up with it earlier.' said Mike taking a sip of his coffee.

'Any surprises in it?' asked Charlie, 'I take it you had a read.'

'No surprises really. He died from exposure as we thought. They can't say exactly when, but they reckon he died of hypothermia a couple of days after he went missing.' Charlie nodded.

'That makes sense. It was very cold at the end of September when he disappeared. If I remember rightly it rained most of the following day. Not surprised he got hypothermia. What did it say about his ankle injury?'

'Almost certainly caused by falling into the ditch. The report said it was sixteen feet from the roadside to the bottom of the ditch, that's a long way to fall.' replied Mike. 'The only other thing I picked up was confirmation that his facial injuries were caused by birds. Some of the close-up photographs are pretty gruesome, so don't say I didn't warn you.'

'I'll have a read of it later. I've a briefing note to prepare ahead of the chief's return so I'm glad we've got the report before he gets back.' said Charlie.

'Look, I was wondering, does the name Mark Tyler mean anything to you?'

Mike thought for a moment and then shook his head.

'Don't think so, why?'

'I know it was well before your time, but I thought it might ring a bell with you.' said Charlie. 'He was in the

228

year below Bull. Drowned in suspicious circumstances near to the Greenbrier bridge. The year Bull was head of school. According to the secretary, Bull and the others in that photograph, might have been with him when he died. She told us they gave themselves the name Mic Sgith. Stands for Sons of Skye apparently. From what she said they seemed like a bit of a crazy bunch.'

'What, Bull Wilder part of a crazy bunch, I'm flabbergasted!' said Mike sarcastically. 'You should check with Phil though. I think he joined in 62, he might know something about it. Was probably still being talked about when he joined.'

'Yeah, I was going to do that.' said Charlie.

'You said you were going to follow up on an address.' asked Mike.

'Yep, it's the only lead we've got from the photograph. One of the boys was killed in a car accident and another has lived in Australia for years. This guy's called Edward Broadley and lives in Harrisburg. Works as a dentist. According to the secretary he was close friends with the boy that died. Sensitive type, not like Bull or the others. He took his friend's death badly and hasn't been near the school since he left.'

'Harrisburg must be the best part of three hundred miles away, are you going to fly up?' asked Mike.

'Don't think so. Bull will be back at work in a couple of days so I'm going to give the guy a call and see if he can see me tomorrow. But I think I'll drive. I don't want Bull knowing about any of this. Not right now anyway. If I flew, he would have to approve the expenses. This might prove to be nothing at all, but I want to speak to Broadley. If Mic Sgith were with Tyler when he died, he might have something interesting to tell us.'

'You're not suggesting Wilder is connected to Jarret's death or the burglaries at the school or the Deans estate, are you?' asked Mike, who was trying to work out where his friend was going with this.

'Just throwing the net out wide, that's all,' replied Charlie. 'After all, that's what you taught me to do wasn't it?' Mike leaned back in his chair and put his hands behind his head.

'Looks like I taught you well then lieutenant.' said Mike in a serious voice. He paused momentarily and then winked.

'Got any biscuits to go with this coffee?' Charlie burst out laughing. That was typical Mike, just typical.

Half an hour later Chris and Sam came into the office talking animatedly.

'What are you pair looking so pleased about?' asked Mike looking up from his desk.

'We may just have got lucky,' said Chris with a beaming smile. 'Zoe has lifted a cracking print from the cigar box, she was also able to tell us that it didn't belong to any of the Buckleys. She had their elimination prints and it's definitely not theirs.' said Chris.

'Holy crap that was quick work,' said Mike.

'There's more good news,' added Chris. 'She says the print is quite unusual, it's got arches as opposed to loops or whorls. Apparently only five percent of people have arch prints so that's going to narrow the field considerably. But get this. The print is from a thumb and it has a visible scar running through it. That's going to disappear in time, but Zoe says she is sure that she's seen that print recently. She can't quite put her finger on it, but she's looking into where that might have been.'

Mike started to laugh. Chris and Sam couldn't see what was funny.

'She can't quite put her finger on it,' chortled Mike, 'unintentional puns are always the funniest.'

'Whatever,' replied Chris who still wasn't getting it.

'Never mind.' said Mike, 'but that sounds very positive, suggest you go next door and update Lieutenant Finch.'

Chapter 19

This must be it, thought Charlie, as he pulled up outside a smart brick building in a quiet residential street in the suburbs of Harrisburg. The black and white sign that hung over the door said Edward Broadley Dentistry. It was approaching one and Charlie had been driving for more than five hours. His back felt as stiff as a board and he was glad of the opportunity to stretch his legs. The thought of another five hours to get back home had already lost its appeal.

Charlie gathered up the empty coke can and various candy wrappers that littered his passenger seat. They may have sustained him during his journey, but he couldn't imagine any dentist approving of his dining habits. He deposited the evidence into a trash can and made his way to the surgery. Inside, the receptionist cheerfully informed him that Mr Broadley was with his last patient of the morning and wouldn't be long. He gratefully accepted the offer of a coffee and for the next five minutes sat in the reception area reading about Patagonian Scallops in a dogeared back copy of National Geographic. Charlie smiled to himself. The only time he ever read that magazine was when he visited the dentist. He wondered if dentists had some financial incentive to carry the magazine as they all appeared to have it. Anyway, five minutes was more than enough to satisfy his curiosity about South American molluscs.

Edward Broadley looked older than his fifty years. Perhaps it was his beard and moustache which although neatly trimmed, had more than a touch of grey about it. He was tall and slim with luscious wavy hair. His wire rimmed spectacles gave him a look of John Lennon.

Having properly introduced himself, Charlie said how grateful he was to be accommodated at such short notice. He thought he would break the ice with some small talk about his own dental habits and his inability to keep up his six-monthly appointments. Broadley made conversation politely, but Charlie could sense his unease. He kept looking at his watch and reminding Charlie that his next appointment would be in at quarter to two and he hadn't yet had his lunch. Time to cut to the chase, thought Charlie, as he started to explain the purpose of his visit.

'I will talk to you,' said Broadley, 'but I won't be giving you a statement. This is strictly off the record. I'm only speaking to you as you said you wanted to talk to me about what happened to Mark. I've waited over thirty years for someone to want to talk about Mark. He seems to have been forgotten in all of this.' Charlie nodded.

'Of course, I understand that. But do you mind if I take some notes?' asked Charlie taking a pad out of his folder. 'No statement, just notes.'

'Fine,' said Broadley, 'just some notes.'

Charlie listened carefully as for the next ten minutes Edward outlined the circumstances of that fateful night.'

'We were all with him. Ewart, Ralph, Vince, Brian and me. All of Mic Sgith was there.' Broadley shook his head ruefully. 'It's pathetic really, but when you're eighteen it seemed important. A band of brothers, all for one, sworn to secrecy.' Broadley scoffed and shook his head again.

'Mark was a brilliant guy. The best Sligachan scholar by a distance in my time at the school. He would have made a great head of school. He wasn't like the others. If it had been down to him there would never have been a Mic Sgith, but that was Ewart's and Ralph's idea. They drove it. Mark just had to go along with it. Same as me I suppose.' Broadley continued as bit by bit he outlined the events of that night.

'Sorry to interrupt but can I just clarify then. Ralph had shot the deer with a crossbow somewhere in the woods on the slopes of the Greenbrier.' Broadley nodded. 'Then Ewart cut off the deer's ear and wiped Mark across both cheeks with it.' Broadley nodded again.

'From the time the deer was killed, Mark had three hours to complete the challenge. Having been blooded he had to run carrying the ear to the cemetery in Fairlea and place it on the Founder's grave.'

'Not the head then, just the ear, is that correct?' Broadley frowned.

'Yeah, just the ear.'

'And the rest of you then followed in vehicles?' asked Charlie.

'That's right. Mark had to run through the woods to the mountain road and then follow it to Fairlea. That's nearly eleven miles. By the time he got to the cemetery it was pouring with rain and getting cold. Mark still had to run the two miles from the cemetery to the bridge. And that's when it happened. I still shudder thinking about it all these years later. It was so unnecessary. It never should have happened.'

'I know this is difficult for you, but can you tell me what happened at the bridge?' asked Charlie. Broadley paused for a moment as if he was gathering his thoughts.

'If he didn't walk across both sides of the bridge, he'd fail the challenge and he would dishonour Mic Sgith and the Founder's memory. That's what Ewart said. I can't believe I'm saying this now; it just seems ridiculous.'

'I understand, and I know this is difficult' said Charlie sympathetically. 'But I need to know how Mark drowned.'

'He didn't want to walk across the bridge. It was nearly pitch black and pouring with rain. The metal girders were slippery. I remember he climbed onto the bridge, but it was obvious he wasn't happy, he was wearing sneakers and he couldn't get a proper grip. It must have been at least twenty feet from the bridge to the river below. The girder he had to walk along couldn't be more than six inches wide. It was incredibly dangerous and incredibly stupid.' added Broadley.

'If it was that dangerous, why did he not just stop?' asked Charlie writing more notes on his pad. Broadley sighed and shrugged his shoulders.

'He didn't want to let us down, or the Founder for that matter. But it was more than that. I saw it with my own eyes, I was there. He wanted to climb down and I'm sure he would have, but Wilder wouldn't let him.'

Charlie looked up, his detective's instincts telling him that he was now getting to the crux of the matter.

'Wilder had picked up a large stick. He started prodding it at Mark's legs and telling him he must keep going. The honour of Mic Sgith depended on it. Several times he jabbed at his legs and then Mark continued to climb. Seconds later I saw him fall. I can't be certain but I'm sure his head hit the girder, there was a dull thud. That was the last time I saw my friend. We searched the river from the bank for over an hour. We even tried to shine the car headlights onto the river, but the angle wasn't right. We headed back to the school but not before Wilder had sworn us to secrecy. We were Mic Sgith, not a word was to be spoken. I was in shock. Honestly, I don't remember much of what happened after that.'

'Presumably you were all interviewed by the police. There must have been an investigation?' remarked Charlie. Broadley sighed and nodded.

'I do remember being spoken to by a police officer the following day. We were all sitting in the headmaster's study. But that was about it. Of course, I didn't say anything. None of us did. But honestly, thinking back, I don't recall being interviewed by the police again.'

'So, nothing came of the police investigation?' asked Charlie.

'Not that I'm aware of. I remember thinking years later that that wasn't so surprising.'

'What makes you say that?'

Broadley gave a wry smile.

'Wilder's father was in the police so it shouldn't be a great surprise. They close ranks, look after their own.' Broadley started to laugh. 'I've seen it in my own profession, they all do it. Doesn't make it right but that's life I'm afraid.' added Broadley glancing at his watch.

'Lieutenant, you're going to have to excuse me, I'll need to grab a quick sandwich, my next patient will be in

236

shortly. But you know, I feel better for talking about it with you. It's been quite cathartic; I must have been needing to get it off my chest.' Charlie smiled and nodded.

'Just a couple of quick questions and I'll be on my way. The test, or challenge I think you called it. Did Wilder just dream that up?'

'Not really,' replied Broadley. 'For decades, next year's head of school had been required to run from the school to the cemetery in honour of the Founder. But in years past they just left a bunch of thistles on the grave. It was Wilder's idea to kill a deer and cut off its ear. Apparently, it was something the Founder had done as a boy.'

'I see,' said Charlie, 'but why the bridge. What was the significance of that?'

'Another of Wilder's ideas,' replied Broadley. 'Greenbrier bridge is made of steel from the Greenbrier Steel Corporation, the Founders company. There's a small plaque on the bridge that tells you that. Wilder was obsessed with honouring his legacy.'

'Huh,' said Charlie closing his notepad. 'I never knew that about the bridge.'

'So, are we done?' asked Broadley getting up from his chair and holding out his hand.

'We are, Mr Broadley,' said Charlie shaking his hand, 'and I'm obliged for your help. What you've told me is starting to now make some sense. But as we agreed, this conversation was off the record, so this will be the end of it. But before I go, can I just say how sorry I am for the loss of your friend, I can see the hurt it has caused you.'

'I appreciate that lieutenant, that's kind of you, and safe journey home. That's a heck of a journey to undertake in a day.'

*

Despite yesterday's long drive Charlie was still in the office for just after six. And just like the previous few days, Sam was already hard at work, ploughing his way through the pile of accounts for the bank enquiry, when he arrived.

Charlie had noticed that the light was on in the chief's office when he was parking his car. He could see Bull, head down, sitting at his desk. He'd thought about knocking his door to enquire if he'd enjoyed his vacation, but then thought better of it. Anyway, he had a lot to do ahead of the morning meeting. He was expecting to be grilled about Charlie Jarret's death, and inevitably, Bull would want an update about the burglaries at the school and the Deans estate. At least today Charlie had an ace up his sleeve. The chief didn't know that they had recovered the stolen cigar box, at least that was going to be something positive to put the chief in a good mood.

'You're in early, I thought you might have given yourself a later start, must have been a long day yesterday. What time did you get home?' asked Mike as he limped in the door.

'It wasn't too bad. I was back in the house by eight. By the look of things that leg of yours still appears to be bothering you?' replied Charlie who was washing the coffee mugs at the sink.

'Yep, it's still pretty sore. You don't heal any quicker when you get older that's for sure. Anyway, more importantly, how did you get on in Harrisburg?'

'Yeah, good thanks, it was well worth the trip. Broadley didn't want anything on the record, but what he told me has helped explain why a deer's head ended up in the Greenbrier river.'

'Interesting,' said Mike filling the kettle.

'I'll tell you more after the morning meeting,' said Charlie, 'but let's just say the Charlie Jarret enquiry has ratcheted up a notch or two. By the way, is there any update regarding the fingerprint from the cigar box? From what Chris said the other day, Zoe was hopeful of getting a positive ident.'

'Spoke to her yesterday and there was nothing then. It was driving her nuts. She's sure she's seen that print recently so was reviewing recent cases.' Charlie sighed and gently shook his head.

'It just seems a really old-fashioned way of doing things. You would think these days we would be able to automatically check prints. Doing it manually is just so cumbersome. Surely it's not beyond the wit of some clever person to come up with something better.' Mike started to laugh.

'I had the very same conversation with Zoe yesterday. But the short answer is we don't yet have an ident but she's working on it.'

*

Charlie glanced up at the clock on the wall. It was now 0915. The meeting had been going for well over an hour and they still had to discuss the Marsco lodge break-in. A week in Cancun may have given the chief a nice tan but it had done nothing to improve his mood. He was just as irascible as ever. Charlie and Angela had fielded endless questions about Charlie Jarret's death. On and on he went, delving deeper and deeper into the minutiae of the enquiry. Charlie was sure that Wilder had only passed round the photographs because he knew that Mrs Dunbar, who had been taking minutes, had a weak stomach. On seeing the state of Jarret's ravaged face, the poor women had to excuse herself and head to the bathroom. She hadn't felt able to return for the next twenty minutes.

Eventually the time came for Charlie to play his trump card. Having gone over the background of the burglary, Charlie explained how Sam had come to discover the box. He then removed several photographs from an envelope and passed them round the room. Dave's team had obliged and provided several excellent photos that showed the cigar box from different angles. They had even provided a photograph of the unusual print found on the brass plate.

The chief's response was not what Charlie was expecting. For a minute or so he didn't say anything. He just glared at the photographs as his face turned the colour of puce. At the other end of the table sat Sergeant Mitchell, completely mute and looking straight ahead as if he was hypnotised. His ruddy complexion replaced by the pallor of a cadaver. Grey with just a tinge of green. Chris, who had been sitting next to him, went and got a glass of water as he thought he was ill.

'What on earth was all that about?' said Angela when they finally got back to the detectives' office.

'Beats me,' said Chris. 'It just seems there is no pleasing some folk. Okay, we still don't have a suspect, put you would have thought he would have at least been pleased that we had recovered some of the stolen property. His mood didn't improve even when you showed him the letter, boss. I give up. I can't begin to fathom the man. I'm sorry, but sometimes he really is a shit.'

'What do you mean sometimes,' said Mike who had been listening in to his colleagues' conversation. Charlie was about to try and bring things to some order when the phone rang.

'Officer Coutts speaking,' said Sam answering the phone. Sam covered the mouthpiece. 'It's for you Chris, It's the lab, they've got some news about your thread.'

'Tell them I'm on my way,' said Chris grabbing his folder, 'I'll be down in a tick.'

'Can I see you in my office for a minute Mike?' said Charlie picking up a pile of papers from a desk.

'Sure,' said Mike. He got up and hobbled across to the door. This sounds ominous he thought, especially if he can't tell me in front of the others.

'Have a seat,' said Charlie closing the door of his office behind him. 'I wanted to speak to you in private. I think I need your advice.' The serious tone of Charlie's voice suggested to Mike that something important was afoot.

'Oh,' replied Mike, 'you've been doing pretty well up to now, so this must be serious.' Charlie nodded.

'I've got a feeling it might be.'

'I take it this is connected to yesterday's visit, otherwise I would have heard of this before now.' Charlie smiled.

'You aren't a detective for nothing! But yes, it's to do with my meeting with Edward Broadley and what he told me.' Charlie stood up and looked out of his window.

'I think I now know why that deer's head ended up in the river.' Mike raised his eyebrows.

'Okay. And do I take it that you've been able to link that to Charlie Jarret's abduction?' asked Mike.

'Yep, I think I can. And the thing is, I'm pretty sure it's also connected to Marsco College.'

'Wow,' said Mike sitting back in his chair. 'Wilder's going to really go off on one now if pupils from the school are involved.'

'It gets worse,' said Charlie. 'Wilder's boy might be one of those involved. And just to top it all off, the chief would appear to have been involved in the death of Mark Tyler, the boy who died in mysterious circumstances in 1960.'

For several moments Mike didn't say anything, so stunned was he by his friend's revelation.

'This is turning into a can of worms,' said Charlie with a weary sigh.

'You're not kidding,' replied Mike who was still trying to get his head round what his friend had just told him.

'Broadley wouldn't speak to me on the record, so I doubt I'll have the evidence to implicate Bull, but the other stuff, the stuff about pupils from Marsco being involved in the death of Charlie Jarret, now that is going to have to be a serious line of enquiry.'

'Yes, of course,' said Mike. 'So how to you want to play this?'

'At the moment it's still circumstantial,' continued Charlie, 'but there are just too many things going on that point to their involvement in Jarret's death. Give me a moment, will you? I scribbled out some notes last night to make sure I've got everything in chronological order,' said Charlie unfolding some paper on his desk.

'Sure, take your time.' said Mike.

'When I was at the school the other day, I spoke to the secretary, Mrs Henderson. As you know, she gave me some information about how the chief and his cohorts came to found Mic Sgith. Talking to Broadley yesterday filled in some more gaps. Were you aware that the chief's son is currently a house captain at Marsco, and that Ralph Portman's boy is head of school?' Mike raised his eyebrows.

'I knew about the chief's boy, but I didn't know about Portman's son. But how does any of that suggest that Wilder's boy was involved in Charlie Jarret's death?'

'It's not just Jason Wilder that's involved. I think that Portman's boy and several others are implicated.' explained Charlie. 'I think all of it connects back to Mic Sgith, the Sons of Skye.'

'Okay,' said Mike nodding, 'what makes you say that?'

'Well, it appears that the group was formed by the chief in 1960 when he was head boy. It was supposed to be in honour of Donald McCaig, the founder of Marsco. According to Broadley, there had been a tradition for years that the next head of school would have to run the eleven miles from Marsco to the cemetery in Fairlea to lay thistles on the Founder's grave. I think it was supposed to be an act of respect.' said Charlie. 'But Broadley told me that when they were in their final year, Wilder wanted to demonstrate that Mic Sgith were special, a band of brothers who were one hundred percent loyal to the school. To prove their worth, he decided to introduce a new challenge, much more demanding than just a simple run.'

'And what was his purpose in changing it?' asked Mike.

'I think he believed it would test a boy's resilience. If the scholars were going to become head of school, then they needed to prove their worthiness. Wilder wanted to ensure that the bloodline remained strong. Well that's what I think he thought. There's some supposition on my part, but I don't think I'm far from the truth.'

'I see, well, I think I see.' said Mike resting his chin on his hands. 'And the designated boy was presumably Mark Tyler.'

'Correct,' replied Charlie. 'He was the Sligachan scholar, chosen because he was the outstanding pupil of his year. Wilder designed a challenge that he thought would test the courage and loyalty of all future scholars.'

'Okay, I think I follow all that,' said Mike. 'But what changed, what did they now have to do?'

'This is where it starts to get a bit bizarre.' replied Charlie. 'It began with the killing of a deer. They cut the animal's ear off and Wilder wiped its blood across Tyler's face. Then like before, he had to run from the college to the cemetery. Only this time it was the deer's ear and not thistles that had to be left on McCaig's grave.'

'Ah, I see. That now ties in with what the caretaker at the cemetery told Chris.'

'Exactly.' replied Charlie. Before he had time to finish his explanation there was a knock on the door.

'Sorry to disturb you, sir,' said Sam poking his head round the door, 'but Mrs Rawlingson is just off the phone. She's asking if Lieutenant Rawlingson might be able to return home as she's been a little sick and has a doctor's appointment to attend. She doesn't want to risk driving and was hoping that you might be able to pop back and take her. She doesn't expect it will take very long.' Mike screwed up his nose.

'Sorry about this.'

'Look, it's not a problem,' said Charlie. 'This will keep. Anyway, I've to call in this afternoon and see the bank manager regarding the compromised accounts enquiry, so don't feel you need to hurry back. We'll continue this conversation in the morning.'

'Appreciate that,' replied Mike gathering up his papers.

'That's why you're working restricted hours and I'm an acting lieutenant.' smiled Charlie. 'It's so we can accommodate circumstances like this. Now you better get going, I'll see you in the morning.'

An hour later Sam found himself alone in the office. The boss had left for his appointment at the bank and Mike had gone home to take Susan to the doctors. Angela had said she was away to get a statement from the guy who had been working the nightshift at Sheetz gas station the day Charlie Jarret went missing. That just left Chris, but Sam had no idea where he was. He hadn't seen him since this morning when he'd rushed down to the lab to get an update about the thread he'd found on Jarret's jacket.

As he hadn't been tasked with anything else, Sam decided to press on with checking the bank accounts. With Mike's assistance, they had already checked more than two thirds of them. If he got a clear run, he reckoned he could finish the remainder by tomorrow at the latest. Cross checking page after page of figures was not everyone's idea of fun, but Sam was in his element, deep in concentration, he was like a dog with a bone. If there were any discrepancies in the numbers, he was determined to find them.

The phone rang several times before Sam zoned out of what he was doing and answered it. Chris was on the other end, excited and looking for the boss.

'He's not here, I'm afraid,' said Sam. 'In fact, I'm the only one here, the others are all out. Can I help?'

'No worries,' replied Chris, 'It will keep till the morning, but I'm at the school and I've just left Mr Buckley. He's told me something very interesting about the button that Screech had in his possession. It looks like the thread I found on Charlie's jacket might be important after all.'

Chapter 20

Wayne Mitchell was a bag of nerves. His attempt to speak to the chief immediately the morning meeting finished had been summarily dismissed. He had wanted to apologise, to explain himself, but Wilder wouldn't listen. He couldn't even bring himself to look at his sergeant.

'I'll speak to you tonight.' he'd spat, the loathing in his voice both palpable and menacing. 'Don't you dare leave the house before I speak to you.' he had hissed before slamming the door of his office.

That had been more than ten hours ago. It was now approaching nine and Mitchell was in danger of cracking up. The phone sat silent on the table. He poured himself another bourbon, his hand shaking so badly that most spilled onto the tablecloth. The bottle, now all but empty, told the story of the turmoil he was feeling. He was gripped by fear.

He picked up the magnifying glass and peered at his thumb. As if it would be different this time! Mitchell scoffed at the irony.

'I've got special fingerprints,' he snorted. 'No loops or whorls for me. No sir, I've got fucking arches and a thumb scar to boot.' Mitchell held his head in his hands. Special fingerprints, I've never been special at anything, he thought taking a slug from his glass.

Always Mr Ordinary that's me. Never made the sports team, always last to be picked.

Mitchell's poor hand to eye co-ordination meant most sports at school and been beyond him. Academically he wasn't stupid, but he wasn't particularly clever either. He was just unremarkable. He had never won a prize in his life. None of that meant he wasn't liked. At school he had had friends. His lack of talent meant he was never a threat. Being friends with Wayne Mitchell wasn't difficult, he would never steal your limelight.

That all changed when he joined the police. Thinking it was smart to tell tales to senior officers, it wasn't long before he alienated most of his peers. Nobody liked a snitch. Not being smart enough to realise his mistake, he continued in the same vein and soon was ostracised by all. He had made his bed and now he had to lie in it. Life as a police officer can be hard and without support from your colleagues it can be intolerable. He had paid a heavy price for his actions, now he was alone, he had no one to turn to.

Mitchell looked up from the table, his icy stare fixed on the wedding photo that stood in a gilt frame on his mantlepiece. A beautiful bride and her groom, full of hope for a lifetime of happiness.

'What are you looking at?' he sneered sticking up the middle finger of his right hand. 'You fucked off too remember. I loved you Mary-Ann. We were a team you and I. Beautiful house, we were planning for a baby for fuck's sake. You even took the fucking dog when you left. And now I'm living in this shithole.'

Mitchell drained his glass. He had been married to his childhood sweetheart for seven years. For the last eight, ever since she left him, he had lived alone above the laundrette in a dingy one-bedroom apartment that smelt of damp.

It was not the bottle that had cost him his marriage. His wife just couldn't reconcile the demands of the job. Missed dinners and cancelled rest days were the norm. For a young wife, eager to enjoy vacations and a normal social life, it was all too much. Strangely, it wasn't his broken marriage that set him apart from his colleagues. That was one of the few things they had in common. Stable marriages were rarer than hens' teeth in the police.

Mitchell picked up his car keys. I could end this now, he thought. Drive into a fucking tree and be done with it. It's not like anybody's going to miss me. It would be over in an instant. If they send me to jail, I'm a dead man anyway. At least this way it would be on my own terms.

Just then the phone burst into life. He wasn't going to answer it but something in his head made him lift the receiver. He braced himself for the tirade of abuse. The voice on the other end was measured and calm. Mitchell was immediately on edge, why was the chief not shouting and cursing at him?

'I don't want your apologies,' said the chief. 'This has gone way beyond that. I need to fix this fuck up you've caused me. But please don't think I'm doing it for you. You've dragged me into this mess through your incompetency. And now I'm going to fix that. It will save my reputation and might keep you out the fucking jail. So, listen carefully.'

Mitchell had no idea what the chief was planning. But his boss was smart, and he'd said he could fix it. Right now, that was Mitchell's only hope of staying out of prison. Perhaps, for once, fortune would smile on him. Could he be given one last chance? That glimmer of hope was enough to banish his suicidal thoughts. The chief had told him to meet him at the old quarry on the Maxwelton road. He had half an hour to get there. Oblivious to the fact that he was still in his uniform, he grabbed the bottle and his jacket and headed for the door.

The old limestone quarry at Maxwelton had long since been abandoned. Now its only visitors were an occasional dog walker, or an intrepid mountain biker prepared to traverse the myriad of undulating paths that surrounded the quarry floor. In the darkness, it was home to bats and other creatures of the night, hidden from sight by the blackness. It was the perfect spot for a secret rendezvous.

Mitchell didn't see the chief's car as he drove into the cavernous car park. He parked up and sat nervously with his engine running wondering what was about to unfold. Over to his left, a set of headlights switched on and he heard a car door shutting. Through the beam of light, he watched as his boss walked slowly towards him. Mitchell switched his engine off and got out of the truck. He felt a knot in his stomach and his mouth felt dry. It wasn't just the effect of the alcohol, the nerves of earlier had returned with a vengeance. He clasped his hands to control the shake, but to no avail. He was a quivering wreck.

'I want to explain. Please sir, I want to tell you what happened,' pleaded Mitchell consciously trying not to slur his words.

'You've been drinking, you're stinking of whisky. I trusted you Mitchell,' said the chief with a look of disgust. 'I gave you a second chance, and this is the thanks I get. Not only did you fuck up but then you went and lied to me. You said you had burnt the box you cretin. I can't believe you fucking lied to me.'

'It wasn't like that,' wailed Mitchell who was now shaking uncontrollably. 'There was nothing I could have done, it was pitch black, I was being chased. I tripped and it fell out.'

Before he could explain further Wilder interrupted, 'I don't give a flying fuck what happened. Bottom line is you lost it and now I have to fix that.'

Mitchell nodded manically as he stood trembling.

'Fix it sir, yes, if anyone can fix it, you can sir.'

'Why are you still in uniform, and why have you got your handgun with you? You're drunk you idiot. And look at you man, you're shaking like a leaf. You're in no fit state to have a side arm. Hand it over to me now you hear me? You can get it back tomorrow when you're sober.' said Wilder.

Mitchell nodded and removed the firearm and handed it to Wilder.

'Right,' said Wilder, 'If we're going to fix this mess, I'm going to need you to calm down. You understand?' Mitchell nodded. 'Okay, now listen to me. I want you to shut your eyes and take some deep breaths. That's it, keep your eyes closed and breathe deeply.'

Chapter 21

The following morning Angela and Chris were in the detectives' office updating the action log for the Charlie Jarret enquiry. At his desk in the corner of the room was Sam, deep in concentration. He had been there since 0530 hrs and now there were less than ten accounts to check. It had been a time-consuming task but thanks to Sam's efforts it was almost complete. Unless something dramatic happened with these last few reports, it didn't look like he was going to turn up anything too remarkable. In fact, out of all the accounts that had been checked, he only wanted to highlight five to Mike and Charlie.

Four of those had withdrawal activity that might need further explanation. But as none were for large amounts, he was fairly confident that they hadn't been compromised, but nevertheless, he wanted a second opinion. The fifth report had stood out because it had several recent transactions that were out with the norm. The confusing aspect was the activity showed money entering the account not leaving it. Over the last six weeks, Sam had noted three sizeable deposits, all made from the same account, that didn't fit the previous transaction profile.

'Looks like you're just about done,' said Chris noticing the dwindling pile on Sam's desk. 'You've done a good job. That's a lot of extra hours you've put in to get that finished.' Sam smiled.

'I've enjoyed doing it. I was hoping it might turn into quite an interesting enquiry, but it doesn't look like it now. I'm pretty sure that whoever accessed the accounts, hasn't been stealing money from them. And I understand that's a good thing. It's just not quite as exciting as I was hoping for.'

'Nature of police work I'm afraid,' added Angela, 'you've got to plough through a lot of mundane stuff before you get any excitement.'

'I'll second that,' said Chis putting on his jacket. 'Can you let Charlie and Mike know that we had to go? We've an appointment to see a Georgina Main in Fairlea. She's the seamstress at Marsco, Donald Buckley gave me her details. I think she might be able to help us with our enquiries about the button.'

'You got a thread to follow up then?' asked Sam in a deadpan voice. Angela burst out laughing.

'Thread to follow up on. That's very funny, I like it.' Sam winked and smiled.

'Yeah, Okay, I get that one.' said Chris who was frequently oblivious to his colleagues' jokes.

'Look, I wanted to update Charlie personally, but God knows how long they are going to be in there. We'll be late if we don't get going now. Do us a favour and let them know where we've gone, will you?'

'No problem,' replied Sam, 'but what about the morning meeting, it's due to start in ten minutes. What will I do if they're not out by then?'

'Give it five and if they've not appeared, go and chap Charlie's door.' replied Angela. 'They've been in there for ages so I take it must be important, but there will be hell to pay if they miss the chief's meeting.'

*

'Anyone know where Sergeant Mitchell is?' asked the chief, impatiently rapping his fingers on the table. 'It's after eight now we need to get started. Sergeant Coutts, any idea where he is?'

'Sorry I don't,' replied Phil. 'I haven't seen him this morning. He usually stops by the front office to pick up correspondence, and to be fair he's not usually late. Perhaps, he has something on and has arranged for someone else to deputise for him.' The chief glared at Phil.

'That's looking unlikely don't you think sergeant as they aren't here either?'

You could almost taste the sarcasm as it dripped from Wilder's tongue. Charlie looked at the ceiling willing his friend to shut up and not say anything else. Although the chief was an ass, you had to have your wits about you whenever you talked to him. He was as sharp as a tack and if you said something stupid, you would know about it soon enough.

'Sorry sir, I was just thinking out loud,' said Phil. 'Do you want me to phone the department and find out what's happened?'

'Too late for that now,' snapped the chief. 'Do it after the meeting and when you get hold of him, tell him I want a written explanation as to why his department was not represented at this morning's meeting.'

'Understood.' said Phil quietly.

The rest of the meeting passed uneventfully. From the detectives' point of view, most of their updates had been given yesterday on Bull's first day back from vacation. But Charlie had still been on his guard. You never knew when the chief might ask you a question. At times it could come straight out of left field, it might not even be connected to your area of responsibility, so you had to be paying attention. It was the reason why Charlie always had another detective with him at the morning meeting. On the rare occasion he missed something, he could usually depend on his colleague to bail him out, particularly if that colleague happened to be Mike Rawlingson. Not much got past his ears or sharp eyes.

When they got back from the meeting, Charlie and Mike had a visitor waiting for them in the corridor. It was Zoe Gibbs from Forensic. She was carrying a manila envelope and had a concerned look on her face.

'Come in Zoe, have a seat,' said Charlie opening his office door. 'What can I do for you? Don't look so worried, I don't bite.'

*

For the last fifteen minutes, Chris and Angela had been trailing up and down various streets trying to find the premises of Georgina's Alterations.

'We're in Fairlea and this is definitely Webster Street.' said Chris peering at an address in his folder. 'It says here it should by 97A.' Angela scanned the street once again looking for a number.

'Well that shop over there says 85 so we can't be far away now.' A moment later Chris's eyes lit up.

'I think this may well be it,' said Chris pointing to a narrow flight of stairs running up the side of a smart wooden panelled building. 'I think 97A might be the office at the top.' Sure enough, etched onto the glass door of a small office at the top of the stairs were the words, Georgina Main, Soft Furnishings, Bespoke Tailoring and Alterations.

A bell rang as the detectives entered the premises and a middle-aged lady with horn rimmed glasses, wearing a blue twinset and matching black skirt appeared from the back shop. Chris introduced themselves and explained the purpose of their visit.

'So, you've met the Dionach?' said the lady with a broad grin. 'He's a bit of an institution at the college alright, but his bark is worse than his bite. Once you learn how to manage him, he's fine. A bit of a pussycat really, but he loves that school and has the boys' best interests at heart. Please have a seat.'

'It sounds like you know him well,' said Angela sitting down at a sewing desk.

'I've done work for the college since 1965, not long after Mr Buckley took over from his father as the Dionach, so I've known him a long time.'

'What exactly is it you do at the college?' asked Chris sitting down on a newly upholstered chair. He yelped in pain. He'd sat down on a cushion covered in pins.

'Whoops, sorry about that, I forgot to say. I'm repairing that chair and as you've discovered it's full of pins.'

'No harm done,' said a relieved Chris checking the back of his trousers.

'You were asking me what I do at the school.'

'I was,' said Chris sitting back down.

'Well my official title is College Seamstress. I suppose my main work is making and repairing soft furnishings. Curtains, cushions that sort of thing. My other area of responsibility is uniform repairs and alterations. You'd be amazed how adept those boys are at tearing their uniforms. But I shouldn't complain, without the college I don't think I would be able to continue my business, there isn't the same demand for bespoke soft furnishings anymore. Folk just go to Macy's for that type of item now. Sorry, but that was a bit of a longwinded explanation. What is it that you think I can help you with?' asked Miss Main.

Chris took the button from his trouser pocket and handed it to her. 'I was hoping you might be able to give us some information about this button. Mr Buckley told us that this was a special button, only worn by the head boy and his house captains.'

Miss Main nodded. 'That's correct officer. They are very expensive buttons. I expect the Dionach explained that they are made of deer antler, imported from the Strathaird estate on the Isle of Skye. They pick them off the slopes of Marsco after the stags have shed them in the spring and send them over here. We don't get them every year, just when we need them. We're down the last couple so I expect the Dionach will ask for more next spring. The expensive bit is getting them hand carved. A guy out in Charmco does it for us. Carves that mountain and thistle onto that tiny surface. Exquisite isn't it?' said Miss Main proudly.

Angela and Chris both nodded.

'Mr Buckley also told us that they are only used for the boys' tartan waistcoats, nothing else, is that right?' asked Angela.

'It certainly is, but that still requires twenty buttons every year for the new head boy and his house captains. Four on each waistcoat. And that doesn't take account of any buttons that may come off and get lost.'

'I see.' said Chris making notes in his pocketbook. 'And does that ever happen?'

'Very occasionally,' said Miss Main, 'though funnily enough I did have to replace two fairly recently.'

Chris looked up. This could be important. He needed to understand why Screech had a Marsco College button in his possession.

'Are you able to tell us when that might have been?'

'I think I should be able to tell you that officer, just give me a minute to find my receipt book. I have to submit an invoice for any work I do for the college, so I should be able to provide you with a date.'

'That would be very useful if you could.' Miss Main disappeared into the back shop to look for her book.

'Fingers crossed,' said Angela. 'With any luck the date will tie in with Charlie's disappearance.' Angela looked across to Chris. 'You didn't mention the thread to her. You weren't forgetting, were you?'

'No,' said Chris frowning, 'I was about to come to that.' Before he had a chance to explain further Miss Main returned with the book.

'Yes, I thought so. I sewed two buttons onto a waistcoat on the 28th September.'

Angela glanced at Chris and raised her eyebrows. The 28th was right around the time Charlie Jarret had gone missing.

Miss Main continued, 'As well as missing two buttons, the waistcoat was quite badly torn. I remember it now. Fortunately, I was able to repair it. That was just as well, as the cost of a new waistcoat, well, I'd blush telling you how much that would cost.'

'Does your book happen to tell you who the waistcoat belonged to?' asked Chris hopefully.

'Afraid not, but the Dionach should be able to tell you that, or maybe Mrs Henderson, the secretary. One of them will certainly know.'

'Quick question then,' said Angela. 'Who pays for the repair?'

'If it's under $40 then normally the college does. If it's more than that then the college bills the parents.'

'And can I ask how much this repair was?' Miss Main looked at her book. '$78 dollars. I know, those buttons are expensive.'

'I also wanted to ask you about this?' said Chris pulling a small plastic bag containing the green thread from his pocket. Miss Main smiled and nodded.

'Oh yes, I recognise that thread alright. It's a very distinctive shade of green don't you think. They call it forest green.'

'Yes, I suppose it is.' replied Chris.

'I only use it for the college waistcoats. Just as well too, like the buttons it's very expensive thread. Made of Egyptian cotton and imported from a Scottish company called J&P. Coats. It's far and away the best colour match for the McCaig tartan.' said Miss Main producing a small reel of the thread from a drawer. 'You won't mistake that colour, it's so vivid, I've never seen a shade of green quite like it. Of course, we could use different thread, and I suppose nobody would notice. Well nobody except me,' said Miss Main with a giggle. 'But the school likes to keep the Scottish connection. It's little things like that that make Marsco such a special school.'

'Any chance I could have some of that thread?' asked Chris.

'Depends how much you want. I've only got this reel and one more I think, so I don't have a great deal to spare.' said a concerned Miss Main. Angela's face broke into a broad grin.

'He only wants a couple of inches so he can get it analysed. He should have said, but don't worry he's not after a whole reel.' The three of them started to laugh.

'Well then, that won't be a problem.' said Miss Main picking up a pair of scissors. 'Just you say when.'

*

'Who else knows about this, Zoe?' asked Charlie switching on the engaged light in his office.

'Other than me, just Dave. I asked him to check it for me. Then I came straight up to see you and Mike.'

'And you're sure there's no mistake?' asked Mike.

'No mistake, it's definitely his. I must have checked it a dozen times before I told Dave and then he spent half an hour looking at it. It had been bugging me for a couple of days. I knew I'd seen that print. As I explained, the arches make it quite distinctive and the scar running through it, that makes it even more unusual.' said Zoe.

'So, when did it finally click, when did you realise it was Sergeant Mitchell's print?' asked Charlie who was now scribbling notes on a pad.

'It was just by chance. First thing this morning I was looking for Neil Planner's prints, for elimination purposes for a break-in he'd attended last week in Alderson, and there it was. I file all our officer prints by department. Makes it easier, especially when doing eliminations. So, Sergeant Mitchell's were sitting in the file alongside Neil's. I knew I'd seen that print recently. When he took up his new job, I moved his prints from his old department into Roads Policing, keeping the prints of officers who work together in one place keeps things simple.'

'I know I don't have to tell you, but I'm going to anyway. You can't speak to anyone about this. Dave already knows so that's fine and I'll speak to him later, but Mike and I are going to have to brief the chief. I can't say if he'll want to speak to you, but I'd say it's likely given the circumstances.' said Charlie.

Zoe clasped her hands and looked at the floor.

'You've nothing to worry about,' said Mike reassuringly, 'you're only doing your job, you've done nothing wrong.'

Phil Coutts was standing in the corridor when Mike opened the door to let Zoe out.

'I saw the engaged light was on, so I didn't want to disturb you, but you're going to want to know this.' said Phil. Mike ushered Phil into the office. He could tell by the tone of Phil's voice that something was up.

'Is there a problem?' asked Charlie looking up from his desk.

'Think there might be.' replied Phil. 'It looks like Wayne Mitchell has gone AWOL. He never arrived at work this morning. When I phoned his office, they thought he was here for the chief's meeting. I've sent uniforms to his flat and he's not there. The pick-up's gone too. They spoke to a neighbour who said they saw him driving off at speed about 2130 hours last night. The neighbour said he clipped the post on the way out and the cops are confirming there's fresh red paint on the gatepost. Mitchell's pick-up is red.'

'Shit,' said Charlie. 'The first thing we need to do is find him, make sure that he's okay. Who've you got looking for him at the moment?'

'Three patrol cars, but I can pull in more.' said Phil.

'Let's speak to the chief first.' said Charlie. 'He needs to know. If we still haven't traced him after we've spoken to the boss, we'll need to up the ante. Get a set of maps and open the incident room. And make sure his licence plate number is circulated to all mobile patrols.'

'Roger that,' said Phil scurrying down the corridor to get things started.

Charlie looked at Mike. 'I know you're thinking the same as me.'

'Possibly.' replied Mike.

'Mitchell's reaction yesterday when I told the chief about the cigar box was really strange. This puts his behaviour in a bit of context doesn't it?' Mike nodded.

'I hope he's not gone and done anything stupid.'

Charlie blew out his cheeks. 'Let's hope not, but I wouldn't put it past him. Look, can you take a seat?" said Charlie sitting down at his desk. 'I think we should take a minute before we head up to see the chief.'

'Agreed.' said Mike sitting down.

'I've been thinking, it wasn't just Mitchell's whose reaction was weird yesterday. The chief didn't seem best pleased either. I know he can be difficult to read sometimes but it did strike me as strange.'

'No, I thought the same.' said Mike. 'So, what are you suggesting?'

'I'm not suggesting anything yet, but it now looks very like Wayne Mitchell has broken into the lodge house and stolen that cigar box. The man's an idiot but why would he do that?' asked Charlie.

'Not a clue,' replied Mike. 'He'd just been made a damn sergeant as well. Makes no sense to me.'

Mike stared at Charlie who was deep in concentration.

'I know that look of yours Charlie Finch,' said Mike biting his fingernail. 'You'd better tell me what's on your mind as I've a feeling I'm not going to like it.' Charlie grimaced and scratched his head.

'Don't tell me that you think that Bull has put Mitchell up to this?' Charlie didn't say anything. 'Oh, my sainted aunt.' said Mike shaking his head.

'Look, I'm not saying he is involved, but with everything else that's been going on you can't say it hasn't crossed your mind.'

Mike rubbed his brow and sighed. 'Okay. It had crossed my mind, but there could be any number of other explanations.' said Mike.

'I'm all ears,' said Charlie, 'fire away.'

'Alright, alright at this precise moment I can't think of an explanation that would explain what's been going on. But equally, that doesn't necessarily mean that the chief's involved. So how to you propose to play this?' asked Mike.

'I'm not going to be cautioning him and interviewing him as a suspect if that's what you were hinting at.'

Mike bit his lip but didn't say anything.

'I'm suggesting that we keep an open mind, but I'm going to give the chief the opportunity to explain what he thinks has happened and why his new sergeant's print is on a stolen cigar box.' continued Charlie.

'Fine by me,' replied Mike, 'I think that's a sensible way to approach it.'

*

'Look guys, I understand why you're asking me that, but the truth is I have no idea what the hell he's been up to. But I'll hold my hands up to one thing, I made a mistake making him a sergeant. I thought it was time to bring him in from the cold, give him a second chance, but it looks like my judgement was wrong on that.' said Wilder frankly.

Charlie and Mike had been sitting in the chief's office for more than half an hour. They had agreed an action plan to try and trace Mitchell. Now every available resource between Lewisburg and White Sulphur Springs was out looking for him. A couple of minutes ago, Charlie had asked the chief why Mitchell would appear to be implicated in the burglary at the lodge house. Mike had known the Chief for more than twenty years. Seldom, if ever, had he seen him so even handed and considered. It left Mike feeling distinctly uncomfortable.

'I've thought of one thing that could possibly explain it.' said the chief getting up from his chair.

'And what might that be, sir?' said Charlie politely.

'It's just occurred to me. Mitchell was in my office the day before the burglary. He was in a good mood as a couple of days previously I'd told him about his promotion. If I recall correctly, I happened to be on the phone to Mrs Wilder. I was ranting on about my meeting with Buckley the previous day and the letter he'd shown me, which as you know was in the cigar box. I'd told Buckley that I would raise the matter at the next board of governors meeting.'

'Can I stop you there, sir. I'm not sure I'm following this. What were you going to raise with the governors?'

'Of course, lieutenant, I should have explained myself better.' said Wilder in an unusually conciliatory tone. 'The letter was to do with Buckley and his right to continue living at the lodge and working at the college. You see the board had previously agreed that he should retire on his next birthday when he was going to be seventy. A not unreasonable position for the board to take I'm sure you'd agree.'

Charlie smiled and nodded gently. This time he didn't say anything. Now was not the time to interrupt the chief. It was a tactic he'd learnt from Mike early in his detective career. Don't fill the dead air. Now was the time to stay silent and let the chief speak. Dead air is difficult and uncomfortable. There is a strange need to break the silence and fill the space. Detectives are taught when not to say anything. Right now, it felt like one of those moments. If he was right, the chief would continue to speak, and he might just tell them something he hadn't intended to.

'Now I'm speculating a bit here, and I know it sounds bizarre, but stay with me for a minute. I'm just wondering, given Mitchell's previous track record of trying to ingratiate himself into the good books of senior officers, that he might have thought he was doing me a favour. He knew I was angry with Buckley as he'd heard me ranting to Bridget about it, so perhaps he thought he'd fix it, make the letter disappear, or something like that. I don't know, none of this is making much sense, as I said I'm just speculating, but crazier things have happened. When we find him, you're just going to have to ask him why he did it. God, what a fool he is.' said Wilder sitting back down in his chair.

'I just hope we get an opportunity to ask him,' said Mike quietly, 'I can't help thinking this might end badly. It's happened before and we all know Mitchell's not the most stable of characters.' The chief and Charlie nodded in agreement.

'Let me know the moment you have any news,' said the chief, 'I'm around for the rest of the day. If there's nothing by three, we'll meet in the incident room and discuss our next steps. We might need to call in the helicopter.'

Charlie and Mike walked back to Charlie's office. Mike filled the kettle to make some coffee.

'Well what do you make of what Bull said?' asked Charlie.

'What? On a scale of one to ten how likely is it that it's bullshit? Very likely I'd say.' replied Mike sarcastically. 'I wasn't convinced by that at all. That was a performance for our benefit. I don't like it when he's calm, I find it unsettling.'

'Couldn't agree more, said Charlie. 'I think it's just as likely he told Mitchell to steal the box. Mitchell's stupid enough to do anything the chief asked him to. But look at me, I'm speculating now?'

'I'll tell you the one thing the chief said that I agreed with, we need to find Mitchell and ask him. He's up to his neck in it anyway, he'll tell us what possessed him to do it.' said Mike.

Before the two friends could continue their conversation there was a knock at the door. Mike got up and opened the door. Standing there holding a file bulging with papers was Sam Coutts.

'Not sure if this is a good time, sir, but I've finished checking the last of the bank accounts and was wondering if I could have a quick word. Most of these have definitely not been compromised, but there are five that I wouldn't mind getting your opinion on.' said Sam holding up the folder.

'Sorry Sam, but we're up to our eyes at the moment so I'm afraid it will have to wait.' replied Charlie shaking his head. 'Look do me a favour, I'm going to need you to stay in the office and man the phones for the Jarret enquiry. Since you'll be here anyway, could you type me up a briefing note outlining the points you want to raise with those accounts.' asked Charlie.

Sam's heart sank. He may be good with figures but the thought of preparing a briefing note for the boss filled him with dread. He was hopeless on paper. Sam tried to force a smile.

'Sure, sir,' he replied meekly. 'Whatever you need.' He was about to leave when Charlie added.

'I know you've worked hard on those accounts. Mike has told me about all the extra hours you've put in and it's much appreciated. If I get a chance, I'll take the accounts home and read your report later. Just leave it on my desk if I'm not here.'

'Thanks, I'll do that,' replied Sam.

'Got a gem there,' said Mike rinsing out his cup. 'Hardworking, keen to learn. The sooner we can get him into the department the better. He'll make a cracking detective.'

'Yep. He's definitely the best prospect I've seen in quite some time.' Charlie clenched his teeth; he'd suddenly remembered something. 'Jeezo Mike, I'm sorry, with everything that's going on, I forgot to ask how Susan was. I take it she's not being sick anymore?'

'It's all good thanks she's fine. The doctor thinks she's just been overdoing it a bit and the sickness, well, we're pretty sure that was the prawns from the previous night's dinner. And look no worries. No need to feel bad about it. You've got plenty on your plate, and for what it's worth, I think you're doing a fine job.'

Charlie smiled and patted his friend on the shoulder. 'I appreciate that thanks. Hearing you say that means a lot.'

'Check us out,' laughed Mike, 'a couple of crusty old detectives being nice to each other, we better be careful, we could ruin the reputation of the department.'

Chapter 22

Neil Planner looked at his watch, it was twenty past two. He had been told by Sergeant Coutts to be back at the office for a briefing update at three, so he just had time to check Sue's diner and the old quarry before heading back to the office.

Apart from an elderly couple and their dog, there was no one in the diner. The waitress hadn't seen anyone fitting Sergeant Mitchell's description and she was sure she hadn't seen a red pick-up in the car park since she'd come on duty at eight.

A further two miles down the road was the Maxwelton quarry. Neil smiled to himself as he turned off the road onto the dirt track that lead to the car park. The last time he was there he had pulled in to find a quiet spot where he could take a pee. He had disturbed an amorous couple hard at it on the backseat of their coupe. They couldn't get dressed quickly enough when they realised, they'd been spotted. The car took off like a scalded cat, wheels spinning and tyres screeching.

The vehicle Neil could see parked in the far corner of the car park would not be leaving in such a hurry this time. Neil's heart pounded against his chest. It was Wayne Mitchell's red pick-up and a body was lying motionless next to the truck. Neil didn't have to check that his boss was dead. A pool of congealed blood, the colour of dark chocolate, had oozed from his temple and had partially solidified at the side of his head. He had suffered a catastrophic head injury. A substantial part of the left side of his head, where the bullet had exited, was missing. A police issue Glock 19 handgun, just like the one that was strapped to Neil's waist, lay a few feet from the bloodied corpse. Neil felt repulsed. He wanted to be sick. He had seen any number of dead bodies during his service, but he had never had to deal with a dead colleague. Blasted through the temple with his own gun. It was like some scene in the movies, it was truly horrific.

*

Back at the police office the chief was about to start the afternoon briefing when a stone-faced Sergeant Coutts appeared at the door.

'If I can have a word, sir?' said Sergeant Coutts leaning round the door.

The chief got up and walked across the room. Charlie looked across to Phil, the briefest of nods an indication that he should follow. Taking his lead from Charlie, Mike got up and joined the others in the corridor.

'Have we found him?' asked the chief. Phil nodded.

'Alive?' asked the chief.

'Very much dead I'm afraid,' replied Phil. 'Neil Planner discovered him lying next to his vehicle in the old quarry at Maxwelton. It appears he's shot himself through the head. Neil's got the car park cordoned off and Sergeant Lang and other uniforms are at the scene. But we need the doc and the detectives up there sharpish. I've left a message for Scenes of Crime. They're finishing at another job and heading straight over. I told them you'd see them up there Charlie.'

'Shit.' said Wilder. 'It seems your instinct was right enough Mike.'

Mike didn't reply.

'I'm obliged to you Phil,' said the chief, 'looks like you've got the initial response well covered. Of course, a consequence of this is we'll now never know his motivation for breaking into the lodge.' continued the chief without the slightest show of emotion.

Callous son of a bitch thought Mike. One of his officers has just blasted himself to death and there's not an ounce of compassion from the man. What an asshole he is.

'Just one more thing, sir' said Phil. 'Neil is reporting that he found an empty bottle of Old Mister in the footwell of the truck. Looks like he's downed it and then committed suicide, poor soul.'

*

Half an hour later Charlie and Mike parked up on the track leading to the quarry car park. A couple of hundred yards further up the path, a young uniformed officer was standing next to some barrier tape that was strung across the car park entrance. The officer politely asked for their details which she recorded in her pocketbook before allowing them entry to the scene. She advised that they should walk along the edge of the grass on the right-hand side, as Sergeant Lang was trying to preserve some tyre tracks that could be seen in the soft mud at the entrance to the car park.

'Hello, sir.' said Sergeant Lang acknowledging the detectives as they approached the truck. Their colleague's body lay face down on the ground about twenty feet away.

'I've not covered his body, sir, as we've got the area sealed off now and he's not going to be seen by any members of the public. I know it looks like suicide, but I didn't want to contaminate any potential scenes of crime.'

'No sergeant you're spot on. We'll need the usual photos taken in situ and an examination of the body and truck, and of course the firearm. And that was a good shout about the tyre marks, you can't be too careful with these things.' replied Charlie as he walked over to join Mike who was standing a few feet away surveying the scene.

'Shot himself while he was still in his uniform, makes you wonder what must go through people's minds to make themselves do something like that.' said Mike looking down at the body of his colleague.

'Guess we'll never know, but he must have been in a really bad place to shoot himself like that.' replied Charlie. 'I know people say it's a coward's way out but I'm not so sure. I think it must take a lot of courage to take your own life. It's a real tragedy though. He wasn't a friend of mine, but it's still a dreadful waste of a life. His family are going to be devasted.' said Charlie solemnly.

As he was looking at the body, a thought suddenly came into his head. The Doc Martins, Mitchell was wearing looked small, certainly no bigger than a size eight. He had never noticed that before. Wayne Mitchell's feet were below average size. Dave and his team will take a print from his shoes, but looking at it now, Charlie was confident that they would find a match for the footprints found at the lodge house.

After several moments of quiet contemplation, Mike left Charlie and wandered back to the entrance of the car park. He crouched down to get a closer look at the tyre tracks that were clearly visible in the soft mud.

'What have you found that's so interesting?' asked Charlie walking over to his friend.

'Take a look at these tyre marks here.' said Mike pointing at the mud. 'You can see that there are three sets of tracks, all of them are quite distinct. And look here, the tread on these two look identical, but I think they've been made by different vehicles as they appear to veer off in different directions just up there.' Charlie crouched down to get a better look.

'This set though are much chunkier, they've been made by a bigger tyre.' added Mike. 'They look to me like they could have been made by Mitchell's truck.' Charlie nodded.

Looking across to the far side of the car park, Charlie could see Neil Planner standing talking to another officer next to his patrol vehicle.

'I would agree with you. It looks to me like those chunky tracks have been made by the pick-up, and as Neil's car is parked over there, it suggests one of these other sets have been made by him.' said Charlie.

'So, who to the other set belong to?' asked Mike.

'Who knows? But it looks like the third vehicle has a similar tread to Neil's patrol car. They certainly look the same. Not sure what any of that proves but we'll get scenes of crime to examine them more closely and see what they can tell us.'

'That looks like it might be the doc now,' said Charlie noticing a middle-aged man getting out of a white coloured saloon that had parked up near to the barrier tape. 'After the doc's had a look can you get him to confirm the death while I go and have a word with

Neil. He must be quite shaken. You don't expect to have to deal with the death of your boss when you rock up to work in the morning.'

*

'They left you all alone again Son?' asked Phil Coutts sticking his head round the door of the detectives' office.

'Someone has to man the fort,' said Sam looking up from his desk. 'And as the junior member of the department it's always likely to be me.'

'You won't learn anything stuck in here manning phones; I'll have a word with Charlie. You need to be out there with them, learning new skills.' said Phil.

'Please don't bother dad. I know you mean well, but it's not like that. They've been great about taking me out on enquiries. I'm only here because I've a briefing note to prepare for Charlie. It's doing my head in to be honest, but it's what I need. If I'm ever going to be a detective, I'm going to need to be at least competent at writing reports.' said Sam with a resigned sigh.

'That's a fair point,' replied Phil. 'I could stay and give you a hand if you want.' Sam shook his head.

'Appreciate the offer dad, but I think I need to learn the hard way. I'm getting there, it's just taking a lot more time than it should.'

'Remember that it doesn't have to be a masterpiece. A briefing note just needs to cover the facts. Keep it brief. Far too many officers like the sound of their own voice. Same when they write a police report. You'd think it was a Hans Christian Andersen story they were writing, they get so carried away. So, brevity is the key.' said Phil heading out the door.

Sam looked down at his report. Brevity wasn't his issue. It was certainly short enough, he just wasn't convinced that he'd covered all the facts, or it was making much sense.

Sam took out a box of milk duds from his pocket and put a handful of the chewy sweets in his mouth as he read through his report. He knew immediately what he'd done. Shit thought Sam putting a finger into his mouth and removing a lump of amalgam the size of a pea. His tongue instinctively probed the ragged edges of the gapping cavity. Breathing in, he winced as the cold air jangled the root of his tooth. Guess that's what I get for eating so many sweets thought Sam.

For someone in his early twenties Sam's teeth were in some state. Almost all his molars had fillings and episodes like this were not uncommon. Five minutes passed and not a word of his report registered, so distracted was he by the discomfort in his mouth. Despite the pain he was in, he couldn't stop putting the tip of his tongue into the hole where the filling had been. The jangly smarting was now giving way to a full-on dull ache.

Sam hated the dentist. He knew fine well that his infrequent visits were a contributing factor to the state of his teeth but somehow, he couldn't help it. If the pain wasn't severe, he always found an excuse not to attend. But this time he knew he'd need to go. This bad boy was going to need attention and quickly.

'You in pain?' asked Chris noticing Sam holding his jaw as he walked into the office.

'Just lost a filling eating some damned milk duds and now it hurts like hell.' said Sam in obvious discomfort.

Chris pursed his lips and nodded.

'Dangerous things milk duds.' said Chris. 'Nearly as bad as salt water taffy, gave that up a long time ago. Couldn't eat the taffy without losing a filling, should come with a health warning. Evil stuff. And milk duds, they're nearly as god damn bad.'

Sam sighed and gently shook his head. 'You're really not helping,' he said stapling the pages of his report together.

'Okay,' said Chris realising that Sam was in no mood for his banter. 'Have you made an appointment for the dentist? If you're in that much pain, you'd better go and see one sharpish.'

'Yeah, I was about to call them when you came in,' replied Sam, 'but before I do, I take it you've heard about Sergeant Mitchell.'

'Hell, yeah that's dreadful news. I just got an update from your dad at the uniform bar. Angela and I were in Fairlea and we must have missed the initial radio message. It was only when we were on our way back and we heard that the doc and scenes of crime were being sent to an incident at the quarry that we put two and two together and realised what had happened.'

'I wondered if you were going to head up, I don't know if they need any more help up there?' said Sam.

Chris shook his head. 'We offered to go, but Charlie told us to stay here. He and Mike are away to Marlinton to tell his poor mother the news. I'm going to head to the hospital to try and see Screech. He's been moved to a rehabilitation facility in Asbury apparently, I want to try and speak to him about the button.' said Chris.

'I thought he wasn't able to speak,' said Sam.

'Last time I saw him he could speak but he couldn't get his words in the right order, so nothing he said was making much sense. I'm hoping things may have improved if he's been moved to a different hospital. Time will tell.'

'Can you make sure you're back here for five?' added Sam 'Charlie wants everyone here for a briefing. Apparently, it's important that we're all here as something big might be going down tomorrow.'

'Sounds interesting,' said Chris. 'I've a feeling I might know what it's about.'

'Oh,' said Sam who hadn't a clue why the briefing had been called.

'It was just something Charlie said when I was talking to him this morning, but I'd better not say, might end up looking foolish if I'm wrong and it wouldn't be the first time that's happened.' said Chris grinning.

Sam wondered if Chris had just said that to tease him. He was desperate to know why the briefing had been called, but on this occasion, he decided not to bite so he kept his mouth shut.

'Look, regardless of what the briefing is about, you'd better make that appointment, you can't operate properly if you're in as much pain as that.'

Sam nodded but before he could reply Angela walked into the office and made a thumbs up sign towards Chris.

'I got to see Zoe and she's going to examine the thread for us. But it's on the understanding that it's not an official report, we'll have to wait for that. She's just doing us a big favour. The good news is she's fairly confident that she should be able to tell if the cotton is the same type of thread that was on Charlie Jarret's jacket and was attached to the button that Screech had on him.'

'That's what I wanted to hear,' said Chris clearly buoyed by the news. 'Did she say when she would be able to do it?'

'She's digging the stuff out now, but don't worry, she's assured me she won't go home before speaking to us. Listen, if you're going to the hospital, I'm going to make a start on dictating the witness statements from the Deans burglary, so I'll be in the report writing room. I told Zoe to phone the general office number, so if she rings come and get me you hear?' said Angela.

'Will do,' replied Sam. Chris looked at his watch. It was already after three.

'I'm having second thoughts about going to the hospital. I'll be pushing it to get to back by five. It can keep for a day or two. Anyway, I don't want to be out when Zoe calls, so change of plan, I'm going to Annie Mack's for a cheeseburger, I'm starving. Do you want anything?'

Angela laughed. 'Not for me, I'm still trying to shift a couple of pounds, so I'll give it a miss thanks.'

'Sam, what about you, do you want anything?' asked Chris putting on his jacket.

'You trying to be funny?' replied Sam still holding his jaw.

'Oops sorry, I forgot about your tooth. Now phone the damned dentist when I'm out, and don't let them fob you off, you're going to need to get that sorted you hear me?'

'I hear you.' said Sam lifting the phone.

Half an hour later Chris was wiping ketchup off his fingers having just polished off two cheeseburgers when Zoe appeared at the door.

'I thought it would be easier to update you in person rather than on the phone.' said Zoe slightly nervously.

'Sure, appreciate that.' said Chris. 'Take a seat will you and I'll get Angela. Sam, do you mind knocking the door and telling Angela that Zoe's here?'

'No need,' said a voice from the door. Angela came in and sat down. 'Good timing it seems, I'd just finished dictating the first couple of statements when I thought I heard Zoe's voice in the corridor.'

'Nothing wrong with your hearing,' said Chris laughing. Zoe smiled politely.

'So, what are you able to tell us?' asked Angela.

'Well, I'm pretty sure the thread sample you gave me is the same type of thread that was on the jacket and the button.' said Zoe.

'You said pretty sure. What does that mean?' snapped Chris butting in. '50% sure, 99% sure?'

'Chris don't be so rude. Will you let the poor girl speak?' said Angela not impressed by her colleague's impatience.

'Apologies,' whispered Chris realising that Angela was right. 'Sorry Zoe, you were saying.'

Zoe looked a little embarrassed. She had only been in the department for just over a year. It was her first job after university and while she understood how important her work was to detectives like Chris, their brusqueness and abrupt manner took a bit of getting used to. She had quickly learned not to take it personally, police work was demanding, they liked to call a spade a spade and there was little room for flannel. They dealt with facts and always needed things done yesterday. Zoe had learnt a lot in her first year. She knew Chris wasn't being deliberately rude, but nevertheless, she was slightly taken aback by his abruptness. She swallowed hard and then continued.

'Without proper analysis I can't guarantee it, but if you're pressing me, I'd say it's almost certainly the same thread.'

Chris broke into a broad smile. 'And that's for both the jacket and the button?'

'That's correct,' replied Zoe, 'they are all the same thread. I'm also almost certain it's Egyptian cotton. I remember getting a lecture at university about cotton. Egyptian cotton is the best quality you can get. It's handpicked so there tends to be less stress on the fibres. They appear straight and intact when you look at them under the microscope. When I compared it with another piece of cotton the difference was stark. It was much more irregular and had many more splices in it. The cotton sample and the stuff from the jacket and button were all top-grade cotton. The colour and structure also looked identical.'

'Fantastic, that's excellent news, you've made my day.' said Chris struggling to hide his delight. 'I think you've just given us the confirmation we're looking for. Charlie and Mike are going be delighted to hear that Zoe. And I appreciate you doing that for us at such short notice.'

Zoe smiled. 'Just glad to be able to help.'

Suddenly, in the space of five minutes, she had gone from zero to hero. That was just the nature of the beast. Police enquiries often depended on the outcome of forensic examinations. Sometimes it exonerated your suspect, at other times it provided the critical piece of evidence that would prove their guilt. For reasons unknown to Zoe, it looked like her examination of the thread was going to be of vital importance to the investigation into the abduction and death of Charlie Jarret, and that made her feel pretty damn good.

*

Charlie and Mike had arrived back at the office at quarter to five. For the last ten minutes Chris and Angela had been giving Charlie an update about their visit to see Georgina Main and Zoe's findings about the thread. As the others waited in the main office for Charlie to appear, Sam found a large manila envelope into which he placed his report. On the front, in large black letters, he wrote FAO Lieutenant Finch.

'Sorry to have kept you,' said Charlie putting a file of papers down on a desk. 'But the last ten minutes have just confirmed we're now in a position to identify potential suspects in the Charlie Jarret enquiry.'

Sam felt a tingle of excitement as he listened to Charlie. For the first time in his short police career he felt he was part of something significant. Reporting traffic violations and petty thefts might be his usual bread and butter, but this felt in a different league altogether. This was why he wanted to be a police officer.

'However, before I get on to that, I want us all to take a few minutes to reflect on what has been a difficult day. As you know we lost a colleague today, in the most tragic of circumstances. Two hours ago, I was sitting with a mother who was breaking her heart having just learned that she'd lost her only son. You don't need me to tell you that this is a job like no other. It takes you to places that other folk don't see. It can be dark and unforgiving. I don't want to speculate about the circumstances surrounding Sergeant Mitchell's death, but I do want you to take a moment to remember your colleague and his family and friends. But I suppose most of all I want to say that we have a responsibility to look out for each other, through the good times and the bad. As I think today has proved, it can be a short journey to loneliness and despair. This job is hard enough as it is, so don't forget to look out for each other. It might be just a supportive word or a kindly gesture, but today has reminded me how important these things are. So, let's try to always stand together, have each other's back. I couldn't do this job without all of you, and after today, I just wanted you all to know that.'

For several minutes nobody said anything as each present were lost in their own thoughts. The room fell silent apart from the gentle tick of the office clock. Today had been a sobering reminder of just how fragile life could be. Nobody in that room would have counted Wayne Mitchell as a friend, but the loss of a colleague was still profound and upsetting. Charlie's words seemed so apt. A stark and timely reminder of how precarious life can be.

It was difficult interrupting the silence, it appeared insensitive, even a little rude, but Charlie knew that things must move on. Police investigations, like life generally, don't stand still and there was important work to be done.

'Before I go any further, I want to stress the importance of confidentiality in this enquiry. What gets said in this room will stay in this room. This is a sensitive investigation, and no-one is going to speak to anyone who is not present just now about it. If I hear that that confidence has been broken, I will find out who did it and I'll guarantee you'll not be working in this department any longer. I'm sorry to start with what you might interrupt as a threat. It's certainly not meant to be, but it's important that I make that clear from the start.' said Charlie.

Only Phil was brave enough to put up his hand and ask the question that everyone was thinking.

'Does that include the chief?' asked Phil who was leaning against the wall at the back of the office.

'That's correct it does,' replied Charlie firmly. 'Most of you know that the chief is a former pupil of Marsco College and is currently head of the board of governors. This enquiry now centres on the school and more particularly some of its senior pupils. After the morning meeting tomorrow, Chris and I will be attending the school, initially to put some questions to Mr Buckley, the school's guardian. If that interview goes as I expect it to, we may well be bringing pupils back to the office for interview.'

Sam's heart sank, his dental appointment was arranged for ten-thirty tomorrow morning. Right when Charlie and Chris would be at the school. He couldn't even cancel as he'd already let Mike know and Chris had unhelpfully chipped in to say how much pain he was in. Mike was now insisting that he got it seen to so there was no backing out. That sucks, thought Sam, just when we get to the interesting bit, I've got a damned dental appointment. How pathetic is that?

'Phil, as you are custody officer tomorrow, I'll need you to set up the interview rooms as required.' said Charlie. Phil nodded. 'I also want a police van on standby in case we need to bring additional suspects in. I'm anticipating up to six, but it might be less. I want the van positioned in the layby off the Greenbrier road, it's only a quarter of a mile to the school from there and we'll call them in as required.'

Phil nodded again. 'Sergeant Robertson is early shift tomorrow; I'll organise that with him.'

'Fine,' said Charlie, 'and remember, he doesn't need to know any specifics, just tell him he's assisting us and needs to be in position by ten.'

'Understood,' replied Phil.

'Can all the detectives stay behind please, and we'll go over the interview plan?' asked Charlie. The detectives nodded as the others left the room. Charlie looked across to Sam who now wasn't sure if he should leave or stay. He wasn't a proper detective, but as he was on secondment to the department, he was in a quandary. His dilemma was resolved by Charlie.

'You can stay as well. Chris told me about your tooth problem, but when you get clear of the dentist tomorrow, radio in and you can rendezvous with us. You won't miss out; I'll make sure of that.'

Sam's face lit up into a broad smile. Instantly, he realised how inappropriate that might appear, so he checked himself and tried to look serious. This was still a sombre moment. Sergeant Mitchell had been his line manager so now was perhaps not the best time to be so obviously pleased. Yet somehow, he was struggling to find the right emotion. He knew he should feel some sadness, but he didn't. He was completely ambivalent and that concerned him. His father had told him the job could make you hard hearted and cynical, but that was only supposed to happen after many years in the job. Sam only had seven months service. If this was how he felt now, he couldn't begin to imagine what he'd be like when he got to his father's age. That thought didn't sit well with him.

At the other end of the office, Charlie was deep in conversation with Chris as the other detectives started to drift away. Sam stood respectfully a few feet away waiting for an opportunity to speak to his boss.

'Is that your report?' asked Charlie noticing that Sam was standing holding an envelope. Sam nodded and handed Charlie the envelope.

'I hope it's okay,' said Sam almost apologetically, 'I've not had to write a briefing note before, so I'm not sure if I've covered everything you need.'

Charlie smiled. 'I'm sure it will be fine. I'll take it home with me and hopefully get the chance to read it tonight. Now time you were off, it's been a long day and tomorrow promises to be just as busy.'

As Sam turned to leave the phone on his desk rang. Sam picked up the phone.

'Yes sir, he's here, I'll just get him for you.'

'Is that the chief?' asked Charlie. Sam nodded and handed Charlie the phone. Charlie put down the envelope and sat on the edge of a desk.

'Yes sir, Mike and I went to see her. She was devastated as you would expect. We arranged for a neighbour to sit with her and her daughter was going to be coming up from Tennessee tonight. A family liaison officer will make contact first thing tomorrow and pick things up from there.' said Charlie. 'No, nothing untoward, sir. Unsurprisingly we haven't traced any witnesses. Dave says he will have the photographs and his report ready by end of play tomorrow at the latest. He's going to expedite things since he was one of our own. Yes sir, I'll do that, if anything comes up, I'll let you know right away.'

*

Susan Rawlingson was making risotto in the kitchen when Mike arrived home. A glass of Glenlivet sat on the work surface awaiting his arrival. Susan hugged her husband and lovingly kissed his cheek as he walked in.

'Tough, tough day darling,' said Susan handing Mike his whisky. 'When you phoned me earlier, I couldn't believe it, it's just shocking, the poor man, what a state he must have been in to do something like that.'

'What a waste of a life,' replied Mike taking a sip of his whisky. 'But can we talk about something else, today has been depressing enough.'

'Sure,' said Susan realising that her husband was not in the mood for talking about it. After more than twenty years of marriage she had learned to read the signals. Now was a time to change the subject and talk about something positive and she knew just the thing that would do that.

'Came in this morning's post,' said Susan handing Mike a letter. 'It looks official and it's got a Chicago frank on it. I think it's the one you've been waiting for.'

Mike sat on a stool and opened the letter which he read without saying anything.

'Well!' said Susan, 'are you going to tell me what it says?'

'Sorry, yes of course. I was just making sure I'd read it properly.' The beaming smile on Mike's face suggested it was good news.

'It says that Bob Thomson will be retiring at the beginning of May, and they're inviting me to apply for the Captain's vacancy that will arise when he goes.'

'That's great news darling, they've followed up their telephone enquiry with a formal letter, they must be serious. Looks like they really want you to apply.'

Mike nodded. 'It does look that way, but more importantly, what do you think?'

Susan leant forward and hugged her husband.

'We've already discussed this. I'm more than happy to move to Chicago. This cancer treatment has made me realise that opportunities need to be grabbed. Life's too short to waste them. I can tell you one thing though; I won't be looking for another teaching post. Well not one in a school. Although the thought of teaching guitar and the piano privately has a great deal of appeal. I could choose my hours to suit myself and there will be no shortage of pupils in a city like Chicago.'

'And what about Keegan? He's got two more years at high school, it's not ideal timing from his point of view.' said Mike.

'He's fine about it, really he is.' said Susan reassuringly. 'As you said yourself, he can go to your old school, and being near your parents would be great, he doesn't get to spend enough time with them.'

Mike started to smile. He had always yearned for a move back to his home town. He had loved living in Fairlea, but from a professional point of view, his police career was going nowhere. After more than eight years as a lieutenant it was time for a new challenge. Anyway, the department was in safe hands. Charlie had proved he was more than capable to take on the role. He would be a shoo-in to be made permanent if Mike was to move, and others, like Angela and Chris might get their turn at a well-deserved promotion. Mike could see many benefits if he decided it was time to move on.

'I know you're right about Keegan, but I'll need to sit down with him and discuss it seriously.'

'He does have one non-negotiable condition about any move though,' said Susan giggling.

287

Mike looked confused. 'Oh, and what might that be?'

'Two season tickets for Wrigley Field. Seems like you two are going to be watching a lot of baseball.' Mike gave a rueful smile and shook his head.

'Not sure how long he'll want to keep those tickets up. Not after the way the Cubs finished last season. They really are terrible just now.'

Chapter 23

Tuesday 10th November

'Well there's a shock,' shouted Mike as he parked his car in the office car park. 'I nearly beat you in this morning.' Sam laughed and looked at his watch.

'Just checking I've not slept in, but it appears that I'm at my usual time and you're early,' replied Sam with a mischievous wink. It was twenty minutes before seven and the darkness was just giving way to a beautiful late fall sunrise.

'Looks like it's going to be another lovely day,' said Mike as the two officers made their way across the car park. As usual, the chief's car was already parked in its spot next to the car wash.

'I'll say one thing for our leader,' said Mike, 'he's always in early and doesn't half put the hours in.'

Sam didn't reply but stopped abruptly as they passed the chief's vehicle. Something had caught his eye. Sam crouched down by the front nearside tyre and ran his hand over the thread.

'Look at the size of that nail in his tyre.' remarked Sam.

Mike came across and bent down to take a closer look.

'Yep, that's a belter. Judging by the size of the head I'd say that was a masonry nail. But it appears he may have been lucky. The tyre doesn't look flat in any way and as the nail's in the centre, it should be able to be repaired.'

'I expect he isn't aware it's there,' said Sam standing up.

'I don't suppose he does. So why don't you call by his office and tell him. He'll want to get it repaired as soon as he can.' Sam looked aghast.

'What me tell him?' he spluttered tapping at his chest.

'Yes, you. He's not an ogre and won't bite. Anyway, you're doing him a favour, he'll thank you for it.' Sam still didn't look convinced.

'Don't be such a pussy, I've got the overnight report to prepare for the morning meeting, that's why I'm in sharp. Charlie's got enough on his plate, so I thought I'd do the report. One less thing for him to worry about. So, I'm going to the office and will stick the kettle on, and you're going to tell the chief he's got a frigging great nail in his tyre. Agreed.' said Mike.

Sam smiled and nodded. 'Agreed.' he replied.

By the time Sam came into the office Mike had made the coffee.

'Well, did it come as a surprise to him?' asked Mike.

'Yeah, it sure did, but you were right, he was pleased to find out. He said he'd get it fixed on his way home tonight.' replied Sam hanging up his jacket.

'Told you so,' said Mike putting down Sam's coffee. As he put down the mug, he noticed the large manila envelope with Charlie's name on it lying on the desk next to Sam's. Discreetly Mike lifted the envelope and put it between the pages of his newspaper. He didn't want Sam to know that Charlie had forgotten to take his report home.

By eight o'clock the others had arrived in the office and Mike had nearly finished the overnight report. A couple of thefts, a break-in to a beer truck and an assault outside a bar in Renick and that was about it. Just as well thought Mike, if anything major had come in it would have dragged resources away from the focus of the day, the Marsco College enquiry.

Charlie was in his office reading witness statements when Mike brought him in a coffee and the overnight report.

'That's another one I owe you,' said Charlie taking the report. Mike nodded and smiled.

'Quiet day fortunately, it won't take you ten minutes to get your head around that, not much in there as you'll see.'

As Charlie took a sip of his coffee Mike produced Sam's report from inside his newspaper.

'You forgot this last night. I found it on a desk next door when I came in this morning.'

'Shit,' said Charlie shaking his head, 'does Sam know?'

'Nope.' replied Mike. 'I sent him up to see the chief when we got in. He noticed a large nail in Bull's front tyre when we passed his car this morning and as I didn't think the chief was aware, I told him to go up and tell him. He was as nervous as a kitten, but he did go. Anyway, as I said, he's none the wiser that you haven't read his report.'

'Well that's something I suppose. I must have put it down when I was speaking to the chief last night and just forgot about it. I never even realised when I got home last night.'

'Don't worry about it,' said Mike. 'You've got a lot on and its not the highest thing on your list of priorities right now.'

'That might be true, but I still shouldn't have forgotten about it.' replied Charlie.

'Look, why don't you leave it with me? I did some of the leg work on the enquiry and I'm pretty much up to speed with it. I'll give it a read and brief you later. You get on with what needs to be done for this morning. How does that sound?'

'Sounds great to be honest,' said a relieved Charlie, 'If I owed you before you can double that now, I appreciate it, thanks.' Mike gave a rueful smile.

'I've been that soldier remember. You can buy me a beer at Bursley's, and we'll call it quits. Seems like it's been a while since we were able to go for a beer.'

'That's for sure, and yeah, you've got a deal.'

'And look on the bright side,' said Mike, 'the chief should be in a good mood, young Sam might have saved him a lot of grief, that tyre could have given up at any time.' laughed Mike.

*

'I thought you were heading to the hospital to see Screech first thing,' said Angela noticing Chris was still at his desk.

'Change of plan. Charlie wants to be at the school by 0915 and as he's not yet out of the chief's meeting, he was right, there isn't time to go this morning.' said Chris. 'Anyway, I'm just off the phone to the hospital and I think it would have been a waste of time. The doc I spoke to said physically he's doing well, but his speech hasn't got any better. He's still not making any sense and jumbling up all his words. He didn't say so directly, but he didn't sound hopeful that things were going to improve. I reckon the poor sod has brain damage, that family has had its share of tragedy recently.'

'That's for sure,' said Angela lifting the lid of the photocopier.

'Someone left something on the copier?' asked Angela holding up a sheet of paper.

Chris raised his eyebrows and nodded.

'Yep, that would be me,' he said, gratefully taking the paper from Angela. 'Glad you found it, that could have been embarrassing. It's the letter from the cigar box, I was photocopying it to give a copy to Buckley when we see him later. He's been bending my ear about getting the letter and box back.'

'I hope you told me him he couldn't get it.' said Angela indignantly. 'The report hasn't been submitted to the DA's office yet.'

'Yeah, I told him Okay. I'm not that stupid,' said Chris annoyed at Angela's tone. 'But I did tell him he could get a photocopy, it's to do with his tenancy, so it's important he gets a copy.'

'Fine,' said Angela sensing Chris's annoyance. 'I wasn't having a go at you.'

Chris shrugged his shoulders. 'I know that, but before you ask, it's been checked for prints. The only ones they found belonged to Buckley.'

'Doesn't look like it'll matter now. With the print on the box and Mitchell's shoe prints on the carpet and in the rose bed we've got all the evidence we're likely to need. The only thing that doesn't stack up is that damned fish. It's really bugging me, I can't work out why it was there. According to Hugh Robertson, Mitchell didn't know one end of a fish from the other, it's just weird.' said Angela.

'You about ready to head?' asked Charlie sticking his head round the door.

'Sure boss, I'm good to go,' replied Chris stuffing some statement paper into his folder. 'Good. I just want to grab a quick word with Mike, so I'll see you at the car in five.'

Chris raised his thumb and went to look for the car keys.

*

'Either will do lieutenant,' said the Dionach who was sitting behind an impressive mahogany desk in his office. 'I'll answer to Mr Buckley or Dionach, just don't call me a caretaker, or we will fall out pretty damn quick.'

Charlie laughed. 'Yes, your secretary warned us not to use the 'C' word and given that you're considerably bigger than me I'll call you Mr Buckley.'

'That will be just dandy then. Now about that letter.' said Buckley rising from his chair.

Chris took the photocopy from his folder and handed it to Buckley.

'As I explained on the phone, you can't get the original or the cigar box back until the DA's office says so and that could be some time yet.'

'Yes, yes I understand that,' said Buckley who was grinning like a Cheshire cat as he read through the letter. 'This will do nicely officer, it's all I'm going to need. I'm grateful to you.' Buckley folded the letter and put it in his jacket pocket.

'Apologies, but I wanted to get the matter of the letter out of the way. Now you were asking about a torn waistcoat that Miss Main in Fairlea repaired.

294

I remember it wasn't that long ago but if you give me a minute, I'll look up my file, it will have all the necessary details.' added Buckley. Chris gave Charlie a knowing look, this sounded very promising.

'Yes, just as I thought, it wasn't long ago. Two buttons replaced and a tear repaired on September 28th. All for a cost of $78.' announced the Dionach.

'Does your note tell you who the waistcoat belonged to?' asked Chris taking down some notes. The Dionach smiled.

'It certainly does, the waistcoat belonged to Jason Wilder, your chief's son. And I can tell you, your boss wasn't best pleased to be billed for the repair.'

'Can you photocopy that receipt for us?' asked Charlie, 'we're going to need a copy for our enquiry.'

'Not a problem lieutenant, there's a photocopier in the secretary's office, but is there a problem I need to know about?'

Charlie looked the Dionach square in the eye.

'Mr Buckley, I'm sure you'll appreciate I can't say a great deal as this is an ongoing enquiry. But do you remember a couple of months ago you found a deer's ear on the Founder's grave?' The Dionach frowned and nodded.

'I wouldn't forget that. Dreadful business desecrating the Founder's grave like that. But how do you know about it?' asked the Dionach.

'I'll hopefully be able to explain all of that later, but for now I'm asking for your assistance.'

'That's a given lieutenant,' said Buckley who was now confused. What did finding the deer's ear have to do with the break-in to the lodge? As far as he knew a suspect had been identified for that and as nothing else had happened at the college that he was aware of, he couldn't think what their enquiry could be about.

'Can we begin then by identifying the whereabouts of your head of school and his four house captains? I'm going to need to interview them in connection to a serious criminal investigation. But before we go any further, can I ask that you make the headmaster aware of our presence, I'd like to brief him in person.' said Charlie.

The Dionach sat down in his chair. He was shell shocked. This had come completely out of the blue. What the hell was going on?

'I've no idea what this might be about lieutenant, but as I said, you can be assured of my assistance.' said the Dionach still recoiling from the shock that pupils from the school might be involved in something criminal.

'However, I'm afraid your timing's not great. The headmaster is away to Franklin with the lacrosse team for the inter state finals. In fact, none of the boys you want to interview are here. Ryan Portman, our head boy, and Jason Wilder play for the team and the other three have gone as supporters, they're away overnight and not due back till tomorrow evening. I'm sorry about that.'

Charlie looked at the ceiling and rolled his eyes. He hadn't reckoned on this happening.

'Boss, it's not a problem, I'll radio in and get them to stand down the van and the interview team,' said Chris realising their plan would have to be changed. 'No harm done; we'll organise it for another day.'

Charlie nodded. He was annoyed with himself. He was usually meticulous in his planning, but this was an oversight and it was entirely his fault.

'Thanks Chris if you would. Oh, and get them to thank Sergeant Robertson and his team for their help, I'll speak to him in person later.'

'On it now,' said Chris stepping into the hallway.

'Listen, I've just had a thought,' said Charlie scratching the back of his head. 'Who's the Sligachan scholar in the year below, the boy who'll be head boy next year?'

'That would be Nathan Young, good lad is Nathan. I'm hoping he'll be a great head of school. He's a smart boy, he's got his head screwed on the right way. He'll be a damn sight better than the present incumbent, that's for sure.' said the Dionach.

'And why's that?' asked Charlie.

'He's got a real smack for himself has Ryan Portman. To be fair it's not just him, Wilder and the others are just the same. They think they rule the school. Nathan Young will be a breath of fresh air, he's not like that at all.'

'Is Nathan in school today, or does he play for the lacrosse team as well?' asked Charlie. The Dionach started to laugh.

'Your luck might have just changed lieutenant. He was supposed to be away with the team. Fine player Nathan, but he injured his leg a couple of weeks ago so wasn't fit to play. And unlike the others who will do anything to be out of school, Nathan thought it better if he continued his studies, he's got important exams coming up. As I told you, Nathan's not like the others.'

Sounds like a bit of a geek if you ask me, thought Chris, who had come back into the room. I would have gone on the trip like a shot if it had been me. He gave an ironic sigh. On reflection, that was perhaps one reason why his own academic career had not been stellar.

'If you could organise it, I'd like to speak to Nathan, while we're here. You said the headmaster was away with the team, I take it somebody will deputise in his absence?' asked Charlie.

'That's correct, our depute head Mr Leishman, is in charge, and Nathan's house master, Mr Innes, is also around.' replied the Dionach.

'I'll need one of them to be present when I speak to Nathan,' said Charlie, 'but before we get to that I'd like to see in their accommodation if that's alright with you.'

'Well that won't be a problem,' replied the Dionach, 'Apart from Nathan, the others all stay in the old boat-house by the lake. Our head of governors, your chief, decided it would be a good idea if the house captains and head of school had their own accommodation. Ridiculous if you ask me. We managed perfectly well in dormitories for seventy-four years. But oh no, that wasn't good enough for this lot. And I'll tell you another thing, it's pandering to things like that that makes them so arrogant. They think they rule the roost here.'

'I can see you don't approve,' said Charlie.

'That's an understatement,' continued the Dionach. 'The previous head of governors would never have entertained it, but nothing seems too much trouble for Wilder's son and his pals. Just wait till you see the house. They spent a fortune converting it, I've stayed in worse hotels.'

As the three men walked down to the boathouse, Charlie took the opportunity to ask if any of the boys drove a pick-up. The Dionach nodded.

'Ryan Portman drives a dark blue Ford pick-up. The vehicle belongs to his father, but Ryan has just about full access to it. If it's here it'll be parked on the other side of the house. That's where he usually leaves it.'

There was no trace of the pick-up when they arrived at the boathouse.

'If it's not here it'll be up at Huntersville, his father runs Deans haulage and lives on the estate. Ralph hasn't driven to Franklin, they went on a coach, so I'm guessing the truck is at his father's place.'

'Not a problem, we can check that later,' said Charlie as the Dionach opened the door of the boathouse.

'I see what you mean,' said Chris as the three men stepped into the airy hallway. 'It's been beautifully done, and you can still smell fresh paint.'

'They only finished decorating the last bedroom the other day. The contractors must have been and removed the last of their stuff. Yesterday there were still tools and rolls of wallpaper and paint tins on the veranda, but it's all gone now.' said the Dionach.

Standing in the hallway, Charlie's attention was immediately drawn to a small wooden plaque that was hanging on the wall.

'I've seen that design all over the school,' said Charlie looking at the intricate carving of a mountain and a thistle.

'The mountain is Marsco, which is on the island of Skye where our Founder was originally from. And, of course, the thistle is just further recognition of his Scottish heritage.' replied the Dionach.

'And what's the significance of the words Mic Sgith 1992, which are written round the edge of the plaque?'

The Dionach puffed out his cheeks and gave a weary sigh.

'Bit of a long story I'm afraid,'. Before the Dionach could explain further, Chris called through from the kitchen.

'Boss, come and have a look at this.'

In the kitchen, Charlie found Chris examining a framed photograph that was hanging above the kitchen table. The photo depicted five young men sitting on a large sofa with their feet resting on a coffee table. They had their arms wrapped round each other's shoulders and they were all laughing.

'Well, that's clearly Jason Wilder,' said Charlie pointing to the youth on the left of the photograph. 'Same haircut as his father, they look very alike.'

As the Dionach explained who the other boys were Charlie was aware that Chris was itching to say something.

'Okay what is it? I can see you're dying to say something.'

Chris's face broke into a wide smile.

'Check out the sole of his boot,' he said pointing at Jason Wilder. Charlie stepped closer to the photograph and peered at the picture.

'Well I'll be damned, it looks like his right heel is missing an insert,' said Charlie stroking his chin.

'Yep, that's what I thought,' replied an excited Chris. 'I'm sure Dave and his team could blow that photo up a bit and tell us for sure.' Charlie nodded in agreement.

'But it gets even better,' said Chris reaching under the table. 'Look what I found in the bin.' Chris held up an empty bottle of chocolate milk. 'Same brand as Angela found at the side of the mountain road.' continued Chris.

'That'll belong to Ryan Portman,' said the Dionach. 'He's addicted to the stuff, doesn't seem to drink anything else. There will be more in the fridge you can be sure of that. Horrible stuff, it can't be good for you, but as I said he's an addict.'

Charlie opened the door to the fridge. Sure enough, on the bottom shelf were three more bottles of chocolate milk. Charlie felt a warm glow, he knew this was potentially very significant. He was beginning to understand the sequence of events that led to the death of Charlie Jarret.

'I brought some production bags just in case,' said Chris placing the empty bottle into a plastic bag that he'd taken from his pocket.

Charlie nodded. 'And if you don't mind, we'll be taking the photograph as well.' said Charlie removing the photograph from the wall. The Dionach shrugged his shoulders.

'Fine by me. Now, do you want to head over and speak to Mr Leishman while I go and find out where Nathan is.'

'That sounds like a very good idea.' replied Charlie.

'Just one more thing before we go,' said Charlie who was now opening various cupboards in the kitchen and the hall. 'Do the boys have a toolbox? A hammer, saw, that type of thing.'

'Not that I'm aware of. I keep a box of tools, so if they needed something, they would come and ask me. But they never have, and I can't think of a reason why they would ever need to. Why do you ask, is it important?'

'No, I don't suppose it is,' said Charlie as the Dionach closed the boathouse door behind them.

*

'I take it everyone is aware that the interviews won't be happening today?' asked Phil who had just come up from the front office. Angela looked up and nodded.

'Yeah, we've just heard. Mike took a call from Charlie, they're going to be at the school a while yet, they're about to interview a boy, but from what Mike said it doesn't sound like he's going to be a suspect.'

'Fine, as long as you know.' said Phil looking round the office. 'I take it Sam's already left for the dentist?'

'Left about five minutes ago,' replied Angela, 'he's the only one who's pleased the interviews are off, means he's not missing anything.'

Phil smiled and laughed. 'That's my boy, you certainly can't fault his keenness. Just between you and me, I know he's loving his secondment.'

'I should damn well hope so, he's working with great people,' said Angela chuckling. 'But seriously though, he's doing well. Great attitude and not afraid of hard work, he'll make a cracking detective one day.'

'Making coffee, does anyone want one?' asked Mike who was filling the kettle.

'Not for me thanks,' said Phil, 'I'd better get back downstairs.'

'Me neither, I'm not long after one.' replied Angela.

'Fine then,' said Mike, 'if anyone needs me, I'll be in Charlie's office, I've got a report to read.'

'Roger that,' said Angela, 'but before you go, any idea where Grassy Meadow fishery is?'

'Why do you want to know?' asked Mike who was curious as to what Angela was up to. Angela looked up and grinned.

'It's been bugging me for days, so I thought I'd compile a list of local fisheries and try and establish where that damned trout from the lodge enquiry came from. I've got a load of information about the type of food that was in its stomach, so as I now have a free day, I thought I'd see what I could turn up.'

Mike looked a little sceptical.

'Fair enough, but I'm not sure what it'll achieve, the evidence is pretty overwhelming, and I don't want to think you're out there chasing red herrings!' said Mike with a wink.

'Ha-ha. That's about the third time that joke's been made since this enquiry started. Anyway, back to my original question. Do you know where Grassy Meadow Trout Fishery is?'

'Funnily enough I do,' said Mike putting a spoonful of coffee in his cup.

Chapter 24

Sam was dreading his appointment. He had been popping painkillers like there was no tomorrow since losing his filling, but his tooth still hurt like hell. As he was driving, he tried to recall why his dentist was in Huntersville. It wasn't exactly local, but he'd been going there since he was a young boy. He knew Mrs Watt, his dentist, had been a school friend of his mother's, but it still seemed stupid to be driving nearly twenty miles for an appointment. To make matters worse he still had the lovely Alexa to contend with. Alexa Hiscock had been the receptionist at the practice ever since he could remember. She was prissy and aloof and always voiced her opinion about his infrequent attendance.

Sam laughed to himself, for a dental receptionist, Alexa had just about the worst set of teeth you could imagine. They looked like a witch doctor's necklace. Despite all of that, she still saw fit to comment on the state of Sam's teeth. To add insult to injury this visit would cost him at least thirty dollars. This was not shaping up to be a good day.

A couple of hundred metres ahead of him, Sam noticed the distinctive red and white livery of a Deans haulage truck parked in a lay by on his side of the road. As he got nearer, he recognised the truck and the driver. It was the truck he'd first seen in Boonville when he was driving to his friend's wedding. The same truck that burst two tyres after an accident with a deer a few weeks ago. The one with the dodgy logbook with the figures that didn't stack up. The driver, still wearing his signature Orioles baseball cap, was speaking to a man who was standing next to a dark blue Ford pick-up.

A dark coloured pick-up, thought Sam, immediately remembering that Mike and the others had frequently mentioned a dark pick-up when discussing Charlie Jarret's abduction. Sam also knew that so far, they hadn't been able to trace the vehicle. Whether it was that, or because it presented him with the perfect opportunity to miss his appointment, he wasn't entirely sure. But for whatever reason, Sam decided he wanted to find out who was driving the pick-up and where was it going.

In his rear-view mirror, he could see both drivers getting back into their vehicles. A mile up the road he pulled into a lay-by and waited for both vehicles to pass. Now following from a safe distance, he watched as both vehicles indicated and turned into the Deans estate, a couple of miles outside Huntersville. Sam wondered what he should do. He couldn't just follow them in, he was all on his own, he needed to be discreet.

Off to his left, a narrow road, no more than a dirt track, followed the line of the perimeter wall to the forest beyond. Making a left turn he followed the track for a few hundred yards. He parked in a clearing between some tall trees taking care not to block the road. Sam climbed over the wall and picked his way through the trees towards the house. If he was quick the driver of the pick-up might still be about. A minute or so later he found himself at the edge of a large car park where five haulage trucks were parked. Sam scanned the licence plates of the trucks. None of them was the one he was interested in. Through some trees at the far side of the car park he could see the house. Again, there was no sign of the truck or the pick-up and nobody seemed to be about.

Over to his right he heard a loud clanging noise. It sounded like someone was shutting a metal gate. The sound seemed to be coming from behind the row of trucks. Using the trees as cover, Sam moved quickly round to his right. Suddenly, there it was. Just beyond the last of the trucks, he could see the pick-up. A man wearing dark clothing was closing the gate. Staying out of sight he watched as the man got into the pick-up and disappeared down a narrow track.

But where was Oriole man and his truck? He looked around the car park one more time to make sure he hadn't made a mistake. But he was right, it wasn't any of the vehicles parked in the car park. He had seen it turn into the estate along with the pick-up, it couldn't have just vanished, so where was it?

As soon as the pick-up disappeared, Sam ran across the car park to the metal gate. He needed to find out where that pick-up was going. A beech hedge, all of six-foot high, ran down one side of the track. Perfect he thought. It would provide all the cover he needed to follow the track without being seen.

Standing on the other side of the gate at the edge of the track was a large plastic trash can. Strange place to have a trash can he thought, it's nowhere near the house. He lifted off the lid. His partner, Neil, had told him that it was always worth checking trash cans, and it wouldn't be the first-time they'd recovered stolen property from one, ditched by a thief desperate for a quick get-away. He sifted through the pile of garbage. It didn't look like stolen property, but the empty tequila bottle and tortilla wraps suggested that someone had a taste for Mexican food. Sam remembered the box of chilli sauce bottles and tortillas that Neil had found when he had checked the rear of Oriole man's truck, this was weird, why would a trash can stuffed full of Mexican foodstuffs be by a gate in the middle of nowhere?

Creeping down behind the hedge, Sam followed the track deeper into the forest. A couple of minutes passed before he saw what he was looking for. The truck and pick-up were parked next to a large rectangular shaped compound. He stared at the building. What in God's name is that? Surrounded by a high fence and with light stanchions at each corner, the austere looking one storey building, looked for all the world like a prison. What the hell was it for? And why had it been built in the middle of the Deans estate? Sam had no idea what was going on, he couldn't make any sense of it, but at least he had found the truck and the pick-up.

The red and white truck was parked with its tailgate only a few feet from a large set of metal doors. Standing next to the truck was the man in the Orioles cap and the pick-up driver. Sam watched from behind the cover of the hedge as the truck driver punched a code into a control box on the door. After a few seconds delay, the compound doors swung open. Another short delay and then another door, this time at the front of the compound, also opened. What the fuck was going on? He was too far away to hear what was being said but it was clear that the two men were deep in conversation. After a few moments the pick-up driver approached the truck and with the palm of his hand banged twice on a metal panel next to the rear wheels of the vehicle. Sam felt tense. Right now, he needed his wits about him and to think clearly. He tingled with anticipation, a combination of nerves and the adrenaline that was surging through him. This was the excitement he craved, this was why he wanted to be a police officer.

Edging ever closer, Sam watched agog as the side panel opened and disgorged its contents. Four men and two women slithered sideways out of the hold onto the ground. Each stood motionless at the side of the truck holding what looked like a blanket. He only saw their faces for a split second, but he thought they looked Mexican. Their black hair and dark olive skin told him they weren't from round here. Immediately, all six covered their heads and walked briskly, one behind the other, into the compound. Neither of the two men followed. After ensuring the gates were locked, they got back into their vehicles and drove up the track towards the truck car park.

Sam retreated to the safety of the woods. He wasn't sure what he should do but he knew he needed assistance. Taking his radio from his pocket he called the control room.

'Acting Detective Coutts, to control,' he whispered into the mouthpiece.

'Control to Acting Detective Coutts go ahead with your message.'

*

Back at the police office, Mike opened the envelope and took out Sam's report. He smiled to himself. He knew about Sam's dyslexia and his struggles with report writing, so he wasn't wanting to be overly judgemental. Even so, this was still a bit of a dog's dinner. He read through the report. All the relevant information appeared to be there, it just wasn't necessarily in a logical order. Mike ploughed on jotting down some notes as he read. He agreed with Sam's concluding paragraph that the reports with unusual withdrawal activity didn't look as if they had been compromised. The amounts taken out were modest and there was no pattern of targeted activity. It was, however, the last of the five redacted reports that now had his attention.

Mike snorted and scoffed. He knew the chief would be on a big salary, but the monthly amount was considerably larger than he had imagined. He had immediately recognised the bank giro credit code that went into Wilder's account on the last Thursday of the month from the West Virginian Police Department. It was the same one as paid his own salary.

In the deposit field of the statement, Sam had highlighted three entries. Mike stared at the entries that had been marked with a yellow fluorescent pen. Three deposits, all of two thousand dollars, made within the last six weeks.

It was the column detailing where that money had come from that sent the alarm bells ringing in Mike's head. Six thousand dollars paid into the chief's personal account by Deans Haulage. Mike knew a rat when he smelt one and this stunk to high heaven. He needed to speak to Charlie, something was seriously wrong.

*

'Okay Nathan, I think I follow all that,' said Charlie who had just listened to Nathan Young describe what happened the night Charlie Jarret was abducted. Nathan had begun by explaining how he'd been challenged by Jason Wilder and Ryan Portman to run from the college to the cemetery in Fairlea carrying the deer's head. He then described how, once he got there, he had been instructed to leave one of the deer's ears on the Founders grave.

'So, just to clarify then?' said Charlie, 'Jason and Ryan had killed the deer with a crossbow earlier in the day and it was their idea that you needed to carry the animal's head, not just the ear?'

Nathan nodded.

'They said that the class of 92 had to be better than their fathers' year, and as a Sligachan scholar, it was my duty to oblige. So instead of just taking the ear, they thought they would take it up a level and make me carry the head during the entire challenge.'

'How did they cut the head off?' asked Charlie.

'Jason had a saw with him, he cut the deer's head off. Ryan then cut off the ear with a knife.'

'Do you have any idea where the saw or knife came from?'

Nathan sighed. 'No, sorry, I don't.' Mr Innes who was sitting in the corner of the room grimaced.

'How gross,' he muttered under his breath.

'Let me get another point clear,' said Charlie. 'I think you said that you didn't see the man fishing under the bridge when you threw the head into the river.'

Nathan nodded again. 'That's the truth lieutenant, I only knew he was there when he shouted at me. He said I'd spooked the fish, or something like that.'

'So, what happened after that?' asked Chris who was trying to take down detailed notes.

'I never left the bridge. I don't think Simon, James or Ross did either. It was just Ryan and Jason that went down.'

'But you knew there was some form of argument.' asked Charlie.

'Sure,' said Nathan shrugging his shoulders. 'They were cursing and swearing at each other, but it was dark and difficult to see. I was starting to get cold, I only had shorts and a singlet on. I think it was Simon who said we should head to Sheetz. The arrangement had always been to go for burgers at the gas station. I can remember Simon shouting to tell Ryan and Jason that we'd see them at Sheetz.'

Charlie nodded. 'And you're telling us that was the last you saw of them till the following day. You never saw Ryan, Jason or the man at the gas station?'

'That's the honest truth officer. Ross drove us there in his Corolla. We got our burgers and waited for them to arrive. We must have waited more than ten minutes, but they didn't show, so we headed back to the college.'

'And the colour of the Corolla, Nathan?' asked Chris looking up from his notes.

'Light blue,' replied Nathan.

'And what about Jason and Ralph, how were they going to get to the gas station?' asked Chris.

'In Ryan's pick-up. It was parked next to Ross's car at the side of the bridge.' replied Nathan.

'And Ryan drives a dark blue Ford pick-up, is that correct?' asked Chris. Nathan nodded.

'Look, I just wanted to get back to my dormitory. I know I shouldn't have been out of the school at that time without permission. Earlier that evening I'd told Mr Innes that I had a bit of a headache and was going to have an early night. I thought that way nobody would be looking for me. All I wanted to do was to get back to school and go to my bed. I had to climb the drainpipe to the first floor to get into my room. Looking back now, it just seems so stupid. But I didn't want to let them down. They said it was my duty. The honour of Mic Sgith depended on it. But I regret it now. I'm sorry I've let you down Mr Innes.' said Nathan looking across to his housemaster.

Charlie could tell that Nathan was hurting. He was sitting head bowed looking at the floor. He appeared genuinely stunned when Charlie told him that the man fishing at the bridge had been found dead in a ditch on the mountain road. Charlie was sure that the boy didn't know anything about it. From what they had found in the boathouse, and from what Nathan was now telling them, it was clear that the finger of suspicion was pointing firmly at Jason Wilder and Ryan Portman.

'That's all we need to know for now Nathan,' said Charlie quietly. 'We'll need to interview you again and take a formal statement, but we'll organise that with the school and let you know when that will be. I also want to thank you for your honesty, you've been most helpful.'

Nathan smiled weakly as the detectives got up and left the room.

'I think he's telling the truth,' said Charlie turning to Chris.

'Yeah, I agree,' replied Chris. 'I feel kind of sorry for him, I hope he still gets the chance to be head boy. Like Buckley said, he seems like a decent lad.'

'That'll be a decision for the school, but I'm with you, I hope this doesn't go against him. Right, time to re-group and see where we are. We may not have got our interviews but finding the photograph and milk bottle has been a real bonus. Look, why don't we swing past Benny's and grab some breakfast and while we're there I'll phone the office, I want a word with Mike.'

*

'Glad I eventually found you,' said Phil walking into Charlie's office. 'Nobody was answering the phone next door, so I thought I'd come looking for you.'

Mike looked up from the desk. 'Sorry about that, but everyone's out. What can I do for you?'

'It's Sam. He's been on the radio asking the control room to contact you. He's over at the Deans estate. He's asking if you could meet him there. He's parked on a dirt track by the perimeter wall. He says it's on your left just before you come to the main entrance.'

Mike raised an eyebrow. 'Did he say what it's about?'

'It wasn't me who spoke to him, but he said it's important and he needs your advice.' Mike stood up and put on his jacket.

'He's not in any danger. We offered other resources but he's asking specifically for you,' said Phil.

'Sounds like I better get going then,' replied Mike.

'And I'll tell you another thing,' added Phil, 'it had better turn out to be important, he's missed his damned dental appointment because of it.'

Chapter 25

In his office on the third floor, Ewart Wilder was trying to ignore the phone that kept ringing on his desk. He was starting work on the eulogy that he'd promised Mrs Mitchell he'd give at the funeral of her son. She was keen that her boy be given a full police funeral, and that being the case, the chief wanted to ensure that his tribute set the appropriate tone, this was a chance to impress, and he wasn't going to pass up the opportunity.

'For fucks sake,' said Wilder slamming down his pen and glaring at the phone. 'You're a persistent son of a bitch, I'll give you that. He grabbed the handset. 'Chief Wilder, who's speaking?'

'Ewart, it's Bruce Innes, from Marsco,' said the voice on the other end of the phone. 'I've been trying to get hold of you, I'm not sure what's going on or if you already know, but two detectives, a Lieutenant Finch and some other guy have just left the college.'

'I haven't a clue what you're on about Bruce, what the fuck were they doing at the college?' asked Wilder angrily.

'I don't know all the details, but they've just finished interviewing Nathan Young about an incident at the Greenbrier bridge, something to do with the abduction and death of a Charlie Jarret. The thing is, Ewart, they really wanted to speak to Jason and Ryan Portman,

I don't know what they've supposed to have done, but from what Nathan told your officers they were both clearly at the bridge the time Jarret went missing. In fact, all of Mic Sgith were there. I just thought you'd want to know.'

Wilder's mouth felt suddenly dry, his neck muscles tightened, and his heart raced. Tiny beads of sweat appeared on his forehead. He was stunned, this had come as a complete shock. He put down the phone and stared into the distance. His mind was in overdrive, he was struggling to think straight.

He already knew that his son had reinstated Mic Sgith, Jason and Ryan had told him at the reunion dinner, but he knew nothing about them being at the bridge the night Jarret disappeared. He knew, of course, that his lieutenant was working on the theory that Jarret had been abducted from the bridge. Wilder didn't like the sound of this one bit. None of his detectives had mentioned that they were going to the school this morning and Charlie Finch had been at the morning meeting. Wilder was long enough in the tooth to know that his lieutenant didn't want to disclose what he was up to. But what did he know? What made him think that Jason might be involved in the abduction of Charlie Jarret. Wilder's blood ran cold. For once, he didn't know what to do.

*

Angela had been driving around in circles for the last five minutes. It must be here somewhere she thought, as she was sure she'd followed Mike's directions to the letter. When you come to the crossroads it's sign-posted he'd said, then it's only another half mile down the road. Well, this is definitely the crossroads, but she was damned if she could see any sign. Just before her exasperation got the better of her, she saw an old man approaching on a bicycle, he was carrying a fishing rod.

'Excuse me sir, I'm a bit lost, I'm looking for Grassy Meadows fishery?' said Angela stepping out of her car. The old man stopped and smiled.

'Folk are always getting lost here,' he said climbing off his bike. 'Someone will have taken the sign down again, happens all the time, I reckon it's the same person that does it. Don't ask me why, but they always leave it lying in the grass.' The old man walked across to some long grass at the base of a large oak tree. He started to laugh. 'Told you,' he said picking up the sign and hanging it on a nail on the tree. 'Happens regular as clockwork. Now just follow the arrow,' said the old man pointing down the road to Angela's right.

Angela smiled and thanked the man 'I'm sorry I can't offer you a lift, we appear to be headed to the same place.'

'Not a problem, ma'am,' said the old man tipping his cap, 'I'm not in a hurry, you can't be in a hurry when you're a fisherman, you need patience for this game.' he said with a smile. 'It's half a mile down the road, you can't miss it. Ask for Crawford Alan, he's the guy that runs the place, he'll see you alright.'

Angela had drawn a blank at the first two fisheries she'd visited. The first place she'd arrived at had been dilapidated and looked like it was permanently closed. The guy she spoke to at the other place had only just started working there and he knew absolutely nothing about trout or their feeding habits. Let's hope it's third time lucky thought Angela as she parked her car.

Over to her left she could see a stocky built man, dressed in camouflage clothing, carrying a plastic bucket standing by a shed at the side of the lake.

'Are you Crawford Alan by any chance?' asked Angela approaching the man. The man put down his bucket.

'That's me,' he said with a smile. 'You don't look like you've come here to fish so how can I help you?' Angela produced her police badge and explained why she was there. The man listened carefully as Angela described the composition of the trout pellets detailed in her report.

'Can you show me the description of the pellets you're interested in?' asked the man. Angela turned to page two of her report and showed it to the man.

'Yeah, I thought so,' said the man nodding. 'It's the same stuff that's in my bucket. We feed all our trout with it, it's the best stuff, I know other fisheries use cheaper feed, but it doesn't produce the same quality of fish as we do.'

'That's good to know,' said Angela reaching into her folder and taking out a photograph. 'I was also wondering if you recognised this man?' asked Angela handing over the photo. Crawford pursed his lips as he studied the photograph.

'You know, there is something familiar about him. Can you give me anymore information?'

'He's a police officer, his name's Wayne Mitchell, if he'd been here it would have been about the beginning of October.'

Crawford thought for a moment before tapping the photo with his hand.

'Yep, I remember him. He came over one afternoon to pick up a rainbow trout. I'll tell you why I remember him, your chief is a friend of mine, we've been in the Buffalo's together for years. Ewart phoned saying he needed a trout and he needed it quickly.'

Angela was taken aback, that was not what she was expecting to hear.

'You're telling me Chief Wilder phoned you?'

'Yeah, that's right. He said, sorry what did you say his name was?'

'Mitchell, Wayne Mitchell,' replied Angela.

'Yeah Mitchell. Ewart said that he would be over to pick up the fish. I did think it was a bit strange at the time. What did he need one trout for? Mitchell wanted to pay me for it, but as your chief is a friend, I just gave it to him.'

Angela was gobsmacked. What on earth was going on? Not only did she now have confirmation that the trout found at the lodge break-in had come from the fishery, she now knew that her chief of police had organised it. She needed to speak to Charlie quickly.

*

In Benny's diner Charlie's breakfast was getting cold. He had been phoning the detectives' office for the last five minutes, but the phone just kept ringing out. He then tried the front office, finally his persistence was rewarded, and he was now speaking to Phil. Chris waved to his boss to come across. His eggs would be stone cold at this rate.

'Sorry about that,' said Charlie returning to the table. 'Everyone seems to be out but eventually I got through to the uniform bar and got to speak to Phil.'

Between mouthfuls of his breakfast Charlie explained how Mike had left the office to go and meet Sam at the Deans estate in Huntersville.

'Phil doesn't know what's going on, but whatever it is, it stopped Sam getting to his dental appointment. Phil said that Sam had radioed in asking for Mike to meet him at the estate.'

'Huh,' said Chris.

'Apparently, we also missed a radio message from Mike. He was looking to speak to me, but I think we were still with Nathan when they were trying to get us. He didn't tell Phil what he wanted.'

Chris nodded. 'Typical. You also wanted to speak to him. Passing ships eh. And what about Angela, where is she?'

'God knows. She muttered something to Phil about heading out to visit some fisheries. Ever since she got that damned report, she can't seem to let it go. Finish your breakfast and we'll head over to Huntersville, it's not that far if we take the back road. We'll rendezvous with Mike and Sam and find out what's going on.'

*

As they drove up the narrow track that ran parallel to the perimeter wall, they could see Sam standing next to his car talking to Mike.

'What's up guys?' said Charlie getting out of the car.

'Not entirely sure,' said Mike rubbing his chin. 'Sam here spotted a blue pick-up and a Deans Haulage truck at the side of the road. He'd previously dealt with the driver of the truck and as he knew we were interested in tracing a dark coloured pick-up he decided he would follow them. Have I got that right?' Sam nodded. 'You tell them Sam, after all it was you that discovered it.'

'Discovered what?' asked a confused Charlie. Sam started to explain.

319

'Both vehicles turned into the estate. I parked here and followed on foot through the woods. I couldn't see where they'd gone initially, then I saw the pick-up disappear down a track into the forest. I found the pick-up and truck parked about a third of a mile in that direction,' said Sam pointing over to his left. 'Both vehicles were parked next to a large compound. It's surrounded by a fifteen-foot fence with barbed wire. There are flood lights at each corner, it looks like a prison to me.'

'A prison!' exclaimed Chris, 'in the middle of the Deans estate.'

'Sounds crazy I know,' said Mike, 'but it does look like a prison, its certainly got a serious level of security. I've been down with Sam to have a look. It's got security cameras everywhere. Someone has gone to a shit load of trouble to make sure that whatever it's guarding doesn't get out.'

'Okay, I'll ask the obvious question, what is it guarding?' asked Charlie.

Mike looked at Sam. 'You tell them what you saw, nobody was around when I went down, but Sam here witnessed something pretty interesting. On you go, tell them what you saw.'

Sam took a deep breath. 'When I discovered the compound, the pick-up and truck were parked outside the main gate. The pick-up guy punched in the security code and the doors opened. He then banged on the side of the truck and a panel over the rear wheels opened and six people got out.'

'A side panel, not the back doors of the truck?' asked Charlie.

'No. They definitely came out the side of the vehicle. I didn't know it was there, it was like a secret compartment. It wasn't very big, they had to slither out sideways.'

Charlie nodded. 'Then what happened?'

'Each of them was holding a blanket, they covered their heads and walked into the compound one after the other.' Continued Sam.

'And did you get a good look at the six of them?' asked Charlie.

'I only got a fleeting glance. But I can tell you there were four men and two women. I think they all had black hair and they were very tanned looking, I thought they looked Mexican. But as I said, I only got the briefest of looks before they covered their heads.'

Charlie took out his pocketbook and scribbled down some notes. 'Another cracking piece of work, Sam. Not sure what it's all about right enough, but it's going to need further investigation, someone's got a lot of explaining to do.'

'Tell them about the trash can, you forgot to mention that.' said Mike.

'Yeah, sorry about that. At the top of the track that leads to the compound, I found a plastic trash can. The thing is, when I lifted the lid, it was full of tortilla wraps and other types of Mexican food. There was an empty bottle of tequila in there as well.'

Chris nodded, before adding, 'That kind of backs up what you said about the people looking Mexican, would make sense that they were eating Mexican food.'

Charlie thought for a moment.

'I don't disagree Chris, but from what Sam's told us, it suggests that the people he saw were arriving at the compound. The stuff in the trash can had already been eaten, in fact it might have been there for days.

It suggests to me that other people, perhaps people already in the compound ate that food. Whatever it is, we're going to need some serious amount of resources to take this on.'

Mike gestured to Charlie. 'Can I have a quick word in private?'

'Sure,' said Charlie walking across to Mike who was now standing next to his car.

'Look, I tried to get a message to you at the school. I read Sam's briefing note about the compromised accounts just before I came here. It's too much of a coincidence for it not to be connected.' said Mike.

'Now you've lost me, what's too much of a coincidence?' asked Charlie. Mike continued.

'One of the accounts that Sam wanted you to know about belongs to Wilder. I know you'd had the names redacted but I recognised the bank giro credit code straightaway, it's the same one that pays our salaries after all. Anyway, Wilder's account has had six thousand dollars deposited into it over the last six weeks. Three separate deposits, each for two thousand dollars, and here's the kicker, the three deposits were made by the Deans estate. Looks like our leader has been on the take.'

Charlie's eyes opened wide and he blew out his cheeks.

'Now that is interesting.'

'And another thing,' continued Mike, 'do you remember that wedding Sam drove to in Oklahoma?'

'Vaguely,' replied Charlie.

'Well, just as you arrived Sam was telling me how he'd previously met the driver of the truck in Indiana. The driver told him they'd just opened a new route and he was on his way back from Mexico. He told Sam he'd crossed the border at Nogales. I smell a rat Charlie. I can't think of any legitimate reason why that money would be going into Wilder's account, can you?'

Charlie put his hands to his lips not saying anything. He was trying to process the magnitude of what Mike had just told him. Eventually he spoke.

'Nope. At this precise moment I can't think of any legitimate reason. Just one thing though. Do you remember after Eustace died the chief wouldn't let me undertake a proper search of the estate, he said he wanted the resources for his new drugs initiative that Mitchell was to lead?'

A look of recognition spread over Mike's face.

'You're right, I'd completely forgotten about that. Something now tells me that Wilder didn't want us sniffing about the estate, he didn't want us to find the compound. That was a convenient excuse to get us out the way.'

Charlie puffed out his cheeks and shook his head.

'This is now getting pretty complicated. From what I found out at the school today I'm convinced Wilder's boy along with Ryan Portman, abducted Charlie Jarret from the bridge and drove him up the mountain road. They left him up there in the pitch black and somehow, he's ended up in the ditch. Either they pushed him in, or he's slipped and fallen. I couldn't get to speak to them today as neither were in school. They're away with the lacrosse team at some tournament and not due back till tomorrow evening, we'll have to wait till then to formally interview the pair of them.'

'So, do you think they killed Jarret? And what about the other boys? I thought we were working on the theory that there might have been six of them.' asked Mike.

'I believe there were six of them at the bridge, but from what I now know, I think only Jason and Portman are responsible for his death. I'm also absolutely certain that the pair of them abducted him. We found evidence at the school that should place them at the bridge and the ditch where he died round about the material time. And the button and thread that was in Screech's possession are from Jason Wilder's waistcoat, Buckley confirmed that for us. But, I'm not sure how any of that connects to what we've found here. My gut feeling suggests that it does, but am I missing something?' asked Charlie.

'Do the two things have to be connected?' replied Mike. 'Ralph Portman runs this estate, and we know he and the chief know each other through the school, but that might be it. Charlie Jarret's death and whatever might be going on here might not be connected at all.'

Before they had a chance to discuss it further Chris shouted across.

'Boss, you're wanted on the radio. Angela has been on and she's asking if you can meet her at the Grassy Meadow fishery. She says she's got important information and needs to speak to you urgently.'

Charlie looked at Mike and shrugged his shoulders. He wondered what Angela had turned up that now needed his urgent attention.

'How far is the fishery from here?' asked Charlie.

'No more than ten miles, probably a bit less in fact.' replied Mike. 'Fine,' said Charlie, 'message her and tell her I'll be there in twenty minutes.'

'On it now,' said Chris.

'Look, here's what I want you to do. I've got a camera in my car. You stay here with Sam and Chris and try and get some photos of that compound, you'll need to be discreet, but we're going to need them to plan our operation. I'll go and see what Angela's turned up. I'll meet you back at the office at two and we'll hatch a plan on how to proceed, this needs to be done right.'

*

'For fuck's sake, can a man not get any peace,' spat Wilder picking up the phone. 'Chief Wilder, what do you want?'

'Ewart, it's Crawford Alan from Grassy Meadow speaking. I'm sorry to disturb you but I thought I should phone. One of your detectives, an Angela something or other, turned up to see me this morning. She wanted to know about the feed I give to the fish. Then she showed me a photo and was asking questions about the officer you sent to pick up the trout a few weeks ago.'

It was only a few words, but their significance ripped through him like a rapier. Wilder's world was about to turn upside down. His face turned a deep shade of purple as the realisation of what Alan had said hit him. If his detective knew that he'd arranged for Mitchell to pick up the trout, then of course she could link him to the burglary at the lodge house. He was incandescent with rage.

'What the fuck did you tell her?' yelled Wilder, now visibly starting to shake. 'Did you tell her I'd sent him?'

'I'm sorry Ewart, I didn't know that I shouldn't. You never said. It was only later when I opened my paper that I realised that Mitchell was the officer found dead at the quarry. I don't know what's going on Ewart, but another guy, who I also think is a cop, has now turned up. They've been talking for the last ten minutes.'

'Tell me you've not spoken to him too,' demanded Wilder.

'I've not said a word to him. I could go out the side door and disappear through the woods if you want me to. Just tell me what you want me to do.' said Crawford who was shaken by his friend's aggressive tone.

'Do what you have to, but don't say a fucking word to him, you hear me. Not one word.'

'Gotcha, and look, I'm sorry if I've messed things up for you.'

Wilder put down the phone. His chest felt tight and he was struggling to catch his breath. These were not emotions that Ewart was used to. Events that he could no longer regulate were spinning out of control. He felt helpless and crushed, there was nobody to turn to.

*

Charlie and Angela had arrived back at the office by quarter past one. Having updated Phil as to the goings on at Huntersville, Charlie was now at his desk trying to make sense of what had turned out to be a crazy day. He had the best part of forty-five minutes before he was due to meet with Mike, so he grabbed a pad and started to scribble some notes. He needed a time line to plot how he should proceed. The interviews with Jason and Ryan Portman would be dictated by their arrival back at the school. That would not be until tomorrow evening at the earliest so, for now, he would concentrate on how best to tackle the compound that they had discovered at the Deans estate.

In the back of his mind Charlie knew he had to address what to do about the chief. That was way beyond anything he had experienced before. He appreciated the gravity of the situation and how sensitive that enquiry would need to be. His earlier suspicions that his boss might somehow be involved in the lodge burglary looked like proving to be correct. And with Mike's revelations about the money that was going into his account, it begged the question, what else might he be involved in? He knew he would have to go through police headquarters in Charleston before he did anything else and that was not a prospect he was relishing. But at that precise moment he needed to speak to his mentor, he needed Mike's wise counsel and advice.

Charlie picked up Sam's briefing note that was still lying on his desk. While Mike had explained the gist of what it said, he now had time to read it while he waited for his friend to arrive. He had only just finished the first page when there was a knock on the door. Charlie looked up, it was Dave Richardson from forensics, and he was carrying a large envelope.

'At last,' said Dave with a smile. 'I've been up and down those stairs all morning looking for you or Mike, but the detectives' corridor has been like the Marie Celeste. And it wasn't just me looking for you. Wilder was coming out your office muttering under his breath, last time I was up.'

Charlie glanced down at the note on his desk and wondered if the chief had seen it when he'd been snooping about his office. Either way, what did it matter? He would be confronting the chief about it in due course, but for now, that could wait.

'Yes, I'm sorry about that,' said Charlie gesturing for Dave to come in and take a seat. 'It's been a really busy day, but Mike will be here shortly. What can I do for you?'

Dave opened the envelope and pulled out several photographs.

'Just got these developed so I thought you'd want to see them. They're photos of the tyre prints we found up at the quarry. Turns out we were both right and wrong.'

'Oh, how's that?' said Charlie taking the photos from Dave.

'Well, we were right about there being three vehicles. The chunky tracks, on photos 'A' and 'B' belong to Sergeant Mitchell's pick-up.' Charlie nodded.

'C' and 'D' are prints from Neil Planner's patrol car.' Charlie looked closely at the photos and nodded again.

'But these are the most interesting prints,' said Dave handing Charlie two more photographs. 'And this is where we got it slightly wrong. At the time, we thought the treads of the second and third vehicles were identical, but they're not. If you look where I've marked with the red arrow, you'll see that the tread is slightly different from the one in the other photograph.'

'Ah-ha, I can see that,' said Charlie holding both photographs up to the light.

'They are both Michelin tyres, but the one in photographs 'E' and 'F' is of a more recent pattern. That make of tyre was just released this year. They are almost identical, but if you look closely you can see that the cross-hatch on the tread is wider spaced on the newer model.'

Charlie smiled. 'You really do have to be an anorak to do this type of work, don't you?'

Dave laughed. 'I've been called worse, but the devil is always in the detail.'

He then pulled three more photographs out of the envelope and handed them to Charlie.

'Take a look at these. They show the print of the third vehicle in more detail. Look at the centre of the tread where the arrow's pointing.'

Charlie leant down and peered at the photo.

'You can just about make it out, it's captured in the other two photos as well. Do you see that small circular shape?' Charlie nodded. 'That looks to me like it's been made by a nail head,' added Dave. 'It's certainly been made by something round that's been attached to the tyre. It's about the right size for a masonry nail, I can't think what else it could be.'

Charlie stood open mouthed as he remembered his conversation with Mike earlier that day. He was stunned.

'Whatever it is, it proves there were three vehicles at the quarry and just one more thing. Look here at this last photo as it shows it best. The tread from Neil's vehicle crosses over both the other two treads which proves that the other two vehicles had been in the quarry before Neil's.'

Dave looked at Charlie who was now sitting in his chair gazing into space.

'Are you alright?' asked Dave, 'You look like you've seen a ghost.' Charlie shivered as he came to his senses.

'I'm fine Dave, just fine. But I think you may have just unlocked the puzzle; this is now starting to make sense.' said Charlie leaning back in his chair.

'Well, if that's the case, I'm glad I've been of some assistance.'

'Who else knows about this?' asked Charlie putting the photographs back into the envelope.

'Just the chief,' replied Dave, 'I usually give him a copy out of courtesy, you know what he's like, he wants to know everything.'

Charlie grimaced. 'When did you give him his photos?'

'Just five minutes before I came to see you. He almost snatched them out my hand, don't think he looked in the best of moods.' replied Dave.

'Huh,' said Charlie, 'and what about Mitchell's gun, is there anything you can tell me about that?'

'Not much I'm afraid,' replied Dave. 'You'll get a full report in due course, but I can confirm that only one bullet was fired, although the cylinder was fully loaded.'

'Prints?' asked Charlie.

'Strangely no, we didn't find a single one. Not even a smudge. The gun looked like it might have been recently cleaned.'

Just then Charlie was aware of footsteps running down the central staircase from the floor above.

'Can you see who that is?' said Charlie gesturing at Dave who was standing close to the door. Dave leant back and looked out.

'It's the chief, looks like he's off somewhere in a hurry, he was struggling trying to get his arm into the sleeve of his jacket.' Charlie grabbed his phone and dialled the front office.

'Come on, come on Phil, answer the damn phone.'

Dave hadn't a clue what was going on, but by the look of tension on Charlie's face, it was clearly important.

'Sergeant Coutts speaking how can I h......' Before Phil could finish speaking Charlie blurted out.

'Phil, it's Charlie, I need you to shut the yard gates.'

'What? You want ....'

'Just close and lock the fucking gates Phil, and don't open them, nobody gets in or out, that includes the chief you understand?'

'Gonna tell me what's going on? I can't just lock the gates.'

Charlie looked out his window. Striding across the car park heading towards his car was the chief.

'Phil, you'll need to trust me on this one, I need you to close those gates right this fucking moment.'

'Okay, okay, I'm locking them now, but there had better be a good reason.' said Phil as he pressed the switch on the wall to activate the automatic gates.

The doors slammed shut just as the chief's car was about to drive out of the car park. Phil heard the sound of tyres screeching and a car door slamming. He looked out his ground floor window. The chief was now screaming into the intercom.

'Coutts, open the fucking door now you hear me, right this fucking moment.'

Phil didn't need to listen to the intercom. The chiefs voice boomed across the car park and through his open window. What the hell was going on?

'Don't fuck with me Phil, you've got one last chance to open these gates,' thundered the chief.

Phil stood motionless by his desk. He was still holding the phone receiver in his hand. The air turned blue as expletives filled the air as the chief continued his tirade of abuse.

'Phil, Phil are you still there, can you hear me?' shouted Charlie from the other end of the phone.

Phil lifted the phone to his ear. 'I'm still here,' he said as he stood transfixed by the scene that was unfolding in front of him.

'He's trying to kick the gates open,' said Charlie as Wilder viciously side kicked the centre of the gates. Again and again his feet smashed into the metal doors.

'I can see what he's doing Charlie,' said Phil sarcastically, 'I'm just not sure how we're going to stop him.'

'I'm coming down,' said Charlie, 'don't do anything until I get there.'

'No worries on that score my friend, I'm not fucking stupid.'

A minute later Charlie and Angela had joined Phil in the uniform bar.

'I'm going to try and reason with him, so let me do the speaking okay.'

'Fine by me. You fill your boots, it's your gig after all. If it all goes horribly wrong it's only going cost me my job, so no big deal.' quipped Phil.

'You both got a mace spray?' asked Charlie ignoring Phil's sarcastic remarks. Angela and Phil nodded and followed Charlie into the car park.

'I'm going to have you for this,' screamed Wilder pointing at Phil as the three officers approached their leader. 'You too Finch, I knew it was a fucking mistake appointing you. I'm having you too.'

The chief was now spitting with rage. How do you remonstrate with someone this angry thought Charlie as they came to a halt a safe distance from their seething boss.

At that precise moment a blue coloured Pontiac turned the corner at Annie Mack's and was now approaching the gates.

'Thank you, God,' said Charlie looking up to the sky. It was Mike and Chris. He watched as his two colleagues got out the car and walked slowly towards the metal doors. Sam's car arrived seconds later and drew up behind them.

'What's going on, are the gates broken?' asked Mike.

Charlie didn't reply. Everyone's eyes were focussed on the chief. Seconds passed and nobody moved or said anything. On the brink of exhaustion, Wilder narrowed his eyes and stared at his subordinates. His chest heaved up and down like an injured bull facing down a matador.

Summoning his last reserves of energy, Wilder launched a final assault. He was almost horizontal when his two feet smashed into the unforgiving metal. Defeated, he crumbled to the ground, hurt and bewildered. Then quite suddenly, like a wounded animal, he picked himself up and bolted for cover. The detectives watched as the chief ran back to the building and up the central stair. It looked like he was heading for his office.

'Open the gates now,' shouted Charlie to a uniformed officer who had been watching from the front office. The gates swung open and Mike, Chris and Sam joined the others in the car park.

'What in God's name is going on?' demanded Phil.

'No time just now, I'll explain later. Mike, Chris, Angela follow me. Sam, I need you to stay here and guard the chief's car, nobody touches it understand.' Sam nodded. 'And Phil, get those gates shut again, they don't open unless I say so.'

'The light in his office has just gone on,' said Chris as the three detectives reached the side door of the building. Mike grabbed Charlie by the arm.

'Can we just take a minute, Charlie. It looks like he's back in his office, he can't go anywhere, so can you tell us what the hell's going on?'

Charlie paused and thought for a moment. Mike of course was right. He needed to take a minute, to remain calm and think rationally. Now was not the time to go off half-cocked. That's when mistakes are made. Now was a time for cool heads. Charlie looked at his colleagues. They needed to know what was about to unfold.

'Okay, listen carefully,' said Charlie. 'Thanks to Angela, I can now prove that the chief was involved in the lodge burglary and I can also prove that he was at the quarry the night Wayne Mitchell died. I'm almost sure that Mitchell didn't commit suicide, I think the chief shot him.'

Angela stood stony-faced as Chris let out an audible gasp. Like the others, he was an experienced detective, but that revelation shook him to his core. Mike looked unfazed by that news. He already knew some of the background, but even so, he was now feeling nervous, this was uncharted waters for them all.

'Holy shit.' said Mike quietly. 'Things have escalated quickly. So how do you intend to play this?'

Charlie looked his colleagues in the eye.

'We're going to arrest the chief for burglary and suspicion of murder, then I'm contacting police headquarters. But right now, our priority is to get the chief in custody.' Mike, Chris and Angela nodded in agreement.

When they reached the third floor, Charlie indicated for the others to wait at the top of the stairs. Cautiously, he approached the chief's door. Crouching down he peered through the opaque glass panel. The light was still on and while he could just about make out the corner of the desk, he couldn't see Wilder. He stood back from the door and whispered to the others.

'I'm pretty sure he's in there. I'm going to knock the door and then Mike and I will go in. I'm not going to beat about the bush. There will be no discussion. I'll tell him he's under arrest, then I'll handcuff him. If he resists, then you'll spray him Mike. I want you two to stay at the door, but don't come in unless I say.' The others all nodded.

Charlie's heart thumped against his chest and his mouth felt dry as he knocked on the door. There was no reply.

'He's definitely in there, I saw him move,' whispered Mike. Charlie knocked on the door again.

'Sir, I need you to open the door. We need to speak to you.' said Charlie calmly.

'Well you can take a flying fuck lieutenant, I ain't opening the door.' said a voice from within.

Charlie put his hand on the handle, but it wouldn't turn. The door was locked. Charlie looked at Mike.

'Try again.' whispered Mike. Charlie knocked for a third time.

'Sir, if you don't open the door, I'll get the master key and open it, we need to speak to you.'

'Go get your fucking key, 'cause you ain't getting in!'

Charlie nodded to Angela who headed down the stairs to fetch the key. As they waited for her to return no one said a word. It was eerily quiet.

'I didn't think another body would go amiss,' said Angela handing Charlie the master key. Charlie smiled weakly at Phil who was now standing at the top of the stairs with Chris.

Charlie knocked the door for a fourth time. 'Sir, I'm giving you a final chance to open the door. Please sir, open the door now.'

There was no response. Charlie turned the key in the lock and grasped the door handle. As he pushed the door open a gun shot rang out, a momentary explosion before the silence returned. Charlie stumbled through the door.

'Do you need an ambulance?' shouted Phil preparing to head back down the stairs. Mike shock his head from the doorway.

'No need,' he said calmly. 'This is now a crime scene.'

Chapter 26

Three Weeks Later

In the corner of Bursley's bar, Charlie, Angela, Chris and Sam sat waiting for Mike and Phil to arrive. They were talking animatedly about the events of the last three months. One thing they all agreed on, none of them had experienced anything quite like it.

'So, the trial is scheduled to start the last week of January.' said Angela. Charlie nodded.

'Just got confirmation of that today. Are all the productions lodged with the DA's office?'

'Yep,' replied Angela. 'Took the last of them down the other day, we're all good to go.'

'What do you think are the chances that they'll be found guilty of the manslaughter charge?' asked Sam.

'Difficult to say,' replied Charlie. 'I think the evidence is overwhelming, but whether a jury will agree is another matter. I'll make one prediction though, with Nathan and the other boys now being prosecution witnesses, I can't see them getting off the abduction charge.'

'I think there's a good chance we'll get a guilty on the manslaughter charge too,' said Chris.

'We'll see. But as only Jason and Ryan were there when they dumped him on the mountain road, I can see proving that charge being much more difficult. Especially if they stick to their stories.' said Charlie.

'I think there might be a plea bargain,' chipped in Angela. 'Plead guilty to the abduction in exchange for the manslaughter charged being dropped.'

'Hmm, I'm not so sure. I think it would be a travesty if they did that. For Screech's and Mrs Jarret's sake I want to see them stand trial for Charlie's death. One thing I know for certain, he only ended up dead because they abducted him and dumped him up there.' said Chris.

'Whatever way it goes, you can be sure it won't be our decision,' added Charlie taking a sip of his beer.

'It was good news about Nathan Young though,' said Chris.

'Yeah, I'm pleased about that.' said Charlie. 'The only thing they were guilty of was being out of school after hours. Nathan and the other three boys weren't guilty of any crime. Letting him be the head of school was absolutely the right decision in my opinion.'

Chris nodded. 'And nine months early too.'

'Oh, how's that?' asked Sam.

'Well, with Jason and Ryan in custody at the detention centre, they needed someone straight away. Made sense to appoint Nathan early. Come September he would have taken on the role anyway.' explained Chris.

'Changing the subject, were you aware that Bridget Wilder's moving?' asked Angela.

'Really. I wasn't aware of that, but I'm not surprised. Who told you she was moving?' asked Charlie.

'The school secretary, Jean Henderson, told us when Chris and I were at the school yesterday. She said that she's selling up and moving to their lake house apparently. She can't bear to be in Fairlea, can't say I blame her.' said Angela.

'No, I can understand that,' said Charlie, 'she'd never be able to get away from it. Not with her husband's suicide and her son awaiting trial. People would always be speculating and gossiping. It must be a living hell for her as it is. I'd want to get away if I were her.'

'Listen, while we're talking about Wilder, did you ever get confirmation from the DA's office about Wayne Mitchell's death?' asked Angela.

'The official findings haven't been published yet, but I'm told its imminent. However, my source tells me it's going to be an open verdict. Which in one way is good. We can't prove that Wilder shot him. I'm convinced that he did, but I can see why the DA won't commit to that. But equally, they aren't convinced that it was suicide, hence the open verdict.'

'It's still not great from the family's point of view is it? I mean not knowing one way or another.' said Chris opening a packet of pretzels.

'Incredible!' said Sam blowing out his cheeks and leaning back in his chair.

'I'll tell you what's incredible,' said Charlie trying to lighten the mood. 'The two-week secondment you've just had, bet you never thought you'd get to experience all of that in a fortnight?' Sam smiled and shook his head.

'And credit where credits due,' continued Charlie, 'It was your eagle eyes that led us to the pick-up and discovering the compound.'

'Don't forget the bank enquiry boss,' added Chris, 'it was Sam that noticed the deposits going into Wilder's account from the Deans estate. All in all, not a bad two weeks work.' The others laughed.

'Seriously though, it was a great piece of work. As was yours discovering the button and the thread on Charlie Jarret's jacket. That was critical to solving the case. And let's not forget Angela's fish, without that we would never have been able to link Wilder to the lodge burglary.' added Charlie. 'In fact, everyone has contributed, it's been a real team effort.'

'So boss, here's a question for you, what do you think made the chief shoot himself?' asked Chris.

'Funny you should ask that; I've been thinking about it for a while now. I'm convinced it was a combination of things. His dispute with Buckley for sure, money worries, finding the nail in his tyre. I think they all played a role.' Charlie turned to look at Sam. 'But I think it was your briefing note that finally tipped him over the edge.'

The others all looked at Charlie, they hadn't heard this theory before.

'Your report was lying on my desk the day the chief shot himself. Dave Richardson had seen Wilder coming out my office when I wasn't there. I'm convinced he read your report. He would immediately have realised that we knew about the money going into his account. From that point on it all started to unravel, he could no longer control things. And we now know about the phone calls he received from the school and his friend Crawford Alan. The chief wasn't stupid, he would have known the game was up, and I don't think he could have borne the humiliation. Sam's report and not being able to get out of the yard to get his tyre repaired must have been the final straw. He was trapped, he had no way out.'

'Wow,' said Chris, 'when you tell it like that it's like something you see in a movie. You'd never expect that could happen in Greenbrier County.'

'That's for sure,' said Angela. 'And just to complete the story, we now know that the people we found in the compound were illegal immigrants brought in as slave labour to make cigarettes that were then smuggled back and sold in Mexico.'

'That's about the strength of it. Six people or thereabouts, desperate for a better life, brought across the border every two months. They had no idea where they were being brought to.' added Charlie.

'They paid a handsome price to be smuggled over the border. Of course, part of the deal was that they would provide the labour to make the cigarettes. That's why the compound was built. It was really nothing more than a cigarette factory. They used their own trucks to bring in raw tobacco from Virginia and North Carolina. Making cigarettes almost twenty-four hours a day, it didn't take long till they could stuff a truck full of contraband cigarettes. Then they would cram the workers into the secret hold in the truck and dump them in the middle of nowhere, somewhere between here and Nogales. And because Wilder had bought off the local police chief and border guards, the truck could cross the border without fear of being searched. The whole sequence of events would then start over again. Simple as that.' explained Charlie.

'Pretty clever if you think about it. By dropping them miles from Huntersville, they would never have known that they'd ever been in West Virginia, and if they ever did get picked up by the authorities', they could never trace them back to here.' said Chris.

341

Sam sat incredulous. This was the first time he'd heard all the details of the raid on the compound. Charlie smiled.

'The law of unintended consequences, Sam. You couldn't have imagined that your briefing note would become the catalyst for all of that.'

Sam didn't know what to say, he just sat gently shaking his head.

'Ralph Portman will carry the can for all of that now. With Wilder dead he's almost solely responsible for what went on. Your truck driver friend, the guy in the Orioles cap, is singing like a bird. He's prepared to testify against Portman in return for a reduced sentence. Looks like Mr Portman will be going to jail for a very long time.' said Charlie.

'He and his boy both,' added Angela.

'I've got everything crossed that he gets found guilty of faking the break-in at the house as well. That son of a bitch took a bit of glass and lacerated Screech's wrist to make it look like he'd broken into the house. What a shit eh. At least Screech isn't getting charged with it. In my opinion Portman should get done for that and be held responsible for Brownie's death and for what he did to Screech.' said Chris.

'Can't say I disagree with any of that,' added Charlie. 'At least we know that Screech and Eustace were only at the estate because of the button. They also knew about the pick-up. They were close to getting to the truth themselves. We can only hope that the evidence stacks up and the jury finds him guilty. It's the least the Jarrets deserve.' The others nodded in agreement.

Chris was at the bar getting a round in when Mike and Phil eventually arrived.

'Sorry we're a bit late, I couldn't get away until the sanitation guy had unblocked the toilets in the cell block. Some idiot had managed to rip up his blanket and stuff it down all the toilets. I'd offered Mike a lift, so of course he was stuck waiting for me.' Everyone laughed.

'And here we were discussing the smuggling of illegal immigrants and the abduction and manslaughter of poor Charlie Jarret, and there you were, dealing with a bathroom emergency.' said Charlie.

'All part of the rich tapestry of being a police officer,' added Mike, who was clearly amused by the whole situation.

When everyone had got their drinks, Phil stood up and tapped his glass on the table.

'Can I have everyone's attention please as I'd like to propose a toast on this auspicious day. Well, in fact, I'd like to propose three toasts.'

The others stopped talking and turned to listen to Phil.

'Firstly, to you Mike.' said Phil looking at his friend who was quietly sipping his beer in the corner. 'I know it's not for a few months yet, but it's been a long time coming and well overdue in my opinion.' Hear, hear cried the others.

'So, can I ask that you raise your glasses to Captain Rawlingson of the Chicago Police Department?'

To Captain Rawlingson cried the others in unison. Mike smiled and lifted his glass to each of his colleagues in turn. Phil then turned to look at Charlie.

'Secondly, to you Lieutenant Finch and the confirmation that your promotion is going to be made permanent.'

'Well that was never in doubt,' whispered Chris who was sitting next to Sam at the table. 'Not after the three months he's just had. After that baptism of fire, whatever comes next will be a breeze.'

'To Lieutenant Finch,' said the friends raising their glasses again.

'And the last toast is to you Angela, for your well-deserved promotion to sergeant. You've also had to wait a long time, but you've more than proved your worth, you'll make a terrific supervisor. And what a bonus, staying in the department, you only have to move desks.'

As the friends lifted their glasses for a third time, Angela glanced across to Chris. She felt for him. The sergeant's job could just as easily have gone to him. Today she was the beneficiary and he had missed out. Winners and losers. It was a fine line between those positions but if Chris was hurting, he wasn't letting it show.

'Congratulations Angela, or should that be boss, you're going to do just great and I'm looking forward to working with you.'

Angela appreciated Chris's magnanimous words. She had been in his position many times before and knew how disappointed he would be.

Just when everyone thought that the toasts had finished, Charlie stood up to speak.

'If I could have everyone's attention for just another couple of minutes, I've got something important I'd like to say.'

Phil and the others put down their glasses and turned towards Charlie.

'I'm sure I speak for both Mike and Angela when I say we're delighted with our promotions and to have that professional recognition means a lot to each of us I know. However, there are some things in life that are far more important than promotions and a few more bucks on your pay-check.' Charlie turned to face Mike.

'My good friend here would probably be too humble to say, but today is a very special day in the Rawlingson household. Mike has just found out that Susan has finished her course of treatment and, as of now, is officially in remission. There's still a way to go but I know Mike, Susan and of course Keegan, are delighted with the report the doctor has given them. That, my friends, is the best news we could have received today.'

Before Charlie could propose his toast, the others raised their glasses and cheered.

'To Susan, Mike and Keegan and to a new future in Chicago,' shouted Charlie as the others offered their congratulations to their boss.

After the noise and excitement had died down Charlie found himself talking to Phil.

'And what about you Phil? Sam says you've put your ticket in and you're leaving in the summer.' Phil nodded.

'If all goes to plan, I'll finish on my birthday, June 14th. I wanted to make sure that Sam was settled in the job and now that's done it's time to call it quits.' Charlie smiled and patted Phil on the back.

'And what then. You're going to miss this place?' said Charlie.

'I might miss some of you, but not sure I'll miss the job if I'm honest. I thought I might take up fishing?'

'Fishing!' said Charlie incredulously.

'Yep, fly fishing. I've already been out with Hugh Robertson. Didn't catch a fish but really enjoyed it. He's a member of a syndicate and can get me a restricted membership, so I thought I might give it a go. Helen will want me out the house, so why not. It's either that or I'll need to write a book, memoirs of thirty years working with you lot.'

'Na, stick to the fishing Phil, we can't afford for you to give away our trade secrets.'

Epilogue

The gathering on the lawn was now starting to break up. It was late in the afternoon and people were drifting away in small groups, keen to get back to the warmth and sanctuary of the school. As the last shafts of a wintery sun disappeared behind the Greenbrier mountain, three figures stood silhouetted in the gloaming.

'Dionach, do you remember Edward Broadley?' asked Curtis Wyles gesturing to the man standing next to him.

'I most certainly do. House captain of Portree if my memory serves me right,' said the Dionach thrusting out a hand to greet his former pupil.

'Spot on Dionach, it's good to see you again,' said Edward shaking his hand firmly, 'It's been a while.'

'It certainly has. But I see you remembered,' said the Dionach with a smile. 'That's what you call a proper handshake. None of that slippery fish nonsense. A handshake should be firm and strong like yours. It sets the right tone and says something about your character.'

'Just one of many things I remembered from my time here, Dionach.' said Edward with a grin.

'How does it feel to be back after all these years?' asked Curtis.

'Pretty good actually. I've surprised myself today, it does feel good to be back. I can't believe it, but It's more than thirty years since I was last here.'

'That's good to hear, I'm delighted you feel like that,' said Curtis putting his hand on Edward's shoulder. 'And it was a fine service and dedication don't you think? The bench is going to look splendid next to your old dormitory overlooking the lake.'

Edward smiled and nodded. 'It does seem like the perfect place. Mark and I liked to hang out here in the summer. We were supposed to be studying, but usually we ended up soaking up the sun and putting the world to rights. Anything to avoid Mr Burt's physics homework.'

'Gosh, now there's a memory.' said Curtis. 'Harold Burt. Must have been dead twenty years and seemed about eighty when he taught us back then. Lovely man but an appalling teacher, it was a wonder how anyone, including me, ever passed physics.'

'I know exactly what you mean,' replied Edward. 'You'd have to work hard to be as bad at teaching as old Burt was. His monotone voice could induce me to sleep in an instant. But happy days nevertheless.'

The Dionach bent down and peered at the brass plaque on the bench.

The words read, 'In memory of Mark Tyler and the friendship and good times we shared at Marsco.'

'I like it Edward, it's a very fitting tribute to your friend.'

Edward smiled. 'Yes. I think it's perfect. I'm grateful to the headmaster, the college and of course yourself, Curtis for allowing me to provide the bench in Mark's memory.'

'I think our new head of governors is going to be more accommodating in that regard than the last one, if I may put it like that,' replied the Dionach.

Edward gave a wry smile. 'The timing now felt right. I wouldn't have dreamed about doing it before, but with everything that has happened, I felt it was right that we remember Mark in this way. With Wilder gone the truth can come out, I know what happened that night at the bridge. I was there. Wilder will never have to answer for it now, but I'm glad it's now out in the open.'

'I wouldn't be so sure,' said Curtis, 'I think God may want a word in Wilder's ear about Mark's death and a few other things to boot. I know I'll take some comfort from that thought.'

'You're a good man Curtis. The college will be in safe hands with you as head of governors. I'm glad you agreed to take it on.'

'That's kind of you to say. I was honoured to be asked and it felt like the right thing to do. It's not exactly handy for me, in fact it's nearly a hundred and twenty miles door to door, but I can stay overnight after board meetings and travel home the next day which is a big help. And other than Founder's Day and a few other special occasions, it's not too onerous a task. I just hope I can make some contribution.'

'He already has,' said the Dionach smiling like a Cheshire cat. 'I'm getting to stay in the lodge house and will be assisting Mr Renshaw, the new Dionach, when he starts in the spring. Works out very well for both of us. Turns out that he'd prefer to live in the boathouse. He's got a wife and a small child with another on the way, so they need the bigger accommodation. Suits Mrs Buckley and Seth just fine as well. Means we don't have to move. I'm very grateful to the board for sorting it out so quickly.'

'So, if Renshaw's going to be the Dionach, what are you going to be called?' asked Edward mischievously.

The Dionach started to chuckle.

'Hmm, I wanted to be known as the Emeritus Dionach, but I don't think Mr Wyles approved.' Curtis shook his head despairingly.

'I'm just kidding,' said the Dionach. 'I think I might become the assistant Dionach, that would suit me just fine.' Curtis looked at the Dionach over the rim of his glasses.

'It's going to be discussed at the next board meeting, but you can rest assured Dionach, you'll be the first to know.'

Curtis looked at his watch.

'Gentlemen, the sun is most definitely over the yardarm and as it's getting cold out here, I wondered if you might like to join me in the office for a dram? I've a bottle of eighteen-year old Talisker to hansel, and I don't intend to drink it by myself, so, what do you say?'

'Now that sounds like a splendid idea,' said the Dionach, 'shall I lead the way?'

In the office Curtis poured three large measures of the liquid gold into crystal tumblers and passed them round.

'Because of the circumstances I thought I'd like to propose a toast. But just before I do, I've got something interesting to tell you both.'

'Okay,' said Edward taking a sip of his whisky, 'now I'm curious.'

Curtis started to laugh. 'You're going to love this, especially you Dionach, I should think this will make your day.'

The Dionach raised an eyebrow.

'Go on then, what is it? It must be funny; you can't stop laughing.' Eventually Curtis regained his composure.

'Okay, okay here goes. You know how Ewart Wilder created Mic Sgith and then got you and the other house captains to buy into it?'

Edward nodded. 'Sure, I remember, I'll never be able to forget it, it still brings back bad memories.'

'Yes of course, and I'm sorry about that, but stay with me. Do you happen to remember what it means?'

Edward nodded again.

'It's the Gaelic for Sons of Skye. Wilder chose the name in honour of the Founder.' Curtis started to chuckle again.

'Well, my friends, it appears Wilder got it completely wrong. Jean Henderson spoke to me earlier, apparently after the police asked her about Mic Sgith, she went and got a book from the library just to check that what she'd told them was accurate. And here's the thing, Mic Sgith doesn't mean Sons of Skye.'

'Really,' said the Dionach starting to laugh.

'Yeah, it translates to 'Tired Sons' or something like that. Sons of Skye should be 'Clann an Eilean Sgitheanaich,' said Curtis checking a piece of paper he had pulled out of his pocket. 'Wilder had somehow managed to get the translation wrong. And for all these years nobody knew. I don't suppose anyone ever checked.' said Curtis.

'Oh, that's brilliant,' said the Dionach now almost in tears with laughter. 'Just brilliant.'

Edward looked bemused and shook his head.

'There is a certain irony to that, but it does seem strangely appropriate that he managed to get it wrong. It was a stupid idea anyway. I think it deserves to be ridiculed.'

'Fair tickled me I can tell you when Jean told me.' said Curtis, 'I knew you'd find it amusing.'

351

'Anyway, enough of that, back to business gentlemen. I've got a gift for you Dionach.'

The Dionach looked surprised. It wasn't his birthday so why would Curtis be giving him a present? He watched as Curtis reached down behind his desk and picked up a slim rectangular package that was neatly wrapped with brown paper. Curtis handed it to the Dionach.

'Now promise me you'll hang it somewhere prominent, where everyone can see it. We don't want any repetition of the last time.'

The Dionach looked confused. He was still none the wiser as to what it could be. Carefully, he unpicked the Sellotape and removed the paper. His face broke into a beaming smile as he stared at his gift.

In a glass covered frame was his letter. The letter given to his father by the Founder. The letter that had been in the cigar box that had originally been a gift from Andrew Carnegie. The Dionach fell silent, he didn't know what to say. He was touched by the sentiment and suddenly felt quite emotional. Tears welled up in his eyes as he struggled to speak. He took a moment to compose himself.

'I'm very grateful for this Mr Wyles. I'll hang it over the mantlepiece in the front room. Everyone will see it there; don't you worry about that. And I'll tell you another thing, I'm going make so many photocopies that you could paper a room with them. I'll never let it out of my sight.'

Curtis smiled and nodded.

'I'm glad you like it. It's an important document, it's helped secure your family's future.' he said topping up the Dionach's glass.

'That letter represents an important part of our history. The history of your family and of our Founder and this great school. Gentlemen, we've come through a turbulent time, a time like no other in the seventy-five years of this institution. It's taken fortitude and a great deal of resilience, the very qualities this school is founded on, to see us through this difficult time. But we have prevailed, and the future once more looks bright.'

Curtis raised his glass.

'Gentlemen, on this special day, will you raise your glasses and join me in a toast.'

The Dionach and Edward held their glasses aloft.

'To the Founder, to Marsco College and to the future, slainte mhath.'

'I'll drink to that,' said Edward.

'Slainte mhath,' cried the Dionach, 'to the Founder and Marsco College, slainte mhath.'